AV

"Father, don[...] -
denly needing[...] d
young man on the ground really was Arron.

His father turned slowly, until the gun
pointed straight at Chris. "They killed her,
boy," he whispered, and tears appeared in
his eyes. "You helped them to kill her."

"I didn't!"

"You brought their magic home with you
that night. I could feel it. I saw it take her
strength. You helped the Roamers kill your
own mother. Now I'm going to pay them
back—and you! I'll kill your friend here."

"Don't be stupid! I hate them as much as
you do."

"Then enjoy this!" His father whipped
the rifle about, pulling the trigger as it
aimed on the Roamer. The gun's explosion
drowned Chris' cry of protest. . .

A SPELL
OF DECEIT

Laurie Goodman

A Del Rey Book

BALLANTINE BOOKS • NEW YORK

For my two sisters:

Jenny, I wrote this for you.

Kathy, I couldn't have done it without your help.

Thank you both for making this happen.

I

CHRIS POURED THE BLUE-GRAY MILK OUT OF THE BUCKET and watched it spill into the dry riverbed, stir up muddy eddies, then soak into the parched ground. He lowered the bucket, still staring at where the sour milk had disappeared. Sour! Milk soured over time, it wasn't supposed to start out bad, the way this milk had. Better to slaughter their sickly cows now, while the meat was still good—if it was still good.

Sighing, he looked around, dead trees rattling their branches at him. He rubbed his eyes with one hand, trying to imagine the land as it had once been, before he was born. His mother had told him stories of how things used to be. He was sick of hearing how things used to be.

He turned and stumped up the path to his house. It had been better then, she had told him. Flowers had bloomed, and all the trees had leaves, and green, green grass had covered the hills. He stared up at the gray sky above him. Blue, he thought to himself, and tried to picture it that way. It had been good before the Roamers, before Shakta cursed the land, cursed his family.

His father and the other men had promised the land would get better if they got rid of the Roamers. But just as Shakta had taken his revenge by cursing the land with his dying

1

breath, so the Roamers somehow continued the destruction, though everyone swore they were all dead.

Chris paused by a spindly tree, resting his hand against the bark, and stared up at the sparse leaves fluttering in the wind. These, too, would be gone soon, gone like the water from the river where he had played as a child. The water back then had been slow-moving and muddied, but he and his friend Thomas had gone down there every day. Katie Topkins had sometimes come along, too, and most of the other children, and they had all splashed about in the water. He had always been searching for tadpoles. His mother had told him about tadpoles. But he had never seen one.

And he never would, he thought sourly, looking back at the dry riverbed. The Roamers had taken that from him. And they would take him at last, too. Damn them.

Chris pulled away from the tree, hurrying up the path to his house. He had dinner to fix yet; no time to waste with this idle dreaming. It would change nothing.

Chris slammed the front door behind him and strode to the peg by the pantry. He did not so much as glance at his father sitting at the kitchen table. He knew he was watching.

"Get the cows milked?" his father's roughened voice asked.

"Yes." Chris hung the empty pail on the hook.

"But . . . where's the milk?"

Chris turned slowly. "It was bad. I dumped it."

His father glared at him a moment, then looked away. "Damn Roamers," he muttered.

"They're all dead. It's been years since the last was spotted." Chris sat heavily in the chair opposite his father, his voice challenging. "It's gotten worse since they've gone, not better, the way you promised it would."

His father's head reared up. "I'll not permit you to talk to me like that!" He grabbed Chris' wrist roughly. "Understand?"

Chris choked back his own anger as it pushed into his throat. "Yes."

"Good." His father let him go, shoving his wrist away. "Get some dinner on this table. I'll go get some more wood." The old man lurched to his feet, puffing air, and shrugged into his coat, pulling it over stiff arms. He wrenched the door open and stomped out, slamming it behind him.

Chris moved to the fireplace. He hung the blackened pot over the fire and poured some water into it. He poured slowly, trying to keep out the scum that always coated the surface of the well water these days. He set the bucket down and pulled some carrots and potatoes from the sacks in the pantry, dumping them on the table. They were small and rubbery.

The knife drawer jammed when he went to open it; he jerked it free with a curse and felt deep in the back for the cause of the problem. His fingers encountered fabric; he recognized the faded blue material he pulled out as an old apron of his mother's. For a moment he fingered the delicate embroidery she had stitched across the waistband, then he grabbed a knife and slammed the drawer shut. "Damn Roamers!"

But as he laid the apron on the edge of the table, he felt a familiar moment of guilt, as if it was somehow his fault his mother was dead. Had he had something to do with it? He shook his head, turning to the potatoes. It was the Roamers.

She had gone to them once, to the Roamers, and come back with a powder that she had sprinkled on all their beds. Why had she agreed to use a Roamer poison? Had she believed it would help them against Shakta's curse? Even after all the Roamers had been killed off, it still hadn't saved her.

Chris remembered that awful night ten years ago. The men of the village had all met at his house to discuss what should be done with the Roamers. They had met late at night, long after his mother had put him to bed. But the low rumble of their voices in the kitchen had awakened him, and he crept down the hallway to peer through the curtains.

A fat man was standing up. It was Mr. McGreggor, his friend Sarah Anne's father. "I hear tell that it's the same in other towns that have the Roamers traipsing through, what with their devil worship, their wild drinking and dancing and lusting after women."

"*Our* women." Mr. Topkins bolted to his feet. "They don't want only their Roamer women. They have need for what's pure, our wives and daughters. You all know I've already lost one of my daughters to them. And my only son, trying to protect her! I won't stand for any more."

The confusion that followed, filled with angry accusations and possible solutions, was finally silenced by a man Chris did not know. The stranger stood and banged his fist on the table, making a loud booming noise that echoed through the kitchen and down the hallway where Chris stood hidden.

"My thinking," the man said in the moment of silence he had achieved, "is that you ought to begin doing what the other towns have already done." Some murmurs followed this.

"There's an awful lot of them . . ." Mr. McGreggor muttered.

"But what about that old tale? What about the Dark Prince?" Mr. Topkins came to his feet again. "The Dark Prince is supposed to right the lands, not us."

Some laughter followed this, but it was more to ease their tension than to ridicule. None of them were so sure they didn't put some stock in the story.

The stranger stood up again, raising his hands for quiet. He nodded to each of them.

"And just what do you think the Dark Prince is?" There was another silence. "Death," the man whispered. Then his listeners all nodded in understanding.

So intent was Chris on listening that he did not hear his mother come up behind him in the dark hallway. He nearly cried out in surprise when her thin fingers bit into his shoulder.

"Get back into bed," she whispered, shoving him in the direction of his room. Her eyes held a wide, frightened look, and that look followed him into his room and into his dreams, where he was carried away by the dark-haired Roamers with their golden rings and wild eyes. Dancing, they had raised him up over their heads in offering to Satan . . .

The next day he had told his friends Thomas, Sarah Anne, and Christine about what he had overheard.

"They're going to kill them all tonight?" Thomas asked. "But what about the curse on your family? This won't help.

My father told me so. Your dad told him you need to find one of those Shaktas, and kill him."

"A Chruston does," Chris snapped back. "A Chruston has to kill a Shakta, and I'm not a Chruston."

"Then I guess you better find a Chruston, too. Or else . . ." Thomas let his voice drop meaningfully.

Chris shook his head to clear the bitter memories, even as his hand tightened on the knife he still held. He pulled the carrots toward him and began chopping them with swift, angry strokes. Thomas had been right, the Extermination hadn't saved his mother. He realized now that she had known it wouldn't.

He remembered her sadness the night of the Extermination. Helplessly, he recalled the way his mother had paced about the kitchen, casting quick glances out the window at the slowly gathering knot of men.

"Clear your dishes, Chris," she had said to him, and he had slid off the window bench where he was watching and dutifully begun to clear the table.

"He'll be all right, Mother." Chris stared up at her as she walked past him.

"Of course." She stopped at the front window, her thin fingers gripping the sill.

"Wish I were going," Chris muttered. "Thomas gets to go."

"Don't you say that!" His mother turned on him with a snap.

Chris shut his mouth, lowering the spoon in his hand.

She advanced on him slowly. "Don't you be like that, Christopher. You promise me. Promise me!"

Chris looked up, bewildered.

"Do you hear me?" she whispered, leaning across the table. He stepped back. "It's wrong—horribly, horribly wrong —what they're doing."

"But—"

"It's wrong!" She turned away from him, her eyes now following the men as they moved away. Her arms wrapped themselves about her to ward off a chill Chris couldn't feel.

"Promise me, Chris. Promise me you'll never kill. Never. Promise me."

Chris looked at the still-uneaten food on his plate.

"Remember the bird? The baby bird you and I nursed back to health? Remember when it learned to fly? Flying golden in the morning. Do you remember, Chris? Do you?"

"Yes."

"Good." She turned back to him. "Remember when I'm gone. Remember that little bird. Your father, he said to kill it, remember? It was a hawk. Remember?"

Chris nodded once.

"Remember the big rat it killed and ate? That was good. It was good we didn't kill it. It flew off free after that, free and alive. It was good."

Chris nodded again, afraid now to tell her that his father had shot it the next day when it ate one of their chickens. She walked closer to him as the torches of the men in the window behind her disappeared into the woods.

"Promise me. All life is precious. Do you promise?" She leaned down close to him, her light eyes looking strangely dark in the dim light.

"Yes, Mother."

She stood straight again. "Go get ready for bed, then."

Chris left in a hurry, anxious to be away from the oppressiveness in the kitchen. He knew this was not the night to beg a few more minutes of staying up. But the feeling of tension didn't leave him, even as he lay in bed and the minutes passed.

He flinched involuntarily at the crack of the first gunshot as it echoed across the valley. He clambered up and pressed his face to the window. Distant gunshots filled the air then, like the crackling at the start of a loud peal of thunder. The base of Mount Klineloch was bathed in ruddy light, and Chris realized with an odd chill that the Roamer camp was afire.

He slid off his bed then, tiptoed back to the kitchen, and peered through the curtains. His mother was curled in the big armchair before the fire. The light flickered erratically, like the shots in the distance. She began sobbing quietly against the back of the chair, her hair pulled down and hanging over her eyes.

Chris hesitated, then stepped through the curtains. He re-

alized he should comfort her. It was expected. She looked up
at him, hearing the boards creak under his approach, then
stood, reaching quietly for his hand. He gave it resolutely.
She pulled him close and hugged him so tightly his breath
was lost.

He remembered hearing her mutter something, her lips
pressed against his hair. It was something about dying. She
said she didn't want to die and that they were all going to die.
Her voice had a high pitch to it, like a chant, or a frightened
squeal. He struggled to pull away, but she lifted him and
carried him back toward his room. Her cheek had been
against his head, and she had grown quiet. Her hair swung
about his neck, tickling the small hairs up.

"Into bed with you." She set him down and smoothed his
hair as he lay down. Her eyes looked swollen and the dim
light cast strange shadows on her face. "Close your eyes." He
closed them, but still he saw her face behind his eyelids.

She tucked the blankets about him, then began singing
softly. Her gentle voice barely masked the random shots that
still echoed on the air.

> It comes to you desired, tired or not
> Sleep, my boy, 'tis a blessed thing
> Trouble will go, light will follow
> Sleep, my boy, 'tis starlight lit
> Ancient orb encircles mind, relieving
> Sleep, my child, promise is in him
> Who takes the gift given you, by me, by him
> To sleep, my little one, all must sleep
> All that was saved by lack of sleep
> To sleep, little boy, it must be
> Come be returned to his trust
> To sleep, little boy, 'tis a blessed thing

The shooting had stopped, and for a moment there was
only quiet. Then Chris heard his mother stifle a sob as she
eased off the bed and left the room. He lay there drifting,
drifting, until he heard the men's voices in the air, laughing
as they returned . . .

Chris started a bit and realized he had been staring at his

mother's apron. Turning, he stoked up the fire under the pot, trying to get the water to come to a boil. Yes, he was certain his mother had known that killing the Roamers wouldn't save her.

And she had fallen sick shortly after the Extermination. At the time, he hadn't thought that the sickness was anything, but she hadn't gotten any better. She just stayed in bed and got thinner and paler, as if she were just going to fade away.

He remembered going to her room one evening, to say good night. But she hadn't seemed to see him there. She was mumbling strangely, and her eyes were rolled back. He just stood in the doorway in horror. In the bed, who was that? His father was in the corner, just a shadow, eyes glittering faintly in the candlelight, hands shoved deeply into his pockets.

"Say good-bye to your mother, son." His father's voice sounded unused.

"Good-bye?" Chris tried to find his father's face, but it blended into the corner, eyes closed.

Chris turned back to his mother then. Her once-long brown hair had become only a few withered strands, thin and dull. Her face was drawn and pinched, her mouth slack as she muttered. Her hands, which had always been cool and soft as they stroked his hair when she kissed him good night, fidgeted spasmodically on her stomach, the skin loose on her finger bones.

"Mother?" Chris started to cry then. The word no longer fit her. His father growled something at him, and Chris moved closer to the bed.

His mother's eyes focused a bit, and a hand reached weakly for him. He pulled back.

"Christopher," she whispered. "Promise? Promise never to kill. Promise."

"Yes, yes, I promise," he said quickly; anything to bring her back. He would love her as he should, if only she would come back! He couldn't love her like this. He couldn't. "I promise. I do."

Her hand fell back to its fidgeting, never reaching him. "The powder," she whispered. "The powder. Roamer." And

Chris knew then that it was the poison she had taken from the Roamers that was killing her.

The next morning she was still and cold as his father buried her out by the old oak—dead, too, long ago. The man had hugged the corpse close as he laid it gently in the dark hole. He hadn't touched Chris, hadn't said one word! He had stared at him as if he were a stranger. Chris had stared back, so empty inside there was nothing. It was the neighbors who had hugged him and had told him how brave he was not to cry and that his mother would always be with him. Chris shivered even now, thinking of that cold, stiff body being near him, remembering his nightmares of the dry earth reaching up like hands to pull him down to her.

Chris tossed the potatoes into the water that was boiling sullenly over the fire in the hearth. It was the Roamers who had killed his mother those long years ago, and he could still sometimes hear her warning in his sleep. *"The powder. Roamer."* The Roamers had killed her, with their poison and their curses.

He frowned, walking toward the cellar, feeling a tension rising in him. He reminded himself that his mother's death— her murder—couldn't have had anything to do with his own dealings with the Roamers as a child, with the strange box that the old Roamer woman had given him. He rubbed his temples, pressing those thoughts from his head. No, it was the powder and Shakta's curse. There was nothing he could have done.

He pulled strips of smoked meat from where they hung in the cellar, carried them to the pot, and tossed them in. He glanced at some of the few remaining spice jars, then grabbed one.

"May as well use it now as later. Doesn't look much like there's going to be any special occasion to hold out for." He dumped the small amount remaining into the stew and stirred slowly. He had time. It would be a while before his father got back with the wood. There was always a reason to stop at the inn for a drink with some old and equally bitter friends.

They would talk about the old days—as if talk would bring them back! Chris released the spoon and sat back on his

heels. There wasn't any sense remembering what was long
gone, wishing it would come back. It wouldn't, and it was
time everyone got used to it. He took hold of the spoon and
stirred once more, then let go and watched it swirl with the
contents. Sometimes things just had to be accepted.

His father crashed back into the room so suddenly that
Chris dropped the spoon into the ashes. "All dead, huh?"
His father panted as he stood there grinning. "You thought
they were all dead. Now I know why the milk's gone bad.
Ha!"

"What are you talking about?" Chris frowned as he poked
the spoon out of the fire, then turned to his father.

"I got me a damned Roamer down at the riverbed, that's
what. And if it isn't the same one that tricked me out of
killing him when you were a boy. Same look, he has, but not
so cocky this time. Oh, he's scared all right. He's been
through trouble, that's for sure. Can barely move. So he
knows he can't go anywhere." The man turned and reached
for his rifle where it hung by the door. He ran his fingers over
the cold metal of the barrel before he lifted it down and
turned back to his son, his eyes gleaming. "And he knows
where I'm going. They can tell those things. You remember."
He hurried out the door then, rifle over his shoulder, the
stiffness in his old limbs suddenly gone.

Chris ran to the door and watched as he disappeared into
the woods. A Roamer? What was his father talking about.
He had said it was the same one who had tricked him . . .

Chris gripped the door frame. Arron? The Roamer whose
grandmother had given him that box? He stepped back
stiffly, closing the door. He had nothing to do with . . . He
shook his head. What was one Roamer more or less, anyway?
He turned back to the pot and picked up the spoon. The
memories of his one meeting with the Roamers pressed into
his mind. He gripped the spoon tightly, stirred once, then
again, the stew splashing over the side. Damn him! He threw
the spoon down and went after his father, unsure if he
wanted the Roamer dead or not.

II

THE DAY HE HAD MET THE ROAMER, HE AND HIS FRIENDS
Thomas, Christine, and Sarah Anne had been playing down
at the river, as always. Thomas had been teasing Chris again
about the Roamers, about what they were doing to his family. It had been Christine who had come to his defense.

"Shut up, Thomas," Christine had said.

And Thomas had turned on her, arms outstretched. "Ooh,
look out! I'm Shakta, come to put a curse on your family,
too. Yah! Yah!" And he chased Christine off into the woods.

"Stop it, Thomas," Chris yelled after him, but he was relieved he had gone.

It was when Christine's screaming stopped suddenly that
he and Sarah Anne thought about going after them. But
Thomas and Christine appeared almost instantly after that,
their faces pale.

"Roamer," Thomas cried in a hoarse voice, and they all
went charging up the path, away from the river. No Homesteader ever wanted to be around a Roamer. The things they
could do with their evil magic gave all Homesteader children
nightmares.

Chris stumbled as he pushed Sarah Anne up the path in
front of him. He scrambled to his feet immediately, not want-

ing to be around when the Roamer stole the fish from his
father's traps. That would be the only reason a Roamer
would be coming down to the river. Roamers survived off of
what they took from the Homesteaders, never staying put in
one place long enough to provide for themselves.

The Roamer was going to steal from his father's traps.
And that thought was what stopped Chris. He had to protect
the traps. Had to. And he turned back toward the river, at
the last minute hiding himself among the dry weeds scattered
about the edges, thinking how proud his father would be of
him for saving the fish and defeating the Roamer.

The Roamer strode out of the woods from the other path.
He was a boy. Chris breathed a sigh of relief at that. There
would be nothing much a Roamer boy could do. And there
he was, striding confidently down to the water's edge. His
bright clothing stood out against the brown scenery. Roamer
clothes were always finely made, of bright silky cloth embroidered with many-colored patterns that seemed to move even
when the wearer was still. But it was the black hair and black
eyes of the Roamers that chilled the hearts of the Homesteaders. The Roamers might try and cover their dark souls
with their colorful clothing, but the blackness of their eyes
betrayed them.

Chris smiled to himself then. He would easily be able to
grab this boy when he tried to steal from his father's traps.
Let the Roamer try and lie away the fish as it hung from his
stealing fingers. Chris would turn him proudly over to his
father.

But the Roamer only stood quietly on the bank. He didn't
go near the traps. Chris watched closely, waiting for the
chance to accuse him. But the Roamer just stood there, staring at a rock at his feet. Then he bent down to it, slowly, and
lifted the stone, weighed it a moment in one hand, then
passed it to the other. He tossed it in the air and watched it
fall. Chris looked on, curious. What was the Roamer doing?
Choosing the right stone to kill fish?

The Roamer picked up the stone once again, his face
thoughtful. Then he nodded, a quick smile coming to his lips.
He placed the rock on the ground and knelt before it. Then
he began humming, eyeing the rock still. He altered the tune,

lowering his head to his chest. What was he doing? His head came up with a snap, the tune breaking off.

Chris smiled at that. The Roamer had hurt himself somehow. That would please his father. But then the smile faded from Chris' lips, and all his nightmares of the Roamers came rushing back to him. The rock—the rock in front of the Roamer, it had moved a bit. By itself! Then again, as if it were alive! It hesitated, striving to rise from the earth. Almost up. Down again, no up—yes, completely up! It hung upon the air, the invisible hand of Satan holding it there.

The Roamer! Chris stepped back. How could the boy do that unless he was with the devil? Chris had to stay still! The Roamer would hear him and bring the whole caravan down upon him.

The stone thumped back to the earth then as the Roamer turned to look at the bushes. He stared for a long time, his dark eyes piercing the reeds, not seeming to notice that the stone had fallen. Chris held perfectly still. The Roamer at last turned back to the stone. Chris closed his eyes and let his breath out slowly, quietly.

He peered out again only on hearing a splash. The Roamer boy was up to his knees in the water. He was leaning out, tugging on something. His father's traps! But Chris didn't dare to move—the stone . . . the magic . . .

The Roamer hoisted the trap up and neatly pulled out the fish inside, then tossed the trap back. Chris clutched at the reeds about him. What could he do? He couldn't just let the Roamer get away with that. How dare he? How dare he!

The Roamer was starting back toward shore. He stopped again, the fish slipping from his fingers. It made a small splash and was gone. The Roamer was staring at the bushes again.

"Come out of there," he said.

Chris started at the sound of the boy's voice and at seeing the dark eyes of the Roamer staring directly at him.

"Are you going to come out?"

Chris just stared back, still not daring to move.

The boy tilted his head as he looked Chris over, his face just as it was when he had examined the stone. He lowered his eyes then, either embarrassed or angry. Chris was unsure.

"I'm not stealing your fish," he said, as if patiently explaining. "It's not yours until you've come and taken it."

"Words for a thief," Chris shouted at him from the safety of his fortress. "You leave none for us. We do all the work, and you leave none for us!"

"There just aren't that many to catch." The Roamer looked back at the murky water as if he regretted dropping the fish.

"That's not true! We always had a lot of fish," Chris shouted. "A lot, that is, until you Roamers came." Chris raised his chin a bit then. "So my father says."

The Roamer only stared back at him, then shrugged his shoulders. None of it seemed to matter to him. "Well," he said at last, "if that's what you were told, then that's what you were told." Then he grinned suddenly, mocking him. Chris clenched his hands into fists, wanting to reach out and slap the smile from his face. "Don't ever question what they tell you, Homesteader. You might find them wrong. Then what would you do?" He leaned slightly toward Chris, daring him out of the bushes. "You're a weak lot all around, you Homesteaders. Having trouble surviving the tough times? That's just too bad."

Chris leaped out of the bushes, prepared to beat the Roamer into the sand. He couldn't just battle him with words—it was more than that. The insults! To the entire Homesteader population, to him and his family. Oh, what they had done to his family! To his mother—and one day to him as well, with the curses the Roamers had brought down on them all. They had no right! He was going to fix it all right there, right then.

But the Roamer had merely stepped out of his reach, humming, unconcerned. And Chris had sprawled at his feet, his foot catching on something.

Then the Roamer had the advantage. Chris was certain the Roamer boy would leap on him and pummel him into the ground—or worse. The coward! Chris felt the tears stinging into his eyes with the force of his anger, his hatred. But he knew the men of the village would take care of the Roamers that night, take care of them all! Chris struggled to get up to defend himself.

"Sorry," he heard the Roamer say. Then he felt a hand come up under his arm and pull him to his feet. Chris stood there in surprise, feeling stupid.

"My name is Arron." The Roamer brushed the dirt from Chris' shirt. Then he caught at Chris' arm, turning it slightly. Chris tried to pull away, realizing the Roamer was trying to capture him.

"You're cut." Arron pointed to a long gash on Chris' arm. He hadn't even felt it when he had fallen on the sharp stone. He stared at the blood as it dripped onto the white sand. "It's closer to my wagon than to your house. Come on. My grandmother will clean it up." Chris tried to pull back. The Roamer gripped his arm tighter. "It's bleeding rather badly. You won't make it home by yourself." Chris hesitated, but Arron took his arm firmly and led him down the path.

Chris remembered how the Roamer wagons had been scattered about at the point where the path had broadened as it emerged from the woods, under the great shadow of Mount Klineloch. Chris had pulled back as he and Arron approached the wagons. The Roamer men were squatting at fires burning dimly in the daylight. Some glanced up at him, their dark eyes raking his figure. He became painfully aware of his Homesteader looks, of his loose-fitting Homesteader clothing. He looked once more at Arron's close-fitted trousers and short waistcoat, brightly colored and carefully embroidered. His own earth-brown, loosely woven clothes stood out here, when they should normally blend in. Homesteader —everything about him fairly shouted it. He felt he should not be there.

"Come on. What are you so scared of?" Arron turned on him, his grip on Chris' arm tightening. Chris stared at the nearest wagon. A Roamer woman sat on a man's lap. She was laughing, her hair falling in long black waves onto his shoulders. Some Roamer children played in a circle, singing strange, crazed songs, spinning and spinning.

"It's just to the other side of camp," Arron said impatiently. "Are you all right? Do you think you can make it? I can help you. We're almost there."

"No." Chris began to pull away in earnest.

Arron grinned. "Afraid, huh?"

"No!" Chris stopped pulling away.

"Yeah. You Homesteaders are afraid of everything. And stupid, too, if you don't get that cut taken care of."

Chris snapped his arm from Arron's grip, raising his other fist. Arron put his hand over it.

"Sorry," he said softly. "Come on. It's not far. That cut really needs to be taken care of. There's nothing to be afraid of."

"I'm not afraid!"

Arron nodded silently at that and took a tight hold on his arm again. The bleeding had slowed. He led Chris forward once more, and Chris plodded beside him, knowing he couldn't turn and run. He couldn't. He wasn't going to let the Roamer know he was afraid. But he wasn't able to help glancing nervously at the Roamers who began to surround them.

The children who had been playing in the circle had stopped abruptly as he approached. They stepped silently to the side as he and Arron passed. They were the ones who were afraid, Chris told himself smugly, afraid of him. He looked at them scornfully, but then he saw it was Arron they stared at so quietly. Chris turned to Arron then, walking beside him with an arrogant stride.

Chris tried to match his pace as some of the Roamer men came forward from their fires to watch them pass. Instead of the fearless stride he wanted, Chris felt himself moving closer to Arron, as if for some protection. All the men were watching the Roamer boy, a circle of quiet stares, from knowing, dark eyes. Chris stumbled then, his legs numbed with his fear, as he recognized the face of the Roamer man who stood ahead of them, nodding thoughtfully toward Arron. Chris was sure it was one of the men from his nightmares, the one who had raised the knife to cut out his heart! Chris' hand came up to his chest as his breathing became troubled. Arron steadied him, grinning again.

Then Arron had stopped and pointed to a wagon in front of them. Chris just stood there shaking his head. He wouldn't go in. He wouldn't. The Roamers were all staring, staring at Arron who had brought them their sacrifice for the evening.

Chris quaked as he realized that the Roamer boy had tricked him into walking freely into the camp. He was to have been the one to bring the Roamer to his father. Instead, he was the one who had been taken, he was the one to stand trembling.

He refused to go farther.

"In there." Arron indicated the wooden stairs once again. Chris remained frozen, body and mind numb. Arron released him with a sigh. He placed Chris' right hand over the cut on his left arm and pressed it tightly over the wound. The blood oozed between Chris' fingers, while Arron climbed the stairs alone.

"Grandmother," he called into the wagon.

Run! Chris had only one thought in his mind. Run! But his body would not respond. All the Roamer men clustered around him, waiting with their shining earrings and knives. Run! But the thought came too late. Arron climbed back down with his grandmother behind him. She smiled at Chris as she came forward with bandages. He saw in her eyes what he was sure she had to be thinking—what a wonderful sacrifice he would make. She knelt next to him, reaching for his arm. He pulled back, staring. She smelled like the spice jars in his mother's kitchen and she had a bright golden ring through her nose, like the one his father's bull had. Chris was sure she was evil, that she was going to kidnap him and sacrifice him to Satan. Images of his nightmares floated before his eyes, like the large, dark Roamer men all around. All he wanted was to beg for his freedom, but he was too frightened to speak.

Arron's grandmother made shooing motions to the men standing about. "Be off with you. Away." They all hesitated, then moved about their business.

"Ah, Arron, you've been beating up on other boys, have you now?" His grandmother turned her small eyes on him, then back to Chris.

Arron looked down and shrugged. "I made him angry," he said softly. He looked up again. "I told him I was sorry. And I brought him here to be healed to show him that I was." He looked at her, as if wanting something.

She reached out casually and ruffled his hair. "Never you mind, Arron, my child. We know you mean well." She turned back to Chris and began wrapping his arm, assuring herself the cut was clean. "Now, what might your name be?" She smiled again.

"He's Chris Douten," Arron said at her elbow.

Chris stared at the Roamer boy, his stomach growing cold. The dark eyes saw everything! Was there anything he did not know?

"Oh?" The old woman glanced at Arron, who nodded. She peered at Chris then. "Chris Douten?"

He just stood there. Was she asking?

"Sheila Douten's son?"

Chris stood at a loss. They knew his mother?

"Arron, my boy, did you steal his voice as well?" She smiled at Chris again.

"He thinks we mean to use him as a sacrifice."

Chris turned to Arron in horror, his face coloring.

"Arron!" The woman stood with a snap.

Arron lowered his head quickly, then tossed it back up, chin high. "Well, he does!"

"Go get some wood for our fire," the old woman said in a low voice. Arron nodded weakly and walked away.

A fire! They really were going to cook him. Arron was only taunting him further. Chris took a step backward, away from the old woman. She turned and clutched at his shoulder.

"That boy." She shook her head after the direction Arron had gone. "Don't worry, little Chris. He'll grow up someday. Can't leave other people's privacies where they belong, in their own heads." She knelt back down, her face close to Chris'. "Really now, we're not going to sacrifice you. You are much too important for that. You'll be needed later." She watched him a moment. "Really now," she added emphatically. Chris nodded. She smiled and patted him lightly.

Arron came back and dumped some wood noisily by the fire, then turned to glare at them. "Oh, all right," he said grudgingly, answering an unheard question.

His grandmother sighed and looked up at the peak of Mount Klineloch. "Arron, Arron."

He kicked at the logs by his feet, making chips of bark fly

into the air. Then he turned a calm face to the old woman. "Do you want me to get more?" he asked officially.

His grandmother nodded, and he stalked off.

She turned back to Chris, shaking her head. "Come, child." She took his hand. "I have something for you before you go, as you must. Your father will worry and be angry."

Chris didn't want to go into the wagon, but, with the old woman pulling him along, his hand clasped tightly in hers, he had no choice. She led him slowly up the creaky, wooden steps.

The light inside was dim. He stood still, blinking, while his eyes adjusted. A myriad of smells floated to his nose, all of them pleasant and homey. The bed, toward the back, was neatly made and piled high with thick, soft-looking blankets. The trundle underneath appeared to be where Arron slept. He wondered where Arron's parents were.

The old woman steered him to a table covered with a softly shimmering cloth. She sat him at a small bench and took the one on the other side. The chair, Chris thought, looked vaguely familiar. Hadn't the Topkins had one just like it on their front porch? It had disappeared just after the Roamers came. Chris stared up at the old woman who was leaning toward him.

"I have something I want you to keep hidden. It's for when you're older. Can you do that, Chris, my dear?"

Unsure, Chris nodded.

"We did the same for your mother once, trusted her." The woman beamed at him from across the table. And Chris thought of the time his mother had gone to the Roamer camp for the powder she had sprinkled in the beds. Was that what the woman was speaking of? Was that how she knew his mother?

"Now you must be like her, and not like your father, for a while." Chris shifted uncomfortably in his seat. She was insulting his father. But he didn't say anything, just watched as she pulled a tiny box from under the table. It was a dusky gray and not particularly interesting in any way. She opened it. A soft, silvery glow came from within, from a small, round sphere sitting lightly inside as delicate as a soap bubble.

She pushed it toward him. "Take it, boy, keep it safe." Her

voice became urgent, frightening him. "Don't open it, except when you are alone and afraid. It will give you comfort then." She watched him a moment. "Don't show it to anyone. Don't speak of it to anyone."

Chris hesitated, then nodded again.

"Touch it this once." She leaned closer to him. "Just so you'll know it's not so fragile as it looks. Go ahead. Touch it."

Chris reached out, carefully. His finger met the soft, smooth surface. It didn't break. A sudden fear rushed inside of him as something terribly cold seemed to pass through his mind. He struggled to pull his hand away. It had him! Then the silvery softness grew warm throughout him, and the fear left. He took his hand, reluctantly, from the sphere.

"You'll keep it safe?"

Chris nodded quickly.

The old woman shut the box and pressed it into Chris' hand. It fit easily into his palm. He curled his fingers about it, and it was hidden away. "Thank you, dear. Now, it's time you went home. Hide the box somewhere safe. Don't tell anyone—not your mother, not anyone." She looked up as Arron came into the wagon.

"Yes, I will," the Roamer boy answered.

She shook her head, lips pursed together.

Arron let out a sigh of frustration. "I'm sorry," he said quietly. "I'm trying, but I forget. It's just as if you asked me . . ." He let his voice drop to nothing.

"Will you walk him to the river, Arron?"

"Yes."

The walk back through the camp, Chris remembered, was worse than the one coming in had been. The Roamer Arron had walked at a leisurely pace, as if he were trying to test Chris, to see just how much he could take—all the time reading his mind to see how frightened he really was. There had been no hiding. And Chris felt both his fear and his resentment of the Roamers grow at each step.

Chris had stepped close at Arron's side, wishing he would hurry. He knew he wouldn't feel safe until he was far from the Roamer camp . . . and far from that strange boy.

Eerie. That's what it was on the shadowed side of Mount Klineloch. Chris could still see the other Roamers growing silent at their soft approach. Their wild laughter and talk died suddenly, and they stared at the two of them. Chris felt sure they all wanted to kill him. And yet, all they did was stare, stare at Arron.

He convinced himself then that they were only trying to make him unsure. Well, he decided, he wouldn't show them he was afraid. They were all thieves, he told himself, living off the Homesteaders.

He began to notice things around the camp. More things than just the bench in Arron's wagon had been stolen. A blanket hanging over a bush near one of the wagons reminded Chris that Mrs. Hoton had claimed things were disappearing from her laundry line. And Chris saw a horse that looked distinctly like the one Mr. Neten had lost the year before—the patch on the breast, and the one white foreleg.

That was when Chris decided that the Roamers wouldn't scare him. They were lousy thieves. He wouldn't give in to them. Though his legs ached to run, he firmly forced himself to match Arron's measured stride.

At last the camp and its gaudily clad Roamers with their dark, impassive faces were left far behind. Chris felt his breath come more easily from his tight chest. He glanced at Arron to see if the Roamer sensed his relief, but Arron only continued to walk silently beside him, not looking to either side, his gaze fixed on some point far ahead that Chris was not able to see. Chris continued to watch him, unable to place this quiet boy in the midst of the wild drinking and dancing of the Roamers. It was impossible even to imagine him living alone with that old woman, her small, dark eyes as bright as the golden ring through her nose. Where were his parents? Chris wondered. And the Roamer boy answered as if he had spoken the question out loud.

"They're dead."

Chris started at the sound of the Roamer's voice.

"What?"

"I said they're dead."

Chris stared, at a loss. "Who?"

The Roamer's eyes narrowed. "My parents. You

asked . . ." His voice trailed off, his eyes never leaving Chris.

The Roamer could hear everything he was thinking! Chris drew back from him, horrified. Then he turned forward, concentrating on the trees, trying to think of nothing.

"You don't have to walk me any farther," he managed.

"I'll take you to the river."

"You don't have to—"

"I'll take you to the river."

Get away! Something screamed inside of Chris. Run! But . . . admit he was afraid? To a Roamer? He wasn't afraid, not of those thieves. They were nothing. Let the Roamer be sure of himself now—it wouldn't be for so very long. The men in the village would take care of them tonight. He would like to see this Roamer then.

Arron stopped. Chris' palms grew cold and damp. The Roamer, he could hear everything—he had forgotten. Chris waited for him to say something, but he didn't. Chris clenched his fists. He wouldn't let a Roamer frighten him. What would his father think?

"Your grandmother said you weren't supposed to—" Chris started sharply.

Arron turned away. "Sorry," he muttered.

Neither said another word until they reached the river. Chris hurried to the water's edge. The murky water seemed to him to be crystal clear now, so relieved was he to see it and to be rid of the Roamer! Chris started away from Arron without a backward glance.

"Wait." The Roamer caught at his arm.

Chris tried to pull away. "What?"

"I . . ." Arron paused as if trying to say words he didn't know. "You . . . you don't understand." He stared at Chris, trying to see something. "It's not—"

"Let go." Chris pulled back.

"I wasn't trying to scare you. Really I wasn't. I wouldn't . . . can you understand?" He stopped. "Most Homesteaders wouldn't have had the courage, actually . . . to stay at the river," the Roamer finished oddly. Chris couldn't understand. The Roamer was complimenting him. He didn't often get . . . He pulled back. Arron was a Roamer, still, praise or no.

"And then I hurt you. I'm sorry. I wouldn't have had the guts—"

"Get away from my son!" Chris turned, hearing his father's voice boom from nearby. The big man stepped from behind the bushes Chris had hidden in earlier and leveled his shotgun at the Roamer boy.

Chris had caught at his breath then. He should have been glad to see it come to that, but his chest tightened as he saw the barrel trained on the small body of the Roamer. He wanted to run to his father and pull the gun away. But— he knew he should be at his side, helping him aim! Instead, he only stared numbly from the Roamer to his father.

"Come over here, son, where it's safe." Chris ran obediently to his father's side. "Your friends told me you might be in trouble," he said, looking down on the Roamer. He cocked the gun.

"He didn't hurt me, Papa," Chris said quickly.

"Nor is he ever going to. I've had it with your kind," his father said to the Roamer, "and your curses. You're not going to take my wife. You'll not touch her. We're going to take care of the lot of you tonight. But I'm going to start with you, now. So you won't be taking any more from us, boy. Destroy my wife, will you? Not while I'm alive."

A strange look passed over the Roamer's face. At first, Chris thought it was fear, but it looked more like he was sick instead.

"The gun will backfire if you shoot," the Roamer said suddenly.

His father's eyebrows came together in a frown. He lowered the gun slowly. "What? Can you work magic at a child's age?"

"It isn't magic," Arron said more boldly, the illness apparently past. "You haven't cared for it properly."

Chris' father growled and raised the gun again.

Arron raised his head a touch. "You'll risk your life to take mine? Who will protect your wife then?"

Chris' father took a sharp step back, the gun still not leaving the Roamer.

"Don't do it, Papa." Chris caught at his sleeve. "He's not worth it."

The man hesitated a moment more, then pointed the gun back to the path. "Be off with you," he snapped. "Mind you, I don't ever want to see you laying a hand on mine again."

"Oh, you won't." The Roamer grinned. "You won't." And he ran lightly off, down the path.

Chris had watched him disappear. It pained him now to remember how relieved he had been that the Roamer hadn't been hurt. He shouldn't have been relieved at all! But the Roamer hadn't seemed quite as evil as Chris had expected. He had tried to be nice, after all.

Chris had looked up at his father then and, in that moment, recognized that he had betrayed him. It had been the Roamer's fault. They were trying to force Homesteader families apart. That Roamer Arron and his grandmother were trying to drive him against his family. A bitterness swelled through him at that realization. They confused him so he wouldn't want his father to kill the Roamer. His fingertips brushed the box in his pocket, and he knew that he had betrayed them all. Yet he could not cast the box away right then. His father would see it and know. Chris decided he would get rid of it the moment he got home.

"We'll take care of the lot of them tonight," his father promised him. "And I'll see to that cocky Roamer myself." Then he turned to their path. Chris followed closely, a hand in his pocket.

His mother was out on the porch when they got back to the farm. She ran to Chris and hugged him tightly against her.

"What happened?" She looked wide-eyed at his father.

"Roamer had hold of him." He stopped and laid his hand gently on her shoulder. "The boy's all right now."

"Did you . . ." She bit her lower lip, then looked down at Chris, her pale, blue eyes taking in the bandage on his arm.

"Kill him?" He brushed her hair back from her face, looping the long strands back behind her ear. He laughed slightly. "You're too soft-hearted, Sheila. But don't worry, I didn't kill him. He claimed my gun would backfire. Didn't think I should risk it." He waited until her eyes met his again,

smiled, then pulled away and sat in the chair on the porch.
He opened the gun and examined it carefully.

Chris' mother squatted down next to Chris and looked at
his arm, then at him. Chris just stared numbly back. His
father glanced up.

"What happened to your arm, boy?" he asked, noticing the
bandage for the first time. "Did the Roamer do that?"

"No," his mother said suddenly, still watching Chris
closely. "He did it earlier, playing. It's nothing."

"Hmm." The man turned back to his gun, then snapped it
closed. "That brat lied to me. This gun is as clean as ever!"
He stood abruptly, aimed at a tree, and shot.

Sheila Douton jumped, then closed her eyes tightly, her
arms wrapping about herself. She stood slowly and took
Chris' hand and led him into the house.

"Damn Roamer. I'll get him for that," his father muttered.

Chris pushed those memories from his mind as he hurried
after his father. It couldn't possibly be the same Roamer.
What would he be back here for? Had he come to get the box
back? Chris had hidden it under a loose board in the floor
under his bed the day he had gotten it. He had never thrown
it away as he had promised himself he would; he hadn't been
able to. Whenever he opened it, it gave him comfort, promising him . . .

Did he have some power the Roamers had needed to hide,
some power they now wanted back in order to do more evil?
Did the box hold such a power? Or had he simply allowed
the Roamers to cause his mother's death? Had he really betrayed them all?

He skidded to a halt at the edge of the trees before the old,
dried-up riverbed. His father already had his rifle pointed at
a dark-haired young man whose face was cut and bruised, his
clothing torn and bloodied. Chris couldn't imagine how his
father was so certain it was Arron; it must be due to the
almost maniacal hatred he had for the boy who had tricked
him out of killing him. But surely Arron had been killed in
the raid so long ago. The Roamer raised his head and caught
Chris' eyes.

"Father, don't kill him," Chris said suddenly, unsure of his reasons. Maybe he just wanted to know if it really was Arron.

His father turned about slowly. The gun now pointed at Chris. "I knew it that day I caught the two of you together. You didn't want me to kill him then. Don't think I couldn't see that."

Chris shook his head, not quite able to deny it, but still unable to face the fact he had betrayed his family. "Father—"

"They killed her, boy." His father was whispering. Chris saw, with a feeling close to horror, the tears that suddenly appeared in his father's eyes. He never . . . never . . . He had loved her. "You helped them to kill her."

"I didn't!"

"You brought some magic home with you that night. I could feel it. I saw it take her strength. You helped them to kill your own mother. And now . . . now I'm going to pay them back—and you! I'll kill your friend here."

"Don't be stupid. I hate them as much as you do."

"Then enjoy this!" His father swung the rifle about quickly, pulling the trigger as it aimed on the Roamer.

The gun went off with a loud explosion, the barrel breaking into pieces. His father, screaming, staggered back and spun, falling facedown in the sand. Chris stood there screaming with him. He struggled forward, the sand sucking at his feet as he tried to run to his father's aid. He fell to his knees next to him, sobbing. Chris turned his father's body halfway over, then pulled back, choking, releasing his grip, letting the corpse drop back again with a dull thud. He turned away, his eyes falling now on the Roamer who lay with his face covered in his hands.

"You," Chris shrieked. "You killed them! You killed them both!" He jumped up and leaped upon the Roamer, beating him with his fists, pounding out the horror.

"Chris! Chris," the Roamer cried out his name in gasps and clutched weakly at his arms, trying to stop him. At the desperate sound of his name, Chris stopped and pulled back, eyeing the Roamer.

"Arron?" he asked in a low voice. The Roamer nodded shakily. Chris shoved him hard, making him cry out in pain.

"Why? Why did you do this? Why did your people do this to us? We've done nothing to you," Chris half sobbed.

"Nothing?" Arron choked on the word, and his face grew dark. Then he let his breath out with a hiss and looked away instead of venting his anger on Chris. "Oh, what's the point!"

Chris stared at him, trying to bring back his own anger so he could release the emptiness by killing this Roamer to avenge his father and his mother. He got up, kicking at the Roamer. Nothing.

He walked back to his father, pulled off his shirt, and wrapped it tightly about the shattered head. He took hold of the arms and began to drag his father slowly home. He could feel the Roamer watching him.

III

CHRIS PUSHED THE LAST SHOVELFUL OF DIRT ONTO THE grave as the sun was going behind Mount Klineloch. He rushed putting the rocks over the mound so the animals wouldn't get at it. Leaning on the shovel handle a moment, he stared at the two graves, then up at the old, rotting tree that stood over them. He hesitated, thinking he should say something, but nothing came to his numb mind. He stood a moment more, then shrugged and stomped back toward the house, glancing once in the direction of the river as the darkness set in.

He pressed the front door closed with his back and leaned against it, fishing in his pocket. He pulled out the wrinkled paper he'd found in his father's breast pocket. He walked to the table to smooth out the small portrait of his mother. The paper was torn in places, and the smooth lines of her face were smudged. Was it from his father touching it? Crying on it? Chris hadn't even noticed it missing from its place above the fire. He put it up next to the one of his father. The two tiny cameos, side by side as they were in their graves.

He bent and ladled himself some stew and sat at the table. He took a mouthful. The taste was flat, uninteresting. The empty chair at the other end of the table stared at him. He put his head down against the cold wood and listened to his own slow, steady breathing, shivering at the emptiness.

Perhaps it was his own fault his father was dead. His father might not have shot so quickly if he had not been so angered. Maybe he would have thought about the fact that the gun had not been cared for.

He sat up straight, pushing the bowl away. No, his father would have shot anyway, not wanting to be tricked a second time by the Roamer. He had been so wild with anger that first time Arron had tricked him . . . Oh, but he'd gotten the Roamer back. His father had killed more of them that night than any of the other men.

Chris stared again at the empty chair, remembering the men's voices floating down to his room from the kitchen when they came back that night, drunk and laughing. Stories about Roamer women screaming, and their children just staring, not understanding what was really happening. And the Roamer men, unable to protect themselves, their families . . .

"Nothing?" He thought he heard Arron's choked reply coming from the chair. Chris turned to look out the window. But the Roamer had tricked his father again. Oh, yes. He had been content to stay quiet about the gun this time. The Roamer had killed him.

Chris stood suddenly, tipping over his chair. It clattered noisily, echoing into the empty recesses of the house. He wanted to go to his room and stare into the sphere until it sucked him inside, into total comfort and forgetfulness. But the sphere would bring no comfort, it reminded him only of the Roamer now. What a mess everything had become.

He found he had walked down to his room. He turned from his doorway and walked to his parents' room. He stood facing the closed door. Why hadn't his father listened to him! Why did he have to shoot like that? And his father had cried, he stood there and cried when he spoke of his wife.

Damn it! Why hadn't his father ever cried for him. If he had held him once, just once . . .

But when had Chris cried for his father? He pushed his fingertips against his eyes, feeling the cold deep inside of him. It ached out from his chest into his limbs. His parents were dead, both dead, and he could never, never feel anything for them. He pressed his forehead against the door, his fingers resting on the knob. He wouldn't go in. He couldn't go in. It was very clear. His father knew Chris had betrayed him, that he had fought for a Roamer's life. Let the Roamer rot out there, then. That would get him back for the deaths he had caused, for the betrayal. It was their fault. Shakta's fault! Let him rot!

His fingers slid from the knob, and he straightened. The slight rustling of his clothes sounded loud in the vacant hallway. He turned, trying to walk silently back to the kitchen. His footfalls boomed against the walls. Where was his mother's pleading, his father's grumbling? Where were his own tears? Damn the Roamer.

He pushed his way through the curtains into the kitchen and stared at the empty room. The window was black with the night. The temperature, he knew, was dropping. He smiled grimly. The Roamer would freeze to death before the night ended. Good! A fitting end, matching the coldness they had made him endure in this house, his mother rotting alive and his father's mind going with her. And now he was next. Cold to the last; it was fitting. He imagined the cold seeping into the Roamer's battered body, down at the empty riverbed. The cold crept deeper into him with his thoughts. Damn!

He grabbed at a drawer, yanked it open, and pulled out the rolled strips of sheet his mother had carefully made for the emergencies for which she was forever preparing. The emergencies, it seemed, were always too sudden for the sheets to be of any use. He took up a lantern and walked out the door.

When he got to the riverbed, the Roamer was gone. Chris walked to the spot where he had been. The sand showed where he had dragged himself. Chris followed the trail up into the woods, through the fallen leaves. He stopped when he came to a small, clear space where he could see the Roamer lying. His breath was coming raggedly, forming faint clouds of steam above his face, as if his spirit were creeping from him in bits. Chris stepped forward, and the Roamer struggled up, suddenly wary.

"It's Chris."

Arron said nothing, just watched as Chris held out the bandages.

"You're hurt. I . . . I thought I might help."

The Roamer hesitated, then nodded weakly.

Taking that as an okay, Chris knelt beside him. Carefully he removed Arron's shirt. It was stuck in some places where dried blood had sealed it to the skin. Arron's eyes were tightly closed, his hands clenched into fists on the forest floor. Finally the shirt came loose, Chris' eyes widening at the welts across Arron's chest and back.

"What—what happened?" he managed to whisper. Then, quickly, he began to wrap the clean strips about him.

"Nothing," Arron said harshly.

"Hey, come on. I'm doing you a favor," Chris said, glancing at the Roamer.

"Thank you."

Chris shrugged, an uncomfortable feeling creeping slowly into his stomach. It wasn't his fault the Roamer was in this state. Arron began to shiver spasmodically. Chris touched his forehead; feeling the fever, he looked at Arron worriedly. The Roamer didn't look up at him. Chris had done as much as he had intended. But he didn't move to leave the Roamer.

"Are you hungry?"

Arron shook his head.

"Come on. When was the last time you ate?" Arron just shook his head. "Come on." Chris stood and reached to help Arron to his feet.

"No!" Arron recoiled suddenly. "No. I . . . I can't leave here."

"Why?"

The Roamer hesitated, then raised a trembling hand to point. Chris swung the lantern around, illuminating the form of another body wrapped in a blanket. He knelt next to it. It was Arron's grandmother.

"I would never have come back here. But she insisted she be buried here. I don't know why. But that was all she asked from me. She did so much for me. I have to do this for her. And I'll not leave her here, alone in the dark. She was always afraid to be alone." Arron looked away. "But I think she is."

He put a hand over his eyes. "I can't hear her. I try, but I can't . . ."

Chris sat near Arron again. He took the Roamer's arm. Arron's fingers caught at Chris' hand as if trying to gain comfort from his presence. "She wouldn't want to live forever, now would she? Come on, she was very old. She had her time, and I'm sure she'd want no more from you than you've given. Arron, everyone dies sometime . . ."

Arron released his grip, tried to pull away. "Oh, your people have done nothing to us!" He stared at his grandmother. "Nothing."

Chris watched him carefully. The fever seemed to be getting the best of him. "Arron, you can't blame us for her death. That raid happened so long ago. You survived. People just die when they're old."

"Not the way she did. I wanted to help. But she said to stay quiet, not to fight it—to live. She demanded it. I could feel how important it was to her even as her mind became fuzzy from the pain. And I could feel my hatred!"

Chris rocked back on his heels. "Arron. Arron, we'll bury her. We'll do it right now. I wasn't there. You know I wouldn't do it, I wouldn't kill her. I wouldn't . . ."

Arron shook his head. "I'm sorry. I didn't mean to . . . I mean, I know you wouldn't." He paused staring at the blanket-wrapped figure. "It's just, I can still hear her pain as her voice told me what to do. I couldn't even promise her. She couldn't hear. I couldn't even tell her yes! Her pain! It echoes in my head and won't stop!" He clapped his hands to either side of his head, eyes wide. Chris thought he had gone insane. It had to be the fever.

"We'll bury her right in this clearing."

"She'll find her."

"Who will?"

"The one. The one speaking to my grandmother when she was dying. Grandmother was so—so scared. Something about me. She shut me out to protect me from her. Something about doing . . . something . . . I can't hear! Why did you shut me out, Grandmother?" He strained toward the corpse. "Talk to me!"

"She's dead, Arron."

"He's not."

Chris shook his head, unable to make sense out of that. "I'll get a shovel, and we'll bury her and pile rocks on it. She'll be safe."

"I think it's too late," Arron said very quietly.

Chris nodded and stood. "I'll be right back," he said slowly, carefully, not wanting to make Arron any more upset.

After she was buried, Arron seemed much calmer.

"Can you leave her now?"

"I guess."

"Here." Chris handed him the shovel to use as a support, then started to lift the Roamer's pack over his shoulder.

"No!" Arron reached sharply for the pack.

Chris paused, sighed in frustration, then lowered it to the Roamer. "Come on, you can't carry that. Let me."

Arron watched him a moment, then opened the pack and carefully lifted something from the top, some sort of musical instrument in a cloth case. Chris watched him fumble with it, then bent to help him sling it over his shoulder.

"I wasn't going to drop it or anything. Can I carry your pack now?"

Arron nodded. Chris slung it over one shoulder, then hoisted Arron to his feet, supporting him with one arm about his waist. They slowly made their way back to the house.

He sat Arron in a chair at the table, ladled some broth from the stew into a bowl, and set it before him. The Roamer took a few slow spoonfuls, looking carefully about him. He set the spoon down, exhausted.

"You all right now?" Chris asked softly.

Arron nodded, shivering.

"I'll clean you up a bit more and then you can get some sleep. Okay?" Chris helped him into his own room. Carefully he removed the bandages, washed the wounds, and put on some of the salve that was left in the house. Arron kept pulling away and wouldn't let Chris touch him. Finally he was rebandaged. Chris helped him lie down and pulled the covers over him. The Roamer caught hold of his hand as he moved to leave.

"Don't . . . don't . . ."

"Don't what?"

Arron swallowed painfully and shook his head slightly. "Thank you." His fingers tightened slightly on Chris' hand, then fell away. Chris stared down at him a moment, his hand still extended to the Roamer, then he turned and left the room.

Early in the morning the fever had grown worse. Chris had set the instrument on the stand by the bed to protect it from Arron's thrashing. The Roamer babbled incessantly. Chris stared down at him, unsure what to do. He kept the bandages clean, changing them when they got soaked with blood as the Roamer tore the wounds open with his movements. He worked to keep the fever down. That was the best he could hope to do. He was no doctor, and getting one was certainly out of the question, he realized as he stared at the Roamer.

"Protect it . . . the box . . . protect . . ." Arron rambled, suddenly louder.

"What?" Chris leaned close to him. What was he saying?

"Grandmother? Tell them! The box . . . don't let them hurt you! Tell them . . . protect? Me? Chris?"

"What? What are you saying?" Chris wanted to shake him awake, but knew this was as awake as he would be until the fever broke.

There was a knock on the door. Chris hesitated, but Arron had grown quiet again. He turned and went to the door.

He opened the front door and stood blinking dazedly at Mr. McGreggor. There was a Roamer in his house! What was he doing? What was he going to say? How . . . what could he tell him? Mr. McGreggor waited, expecting some sort of greeting, then looked closely at Chris, seeing the fatigue and confusion that lined his face. He took Chris' arm to steady him.

"Christopher? Are you ill? Where's your father? We expected him at the inn last night. Is everything all right?"

Chris shook his head, numbly trying to sort out the questions and his own thoughts. What was he to say? He hadn't slept last night, he'd been up tending the Roamer. A Roamer! How could he explain that? He just kept shaking his head.

Mr. McGreggor pushed him worriedly back into the house and sat him down gently. "Now, where's your father? Christopher, are you all right?"

"Dead. He's dead," Chris finally managed. It seemed so long ago, yet it was just last night.

Mr. McGreggor pulled back, his face growing pale. Now it was Chris who was reaching out to steady. But the man had regained his composure and was putting a strong arm about Chris' shoulders. "Oh, Chris, I'm so sorry. How did it happen? You should have come and gotten someone."

"His gun backfired. He . . . he was hunting something. I . . . I never saw," Chris stammered out. He was lying! Lying to his neighbor, someone who trusted him.

The heavy-set man nodded slowly and smoothed Chris' hair. "Is he back there?" He pointed to the curtain that closed off the back of the house.

"No!" Chris stiffened. "I—I already buried him. Next to my mom."

The man patted his arm comfortingly. "You're taking this very well. I'm proud of you. Come on now, get your things together. You can stay with us awhile."

"No! I mean, no, I'm fine. I want to stay here. I don't want to leave . . ." He paused to see Mr. McGreggor's reaction.

"I don't think you should be alone—"

"I have to. I can't go into the village," Chris interrupted. "I have to sort this out on my own. I . . . I just can't face anybody right now—them not knowing what to say, and me not making it any easier. No, I have to stay here. I . . . I just have to. Can you understand?"

The man looked him over briefly, then nodded, smiling one of those meant-to-be-comforting smiles. "Of course, of course, Christopher. As you wish. But our door is always open. You know that."

"Thanks. I appreciate it."

"I'd like to pay my respects, if you don't mind."

"Of course." Chris hesitated. "Do you . . . do you mind going alone? I . . . I'd rather . . ." He couldn't stand the thought of going out to the grave when he was tending his father's murderer right at this moment. He opened his mouth to tell Mr. McGreggor about the Roamer. But no words came out.

"It's all right, Christopher. I would rather be alone. Your father and I, well, we were . . ." Mr. McGreggor squeezed Chris' shoulder warmly. "I'll be up to check on you again. And do come down and get some supplies at my store. No charge, of course."

"Thank you," Chris whispered, feeling ashamed.

Mr. McGreggor patted him on the shoulder and left the house.

Chris sat back down in the chair and stared toward the back of the house, unable to make himself go back into the bedroom. What was he doing? Caring for a Roamer. He should have killed him. His father. His mother. He rested his face in his hands, unsure.

IV

CHRIS CLOSED THE DOOR TO THE STORE QUIETLY BEHIND him, but Mrs. McGreggor noticed him instantly.

"Christopher!" She hurried over and took him firmly by the shoulders. "My, my, I've had a mind to go up to your house and give you a good talking to. Why, I've been worried sick! You should've come down days ago. I could've just killed my husband when he didn't make you come down here with him that day. Well, we'll just have that room all set up for you in a jiffy."

"No, no," Chris interrupted at her first breath. "I just came down for some supplies. I'm fine. Really."

"Now, Christopher, four days is quite enough time to lock yourself away. You needn't make a hermit out of yourself with grief. Why, we'll come up and give your house a good cleaning. The freshness will do you good."

"Please," Chris said, pulling away. "It's fine. I'm fine. I'd just like some supplies."

Mrs. McGreggor clucked her tongue once. "We're just worried about you, Christopher. Your parents were, well, we were all so close. You're like a son."

Chris looked down. "And I think of you as I thought of

37

my parents." He paused. "But, I'm just not ready, not to talk to anyone. Please. I'm really tired."

She lifted his head. "You look like you haven't slept a wink."

Chris shrugged. He hadn't, not really. He slept in the chair in front of the fireplace or in the one at the Roamer's bedside. He stiffened up thinking of the Roamer.

"I really do need those supplies. Then I'd like to get home and get some rest."

Mrs. McGreggor nodded. "All right. But you come down and see us."

Chris smiled and promised, handing her the list. She took it and went to the back of the store.

The bell on the door jangled, and Chris glanced up to see Mrs. Neten coming in with Christine close behind. Thomas, he could see, was outside taking care of the horses. Chris moved quickly to the counter. He didn't want to see them, not now. But Mrs. Neten had spotted him already and made her way to him.

"Chris? Oh, Chris. I just wanted to give my condolences."

Chris smiled and nodded. "Thank you."

Christine took his hand gently and squeezed it. Chris squeezed it back, grateful for her quiet understanding.

"So when's the happy day?" he tried to say brightly. He didn't want to talk about his father. He just couldn't.

Christine smiled broadly, her hand going to her belly. "A month, maybe." She was beaming.

"That's great. That's really terrific." Chris grinned harder as he realized he had backed himself up against the counter. Where was Mrs. McGreggor with his supplies?

Thomas came in and walked over. He thrust out his hand. "Chris."

"I hear another month before you're a father," Chris said, the smile pasted on his face.

"That's right." Thomas puffed himself up a bit and put an arm about Christine's waist.

"Well, that—that's great." He was out of words and just stood staring.

"Listen, Chris," Mrs. Neten caught hold of his arm and pulled him closer. "Well, you know Thomas has just about

gotten that house of his built. And then he and Christine will
be moving out. Well . . . that is, Mr. Neten and I thought
that maybe—I mean, we'll be all alone and you're alone. It's
sort of . . . well, Chris, there's no sense in both of us being
without family." She smiled quickly.

Chris jerked his hand from hers, not meaning to be rude,
but . . . without family. It struck him cold. He backed
away from them. Did they think he cared so little for his own
parents that he could just trade them in? Did they?

"Chris?" Christine reached out for him. Chris looked nervously at her swelling belly, then up at Thomas and back to
Mrs. Neten. They all knew his own family had been destroyed because of the curse of the Roamer Shakta, that he
could never have a normal family like Thomas and Christine
were about to have. They knew that in the end, he would
waste away as his mother had, and the same would happen to
all his children.

Mrs. Neten's offer, was it so much pity, pity that he could
never have what they all had? All the descendents of Chruston were doomed to fade away to nothing, their minds and
bodies withering like the land about them, until the curse was
destroyed—if it could ever be destroyed. Everybody knew
that.

His eyes fell on Christine's and Thomas' hands, inter-
twined. He could never . . . There would be no point in his
ever trying to have a family. Is that what they thought? Did
they think they could replace this? Make it up to him?

"I'm sorry," he whispered, shaking his head. He hurried
toward the back. "Mrs. McGreggor! Mrs. McGreggor," he
cried out.

She came out with the last of his supplies. "That's all of
it."

"How much?"

"Oh. No charge."

"How much?" He dug into his pocket.

"No, Christopher."

Chris took a deep breath, his hands were shaking.
"Please."

"No, Christopher, it's our gift."

"You don't owe me anything. I owe you. Please!" He

pushed some money into her hand, hoping it would cover it, then gathered up his packages and hurried from the store.

"Chris?"

Chris started awake. He glanced at the bedroom window; it was light out. He looked at the Roamer who was staring back wide-eyed—frightened, it appeared.

"Arron? How do you feel?" Chris straightened up and watched the Roamer recoil.

"I'm fine." His voice came in a whisper. He looked around the room nervously. "I don't . . . how did . . . when?" he started, then stopped, at a loss.

"It was about five days ago."

Arron's eyes opened wider.

"You were pretty beat up." Chris tilted his chair back.

"Yes. I remember—"

"You met my father."

Arron nodded, remembering. "Yes . . ."

Chris stood up. "I fixed you up as best as I could and brought you here. You were really sick." He walked to the window and ran a finger along the glass.

Arron sat silent, waiting.

Chris spun about. "You knew the gun would backfire and kill him. You knew it! Why didn't you try and stop him? You just sat there, content to let him die!"

"Did you heal me just to ask that?"

Chris glared at him. "I don't know why I healed you. Yes, perhaps that is the reason."

The Roamer nodded.

"How can you be like that! Don't you realize I have no one left now? I'm all alone."

"And so am I," Arron said very quietly and very precisely.

Chris stopped in surprise. "I . . . I helped you bury your grandmother," he said, feeling stupid.

"Thank you."

"How . . . how did she die?"

Arron looked away and shrugged. "She was very old."

Chris watched him, thinking of the things the Roamer had said during his sickness. Whatever it had been, it hadn't been old age.

"Oh, I told you, then," Arron whispered, his eyes on the wall.

"You can still hear my thoughts?"

Arron turned back to him. "Didn't you . . . I thought . . . yes, I suppose so," he sighed.

Chris nodded slowly, trying to clear his mind. He'd forgotten the eerie feeling this Roamer gave him. "You were very sick." He repeated an earlier statement to fill the quiet.

He sat back down in his chair. Arron watched him, unsure, like Chris.

"How is it that . . . well, I mean, after all these years. I thought all the Roamers had been killed," Chris said finally.

Arron nodded slowly. "Perhaps. Back when we were little, after I left you at the river, Grandmother and I left camp. We were gone before . . . before . . ." He stopped again.

"The raid?" Chris filled in for him.

Arron's head snapped up. He glared for a moment, then his face became more passive, searching, it seemed, for something in Chris' face—and not finding it. "Yes. We packed and left. Roamers don't question each other. They certainly would not ask us . . . It was to be." He stopped, again searching Chris' face, then shaking his head. "We were nowhere near when . . ." He looked down at his hands.

"When the raid happened," Chris finished once more for him. "And then?"

"Well." Arron looked up, his face plain with disbelief. One of his hands caught hold of the quilt, clutching it. "Well," Arron forced himself on. "We spent time in hiding. It was . . . rather dangerous for a Roamer, one might say." His voice level had dropped. He looked at Chris, who simply nodded for him to continue.

Arron turned away sharply, his lips pressed together in a thin, white line, eyes tightly closed. "Why! Why do you think this way?" He clenched both his fists tightly on the quilt.

"Arron, are you all right?" Chris stood anxiously, unsure what was wrong.

"Yes," the Roamer hissed. "Perfect!"

Chris sat slowly back into his chair. "I . . . I don't understand. What is it? What's wrong?"

The pained look returned. "You really don't, do you?"

Chris shrugged.

"I'm that much below you, am I?" Arron watched his hands as they fidgeted with the blanket. He looked back up at Chris, a guarded look. "What do you plan to do with me now? Sell me?"

"What do you think I am?" Chris said, rising.

"The question, I think, is what you think I am." He waited, then sighed. "Sorry, it was a stupid thing to say. I should be grateful. And I am. Really."

Chris nodded and sat down.

"Really."

"All right. All right." Chris smiled, uncertain. It was quiet a moment and then he signaled Arron to go on with his story. Arron nodded wearily.

"Grandmother and I stayed hidden a long time. Then about—oh, what was it? Two or three weeks? I . . . I've lost track." He paused. "We were found."

"They didn't just kill you?"

Arron looked annoyed. "No. They wanted something, thought we had information about something, so we were worth more than your average run-of-the-mill Roamer. Does that help you any?"

Chris had the feeling he was being insulted, but for what he wasn't sure. Something in the Roamer's tone warned him. "Look!"

Arron held up a hand in apology. "I do it merely for the response."

Chris settled back in his chair, embarrassingly aware that the Roamer could hear everything he was thinking.

Arron's gaze went to a far point in the room, his voice became flat. "They tortured my grandmother until she died. They hit me only when I fought."

"Looks like you fought a lot."

"At first. Until she ordered me to stop. She was so old. She wasn't going to last . . . She was telling me quickly, too quickly, what to do. It was mixed up. It wasn't clear! She was in so much pain and then—and then there was someone else in her mind, reaching, searching . . ."

"In her mind? But . . ." Chris stared at the Roamer, that strange horror creeping into his stomach.

"That's when she . . . she said she wanted to be buried here. I had to. Please. She begged." Arron sat up staring at the far wall. "She never said a word to them. Nothing. But she was begging me!" Arron looked at Chris again. "There was something . . . something I was to do. I was prepared. I was . . . She pushed me out, closed me out. There was danger. She was afraid. I had to get out of the danger. I felt it tearing into her mind as she forced me out. Ripping apart her mind. I could've blocked it! I might have . . . She faced it alone . . . and died . . . alone."

"Why . . . why didn't they kill you, too?"

"I can see the future . . . sometimes." He didn't look at Chris. "Grandmother told them that to keep them from killing me. That sparked their interest, all right. They thought to keep me to predict for them. Tell them their futures . . . when they would die. But after Grandmother was dead, and they left us alone, finally, I used some of my other skills and escaped. They'll be looking for me." He paused. "I don't have to be able to see the future to know that some of their deaths will be by me!"

"Like my father's."

"You can't blame that on me."

"You can see the future. You knew when you were little. It was convenient to tell him then—"

"It was different—"

"But now, oh, now it was much better just to let him blow his head off! You knew and didn't tell him. By doing that, you killed him just as if you pulled that trigger yourself!"

Arron shrugged and looked down.

"Nothing! You did nothing!" Chris stood, his hands clenched.

"And when they massacred that whole camp of Roamers, did you open your mouth? If they went off again to kill more, would you stand before them and say no?" Arron tried to sit forward. He took a slow, painful breath. "No? Well, you've killed hundreds—and I've killed one. You've got me beat there, that's for sure. I see now why I'm so far below you."

Chris strode briskly to the door. "I should have let you die!"

"By all means. What's one more!"

Chris whirled back, his fist raised.

"Go ahead. What's one more?"

Chris stared at the purple bruises on Arron's face and lowered his hand, shaking his head.

"I'm sorry," Arron said quietly. "You're right. I have no right. You have done a lot for me."

"Stop it! Your grandmother told you to stay out of other people's thoughts. Well, do it!"

"Sorry."

Chris spun around, slamming the door as he left. He stormed into the kitchen and sat in the armchair before the fire. He should kill him. He should kill the Roamer. He leaned back and took a deep breath. He should turn him over to the Town Chief. He would know what to do with him. He should do it. He should.

Chris got up and walked out the front door. He'd go get the Town Chief. That was what he would do.

By the time he got to town, he was even more certain. This was right. This was the right thing to do. He would feel much better.

"Chris!" He stopped short and looked up. Katie Topkins jumped down from the ladder standing in front of her father's carpentry shop. She quickly set her paintbrush down on the bottom rung and tried to brush some of the paint away from her skirt. "Chris, hi." She stopped when she got to him. "I was going to come up . . . come up to see how you were." She paused uncomfortably.

"Fine. I'm fine." He nodded. "Fine."

She smiled and looked down. "Yep. I really just wanted to tell you, you could come down anytime. To talk or something. Whatever's on your mind. The weather. Tadpoles?" She squinted up at him.

He gave a slight laugh. "Thanks, Katie. And everything's fine. Tadpoles." He shook his head and sighed. "It's been a while since I've looked for those."

"I know."

Sarah Anne McGreggor came out of the carpentry shop and stopped, seeing Chris.

"Chris, how are you?" She came quickly to his side. "I've

been really worried about you. Mother and I were going to stop up today and see you." She put a hand gently on his shoulder. Katie turned back to the ladder.

"Mother wanted to talk to you," she went on. "Katie, could you call into your father's shop for my mother. I think your mother wants you anyway. She's starting to make lunch, you know."

Katie hesitated, glancing at the paintbrush, then nodded. "Sure," she said, and walked inside.

Mrs. McGreggor was out a second later. "Christopher, I'm so glad to see you. Come and have lunch with us." She took his arm and Sarah Anne took the other. He couldn't argue, couldn't tell them about the Roamer. He had to discuss that with the Town Chief. He would go there right after lunch.

"Now, Christopher, I've organized all the women, and they'll be at your house tomorrow to do a thorough cleaning."

"Oh, no, that's really not necessary." He couldn't let them in his house.

"We'll discuss it later," Mrs. McGreggor said soothingly. "But mind you, I will have my way." And she would hear no more about it until after lunch.

The meal was pleasant enough, the food good for this time of year. No dairy products, though, Chris noticed. That would change when the Roamer was taken care of. The milk wouldn't be bad anymore. The tadpoles Katie had reminded him of might even return.

"Christopher, we actually have been rather worried, with you up there by yourself. I don't suppose you heard about the Roamers."

Chris looked up sharply, nearly dropping his sandwich. "What . . . what about them?"

"Why, it's the talk all around," Sarah Anne jumped in. "They found two of them. Up in Buernston. One was so old, it just died. But the other escaped—and stole something, too. They're combing the entire area for him. Seems they tracked him in this direction, but they lost him up around Mount Klineloch."

Chris nodded. That instrument the Roamer held so close,

that must be what he stole. What was he going to tell the Town Chief? That he found the Roamer and healed him . . . and then turned him over? What would they think? He . . . he could tell them the Roamer held him under a spell. A spell—that was it. He saw in his mind the frightened face of the Roamer when he had awakened that morning, the mix of fear . . . and hope?

"Well, when they find him, what are they going to do with him?" Chris heard himself asking.

Mrs. McGreggor shook her head. "There's only one thing to do with a Roamer."

Mr. McGreggor stomped into the room. "Chris." He nodded in greeting, then turned to his wife. "My lunch ready?"

Mrs. McGreggor got up and set some food before him. She looked extraordinarily small next to the big man. She had seemed so large before.

"Telling him about the Roamer, huh?" Mr. McGreggor nodded to Chris. "Glad to see you're safe, boy. No trouble up at your place, is there?"

He would have to tell them about Arron, tell them now. "No."

Mr. McGreggor nodded and bit into his sandwich. His thick fingers wrapped about the bread. "Well, they'll find him. And when they do, he'll get his. They'll make that Roamer pay for all the suffering he's caused."

"What . . . what'll they do to him? Kill him?"

Mr. McGreggor shrugged. "There's some that would settle for that. But folks are awful bitter now. No milk." He stared at the sandwich in his large hand. "Bug-infested flour. No, there's some that'll want a little compensation for the discomfort."

"What do you mean?"

The heavy man shrugged again. "Give the Roamer a taste of the pain we've gone through."

"Oh." Chris nodded.

"I'm not for that kind of thing myself, mind you. But there are some that are."

"Yes, I . . . I see. Well, I do have to be going." Chris stood up. "Thank you, Mrs. McGreggor, Sarah Anne."

"We'll be there tomorrow, Christopher," Mrs. McGreggor reminded him.

"Oh. No, you can't."

"Come on now, why not?"

"My . . . my cousin. He's there. I . . . I've been taking care of him. He's been through some rough times. His farm was burned and all by thieves. He lost everything. I don't think he'd be up to a bunch of people coming up."

"Christopher! What have you been doing? Tending someone when you're poorly yourself. You should have told me earlier. You in mourning and all. Dear child . . ."

"Well, it helped to have someone to take care of. Took my mind off other things."

"Yes, well, we'll be up tomorrow and see to it that your house is cleaned and the two of you properly cared for. And that is the end of it."

Chris hesitated. He couldn't very well keep saying no. They might suspect something was wrong. But he couldn't have them in there with a Roamer. He looked at Sarah Anne to see if she would be of any help. But she had the same determined look as her mother.

Chris smiled suddenly. "All right," he said softly. "I appreciate it." He nodded to Mrs. McGreggor and then to Sarah Anne, his eyes on her very blond hair. She bleached it, everyone knew.

Chris finally got back to his house. He went quietly into the bedroom. Arron was sitting, holding that strange instrument he hadn't allowed Chris to touch, the one that he'd stolen. He looked up at Chris.

"What are you going to do with me?" he asked. Chris noticed the higher pitch to his voice, his wide eyes.

"I thought you could see the future, Roamer."

"Not always." He glanced at the bottles Chris held in his arms and the tub of water outside the door. "What's all that?"

"Some stuff to bleach your hair."

"What? Why?"

"You look like a Roamer." Chris set the bottles down by a chair and went back to get the water.

"I am a Roamer."

"Yes, well, that's a bit dangerous for now."

"I'm not going—"

"Yes, you are," Chris said firmly over Arron's protest. "Some of the ladies in town informed me that they are going to come up here tomorrow to clean this house whether I like it or not. I have been in mourning too long, they said. Mourning, ha!"

Arron looked down. "I'm not your father's killer."

"And who said you were?" Chris snapped.

Arron looked up. "No one," he whispered.

"Look! I told you to stay out of my head." Chris held up one of the bottles threateningly, then lowered it. "Listen. Those women are coming. I told them my cousin was here and that he'd had some hard times. They said they'd take good care of you, too. So . . ." He brandished one of the bottles. "Instant cousin."

The Roamer was shaking his head.

"You can be as stubborn about this as you like, but if we don't do something about your appearance . . . Well, they won't just kill you, they'll kill me, too."

"Why don't you just turn me over to them now?"

"If you don't stop acting like this, I just might. Now, can you get out of bed, or do I have to do it there?" Arron sat still. "Arron, I'm going to do this whether you like it or not. I'm stronger than you. It'll probably be less painful, though, if it's not a struggle." Arron sat still a moment more. Then, grumbling, he set the instrument aside and began to slide stiffly toward the edge of the bed. Chris reached out to help, but Arron shoved him away.

"Sit there." Chris indicated the chair. Arron tottered over unsteadily and sat down.

"I'll make it just a bit darker brown than mine. I don't want your eyes to stand out too much."

"You mean you're not going to bleach my eyes blind, too?"

"Sit still!"

He worked quickly, not talking and trying not to think. Arron kept an angry silence. When he finished, Chris nodded happily. "I suppose you could pass for my cousin." He paused. "Except your clothes. I'll get you some of mine.

They'll fit." He went to the dresser and pulled a p
out and tossed them to Arron. They fell to the fl
him.

"Put them on," Chris said softly. Arron held stil ut
them on!"

Arron bent over quickly and snatched them from the floor.
He gasped as he wrenched his wounds.

"Serves you right." Chris sat down on the bed. "I'm only
trying to help you."

Arron slid the slacks on carefully. "I don't know why."

Chris ignored him. "Hey, you look less like a Roamer already. But you've got to stop glowering, like you have something against us."

"I do!"

Chris stood. "Well, I have something against you, but I'm
trying to help you."

Arron rolled up his own pants. "You're doing it for your
mother, not for me."

Chris stared, his mouth falling open as if to say something.
He snapped it shut and strode from the room. Arron looked
down, crushing his slacks against himself. "I'm sorry," he
whispered.

He pushed his clothes into his pack, then tottered over to
the mirror above the dresser. He gripped the stand with one
hand to steady himself and touched his hair distastefully.
"Grandmother? I try. I really do . . . I'm sorry." He crept
back to the bed and pulled the instrument close against his
chest.

V

CHRIS SET A SMILE ON HIS FACE AND STEADIED HIS SHAK-
ing hands, then pulled open the door. Mrs. McGreggor stood
on the porch, a bucket in one hand, a mop in the other, and
all the town's women behind her.

"Are you going to let us in now, Christopher?" She bent
her head toward him.

"Yes, yes, come in. But, really, you needn't go to the trouble . . ."

Mrs. McGreggor pushed past him. "Quiet down, Christopher. You need your house polished up. It'll do you good."
She stopped suddenly and turned to look at him. "Poor boy,
you look like you haven't slept a wink since his death. Probably haven't eaten much, either, sick with grief." She set the
pail down.

Chris rubbed his fingers against his damp palms. "Actually
I've been busy taking care of my cousin. He's been very
sick." Chris stooped to help Mrs. Neten, who had begun to
clean the fireplace. "I haven't thought much about—"

"Never mind this." Mrs. Neten slapped his hands away.
"You should have called us sooner. We could've cared for
your cousin, you in mourning and all." She twisted about to
look at Mrs. McGreggor, who was still standing over them.

50

"Go see about his cousin, Helen. The boy has probably nearly killed him. They don't know how to take care of these things."

Chris frowned at that, but Mrs. McGreggor caught him by the hand. "Come on. Show me where he is. What's his name?"

"Arron," Chris said numbly. There were women everywhere. He began to worry anew about what they would find cleaning up. The Roamer's pack . . . the box . . . the Roamer . . . They hurried back and forth about him. At this rate the place would be clean in five minutes.

"Arron," Mrs. McGreggor was muttering. "That's a strange name. It almost sounds . . ." She paused, thinking. Chris hadn't thought about the name. He felt stupid at his oversight, and afraid. "It sounds, well, peculiar."

"Yes, his mother was very strange. She named him before she died—right after he was born. And you can't say no to a dying woman," Chris said quickly.

"That's true. Ah, they probably misunderstood her anyway. Poor boy, no mother to bring him up." She pushed open the door to Chris' bedroom. It was then Chris began to feel sick about his second oversight. Arron might say or do something dangerous. Chris realized he should have made peace with him after last night; he should have at least said something this morning. The Roamer might do something out of spite.

"Oh, you poor boy!" Mrs. McGreggor sat down on the edge of the bed and put her hand gently to Arron's forehead. Clucking softly, she said, "Hmm, a slight fever, not too bad." She touched his cheek. "And your face, so bruised." She smoothed his hair back and looked carefully at the bandages wrapped about his chest. "What else?"

"A lot of cuts, maybe a broken rib," Chris answered. Arron winced when she pressed against his side. She shook her head. "Chris, you should've gotten the doctor."

"I couldn't pay," Arron said suddenly.

"Now that wouldn't have mattered. We would've gladly . . ." Arron was shaking his head. "I see," Mrs. McGreggor said softly. "Now, what happened?"

Arron cleared his throat and glanced nervously at Chris. "I . . . my house was raided."

She took a sudden interest. "They didn't happen to be . . . It wasn't a Roamer, was it? They've spotted some, you know."

"No, they were just like you," the Roamer said sharply.

"Us. He means like us." Chris moved quickly to the bedside. "He thinks it was some townspeople near him who wanted his land."

Mrs. McGreggor looked shocked. "Why, how could decent people do something like that? When people do things like that, I really think the men may be right and there is a Roamer influence around."

Chris saw the Roamer's eyes widen. *Arron, please. Please!* Chris thought desperately. The Roamer looked up at him and closed his mouth.

Mrs. McGreggor stood. "Well, here, let me help you into the other room. You can sit by the fire. My daughter will get the two of you something to eat, and we'll see about cleaning up this room."

She bent and carefully helped Arron up from the bed, then pulled his arm gently over her shoulders and walked him from the room. Chris stared a moment after her. She was incredibly strong for a woman of her age, probably from helping her very overweight husband about during his frequent illnesses. She was fairly amazing in some ways, a constant source of energy, a firm foundation . . . She was also truly annoying.

She sat Arron in a chair by the fire and tucked a blanket about him.

"Thank you," he said hoarsely.

"You deserve to be taken care of, after what you've been through. Did you lose your father in the raid?" She placed a steady hand on his shoulder.

"My grandmother. My father has been dead a long time," Arron whispered.

She clucked sympathetically and ran her hand gently through his hair. "Poor boy. My word, Christopher, your family has not had the best of luck, it seems. Sit here, dear." She patted another armchair for Chris. He sat obediently.

"Now, you're not to do a thing. We'll take good care of you."
She smiled once more at Arron. He smiled back, quickly,
gratefully. She patted his shoulder and walked away. Chris
supposed she was going to find Sarah Anne. He let out a long
sigh. Perhaps it would only take five minutes to clean the
place, but it would be the longest five minutes . . .

"What are you smiling about?" Chris glared at Arron.

Arron turned to him in surprise. "Nothing."

"Hi, I'm Sarah Anne." Sarah Anne came up on the side of
Arron's chair.

"Sarah?"

"Sarah Anne," she corrected smiling.

Arron nodded slowly. "And I'm Arron. Ar-ron," he
added, then grinned. Sarah Anne smiled somewhat uncertainly back, unsure if he was making fun of her. She turned
to Chris instead of dealing with it.

"How are you feeling today? You looked a bit flustered
yesterday. You left so suddenly."

"He had a lot on his mind," Arron answered for him. He
turned to Chris. "Didn't you?"

"Y–yes, a lot," Chris said mechanically. "My future is
somewhat open now . . ."

"Well, I'll help you fill it," Sarah Anne laughed and leaned
closer to Arron. "And yours, too." She straightened up. "I'll
get you some soup and sandwiches. Mrs. Topkins made
them. She's the best cook, even if she is a little off." Sarah
Anne touched her head lightly.

"Say, is Katie here?" Chris turned to try and spot her.

Sarah Anne laughed again. "On a women's clean-up crew?
You've got to be kidding. Besides, her father's got a big order
to fill." Her face darkened somewhat, and she shook her
head. "Well, I'll get you that food." She put her hand on
Arron's shoulder. He flinched.

"Did I hurt you?" She turned, concerned.

"No, no, I'm all right."

She shrugged, then smiled and bounced off.

"What's this?" Mrs. Neten said, pulling the Roamer's
pack from behind the counter. Chris stared, unable to speak.

"That's all the things left from my home," Arron spoke up
in Chris' lapse.

"Well, we'll just wash the clothes in here for you." She bent to undo the ties.

"If you don't mind, I . . . I'd rather it not be opened just yet. Chris put it there so I wouldn't have to think about those things and all that right now . . . if you don't mind?" The Roamer's voice cracked just slightly, just right for effect. Chris watched, amazed at the prowess he had in lying. Its effect was immediate. Mrs. Neten shoved the pack behind the counter again and was at the Roamer's side, arms about his shaking shoulders.

"Oh, you poor thing. Look what I've done. I wasn't thinking. I'm so, so sorry." She hugged him tightly against her, then set him gently back in the chair. "There now, don't think about that now. You've plenty of friends about you, and we all care deeply for you." She ruffled his hair much as Chris had seen Arron's grandmother do those many years ago. Arron shuddered and looked away as Mrs. Neten gently tucked the blankets about him.

Sarah Anne popped back with the food and began to set it carefully on the table between them. Mrs. Topkins followed with two glasses full of fruit juice.

"Mrs. Topkins, you make the best soup," Sarah Anne said, turning to the overly thin woman.

Mrs. Topkins focused on her a moment and smiled in a vague sort of way. "Sweet of you to say . . . yes." Her smile broadened a bit. "But it used to be so much better. When my Julie was here, cooking with me. Yes . . ." Arron started to get up, looking sick, but Mrs. Topkins turned to him with a start.

Sit still, Chris thought wildly. Why did the Roamer have to react to everything?

"Ah, poor boy." Mrs. Topkins forced Arron back into his seat, her bony hands on both his shoulders, pressing him down. He squirmed under her touch. "Poor boy." She let out a sigh, still looking at him. Her face became puzzled. "James?" She leaned closer to him, gathering him in her arms. "James!" Arron tried desperately to pull away.

"Mother!" Sarah Anne called, turning about. "Mother!"

Mrs. McGreggor came quickly and separated Mrs. Topkins from Arron.

"James! Oh, James!"

"No, Jackie, this is Arron." Mrs. McGreggor forced her to look at him closely. Arron cringed under the gaze of the woman's pinched face.

"Arron? Oh, my poor James." The woman covered her face with her hands. Arron pressed himself further against the back of the chair.

"Come along, Jackie, there's work to do." She led the woman away, smiling apologetically at Arron.

Sarah Anne put a calming hand on Arron's shoulder. "She doesn't know what she's doing. Are you all right? You don't look well."

Arron shrugged her hand off. "Fine, I'm fine." The color began to return to his face. Sarah Anne nodded and straightened the dishes, then glanced at Arron.

"Yes, I can. I'm fine," Arron said, looking up at her.

Chris started, then shrank down in his seat. *Arron!* he thought angrily. Sarah Anne pulled back from the Roamer. Arron looked from one to the other in confusion.

"How did you do that?"

"Do what?"

"Answer me . . . before I asked."

"You hesitated. I assumed you were wondering if I was capable of feeding myself in my condition. I mean, that's a natural assumption." He stared innocently.

She laughed slightly. "Yes, I suppose it is. It was just the way you answered, you know . . . You're very observant." She stared at him thoughtfully a moment, then touched his cheek with the back of her hand. "Well, enjoy. I've got to go help." She swished past them and went into the bedroom, smiling once more at Arron.

"Arron," Chris said warningly.

"They don't even suspect."

"Well, I don't know why."

"Because they trust you." Arron turned to look at him. Chris shifted slightly in his seat and took a bite of his sandwich. Mrs. McGreggor came from the back rooms, the small, gray box in her hand. He choked on the sandwich.

"Christopher, there was a loose board under your bed. Did you know this was there?"

"Yes," he managed. "Don't bother with it. I'll take care of it." He stood up, a little too quickly, to retrieve it. If he'd realized how many things these women were going to dig up, he would have fought much harder to keep them out.

"Well, what is it?" She twisted it about in her hand, looking for the catch. "Oh!" The box seemed to leap from her hands as it fell to the floor. Arron was up from his chair and snatching it in an instant. He staggered back once it was in his hands. Grabbing at the armchair, he steadied himself, looking much paler than previously, the box crushed tightly against his chest.

"Sorry, I thought it might have broken," he muttered weakly, then tottered backward again, losing hold of the chair. Mrs. Neten was behind him and caught hold of him, kept him from falling.

"I think I'd like to go lie down." He gripped the box tighter.

"Of course, of course." Mrs. McGreggor moved to help him. "Let me take that from you. Christopher can take care of it."

"Yes, I'll take care of it." Chris finally gathered his wits and reached out for the box.

"No, no." Arron shook his head, looking dazedly about the room. Tears suddenly filled his eyes. "Grandmother had one like it."

Mrs. McGreggor's heart seemed to be breaking as she looked at him. She put her arms more firmly about him, protectively. "You just hang onto it then, if it gives you comfort." She shook her head, dabbing at her own eyes, as she led him slowly toward the back rooms. "I think there's been a bit too much excitement for you today." They disappeared through the curtain.

Chris gripped the back of the chair. He couldn't go in there and demand the box from the Roamer, not with all these people here. He would have to wait to confront him. He forced himself down in the chair. It was quite obvious to him that the Roamer had meant to steal the box all along. That was why he had come back here. All those lies he had told him! And they were lies, and he'd fallen for them, just as these foolish women fell for his poor, sick boy act. He clutched at the arms of the chair and waited for the women to leave.

Finally they slowly began to pack their cleaning gear. They had really done a complete job. Too complete, Chris thought, slapping his hand against the side of the chair.

As soon as they began to file out, he gave quick thanks and good-byes and backed toward the bedroom. Once in the back hall, he raced toward the room.

Sarah Anne was sitting on the bed beside Arron, telling him stories. If Arron had been a Homesteader, Chris would have felt sorry for him. Sarah Anne often dragged out her stories, picking at unimportant details. Everyone knew what she was going to say long before she said it. He smiled. For the Roamer, it was probably even worse. Served him right.

Arron looked up at him. It took Sarah Anne a moment more for it to register that she had lost her audience, she was enjoying her story so much. Then she turned to follow Arron's line of sight.

"Oh, Chris, I was just telling Arron about the time our families went on that picnic up Mount Klineloch. Now, how many years ago was that? We were just kids!"

Chris nodded. "Ten."

"Oh, it can't have been ten. Wasn't it more like eight or nine?"

"Yeah, eight or nine," Chris said quickly. She got caught up in the stupidest things.

"No, maybe it was ten," she added thoughtfully, counting on her fingers.

"I think they're getting ready to go," Chris interrupted her counting.

"Oh, that doesn't matter, I can stay a little longer." She slid one of her legs up onto the bed, letting her skirt fall back, showing off her leg to the knee.

Chris groaned inwardly; he'd seen it all before. It was this behavior that had finally made him lose his boyhood crush on her. Now she was trying to seduce Arron. God! If she knew he was a Roamer, her reaction would have been very different.

Arron sat forward slowly, his eyes locked on Chris, then he glanced thoughtfully at Sarah Anne.

"My, I've never seen such dark eyes," she said softly, staring him full in the face.

Arron shot a look at Chris again. "They think some of my ancestors may have been Ro—"

"Rotesians!" Chris practically jumped forward.

"Rotesians?" Sarah Anne turned to Chris.

"Yeah, don't you remember them from history?" he said in a breath. *Arron!* If he could have hit him with the thought, he would have.

"No, not really . . ."

"Oh, well, maybe you never got that far. Forget it. I think Arron needs some rest."

"Do you?" Sarah Anne turned back to him. "I'm not making you tired, am I?"

Arron opened his mouth to speak, but Chris cut him off. "What kind of question is that? If he says yes, he'll insult you." Chris realized that that was exactly why she had posed the question in just that way. Sometimes the games she played really were too much. "So, I'll have to be rude for him. He's got to have some rest. Why don't you stop back another time." Chris had her by the elbow and was steering her from the room.

"Well . . ." She really didn't seem to have much choice. "I'll stop back again tomorrow and see how you are, Arron," she called back to him. "Bye."

Chris strode quickly back into the bedroom as soon as he had seen her out. He shut the door with a firm hand. Arron waited.

"Did you enjoy yourself?" His voice was pitched strangely high.

The Roamer ran one hand along the quilt, but remained silent.

"Did you like scaring me half to death trying to insult them? All but telling Sarah Anne what you are! You don't seem to be quite aware of the consequences!"

Arron lowered his eyes and ran his hand over the bandages about his chest. "The thought never crossed their minds."

"Well, it might have!"

"They liked me." Arron spoke softly. "They don't like

Roamers. Therefore, it could never occur to them that I was a Roamer."

"I certainly don't know why they liked you."

"Because they saw me as a poor child in need of the wonderful care that only they can offer. They felt needed and, therefore, felt good. I was the person who gave them that feeling."

"Well, you certainly are cocky."

Arron grew silent again.

"And don't think I missed your little magic trick, either. Mrs. McGreggor didn't drop that box."

"You were afraid she would open it."

"I told you not to read my mind!"

"Then why did you keep sending me all those messages!"

"There's a difference between me sending you a message, and you just taking it!"

Arron jerked forward. "You're wrong! There's no difference! They sound exactly the same!" He stopped, his breath coming in short gasps. "You don't know! You've never heard. Most of the time I can't tell whether it's from someone's mind or mouth!"

"Give me the box!" Chris screamed over him.

Arron snapped his mouth shut and glared at him.

Chris grabbed him roughly by the shoulder and jerked him up from the bed. "Give it to me!"

"You think you can do worse than what people have already done?"

"I can try." Chris yanked him closer, his knuckles turning white in the tight grip.

Arron glared back a moment more, then looked away blinking hard. "You would, wouldn't you?"

Chris shoved him away and straightened, staring at his hand as the blood rushed back into it. "I don't know," he said a little shakily. "Just . . . just give it to me."

"What did Grandmother say when she gave it to you?"

"She said to keep it hidden. It was for when I was older."

Arron nodded and slid the box from under the covers. He looked at Chris. "She died for this. They wanted to know where it was. They would have killed you if they found it here. She died for this."

Chris reached for it, but the Roamer pulled it away.

"Why would they want this?" Arron asked Chris.

"Give it to me."

Arron fingered the catch, and the lid sprang open, a silvery glow filling the room.

"Arron, I'm warning you . . ."

Arron touched the sphere, gasping slightly as his fingertips met the surface. Tilting his head, he looked as if he were listening, intently listening.

Chris snatched the box from him. Arron cried out in surprise. The box snapped shut. The glow stopped.

"You are not going to steal this from me, too, Roamer." Chris held the box just beyond the Roamer's reach. "You're nothing. Do you understand that? If I killed you now, people wouldn't mourn, they would cheer! How do you feel about that?" Arron stared up at him, shaking his head slightly. "So, don't play games with me, Roamer. You'll lose. You have nothing. No one will give a second thought to your death. I have friends at least. Your grandmother is dead. No one will miss you." Chris stopped, shocked by the surprise and hurt on Arron's face. Arron looked away.

"Fine," he said so very quietly. Chris pulled the box against his chest and swallowed. His arms trembled. The Roamer covered his face with one hand. Chris suddenly wanted to take it all back, take it all away, comfort him as he had wished his father might have given him comfort, once.

"Arron . . ."

"I said fine!" the Roamer shrieked at him.

Chris ran from the room, ran to his parents' room. He flung the door open for the first time since his father's death and fell down on his mother's bed, clutching the pillow against him, pinning the box between himself and the pillow. He let out a sob, the anxieties of the day getting the best of him at last.

VI

HE WOKE SLOWLY, WITH A RINGING IN HIS EARS, A HUM-
ming against his chest. He sat up. The box, it was vibrating.
Music . . . coming through the box, through the door. He
half remembered his mother singing a tune like it when she
had put him to bed at night. Getting up, he brushed the hair
back from his eyes. The box hummed in his other hand.

He opened the door and peered into the hall. A glow was
coming from the front room, flickering through the curtain
at the end of the hall, firelight. He walked toward it, toward
his mother singing in the armchair before the fire.

He stared at the form in the chair. It was softly singing the
tune, playing lightly on some strange instrument. The vibrating box made the music flow into Chris' hand and through
his entire body. He began swaying in time to the music. The
form in the chair leaned forward and the firelight caught at
its face. Chris snapped out of his trance with a jolt.

"What are you doing?" he demanded.

Arron started, nearly dropping the instrument. Then he
hugged it against himself.

"Are you trying to weave some Roamer magic? I've heard
about what your singing can do. And I've broken out of the

spell you were trying to put me under!" Chris stepped completely into the room.

Arron gave him a bland look. "The only magic it has is the comfort it gives me."

"And why would a lullaby my mother sang to me be of any comfort to a Roamer?"

Arron grinned. "Because—" His smile widened. "—it's a Roamer lullaby."

"It is not!"

"Oh, yes it is. Where did you think your mother got it?"

"Got it? She wouldn't get anything from you. You killed her!"

Arron turned away from him and began to strum softly on the instrument. "She got the song from my grandmother," he said firmly. "And, if it weren't for her, your mother would have been dead much sooner."

Chris stepped closer, his shadow thrown up on the wall along with Arron's. "What do you mean?"

"I mean, my grandmother was treating her for some illness."

"What?"

Arron stopped playing and looked up at him. "Your mother was dying. She felt it. She came to my grandmother for treatment. Grandmother gave her a powder or something."

"That's what killed her!" Chris shook his head furiously.

"What killed her was the lack of Roamers from whom to obtain the powder. If anyone killed her, it was your people." Arron resumed playing his instrument.

"You're lying."

"She gave her the powder and the song."

"Why would my mother go to you?"

"She was dying. It was a chance. She took it."

Chris turned away, remembering his mother's final words. "The powder. Roamer." Had it been an accusation or a plea?

"Not a plea, I don't think. Perhaps she was just trying to tell you."

Chris spun back around. "I warned you!"

The Roamer's eyes widened, then he looked down. "Chris, I didn't . . ." He didn't finish.

"I can't understand this," Chris was muttering. "Why would she do that, go to you. I can't see."

"She wanted to live!"

"And why would you help us? After all the destruction you Roamers have done, why would you suddenly change?"

"We have nothing more to do with the poorness in the land than you do. Don't you think it affected us, too? It struck us all. All."

"Oh no, oh no. I know the old tales about Shakta. I know what he did. He cast a spell on the land."

"What do you know about Shakta?"

"Ah, now the fear comes out. You realize that we do know. You can't work your lies on me."

"You don't know anything."

Chris smiled broadly. "Everyone learns the story. We're taught it as children. Shakta, that great, mighty Roamer Chieftain, kept something from our leader Chruston, causing the first warfare and distrust between us. Chruston decided to take Shakta prisoner in order to obtain the hidden object for the sake of obtaining peace. Shakta would not give it up at first, but was finally persuaded. Peace could have followed, but Shakta was not to let that happen! He cursed the lands and Chruston's family. I'm a descendent. He cursed my family!

"After that, Shakta flung himself from a tower, his mind completely gone by that time. That curse has forever driven our groups apart." Chris watched the Roamer a moment, watched his face. "But there was a prophecy. It is said that there will come a time when one who can right the lands will be. He is called the Dark Prince, and the curse will end. The Dark Prince, as you are probably aware, is death. Death for the Roamers, and a new life for us."

"That is the story they teach you?" Arron looked at him without blinking.

"And you thought I didn't know."

Arron gave a derisive snort. "You don't."

"Oh, yeah!"

"Listen. The real reason Chruston took Shakta prisoner is because he would not reveal when Chruston's death would be. You see, Chruston knew many Roamers are farsighted and he knew Shakta was one of them. He demanded Shakta tell him when he was to die. Shakta said no. Chruston tortured him until he finally revealed his end. I'll agree Shakta was no longer in his right mind, he couldn't have been to release that information. But I think it was shame at the realization of what he had done that drove him to jump. The only curse uttered was the telling of Chruston's death."

"What's wrong with telling someone's death? If you Roamers were as good as you claim to be, you would be helping people out of their tragedies by forewarning them." Chris paused. "My father wouldn't be dead."

Arron stared, wide-eyed. "But . . . but if they got out of their deaths, when would they die?"

"Another time. Later."

"It doesn't work that way, Chris. That is their time. If they get out of it—" Arron's voice dropped to a harsh whisper. "—they don't die!"

"So?"

"So! Everything goes awry! That's why the land is falling apart; apparently Chruston didn't die."

"You're blaming him for all this?" Chris pulled on the back of the armchair, turning it and Arron sharply toward him. "If you insult him, you're insulting me! I told you we were related."

Arron leaned back. "I'm amazed at your loyalty. But then, there is nothing else in you, is there?" Chris expelled a sharp breath, balling his fists. Arron looked down, ignoring the reaction he had evoked. "I would never make any such ridiculous comparisons between myself and Shakta. He was a fool to have ever revealed that information. The only possible comparison I might make is the farsightedness. I take nothing beyond that. He was a fool."

"You mean . . ." Chris leaned down closer. "You mean, you could foresee my death, like you did my father's?"

The Roamer leaped to his feet, nearly knocking Chris over. "Don't ever let that thought cross your mind!" Arron's face was stark white in the firelight. "I don't want to hear it from your mind or from your lips! Whatever happened between Shakta and Chruston will not happen between us. It will not!

Do you understand?" He clutched the back of the chair with a shaking hand. "Do you?"

Chris just looked at him.

Arron shook his head and sat down. He stared into the fire a moment. "Chris, I know you don't like me for what I am, but . . . sometimes, I feel that maybe you do like me for who I am." He looked up briefly, hopefully. "Don't let one cloud the other. We really did help your mother. Really. We trusted her with our cure. Grandmother trusted her for something more—I don't know what. And Grandmother trusted you with that box. That box that she died for! Died in great fear for me . . . and, strangely, for you, too. I still can't reason why . . ." He bowed his head and stared at the instrument he had pulled back into his lap.

Chris shuffled his feet on the age-roughened wood floor.

"There's something that has to be done, Chris, something I have to do." The Roamer's voice had become more contained. "I don't know what. There's so much I can't see." He turned back to Chris. "Grandmother trusted you for something. Your mother, too. This all has to fit together. I . . . I just don't know. I can't think. There are so many images in my mind. Do you know? Did anyone tell you?"

Chris stared at him, then realized his mouth was hanging open. He closed it, pulling back. "How am I supposed to believe you? You . . . you're a Roamer. Roamers lie." He jabbed a finger at the instrument in Arron's lap. "They say you stole that. And now you want to steal my box. I don't believe you're trying to help anyone but yourself, Roamer."

Arron stood up and lifted his pack from where it leaned beside the chair. He pulled the instrument close. "I didn't steal this." He watched Chris a moment, then lowered the instrument. "No, why should you believe me? There's no reason." He turned and moved to go back to the bedroom. "Please excuse my foolish outburst. I have to learn to read the coldness in your mind better." He stopped at the curtain, but didn't turn. "That coldness has got you, hasn't it, Chris? Alone in the crowd, huh? Tied in a web of loyalty, and no comfort for it all."

"Get out of here!"

Arron pushed through the curtains.

Chris sat down slowly. His hands were shaking again. He pressed his head against the back of the armchair. One of the clean-up women had put his mother's portrait back in its little frame. His parents stared silently down on him. The shadowy light made their faces look gloomy and disapproving. "What are you doing with a Roamer?" they asked. "Don't you realize what they've done to your family? Didn't you learn anything from us?"

Chris pulled his eyes away from them, shuddering. Is that what they would think of him? He shrank down lower in the armchair and quickly fingered the catch on the box and held it before his eyes. The sphere's light seemed to pulse softly in rhythm to the remembered lullaby.

"It comes to you desired, tired or not, sleep, my boy, 'tis a blessed thing," Chris sang, half remembering the lullaby. "Trouble will go, light will follow . . ." He stopped, remembering his mother's cool hand on his forehead as she kissed him good night. Her hands were cold . . . cold and stiff as they had been when they buried her. He stared into the sphere and saw those hands sprinkling the powder into her bed. It shimmered in a gray sort of way.

"Mamma, what's that?" he had asked.

"Something for me and for you, to make us happy," she had murmured.

"How?" he had asked, but she would only smile, and he thought her under a Roamer spell. His father had told him the kind of things Roamers could do. He was afraid of her.

He shook his head, pulling his eyes from the sphere. He snapped the box closed and walked toward the back rooms. He hesitated at the bedroom door. The box continued to pulse steadily in his hand. He pushed the door open and walked in, startling Arron who sat curled up in a chair in the corner. The instrument leaned against the leg of the chair. Chris sat on the bed and opened the box. He set it beside him, the glimmer growing to fill the room.

"Play the instrument—what is it?"

"A kithara."

"Please. Play the lullaby."

Arron watched him a moment, then nodded and gently

raised the instrument. He set it in his lap, against his stomach, his fingers poised, ready to play.

"Sing the words, too," Chris added.

The Roamer nodded again as his fingers began to move lightly over the strings. The sound rang sweetly, the silver light from the sphere pulsing brighter with each note. Arron's rich, tenor voice blended easily into the music.

> It comes to you desired, tired or not
> Sleep, my prince, 'tis a blessed thing
> Trouble will go, light will follow
> Sleep, my prince, 'tis starlight lit
> Ancient orb encircles mind, relieving
> Sleep, my child, promise is in him
> Who takes the gift given you, by me, by him
> To sleep, my little one, all must sleep
> All that was saved by lack of sleep
> To sleep, little prince, it must be
> Come be returned to his trust
> To sleep, little prince, 'tis a blessed thing

As the last chords died away, Chris and Arron sat silently, each remembering cold nights. Chris' mother dutifully tucking him into a warm bed, her cool hands stroking his hair as he drifted off. Arron sitting warm against his grandmother by a bright fire, her arms wrapped protectively about him.

They both leaped up at the sharp banging on the front door. Arron quickly snapped the box closed, and they were in the dark. He caught Chris' arm as he turned to go to the door.

"They come in the middle of the night. That isn't good," he whispered. There was pounding again. Chris grabbed at the box and went to put it under the bed. Arron pulled him back.

"No. They'll look there."

"What?"

"Give it to me. Go answer the door. Tell them your cousin is very sick, perhaps they will not look past the hair." Chris just stared at him. "Hurry!" Arron shoved him toward the door, pulling the box from his hand.

Chris paused a moment outside the bedroom, then turned as the banging began again. "I'm coming! I'm coming," he shouted, running his hand through his hair to dishevel it.

"I'm coming!" Chris yanked his shirttails out of his pants and glared at the door as if it were the cause of the pounding. He jerked it open. "What do you want!" He stepped back at the sight so many men with torches, standing on his porch, in his yard. "Say, what is this?"

"There's a Roamer we've tracked to this area," the front man said quickly. "It's urgent. We have orders to check every house for him and for something he stole."

"And this can't wait until morning? There's no one here. I think I'd be the first one to know if there were. I've been about all night. My cousin is very ill, and your banging isn't doing him any good. Come back tomorrow." He started to swing the door closed, but the man stopped it with a hand.

"It is important. We're authorized. We've already searched several houses in this area, yours is not being specially selected."

"But my cousin is too sick to be disturbed. He's been through quite a bit." Chris felt his jaw muscles tightening at their assumption that he would just allow them into his house in the middle of the night as so many of his fearful neighbors had.

"I said it was important, and we have the numbers to force entry if we have to."

Chris peered at the man, his features barely discernible in the torchlight. He looked familiar, Chris thought, like the man who had been at his house long ago, the night before the raid on the Roamers, the one who had suggested the raid. "Who are you? And under whose authority?"

"My name's Doug Craftan. Right now I'm under your Town Chief. He gave us the direct go ahead. More distantly I'm from Buernston, where the Roamer escaped. Now, shall I force my way in?"

Chris glared at him, unsure if the man didn't already suspect him of harboring a Roamer. Maybe he hadn't fooled all the women.

"I'll only ask you once more to come back in the morning," Chris warned.

The man shoved him backward hard. "We take our orders only from only one person, and Dempter claims that the Roamer's in this area. So this area is where we search. Your farm is in this area." Chris stumbled backward over a footstool.

"Now look!"

"No, you look! We are going to search. If you want us to do it quickly and quietly so as not to bother your cousin, then you'll quit arguing. Unless you have something to hide . . ."

"Search and be done with it," Chris snapped, turning away from them. The men spread out quickly on that, thrusting their torches in dark areas, looking behind furniture, opening cupboards.

"Stay out of that room." Chris pushed his way through the men and through the back curtains. "My cousin is sleeping in there." He glared at Craftan. "Or trying to!"

"Check his cousin."

"What are you accusing me of?"

"Nothing." Craftan ran a hand over his cleanly shaven face. "Nothing, yet."

The door was pushed open in a rush of men, and Chris found himself forced in with them. As far as Arron being sick, he may as well have been a sack of rotted flour for the way the men treated him. One of them went over and pulled the covers back from him, turned him over roughly, and put his hand to the Roamer's forehead. Arron feigned a barely conscious wakefulness.

"He's sick all right. Really hot. This ain't no Roamer." He shrugged, touching Arron's hair to indicate the color.

Craftan looked about the room. "Well then, look for it!"

"What did you think?" Chris caught at the man's arm. "Did you think I'd be protecting some damn Roamer? They killed my mother."

"Well, someone is protecting him. He's hiding somewhere."

Chris noticed one of the men scrambling under the bed. He began, nervously now, to wonder what Arron had done with the box and his things. He watched the men closely.

"Loose board under here," the man under the bed cried out.

"Look," Craftan demanded.

"Nothing."

"Wh–what's going on?" Arron murmured, barely heard above the rushing about in the room. Chris stared a moment, wondering at how well the Roamer playacted, then remembering himself, turned to Craftan.

"Will you get these men out of here so he can get some sleep!"

Craftan stared down at him a moment. Chris got the strange feeling that the man was barely seeing him, the same strange feeling the Roamer gave him when he saw his thoughts. He clamped his teeth together.

"Okay, let's move on," the man said finally. The others began to clear the room immediately.

Chris followed them to the front door. Once they were all out, Craftan turned back to him. "If you see anything out of the ordinary, please report it to your Town Chief."

"I don't even know what you're looking for, or why."

"We're looking for a Roamer. He escaped from Buernston."

"Well, why didn't you just kill him when you had him?"

"We were going to, but as I said, he escaped. Killed two people doing it, too. One was my oldest son."

"Really?" Chris felt his own breath catching in his throat. "Well . . . well, had they done anything to the Roamer . . . you know, tortured him or anything?"

The man stared, surprised. "We're Homesteaders, man. Not Roamers. Why would you ask such a question?"

"Well, you said he stole something. To find out where it was, I thought maybe . . . Well, what did he steal, anyway?"

"That's not of any importance to you. We just want the Roamer."

"Who is we?"

"All of us. You know the trouble they've caused."

Chris thought to ask some more questions, but the man was looking at him curiously now. It was best to let them go away—far away. He nodded smartly to the man and went back into the house. Waiting by the door, he watched through the side window until he was sure they were away and heading for the next farmhouse. Then he turned toward the back rooms. He carefully cleared his mind of the things Craftan had told him, then walked into the bedroom and seated himself in the chair by the bed.

"How did you manage the fever?"

The Roamer shrugged. "Body temperature control."

Chris stared at him. The Roamer apparently thought that was a sufficient answer. If he could control his temperature now, he could have done it when Chris had found him. Had the Roamer really been sick then? He cut that thought off when he saw Arron watching him closely. He turned and looked about for the box the Roamer had taken.

"And where did you hide your things? I thought for sure they'd find them, the way they were searching."

Arron pointed to the dark corner in the tall ceiling, humming to himself, and the objects drifted down to the floor. Chris stood up slowly, his mouth falling open. He turned to Arron. He cleared his throat once, then again.

"It's sort of like lightning," Arron was saying quietly. "Little bits of it are in the air all the time. They're in everything—tiny, tiny particles. I . . . I know this." He touched his head gently. "They're all mixed up with other things in the air. And . . . well, I figured it out, you know. How to separate them. It came to me one day; it just sort of seemed obvious. I was humming and . . . and it separates them. They vibrate, vibrate differently at the right note, you see. Then I figured that I could mix them with other things, like with my kithara. They make this force that counters the downward force of the ground. The amount of particles determines the lift." Arron nodded hopefully at Chris. "It just came to me one day."

Chris nodded stupidly, not really understanding.

"What's wrong?" Arron pulled back slightly.

"I . . . I didn't realize. I mean, I saw you lift the stone when we were little, and make the box jump from Mrs. Mc-Greggor's hands. But, but to lift all those things and . . . and hold them there . . ." His voice trailed off.

"It has nothing to do with the devil!"

"It's just so strange."

"Well, you'll get used to it. Then it will be like nothing."

Arron leaned back against the pillows, shifting uncomfortably. Then he looked down, running a hand through his hair. "Damn."

They sat a moment in uncomfortable silence, then Arron sat forward again, a determined look on his face. "I want you to understand."

Chris just shook his head. "You can see right into my head. How can I understand that? It's too unnerving. It's not right. Why, you even knew they were going to look under the bed. You see things and do things . . ." He raised his hands, giving up.

"It's not so simple as that. I hear only some of your thoughts, Chris. I can't dig into your mind for them. Some people's thoughts are stronger than others, and I can hear them. Some people I can't hear at all. And deep-seated desires and thoughts, buried intentions, there is no way I can get at those. Do you understand?"

Chris stared at him blankly.

Arron shrugged. "No, how could you. Look, sometimes I see things, the future or people's thoughts, whatever. But it's not so clear-cut. Sometimes it is very strong, very clear. I know what is going to happen, or what someone is thinking. But sometimes it's just a vague feeling of foreboding, and I'm unsure. That's always the worst. That uncertainty when I'm sure something bad is going to happen, but not exactly what.

"And then there are other times when there is absolutely nothing. It depends on so many things. Things I haven't even begun to learn to control. And I'm not at all sure that I can control them. If you could only see the way I do! You'd see the confusion, little whisperings and warnings that I try and make some sense out of. And then voices that I think are spoken, but they're not always . . ." Arron shook his head. "Is that any clearer?"

Chris stared at him a moment and then shrugged. "It doesn't matter. It sounds to me like you don't really understand." He got up and went over to the corner. He hesitated, then carefully lifted the box and scooped up the kithara. He tossed the instrument on the bed before he sat down.

The Roamer reacted violently. "Careful!" He took the instrument in his arms, cradled it, glaring at Chris.

"Sorry. I didn't realize it was fragile."

"It is."

"Sorry."

"Well, just so long as you know now."

Chris nodded. "I said I was sorry." He paused. "What is it they think you stole, if it's not that instrument?"

Arron grinned suddenly. "You must know, or you wouldn't be so protective of it. That box."

Chris turned it thoughtfully in his hands. "You think that lullaby is connected with this?"

"I do."

"Well, can you play it again? Maybe there's something in it to answer the questions you seem to have. Why don't we take it line by line. Okay?"

Arron didn't say anything, he just shifted the kithara in his arms and began to play. "It comes to you desired, tired or not." He stopped and looked expectantly at Chris.

"Well, sleep . . ." Chris said uncomfortably. He didn't really think there was something there. He was just doing this for the Roamer.

"That's rather obvious," Arron said.

"Well, what do you think it means?"

Arron shrugged and began to play the next line. "Sleep, my prince, 'tis a blessed thing." He stopped, looking at Chris.

Chris twisted about in his chair and set the box on the night table. "Well . . ." He stared at an invisible spot on the floor. "Well. I think the words 'my prince' are not important because my mother sang it differently. She sang it 'my boy.' So I guess it doesn't matter . . ." He left off, not knowing what else to say.

Arron nodded and replayed the second line. "Sleep, 'tis a blessed thing." He stopped and looked up.

"Well, why do I have to do all the work?" Chris banged his fist on the arm of the chair.

Arron smiled. "Okay. Let's make 'sleep' part of the sentence, instead of a command."

"What?"

"Look. It's like this. Instead of telling us to go to sleep and then saying it is a blessed thing, we'll simply make it that sleep is a blessed thing. The song isn't telling us to go to sleep. It's telling us that it is a good thing."

"But that's all guesswork."

"So is the idea that this song means something."

Chris nodded and stared at his hands.

Arron set the kithara down on the nightstand, in front of the box. "Look, why don't we get some sleep."

"Yeah, okay." Chris got up yawning. "Good night, then."

"Good night."

Chris left the room quietly. Arron picked up his kithara and noticed the box behind it. He looked at it for a moment, then reached over and opened it. Light filtered out. He lifted his kithara and began playing quietly, watching the light of the sphere.

VII

CHRIS PUSHED THE DOOR TO ARRON'S ROOM OPEN WITH his elbow, trying to keep the breakfast tray balanced. He slid quietly into the room. Arron was still sound asleep. The Roamer had to be exhausted, sleeping through all the noise he had made getting breakfast ready, Chris thought. He continued into the room and set the tray on the nightstand, then turned to awaken Arron. He paused, watching him. Arron still hadn't moved, he just lay there, seeming dead but for his slow, quiet breathing. One arm was extended over the bed, his fingertips just brushing the kithara where it lay on the floor.

Chris gently brushed back the hair that hung across Arron's face. The Roamer moved slightly and blinked open his eyes. He started back at the sight of Chris leaning over him.

"I . . . I didn't hear you come in."

"Yeah, you were really out." Chris turned quickly to the breakfast tray. He went to hand it to Arron, but the Roamer waved him away.

"Wait, wait. I have to show you. Close the door and the curtains."

Curious, Chris hurriedly did as he was told. Arron opened the box, letting the light come into the darkened room. Chris stared, realizing he had left the box behind last night. Still, he said nothing.

"When I touched it the other day," Arron was saying, "I heard the lullaby. Or rather a perversion of it. That's why I was playing it last night, trying to figure out the way I had heard it."

"So?" Chris leaned forward as he sat down.

"So, listen. But watch the sphere."

Arron played the lullaby again, and Chris watched as the light intensity increased and decreased and the color of the sphere changed, all of it irregularly.

"Well?" Chris asked when the song had ended and the light softened.

"Well, I noted the places the light decreased and I dropped the words where the light dropped. You see . . . it was humming a song without those parts."

"And?"

"And listen." Arron tilted the kithara in readiness and began to play.

> It comes, tired or not
> Sleep is a blessed thing
> Go, light will follow
> Sleep is starlight lit
> Orb encircles sleep
> Promise given you, by me, by him
>
> All must sleep
> All that was saved by lack of sleep
> Must be returned to sleep
> It is a blessed thing

The whole time the sphere glowed with a bright, white light. Arron set his kithara back on the bed.

"Hmmm." Chris looked at the sphere. "What about the colored light?"

"Well, that comes with certain words and word phrases. I couldn't make any order out of them. They're just random, it seems." He took his kithara and plucked the strings, playing out the chords for each color group. The sphere changed colors with each note. "Desired. Trouble will. Ancient. Mind. Relieving. In him. Come. His. Trust." He looked at Chris. "I didn't really try to arrange it. I was tired. Too many possibilities."

"Hmmm. Let's see. The colors came in this order . . . the way you just sang it. Green, purple, blue, green, red, gold, red, blue, purple. Not much order to that. But what happens when you play it?"

Arron nodded. "I tried that much. Nothing. Just the color changes. And I can't make any sense of the words in that order."

"Well, maybe if we patterned the colors, like making two sequences such as red, blue, green, purple, red, blue, gr—"

"Or blue, green, red, purple . . . or purple, green, red, blue. And where does the gold come in? And for that matter which red group first? Hmmm? Does the red group of 'come' or the red group of 'relieving' come first?"

"Okay, okay. I get the point. Too complex. Well, we'll think of something. Go ahead and eat." Arron nodded, smiling, as he reached for the tray. Chris smiled back, then got up, closed the box, and opened the curtains. He sat back down, watching Arron eat. He leaned forward after a moment and gingerly took hold of the instrument. He looked at Arron for permission. "I'll be very careful." The Roamer nodded, biting into a thick slice of bread.

Chris took it and slid it gently into his lap. He ran his fingers slowly along the smoothly varnished wood. It was a mellow, brown color, as rich as the music it gave. He experimentally plucked one of its strings, then laughed slightly. Somehow, his plucking was vastly inferior to Arron's.

"It takes a lot of practice and a good teacher."

"Who taught you?" Chris looked up.

"My mother, first, and then Grandmother."

Chris thought to ask what had happened to Arron's mother, but thought better of it when he saw the guarded look Arron suddenly took on when he thought this. He turned back to the instrument. Its thin, delicate neck, like a bird's, was just perfect for wrapping a hand about. The handle was lightly coated in an intricately designed coat of gold. The body fit snugly in his lap, the smooth, oval shape pressing comfortably into his stomach. He tilted it to look at its face.

"What are these markings?" He ran his fingers over the colorful design on the front. It was beautiful, in a way, but it looked more like writing than a design.

"That's my family name. The kithara is an heirloom. My inheritance, one might say."

"What's the name?"

The Roamer set his fork down slowly, looking at Chris. He hesitated. "Shakta."

Chris started up. "But you said—"

"That he was a fool."

Chris looked down and ran his fingers over the kithara again. They trembled.

"The kithara was his. He gave it to my grandmother, his granddaughter. She gave it to me."

"So your name isn't Shakta." Chris felt the tightness in his chest giving way for air. He knew what must be done with a Shakta. He remembered Thomas' taunts when they were little, that he had to find a Shakta, had to somehow bring about the death of a Shakta at the hands of a Chruston; the cure to the curse.

But this Roamer here was not a Shakta in name, as he was not a Chruston in name.

"Roamer lineage is a matriarchy," Arron was saying. "The husband takes the wife's name. I am Arron Shakta. Does that trouble you?"

Chris averted his eyes, his breath lost again.

The Roamer smiled a tight smile. "Two counts against me now, is that it? A Roamer and a Shakta."

"I wasn't thinking that!"

"No?" Arron said knowingly. "You are not a Chruston in name. He was on your mother's side. Why are you thinking that is so important?" The Roamer stared hard at him, then turned and gazed out the window. "You know, your mother and my grandmother were able to work together." He looked back at Chris. "Do you think we can? Can you forgive my hereditary misfortune for a moment? I can understand, sort of, your revulsion to Roamers. But . . . does the name really matter?"

Chris looked down at the kithara. He was a Shakta! What did he want from him? What did he really want? To do more to his family? Chris' thoughts held there a moment. The curse on his family . . . the cure . . . Here was a Shakta. If his great-great-grandfather, a Chruston, was truly alive as the Roamer said . . . if he could get Arron to him . . . But what did the Roamer intend? He licked his lips and tried to clear his mind.

"I guess it does," Arron said softly. "Although, I can't see why. And I suppose for the moment you are unwilling to tell me."

Chris stared hard at the kithara. He had to block his thoughts. He stared at the design, taking it and only it into his mind. Purple, red, blue, green, red, blue, green, purple, gold. He recited the color pattern over and over in his mind.

He looked up suddenly. "Look! Look here. Look at the colors."

"So?" Arron watched him warily.

"So! The words! The words to the song in this order."

"Which order? There are two words to each color."

"No. There are some colors that have more than one word to them. Like purple. It has a two-word group, 'trouble will,' and a one-word group, 'trust.' "

Arron leaned forward, his hand out for the instrument. Chris gave it to him. The Roamer looked at it closely, counting. "Look," he said at last, tilting the face toward Chris. "See here, the Roamer S has three strokes, the H has one, and this two-stroke here that indicates the S-H sound that you just assume in your language. And then the A has—"

"Now what are you getting at? I'm not trying to learn your alphabet."

"Well, what if whoever wrote this song was trying to give us some code here? What if he looked at the letters and picked words with the same number of syllables as strokes, then painted this the colors that the sphere turned at the notes."

Chris gave him an unconvinced look. "And who would ever think we would come up with that idea? And how would they know that the two of us would be trying to figure out this song? Why would they—"

"Shakta would," Arron said softly. "Or maybe Grand-mother."

Chris leaned back. "Well, play it then, if you think it's going to work." He folded his arms across his chest.

Arron looked down at the colors again and seemed to be trying to arrange it in his head, the words and the notes. Then he turned the kithara right and played it out slowly. "Trouble will come ancient desired relieving his mind trust in him."

Chris burst out laughing. "That makes a whole lot of sense. Trouble will come ancient . . . Well, now at least we know the real reason Shakta threw himself from the tower. Lyrical difficulty." He laughed even harder.

Arron shot him an angry look, then began to mutter the words under his breath. "Trouble will come ancient . . . no. Trouble will come. That's okay alone. Ancient desired . . . Ancient desired relieving? No. Well? Ancient-desired-reliev-ing-his-mind-trust, hmmm. Trust in him. That's all right alone. That leaves ancient desired relieving his mind. Does that make sense? Well, if ancient is a noun, it would be okay."

"Are you still going on with that? You've got to be kidding."

Arron got up stiffly and crossed over to the window. He drew the curtains, then turned to open the box. He sat on the edge of the bed, took up his kithara, and began to play.

"Trouble will come. Ancient desired relieving his mind. Trust in him." The sphere flared up, a golden-white light that struck sharply at Chris, tossing him and the chair he sat on over backward with a crash. Arron leaped upon the box and slammed the lid shut, cutting off the light that still bored into Chris.

"Chris?" Arron leaned anxiously over the chair. "Chris?"

Chris stared up at him, dazed. Arron bent to pull him to his feet, but did not quite have the strength.

"Can you get up?"

"Not yet," Chris said weakly.

"What's wrong? What did you hurt?" He knelt next to him, trying to feel his neck and spine.

Chris groaned and sat up. "No, no. I'm all right." He pushed Arron away roughly.

"I . . . I wouldn't have played it if I'd known . . ." Arron stopped and stared at Chris.

"Stay out of my mind!"

"I wasn't . . . I mean . . . I . . ."

Chris waved him to be quiet as he got to his feet.

"That was meant for you, wasn't it?" Arron said, still on his knees. "It said something to you, didn't it?"

Chris shook his head irritably. "It said the same thing you just sang. Only louder, and many, many times . . . like it didn't want me to forget . . ."

"But why?"

"How should I know," Chris said sharply, then looking at Arron. "Stay out of my thoughts, Roamer," he warned.

Arron stood up. "I'm not probing. You are transmitting!"

"Well, don't listen!" Chris straightened up the chair, grabbed the breakfast tray, and left the room.

Chris stacked the last of the breakfast dishes in the cupboard, then turned to wipe off the counter. A light knock came on the front door. Sighing, he tossed the towel down on the counter. He swung the door open with a jerk and stood staring at Sarah Anne and Katie.

"Well, hi yourself," Sarah Anne said.

"Oh, hi! What are you doing here? I mean, come in, come on in." He swung the door open wide, feeling stupid. "I was just cleaning up from breakfast."

"Oh?" Sarah Anne raised her eyebrows, a slight smile briefly touching her lips. She looked around the room slowly, taking obvious note of the general dishevelment of the place due to the night's visitors. "I see you had those men come search your house, too. To think they suspected someone of harboring a Roamer! Now, who would do such a foolish thing as that?" She bent to straighten a stool.

"Don't bother with that. I'll take care of it later."

She shook her head to indicate it was no trouble. "What really frightens me, though," she said turning back to look at him and Katie, "is the fact that there are any Roamers left. And that the one that is, might be in this area." She nodded slowly. "Although, it's not entirely a surprise to me. I mean, it's gotten to where our cows have stopped giving milk! Well, I know something has got to be causing it. We have to assume our fathers didn't get them all, like we thought."

"Uh, yeah," Chris agreed.

"Come on, Chris," Katie said quietly. "We'll help you straighten up the room."

"No, no, I'll take care of it later. How about something to eat?"

Katie raised the basket she had on her arm. "I packed a lunch . . ."

"You did?" Chris raised his eyebrows.

Katie's eyes widened, and she flushed, frowning, and looked down quickly. "Yes. I packed a lunch. I thought maybe you might like to go on a picnic, to get out for a while." She looked back up at him coolly. "I ran into Sarah Anne on the way here. She was coming up for a visit. So, we can all go, after we help you straighten up. Your cousin, is he up to it?"

"Yes, where is Arron?" Sarah Anne asked, turning about.

"Oh, he's still in the bedroom." Chris tried to catch Katie's eye, to apologize.

"Well, go and see if he's up to it," Sarah Anne pressed. "If not, I'll forfeit the picnic and baby-sit while you two go off and get some air. Go on, bring him out here to meet Katie. He didn't get to meet her yesterday, remember." She pushed him toward the bedroom.

Chris continued on in the direction she had pushed him, thinking it was going to be another very long day. And there were going to be plenty more, he realized, until something was done with the Roamer. What was he going to do with him? He certainly couldn't just let him go. He really had to get him to . . . well, the curse and all. Arron was a Shakta. He stopped his thinking there and opened the bedroom door.

The curtains at the window flapped lazily in the day's gentle breeze. The window was open. The Roamer was gone! Chris rushed to the window, but there was no sign of the Roamer. He had run away! Chris turned in a sudden panic, trying to locate the box. It was gone, too. The Roamer had stolen it. He ran back out of the room, but stopped short at the curtains separating the back of the house from the front. Katie and Sarah Anne were in there.

He forced himself to walk casually into the main room.

"Well?"

"Well, Arron must have gone for a walk. He probably left when I wasn't looking. He knows I don't think he should be alone in his condition, but he does have a lot on his mind. Look, you just stay here, and I'll go and find him. It'll just be a short while."

"We could help . . ." Sarah Anne started.

"No, no. He . . . he's kind of emotional now. He's been through quite a bit. He may be embarrassed with you there. I won't be long, and if I am, well, we'll have the picnic another day, okay?" He didn't wait for an answer. He had backed his way to the front door while talking and was out the door on the last words, his pace brisk. He broke into a run as soon as he reached the woods. He had an idea where Arron might have gone.

He slowed up when he reached the spot where they had buried Arron's grandmother. Sure enough, Arron sat crouched by the grave, his knees drawn up to his chest, his kithara close. His head rested on his knees.

"Shakta!"

The Roamer snapped his head up. "My name is Arron."

"Arron Shakta. And Shakta suits you better. You're a thief like he was."

"I've never stolen a thing in my life. And neither did he."

"Ever steal any fish, Roamer?"

"I . . ." Chris smiled, seeing him look away.

"No . . . oh, no, you're not a thief. A liar, perhaps, but never, never a thief."

"Yes, I've stolen things. You needn't be so—I did all that when I was a little boy."

Chris folded his arms across his chest. "And you've never stolen again? And you've repented, I suppose."

"A thousand times over." Arron still didn't look at him. "Now most of all."

"You probably vowed to yourself that you would never steal again."

"What is this leading to?" Arron turned to look at him, his

eyes narrowed. "That was all long ago. We've both changed, things have happened. What do you want from me?"

"I want to know where my box is!"

"In the space under your bed to keep it safe."

"It . . . it is?"

"Yes."

"Oh." He stood quiet a moment, then thrust a finger at the kithara. "What are you doing out here? And with that thing? Someone could come."

"And I would be killed. And why would you care?"

Chris stared, at a loss.

Arron waited a moment, something in his eyes begging Chris to answer. He turned to the stones piled on the grave. "Well, I wanted to be with someone who . . . someone who did care."

"Come on back to the house."

"Why?"

"Why? Well . . . because . . . because you're sick, that's why."

"So?"

"So . . . and Sarah Anne and another friend of mine, Katie Topkins, are there waiting for us to go on a picnic with them."

"A picnic," Arron said. He stood up slowly, the kithara close against his chest. "I'm leaving soon, Chris. I'm going to find Chruston."

Chris started at that. "He—he's dead. My God, he was my great-great."

"He's not dead." Arron looked sharply at the grave. "I'm going to find him. And if he didn't have a death before, by God, he has one now. I'll kill him for what he did to her. No one should be allowed to do that kind of thing." He turned to Chris. "No matter what you think we are." He looked down, his voice cracking a bit now and then. "But how can you stop them when there are so many? I didn't want them to hurt her. My God, she never said a word. Except in her mind, I could feel her screaming. Feel it, until it burned through me . . . burned. She wouldn't tell them where the box was. That's what they wanted, Chris. They wanted it badly. She wanted it safe worse. Much, much worse." He glared up at Chris.

"Arron . . . Arron, come back to the house. You're not well enough yet."

"I need the box, Chris."

"No!" Chris pulled back, then narrowed his eyes. "You . . . this is all an act. An act to get the box! You probably killed her yourself!"

Arron sucked in his breath, then sat down slowly. "I don't deserve that."

"So you're telling me."

Arron watched him a moment more, then, as if coming to a decision, he began to play the lullaby softly on his kithara. "It comes, tired or not," he sang, then looked up at Chris. "Death, not sleep."

Chris stared at him, confused.

Arron continued. "Death is a blessed thing. Go, light will follow, death is starlight lit. Orb encircles death." He looked up. "That sphere holds Chruston's death." He played again. "Promise given you, by me, by him—to me by my grandmother by Shakta . . . All must die. All that was saved by lack of death—Chruston—must be returned to death. It is a blessed thing." He looked back up at Chris.

"You can't have it, Roamer."

"Then come with me."

Chris paused, thinking. Go to find his grandfather—a Chruston. With Arron—a Shakta. He stopped his thoughts there, his heart banging suddenly in his chest. "We'll talk about this tomorrow. My friends are waiting. Please . . ."

Arron sat a moment longer. "How can you live with those two conflicting thoughts. Do you hate me, or don't you?"

Chris stared at him in surprise.

Arron started laughing. "You really don't know, do you? I'm that far below you that it doesn't make a difference. Okay, let's go then." He sighed and stood.

Chris pulled Arron to a halt as they approached the house. "You have to leave that thing out here." He pointed to the kithara the Roamer had cradled in one arm.

Arron pulled it closer.

"Arron, don't be stupid. What will they think if they see that? They'll know you're a Roamer."

Arron relaxed his grip on the instrument. "When have they ever seen a Roamer instrument? They'll have no idea. Homesteader women are overprotected. I doubt most of them have even seen a Roamer. I'm not leaving my kithara out here." He strode on toward the house.

"Arron!" Chris tried to stop him, but Sarah Anne had come out on the porch.

"Well, it's certainly about time you got back! Katie and I are famished. We were just about to eat the lunch ourselves." She put her hand gently on Arron's shoulder as he stepped up to the porch. "Are you all right?"

Arron nodded. She slid her hand under his elbow as if to help him up the steps.

"I can manage," he muttered. She released her grip immediately and backed toward the door to hold it open for him, her mouth a small, tight line. Arron stopped, looking at her, then smiled. She smiled back uncertainly.

"Thank you, I really am fine," he whispered.

Her smile broadened, her eyes falling away from his face coyly. "What's that?" She eyed the kithara. "Do you play?"

"Yes."

"Oh? Oh, please bring it along on the picnic and play for us."

Chris stared at the two of them as they disappeared into the house. She really didn't suspect the truth. She really thought Arron was his cousin. He took a deep breath, swelling his chest, and strode to the porch, grinning. A Roamer right under their noses, and they didn't even know it. He had fooled them all. They really didn't know.

The three inside came out on the porch as Chris put his foot on the first step.

"Shall we go then?" Sarah Anne asked. Her fingers rested on Arron's forearm.

Chris shrugged and looked to Arron. "Are you up to it?"

"I am."

"Okay then . . ."

Why don't we go up Mount Klineloch," Katie suggested.

"Oh, yes, let's. We haven't been there in so long," Sarah Anne chimed in.

"Well?" Chris looked sideways at Arron.

"I'm fine."

"Mount Klineloch it is, then." Chris took the basket from Katie and led them all off toward the mountain.

VIII

THE DAY WAS RATHER NICE, AND THEY SAT TOGETHER ON one of the few grassy patches that remained. They were up high enough on the mountain that the houses below looked boxlike and unreal.

Despite himself, Chris found the company enjoyable and the food absolutely delicious. Even Arron had defrosted and come out of his moodiness. Sarah Anne had gotten him to play light, funny songs on his kithara. At their laughter, the Roamer grinned back, almost gratefully, and played more. Some of the songs were so comical, he had them laughing till tears came to their eyes. What a change, Chris thought, from the bitter Roamer he had spoken with only an hour or so ago.

Chris rocked back and bit into a small cake, still chuckling at the last tune. He stared at Arron a moment. He had been right in saving him. Arron looked up and smiled, quite suddenly, at him. Chris nodded indulgently and laughed, taking another bite of the cake.

"This is good! Where did you get the good flour?" he said to Katie.

"I don't know that it is good flour, but it's certainly better than what we've been having. Papa says it's black market," she whispered conspiratorially, the way they used to do when they were kids. "My mother says that it's all right, but she remembers—"

"Let's not talk about all that now," Sarah Anne cut in. "We've heard all that. It's so beautiful up here. We've some grass to sit on, and, why, there are even some birds. The town looks different from here. Better. Happier."

"That's because up here you can't see the boarded-up shops, the broken porches, the people's faces . . ." Chris started.

"Shhhh!" Sarah Anne waved her hands in the air. "Eat some more and be quiet!"

Katie lay back in the grass, her hands clasped behind her head. "My mother says she remembers when this mountain had trees with all their leaves, instead of these dead ones. All the trees had leaves." She sat back up. "And all these bare patches, there and all over there, well, they were all covered with grass, much, much greener than this." She flopped back down. "Someday, maybe it'll all come back."

Chris glanced at Arron, but the Roamer was fiddling with his instrument. He turned back to Katie who lay gazing up at the gray-blue sky. He tossed a small piece of fruit at her. "Dreamer."

She tossed the fruit back with a gentle overhand throw. "No more of one than you." She pulled up tufts of dried grass and let it blow over onto Chris, getting stuck in his hair and cake. Laughing at his mock anger, she jumped to her feet and raced for the trees. Chris got up quickly and tried to match her pace.

Arron smiled slightly, watching the two of them darting in and out of the trees, Katie dodging Chris as easily as a little brother might, quickly changing directions, darting into the smaller spaces.

"You two seem pretty close," Sarah Anne cut into his thoughts.

Arron looked back at her and shrugged. "At times, I suppose. We do have our differences." He slid his kithara into its soft case.

"Oh! Don't put it away," Sarah Anne protested.

Arron gave a short laugh. "No, it's had enough."

"Oh, I forgot. You must be exhausted."

Arron smiled again. "No, I'm all right." He stretched his arms out. "I feel really good right now."

"That's good. My mother was very worried about you."

"Was she? Was she really?"

"Of course, silly! Why, she had it in her mind to insist you come down and stay with us, you looked so poorly. But you're looking much better now. Even the bruises on your face are fading." She touched his cheek gently. "But . . . I still hope you'll come down for a visit, maybe?"

Arron stared at her. She was extremely charming in looks, it was almost a wonder no one had taken up with her by now. Then Chris' thoughts from the day before burned across his mind. He was a Roamer. Whatever was he thinking? She would never accept that, never forgive that. He looked down at his hands.

"I might stop by," he said softly.

"Oh, that would be marvelous!" She moved close against him. "You could come by tomorrow, maybe?"

Arron shook his head slowly. "It'll have to be the next time I'm in town. I have some . . . family matters to take care of."

"Oh, but—"

Arron laughed at her. "Yeah, nothing's fair."

"You always seem to know what I'm thinking. I like that."

Arron looked down. "Yeah," he said. The gap between them was too wide. He looked away toward the woods. "I wonder where Chris and Katie have gotten off to?"

"Well, we could go look for them," Sarah Anne suggested. "If you're up to it."

"Yeah, let's go find them. It's getting cold."

Sarah Anne squinted up at the hot sun. "Are you sure you're all right?"

Arron nodded and slung the kithara over his back. "They went up that way." He pointed.

"Maybe they don't want to be disturbed."

Arron looked at her curiously.

"Well, you never know," she added, smiling. "Even with Katie."

Arron shook his head and turned to look back up the

mountain, trying to spot movement in the trees. Nothing. There weren't even birds now.

"Come on, hurry," he said, his stomach turning cold with the rest of him.

"What's wrong? What are you getting so worried about? Arron . . ." But he had broken into a half run, leaving her calling after him. She ran to catch up. They ran through the clumps of trees, where some shaded the ground with broad-leafed branches, but most stood barren and dead as if an odd fire had swept through the area and left only certain trees scorched. Arron stopped, wheezing, a hand coming up to relieve the straining in his chest.

Sarah Anne came up next to him. "I don't think you should be running. And I do think you're working yourself up over nothing."

He peered through the thin trees. *"Chris,"* he called out. *"Katie!"* He stood still, listening.

"Arron . . ."

"Shhh!" He continued to listen, and Sarah Anne, too. But she only heard the slight breeze ruffling through the leaves, rattling the bare branches. Arron rubbed his eyes slowly with his fingers. "Let's try this way," he said at last, pointing up a row of long-dead pines.

"Why would they go that way?" Sarah Anne said, shrinking back. "I don't want to go up there."

"Why not?"

"Because, it's . . . look at those trees. They say there were Roamer camps up here a long time ago. Maybe that Roamer they're searching for is hiding at one of them."

"Uh, I really don't think so. Come on." He took her hand.

She jerked her hand from his. "No, I don't want to go up there."

He glared at her, then looked back up the hill. He had begun to shiver, the sweat from running chilling his body. "Stay here, then." He started up the hill, surrounded now by the dead pines. He stopped again, hearing something.

Sarah Anne scurried up to him. "That sounded like Ka-tie," she whispered. "I'm scared. You're scaring me!"

"Hold this," Arron said, swinging the kithara from his

back. He handed it to her, his hands lingering on it a moment. "Don't let it out of your hands," he ordered.

She nodded, clutching at it. Arron turned and ran up through the line of trees. Sarah Anne watched him a moment, the dead trees closing in behind him like so many doors slamming shut, cutting her off. She raced after him.

Now Arron could hear Chris and Katie yelling in earnest. He doubled his speed, trying to follow the sound of their voices, but they echoed off the rotting trees and mountain cliffs, seeming to come from everywhere and nowhere.

"No. Don't do this to me. Don't do this. No more," he muttered, stopping, trying to sort out the sounds. He ran off to the right.

The trees ended abruptly in a line of cold, white trunks, and a mountain meadow stretched up to a sheer cliff. He spotted Chris and Katie at its base fending off what appeared to be a bear.

He hesitated, then slipped a knife from his boot and ran across the field, quietly, so the animal wouldn't turn.

Chris whacked it hard with a branch he held. The stick snapped in half across the animal's back. It didn't seem to notice. Startled, Chris froze, and the creature lunged at him. Then Katie attacked it, beating its head and back with another stick, screaming at it. But Chris was down. Then Arron was there, too, stabbing it and trying to knock it away. Sarah Anne came running and stood well back, screaming and stamping her feet. Katie dropped her stick and went down on her knees, grabbing at its legs and pulling at it. Suddenly it gave way, rolling over on top of Arron, who had his knife thrust deeply into its side.

The creature bellowed and wrenched itself away. Arron got up quickly, his legs trembling, threatening collapse. But the bear had turned and run off, as if it had had enough.

Arron stared after it, a strange look on his face.

"That . . . that's so odd." Katie gasped out, trying with difficulty to get her breathing under control. "It attacked so suddenly, and now it just runs off."

Arron turned to Chris. "Chris?"

Sarah Anne was still screaming.

"What . . . what happened?" Chris asked weakly. Arron's legs gave way, forcing him to kneel next to Chris. He reached to pull back Chris' shirt where it was soaked in blood.

"It bit my shoulder."

"Yeah, I see." Arron struggled to ease him up and remove his shirt. He glanced up at Sarah Anne, who was now sobbing uncontrollably, kneeling in the dirt.

"He's dead, my God. Oh, my God!" she wailed. Arron turned pleadingly to Katie. She nodded and went to comfort her.

"You stabbed it . . . with a knife," Chris said. Arron nodded. "You had a knife."

Arron pulled off his own shirt, folded it up, and placed it firmly on Chris' shoulder.

"What were you doing carrying a knife?" Chris asked.

"For protection." Arron wrapped Chris' shirt over his own and tied it tightly to stop the bleeding. "Sarah Anne! Be quiet!" She sucked in a breath and was silent.

Katie left her a moment and retrieved Arron's knife. She wiped it clean on the grass and brought it to Arron. "You dropped this."

Arron looked up. "Thanks," he said softly. He slid it back into his boot. Katie watched him. Arron turned to look at Sarah Anne, then back at Katie. "Will you take my kithara from her? She's too upset." He bent over Chris again.

"Your kithara?" Katie asked, not moving.

He looked up. "Yes."

She nodded slowly and walked to Sarah Anne. Arron started to turn back to Chris, then spun back to look at Katie. "You—" He choked the words back and bent back over Chris before she noticed he had spoken.

"I didn't know you had a knife. You didn't tell me," Chris was saying. "I should have checked. Everyone knows Roamers keep knives in their boots."

"You and Katie would be dead if you had."

"Why'd you save us? You could have had it if I had died, Shakta."

"Chris!" Arron sat back on his heels looking at Katie and Sarah Anne. Had they heard?

"What's wrong? Is he all right?" Katie started forward.

"Yes, yes. He's muttering, that's all." Arron investigated the wound more carefully.

Chris blinked a few times, then his eyes focused on Arron's face, close to his. "Arron?"

"Yes, Chris."

"You saved us?"

"Yes."

Chris nodded. "I . . . I feel strange. Sort of."

Arron smoothed his hair back and looked at him closely. "Do you think you can walk? I'll help you."

"Are you up to walking me? Or will someone have to walk you, too?" He smiled imagining a chain of people supporting one another marching down the hill. Then he frowned, seeing Arron smile, too. "I'm okay. It just bit my shoulder, that's all."

Arron watched him a moment more, unconvinced. Then he forced himself up again and bent to help Chris rise. Katie came over and helped him lift Chris, then slid carefully between them.

"You're not strong enough. I'll walk him down."

Arron smiled slightly, looking doubtfully at her small stature.

"Don't worry, I've got him," she said gently. One arm was secured about Chris' waist, the other holding his good arm over her shoulders. She stood firmly.

"All right." He scooped up his kithara.

They made their way slowly down the mountain. The main burden had become not Chris, but Sarah Anne. She was paralyzed. Arron had to coax her along. She was continuously looking over her shoulder, painfully begging them to hurry. And yet it was she who slowed them, watching every tree as if it were going to come alive.

Arron was at his wits' end, exhausted himself. And he was frightened about the effect Chris' wound was having on him. He suspected the animal attack had been meant for himself, not Chris. But there was no time to think about that. He turned angrily on Sarah Anne. She fell immediately silent, huge tears welling up in her large eyes.

Arron sighed. How could he blame her? He was really

lucky Katie had her head together. Things could have been much worse. He took Sarah Anne's hand gently. "I'm sorry," he whispered. "It's all right, really."

"I'm sorry," she said back in a tiny voice, then she jumped at a noise in the trees.

"Sarah Anne," Arron squeezed her hand and pulled her closer. "Nothing is going to happen. Chris is fine, and there is nothing else up here."

"But—but that bear . . ." She sniffed and stifled a sob. "It's still around. Waiting up here to kill us." She tried to pull away, but Arron held her tighter. "Up ahead! It's up there! Waiting!"

"It's not waiting! We scared it off." Arron tried to push her forward. "Come on." He thought briefly about taking his kithara out. A little music to calm her? But it was not the time, it would look odd.

"No." Sarah Anne remained frozen.

"You can't stay here."

She just stared helplessly at him.

"Sarah Anne, come on."

She didn't move.

Arron forced her forward with a hand about her waist. "Nothing is going to happen. Now, you and I have to help Katie get Chris down the hill. Okay? That's what we have to do, just get Chris down the hill."

She nodded slowly and stopped resisting his pushing.

"That's better." Arron smiled at her.

"I . . . I'm sorry. I don't mean to be so silly." She laughed slightly, then cried a bit more.

Arron tightened the hand about her waist. "It's not your fault. It's not. And I won't let anything happen to you, don't worry."

"Really?"

"Really. Come on, now." She leaned close against him, her stride, though still hesitant, strove to match his.

Finally they made it back down to the cabin. Arron was relieved to switch burdens with Katie.

"Take her home. I can take care of Chris," he said.

"Should I get a doctor?"

"No! I mean, it's not that serious, there's no need to trouble anyone."

"All right." She watched him a moment, then took Sarah Anne by the arm and propelled her home.

Arron took Chris into the house, carefully cleaned and rebandaged his arm, and put him to bed.

"Where's my box?" Chris demanded as Arron turned to leave him.

Arron froze. "Under the bed."

"Let me see it."

Arron nodded slowly and crawled under the bed. He reappeared with the box.

"Give it to me." Arron did. "You can't have it, Shakta," Chris said in a low voice.

"Chris—"

"I said no!"

Arron stared at him, a hand against his stomach trying to quell the growing terror there. He backed slowly from the room. "I'll be right back."

"Just stay away from the box, Shakta!" Chris held it tightly against his chest. Arron nodded and backed out of the room, scooping up his pack as he left.

Back out in the main room, he set it on the counter and looked through the contents. Pulling out a few odd jars and a bowl, he set them alongside his pack. He quickly poured some of the contents of the jars into the bowl and added water. His shaking hands spilled some of the mixture. He capped the bowl and pushed it under the ashes of the fire, then stoked it up. He sat at the table drumming his fingers on the smooth wood.

A knock on the door made him jump. He opened it to see Katie standing on the porch with another basket.

"Hi." She smiled. "I brought some food over for dinner. I didn't think you'd be up to making it." She peered curiously into the room. "Something smells good, though."

Arron laughed, a little too loudly. "Not dinner. But come in. Chris is resting."

"He's okay?"

"Yeah." Arron turned away.

Katie set the basket on the table.

"He's in the bedroom," Arron said, staring at the fire, his hands resting nervously on the back of the armchair. "Maybe he'd like something to eat."

Katie pulled some plates from the basket and dished some stew and bread onto one. "I'll just take some in for him, then."

Arron nodded as Katie disappeared into the back. He leaned against the chair and rubbed his face with his hands. Katie came back into the kitchen.

"He's acting . . . well, really not himself."

"Yeah, I—I think there may be some poison or something in the wound." He walked to the fire and poked the bowl from the ashes, then carried it in a towel back to the counter. Bluish-colored steam puffed out and wafted away when he removed the lid.

"What is that?"

Arron looked at the bluish-green paste. "Something to take out the poison." He fanned it with the towel.

"That looks like poison." She watched him closely.

Arron stared back at her. "Well, then, I guess you'll just have to trust me." He lifted the bowl and walked to the back. "If you can," he shot over his shoulder.

Katie moved to follow him, then turned back to the basket and set out two plates for dinner. Chris yelled suddenly from the other room. She turned, raising a plate protectively, then forced herself to set it down. Carefully, she dished food onto first one plate, then the other. She lowered herself into a chair, sitting very straight.

Arron came out at last. He thoroughly washed the blue stuff from his hands in the water basin, then walked over and sat down, eyeing the food.

"It's good," Katie managed to whisper.

Arron nodded and picked up a fork, then lowered it again and looked up at Katie. "So. What are you going to do?"

"Do?" She opened her eyes innocently.

"I know that you know."

"Know what?"

Arron sighed. "Look. All I want to know is what you are going to do."

Katie sat quiet a moment, uncertain. "Well, you did save

us. And that seemed a bit strange, logically speaking. Right now, I'll do nothing. I think that keeps us both safe."

Arron stood up, knocking his chair back. Katie grabbed at a knife on the table, raising it protectively in front of her. Arron stared at it, disgusted. "If I was going to kill you because you knew too much, I would have done it up on the mountain!" He grabbed his chair up and sat down hard, then, embarrassed at his outburst, he looked down. Katie set the knife down slowly. "How did you know?" he said at last.

"The knife—you put it in your boot. And your eyes are so dark. And a kithara is a Roamer instrument." Arron sighed and nodded. Katie indicated his hair. "That will throw a few people off, though."

"A few?"

"Most."

"But not you."

Katie shrugged. "Is Chris going to be all right?"

"Yes."

"That stuff you gave him?"

"It removes poisons. My grandmother was good with medicines. She taught me. She taught me a lot." He stopped, staring off. "Some poisons affect the mind. I just hope I got to it in time. I . . . I didn't realize."

"Why are you helping him?"

"Because he needs help."

"It's not to pay off the debt of him helping you?"

Arron leaned forward. "You think I would have let you two die, except that I owed him something? Well, you're wrong."

"I really don't know what to think."

"Well, it really doesn't make any great difference to me, so long as you don't tell anyone," Arron snapped.

Katie smiled. "It does make a difference to you."

Arron shrugged and started eating, then stopped again and stood.

"What is it?"

He hurried over to his pack and put in the jars and bowl, sliding his kithara in last. Then he pushed the whole thing behind the counter. A sharp rapping came on the door. Katie moved to answer it, but Arron signaled that he would. He opened the door and nodded politely to the man who had led the search on the house the night before.

Craftan narrowed his eyes, taking in the bandages about Arron's chest. "Weren't you sick last night?"

"Yes, I was."

"Well?"

"Well, what?"

"Well, what are you doing up?"

"I felt much better this morning."

"Good enough to go on a picnic?"

"Fresh air is good for you."

The man stood a moment more, then pushed his way into the room. "I'm Doug Craftan," he said sitting down. "I was told about the incident up in the hills by a Mrs. McGreggor. Her daughter said she was up there with you boys and another young lady. Might that be you?" Katie nodded. "Well, tell me about it. Did you see anyone up there? We have reason to believe a Roamer might be involved in all this. Protecting his hiding place, perhaps."

Katie froze, but Arron just shrugged his shoulders unconcerned. "I could draw you a map to show you where we were. You could go up and investigate. We didn't see anyone up there, though."

"I heard your cousin was bitten by this thing. Any poison or sign of magic?"

Arron sighed. "You don't seriously think it was a Roamer, do you? My God, didn't we kill them all?"

Craftan shook his head. "A town had a pair of them. One died, the other got away after killing two people."

Arron nodded, obviously interested. Katie sat back slowly. He lied so smoothly. He couldn't be the Roamer Craftan was speaking of. He took it all so easily, even the accusation of killing those people. Was he so unconcerned about what she thought of that? Was he so sure she would keep quiet?

"Did you see this Roamer?" Katie leaned toward Craftan.

"I never saw either of them. I'm from the town, though. My . . . son was killed by that monster. And so was a close friend."

"I'm sorry," Arron said gently.

The man nodded. "Yeah, isn't everyone. But I know the Roamer is in this area."

"How do you know?" Arron asked.

"Dempter, the person who's ordered the search, knows. Now, is there anything else you can tell me?"

"Sarah Anne probably had the story down pretty well," Katie said.

"Arron?" Chris walked unsteadily into the room, still holding the box close. "Arron, I'm sorry . . ." He stopped and stared at Craftan.

Craftan looked up. "How are you, young man?" His eyes fell on the box. He stood up slowly and turned to look at Arron. "Your eyes are awfully dark, boy," he said very softly.

Arron lowered his head. "What's that supposed to mean?"

Craftan looked warily about the room. "Did you two know he was a Roamer?"

Katie didn't move, and Chris shuffled nervously in the doorway.

Craftan reached down and jerked Arron roughly up by the arm. "What black magic did you use on these children!" Then his mouth hung open in a painful surprise, his grip loosened and then released. He fell to the floor. Arron stared down at him, his knife dripping at his side. No one moved.

"You killed him?" Chris finally choked out.

Arron looked up at him sharply. "And what do you suppose he was going to do with me?"

"But you killed his son."

Arron shook his head. "That doesn't mean anything right now!"

"But . . ." Katie started. The sound died away from her lips as Arron turned on her, the knife held loosely at his side, dripping blood onto the floor. He was looking as if he had done this many times before. Arron turned away then, knelt by the body, and wiped the blade on Craftan's shirt.

"Are you going to rob him, too?" Chris whispered in horror.

"No!" He shoved the blade back into his boot.

"Oh, no, you don't." Chris marched over to him. "Give me that knife."

"Chris, don't," Katie said, her eyes on the Roamer's hand as it hovered near his boot.

"No, Chris, I'm not going to give it to you." Arron looked away. "Why did you bring that box out with you? Why would you do that, Chris?"

Chris stared down at the box still clutched in his hands. "You . . . you would steal it if I left it in there alone."

Arron nodded slowly. "Will someone help me take this man somewhere?"

"Only if you give me the knife first."

Arron stood abruptly. "What did you expect me to do! You couldn't see what he was thinking! The pain he wanted me to feel . . . You didn't see that. I did!"

"You killed his son!"

"Oh, so I should have said to him, 'Please take me and torture me and then in all your wonderful mercifulness kill me!' Is that what you expected me to do? Well, maybe you would have, you with your infinite Homesteader goodness. But not me, no, not me. You weren't there! Watching your grandmother, a woman in her nineties, your only family, tortured until she died! When they struck me for any protest I made. Any human sound! And her screams, pouring into my mind, as they questioned her, slowly peeling away the skin on her hand—"

"Stop it! Stop it! I don't want to hear it," Katie screamed at him.

"Oh, of course not! I wouldn't ever want your ears to hear anything but, 'Isn't the weather so very nice?' and 'Oh, this food is just marvelous,' and 'All those damn Roamers must be dead for things to be going so well!'"

"You have no right to speak to her like that!" Chris jerked Arron around by the arm.

Arron snapped his mouth closed, then ran his hands slowly over his face and through his hair. "You know," he said very quietly, "you know, it would be so nice to have someone who trusted me. You don't know what it's like not to have anyone trust you—and no one to trust." He bent down and slid the knife out of his boot and handed it to

Chris. Then he turned and bent to pull Craftan to the door.
Katie stepped forward and took the man's ankles, hesitating
just slightly before she touched him. The two of them
dragged him outside. Chris stooped to clean up the blood.

IX

"WHAT DID YOU DO WITH HIM?" CHRIS ASKED.

"Buried him," Arron said shortly as he walked into the back room.

Katie listened for the bedroom door to click closed, then sat at the table next to Chris.

"What are we supposed to think?" Chris asked. His fingers played on the hilt of the knife. "What does he expect of us?"

Katie shrugged.

"And what should we do now?"

Katie looked down. "He's killed someone. Apparently he's killed before."

Chris nodded.

"But, what he's been through . . . Do you think it's the truth? Could people really do that? I thought only Roamers . . ."

"He lies very smoothly. I've seen him."

"Me, too. Everything is so strange." Katie looked back up at Chris. "Do you think we ought to get someone with authority?"

Chris nodded very slowly, then stopped, hearing the bedroom door open.

Arron walked into the room and came over to the table.

He stood behind the vacant chair, gripping the back. Chris and Katie exchanged looks.

"So, do I stand guilty? What is my sentence, then?"

"Well, Arron . . ." Chris started, then looked at Katie. He turned back to the Roamer. "Look, you just killed someone and, Arron, you've killed before—his son, and his friend. How could you expect him—"

"Don't you see? I had to get away. I had no choice! I didn't want to kill them. I don't enjoy that. I tried to get away without doing that. I didn't hunt them down, not like they're doing to me! I tried to leave. That's all. And they tried to stop me. They had their fun . . . and then . . . I killed them." He stared wide-eyed. "I tried to just . . . get away. I had no choice!"

"And what choice do we have? We have no idea what you can do."

"Did you ever think about what I will do?"

"You just killed someone! And you've killed people before! What's to say we're not next!"

Arron leaped forward and grabbed the knife from under Chris' hands. "This is how you can know! I could've killed you both so easily! But I haven't. Doesn't that say anything to you?"

They stared at him, more frightened than convinced. Arron sat down. "Okay, I'll tell you what I will do. If anyone comes to this house and discovers I am a Roamer and thinks about killing me or . . . or torturing me . . . I'll kill them first." He glared at the two of them, then his look softened. "But if you two choose to turn me over to them . . ." He shrugged and pushed the knife toward Chris. "I don't see how you could think I could kill you."

"What makes us any different?" Katie asked.

Arron looked at her steadily. "At least you took the time to allow me to prove whether or not I am what you would consider your typical Roamer. If I have proved that I am— well, then I deserve death if I'm as horrible as that. But you did take the time and have shown me that you are not what I would consider a typical Homesteader."

Chris rubbed his injured shoulder. "Okay, we'll not turn you in . . . yet."

Arron stood up. "Well, this is the only chance you'll have. I told you I was leaving."

"You—you can't," Chris blurted out.

"What do you mean? Why?" The Roamer watched him suspiciously. "Are you trying to tell me . . . No, it's not that." Arron continued to stare at him. "I'm leaving tomorrow. I'm going to find Dempter, the person who has ordered this search for me. He must be the mouthpiece for Chruston."

"And I think my grandfather is dead."

Arron leaned down on the table. "Come with me and find out. I can't do what I must do without the box. And you won't give it to me."

Chris rubbed his shoulder.

"I can feel you want to go," Arron went on. "Want to . . . to find out about . . . your family?"

Chris stood up. "Stay out of there, Roamer."

Arron backed up with his hands raised. "Okay, okay."

"What are you talking about?" Katie asked, looking from one to the other. "That old folktale we were told when we were little?"

Arron nodded. "What's left here to stay for, Chris?"

"This farm is my home, remember?"

"This worthless piece of land? You know it's going to get worse, not better. Look, either way, we'll find out what's causing the destruction of the land. Chruston's life or mine." He took the knife and pressed the hilt into Chris' palm. "And if it isn't Chruston, you kill me."

Chris rubbed his shoulder and eyed the blade in his hand.

"Can someone explain what's going on?" Katie leaned forward.

Chris nodded and pulled the box from his lap and opened it, staring at it thoughtfully. Katie sat back slowly as he explained Arron's theory about Shakta, Chruston, and the box. He stopped there.

"Okay," he said with sudden determination. "I'll go. If he's alive, he's my only living relative." He turned on Arron. "But, I warn you, Roamer, I'll give him the same chance to explain that I've given you."

Arron nodded.

Chris stood up. "Then I suggest we get some sleep. Can I see you home, Katie?" He turned to look at her.

"Can I come with you?" she asked softly.

"What? No."

"Why not?" She looked up at him now.

"Katie, you should know better than I do that a woman can't travel as safely on the road as a man. And we're going on foot, yet. Look, wasn't your sister—"

"And so was my brother," she snapped. She stood immediately and began to gather up the plates and food and put them in the basket.

"I'll see you home," Chris said gently.

"No. I'm fine."

"You sure?" Arron asked.

"Yes. I'm sure."

"You won't tell anyone about this—where we're going— will you?" Chris followed at her heels as she strode to the door.

"No. Don't worry. I won't." She hesitated a moment, her hand on the knob, then turned back to them, with an apologetic smile. "Good night, Arron, Chris. Take care of your shoulder." She touched it gently, then went out the door. Chris watched her walk down the path, then turned and shut the door.

"At least I know where the only Roamer is," Chris said, glancing out the window, then he turned back to the table to see Arron glaring at him. "Well, it's true."

Arron waved a hand at him in irritation, then changed the subject. "What happened with her sister and brother?"

"Oh, they were killed when they were going to visit relatives up north. It was just . . . oh." Chris sighed, shaking his head. "Well, it just really shook up the whole family when they found the bodies. I mean, you saw her mother. Well, everyone's sure it was some band of Roamers."

"More likely a band of thieves."

"Same thing." Chris swept some crumbs from the table. "Anyway." Getting no rise from Arron, Chris went on. "It was a real mess. Katie was the only child left. Losing James, though, was especially hard, him being the only son. Her father . . . Well, look, there was no one to follow in the father's footsteps, so to speak."

"Katie's doing a good job," Arron said, recalling her boyish mannerisms.

"That's just it." Chris walked to the back rooms. "Good night."

Chris awoke at a noise. It was morning and someone was moving about in the front rooms. He climbed out of his mother's bed, his body stiff and his shoulder sore. He rubbed it thoughtfully as he stared out the window, watching the sun just coming up from behind the scattered farmhouses. Shivering in the morning cold, he turned to get dressed.

Arron was at the table pulling the drawstrings on his pack when Chris entered the kitchen. The Roamer looked up.

"Are you ready to go?" he asked, setting his pack on the floor.

"You mean, am I packed? No."

"Yes, you are." Arron pointed to a pack by the fireplace.

"The box?"

"It's in there. Go ahead and look."

Chris did. "All right. I guess we can go." He sighed and turned, looking all around the room. His eyes lingering on the now-ragged curtains his mother had sewn, the splintering legs of the table that he and his father had made together long ago. He stopped at last, staring at the pictures above the fireplace. This is for both of you, he thought. I did love you. This will show you I did.

"Not much to leave behind," the Roamer said, shrugging.

"What do you mean?" Chris turned on him. "This is my home! My entire life."

Arron raised his eyebrows. "Sorry. I didn't realize your family duty stretched to encompass the very boards of this house." He shrugged his pack over his shoulders and strode unconcerned to the door.

"And what would a Roamer know about family, anyway?"

Arron paused at the door, a hand catching at the frame, either to stop his movement or to steady him. "And what would you know about anything at all?"

"Now, listen!" But the Roamer had opened the door and

gone out. Chris jerked his pack up and yanked it on. It bit sharply into his shoulder, but, strangely, made it feel better, taking away the peculiar tingling it had. He pulled the door closed behind him, with a last look at the pictures above the fireplace. They belonged here, and he would be back to them when he had shown them that he belonged here, too.

They walked down the road, a thick silence between them. Chris watched Arron out of the corner of his eye. But the Roamer walked, it seemed, without a thought for him, as if he knew Chris would follow. Chris drove his fists into his pockets and trudged doggedly beside him.

Arron stopped quite suddenly, a curious look on his face. Chris followed his gaze back toward the way they had just come, but saw nothing.

"What?"

"I don't know . . ." He continued to stare. "Something."

Just as Chris was about to suggest they continue on their way, he heard the light sound of someone running, and a figure came into view around the bend in the road.

"It's just some kid," Chris said, shrugging in the direction of the little boy running up the road. "Or is he some threat to you?"

Arron gave him a bland look. "No, but I think he's following us. See, he's looking here. I think he has something for us. I . . ." Arron stopped.

"What?" Chris asked, but Arron had fallen silent again, waiting for him to catch up.

"Morning," the boy called out as he came up to them.

Chris stared. "Katie?"

She nodded.

"But . . . what? What are you dressed like that for?" He stared at her, never having seen a girl in pants before. Her long, curly brown hair was pulled up tightly under her cap. With her small size and her mannerisms, she appeared to be a twelve-year-old boy.

"I'm going with you," she said, still a little out of breath from the run.

"But—Katie. You're . . . No, you're not." He finally found the words he was looking for.

"Why not?"

"Well, it's dangerous."

"I can handle myself. I fought next to you against that bear yesterday. And I've taken away any of the problems you, uh, referred to last night." She spread her arms, indicating her attire.

Arron nodded in agreement. "That's true."

Chris shot the Roamer a silencing look. "But, Katie, what about your . . . mother? Your family?"

"I left a note."

"What? What did you say to them?"

"Nothing about what we're really doing, so don't worry."

"They'll worry."

Katie shrugged and looked down. "They worry when I'm there." She stared down at the slacks. "Every time they look at me, they worry." She glared back up at him. "Now, I'm coming with you, or I'm following you," she said with force.

Chris gaped at her, then quickly turned to Arron.

"I guess that means she's coming," he said quietly.

"But . . . but . . ." What was that Roamer saying! "Fine," Chris said at last. "But this isn't going to be easy on you, you know."

"And does it seem like I expect it will be?" she demanded.

"No . . ." Chris said, looking her over again. "Okay, okay. You can come. Let's just go then."

"Which way?" She turned to Arron.

"Dempter is the person Craftan got his orders from. I believe Dempter lives in Sernet, a town to the north of Buernston where Craftan lived. At any rate, Craftan was thinking about the fact that he'd been in Sernet when my grandmother and I had been taken in his town. That's what he was thinking when you asked him if he'd seen me before." The Roamer stared steadily at Katie until she looked away. "Anyway, that's where we'll head."

"You think Chruston is there?" Katie met his gaze again.

"No, but it's a start."

Chris raised his eyes to the sky. "This is crazy."

"Well, just give me the box, and I'll save you the trouble!"

"I suggest you think about something else," Chris warned in a low voice. "You're just making me more and more sure that this is some Roamer scheme."

"Then why are you going?" Arron asked, intently interested.

Chris backed up. "I may not," he said guardedly.

"Yes, you are. Yes, you are." Katie shoved him, laughing lightly. "Because I'm not going back home." She turned at that and started off down the road. Arron turned without another word and followed her. Chris glanced once more back toward where they had just come from, then followed them, keeping a few paces back.

"So," Katie said, walking lightly beside Arron, "you and Chris have decided all this from that lullaby?"

"Well, does it seem logical to you?"

"Logical?" She gave a short laugh. "Chruston still alive?" She shook her head, then paused, thinking. "And what about that last part of the song? The one you said upset Chris. What does that part mean?"

Arron glanced back at Chris. "I don't know."

Katie looked back. "You think he knows?"

Arron shrugged, then shook his head and stared off up the road, watching the dust clouds rolling back and forth in the hot sun. Now and then he thought he might have caught sight of a squirrel scampering across the road or inhabiting one of the few trees still living. The road was narrow, closed in at the sides with the dead trunks of what once might have been a magnificent forest. Their voices, when they spoke, echoed oddly off the rotting trees, as if it were the stumps that spoke. Even now that they had grown silent, Arron thought he could hear words whispering in the humid air. He rubbed his forehead with the back of his hand, trying to press the words into order as they flitted in and out of his mind, some spoken, some thought, some remembered. They ebbed and flowed, confusing him, pushing him first forward, then back, until he didn't know where he was, or who was next to him.

A voice came next to him. He turned and saw his father.

"Get the boy under the wagon," his father commanded.

And his grandmother's strong arms swung him from the ground and carried him to the wagon. She pushed him underneath, spiderwebs sticking to his face. He cringed, pushing back, but she pushed him further and then struggled under after him. She crouched in the darkness, pulling him tightly against her chest so that her heart pounded against him. She was whispering in the most frightened voice he had ever heard.

"Please don't cry! Please don't cry," she was begging him, the words almost blurred in terror. He looked up at her to hear her better, but her lips were still as she spoke. "He'll not get you. Oh, no, not yet. Not until you're ready. Please don't cry." Fear poured over him, through him, nearly dragging him under as the sound of horses' hooves came echoing under the wagon. Her arms tightened. It was her fear, not his. He tried to separate himself.

He could see the horses' legs now, and their riders' feet came swinging down. A rumble of voices, and then his father's more clearly. The rumble, more loudly. Grandmother squeezed him tighter so suddenly he almost cried out. A cracking thud from above masked any sound he might have made. His father! He could see him now, fallen, blood puddled about his face, his open eyes staring at him. He stared back as a warmth, sad, so terribly sad, oozed into him, and he felt his father's once-strong arms encircling his thoughts. Then a coldness, slowly, like the cooling of his father's blood, a cold isolation went through him as his father's thoughts drifted away, leaving only his grandmother's trembling arms about him.

The wagon above rattled and shook as it was ransacked. The horses rode off only after a very long time. His grandmother kept him under the wagon after the horses had gone, rocking him and crying. The eyes of his father watched them unconcerned, gaping like the hole in his head. His own mind felt empty like his father's. Everything had poured out.

Grandmother rocked and whispered over and over. "He'll not touch you. Not yet. No, not yet. Remember, he cannot touch your mind unless you permit it. You have the gift, the strength. He cannot have your mind. You will win. You'll get him back for this. You will." And she cried against his hair. He lay in her arms and pulled her sadness and anger and hatred inside himself, filling the gaping emptiness.

He stumbled and saw the road before him with a shock.

Not the wagon. It was Katie who grabbed at his arm, not Grandmother.

"Arron? Did you hear me? Are you all right?"

"Ancient desired relieving his mind," Arron muttered under his breath.

"What?"

"Huh? Uh. Oh. Nothing . . . nothing."

"But wasn't that part of the tune?"

Arron nodded, blinking a few times, trying to reorient himself. He hated the confusion most of all. He shook the fuzziness away and turned to look at Chris. "Is that pack bothering your shoulder?"

"No. Why don't you just worry about your own wounds."

Arron turned back, face forward. Chris noticed the tautness in the Roamer's shoulders, the sharp edges his boots dug into the dirt road. He sighed, trying to sort out why exactly he was behaving this way. The Roamer hadn't done anything to him, really. Something twisted inside him in indecision.

"Hey, I'm sorry," he felt himself saying. "I'm sorry for the things I said. I—I don't know why I said them."

Arron barely acknowledged this.

"Really, Arron. Here." Chris pulled the knife from his belt, caught up to Arron, and held it out to him. Arron stared, first at the knife and then at him.

"Take it," Chris insisted.

"You sure?"

"Hey, I want some protection. I don't want my other shoulder bit off." He smiled quickly.

Arron grinned back and took the knife, bent, and slid it into his boot. He glanced up at Chris. "Sorry, it's the only place I know how to keep it. We only do as we've been taught." Again he flashed that same grin Chris remembered from his boyhood.

Chris laughed. "Just so you keep reminding us of what you are. The hair—sometimes I forget."

Arron looked down at his boot again.

Katie caught hold of Chris' arm. "Come on, sour-face, now it's your turn to keep me occupied. Poor Arron's been doing it all, so far."

"Well, he's had a more entertaining life than I have."

"I don't know, yours seems pretty full of excitement lately. Why do you think I came along?"

Arron stood. "Excitement! Entertainment? What is this? A game?"

"Come on, Arron," Katie said softly, a bit taken aback by his sharpness. "You must admit, the life of a Roamer is more interesting than that of a Homesteader."

"And at what price?" He looked away.

Katie stared down at her dusty boots. "I was just . . . I didn't mean . . ."

Arron glanced back at her. "Never mind!"

"Cut it out, Arron," Chris snapped. "You have no call to act like that! That's not fair."

"No, it's all right," Katie said, looking up again. "Arron, I'm sorry. I wasn't thinking."

"No, Katie, don't you apologize to him! What's done is done. You had nothing to do with it." Chris strode off down the road again. "The sooner the Roamer realizes that, the better off we'll all be. It's not our fault he's in this state."

Katie stared at Arron, his back to her as he followed Chris with his eyes. His hands were trembling as they clenched into fists. He stared after him with such . . . she thought for a moment he might kill him. She reached forward as if to catch hold of his arms and stop him, but he relaxed quite suddenly and started after Chris, entirely at ease. She walked after him slowly, keeping a close eye on him.

The air had grown increasingly humid and there was a trace of thunder. Katie pulled her hat down tighter and caught up to the two of them, now walking side by side.

"It's going to rain," she whispered after they had trod along in silence for quite a while.

"Yes, it is," Arron agreed.

"It is?" Chris looked up and noticed for the first time the black clouds building up behind them, accenting the bare whiteness of the tree branches. It looked strangely like a fierce winter storm coming up over the leafless horizon, but it was summer. "Oh, it is." He looked about for some form of shelter.

Arron and Katie set their packs down and pulled out their rain capes. Chris watched.

"I packed one for you, too." Arron nodded toward Chris' pack.

"Oh." Chris swung his pack down and delved into it. "Yeah, you did." He pulled it out and put it on, then looked around once again. "Shouldn't we . . ."

"There's a cave not too far from here. We won't beat the rain, though." Arron shrugged and started walking again. Chris hesitated, looking around once more, then followed. He was becoming very aware of the fact that he had no idea where he was. He turned to Katie walking easily at his side.

"Do you know where we are?" he whispered.

She nodded slowly. "Generally. I used to pore over Papa's maps at home. Planning . . . something, I don't know." She smiled, remembering. "But, anyway, I've got a fairly good idea of where everything is. We're just inside the southern edge of what used to be a huge forest called Aetern Timber." She paused, hesitating. "There's something else. I've been thinking. Well, last night I looked on the map for the village where Arron had been taken. Now, we're supposedly heading for a town just north of it, called Sernet, and I've seen that, too." She stopped again.

"Go on," he urged.

"Well, don't you think a Roamer would know some shortcuts? This is the long way. We're making a big loop on this road. I would think we could just cut through the forest. He must know the way." She looked after Arron nervously as the first heavy drops began to fall.

"By this route, it's going to take us weeks and weeks," she went on. "If he doesn't know a short cut, Chris, then how did he get down here with all those injuries he claims he got at Buernston? They would have healed. He's healed pretty quickly since he's been down here . . . It seems odd, don't you think?"

"We've got to be careful. Keep an eye on him," Chris said softly.

Katie nodded.

X

"JUST HOW FAR IS THIS CAVE YOU KEEP TALKING ABOUT?" Chris shouted at Arron above the downpour.

"Not too much farther," Arron promised, pulling his rain cape more tightly about him. The strong wind kicked up its ends, making it all but useless. The three of them were thoroughly soaked.

"Is that it?" Katie raised a dripping finger to point at a blurry, gray hillock rising slightly above the dead trees.

"Yeah, that's it." Arron nodded and increased his speed. Chris started to run toward it.

"Hey, don't," Arron called after him. Chris kept on going. "Chris!" Arron ran and caught him by a slippery arm. "Don't!"

"I'm soaking wet! What do you mean, don't!"

"Being out here one more moment isn't going to hurt you," Arron said heatedly. "Anyone who travels might be using that cave. It's pretty well known."

"So? They'll share. Anyone who travels wouldn't let people go about on a night like this. It's bad out here, in case you didn't notice. It's not real safe, in case you didn't notice that! And if Roamers are immune to natural disaster, Homesteaders aren't!"

"There might be thieves up there."

"All the Roamers are dead, I thought."

Arron shoved him roughly away, almost pushing him down into the ankle-deep mud. "I hope you die up there."

Chris peered back at him through the rain a moment, then turned toward the cave again, running into Katie, who was coming back from there.

"No one's there," she told them. "No light from a fire at any rate." She shrugged.

"Now, may I run?" Chris asked, raising his chin a bit.

"Go ahead." Arron scowled at him, then stooped to pick up a piece of wood floating by.

"A fire?" Katie asked.

"We'll need to dry off, or we'll all get sick." Katie nodded and began picking up pieces of wood as they made their way up the slope.

They dumped the wood in a corner of the cave. It was dry inside, but cool. Chris bent, shivering, to help Katie with the fire.

"I'm freezing. Let's get this going."

Arron laid their capes out carefully to let them dry, then turned and watched as the two of them struggled to light the wet wood.

"It's no use." Katie sat back, hugging her knees. "It's just too wet."

"All the wood is wet?" Chris eyed the other pieces all dripping on the dry dirt floor. "Damn!" He leaned against the cave wall, wrapping his arms about himself.

Arron moved in closer. "All of it can't be wet."

"It's pouring out there!" Chris glared at him. "Of course it's all wet."

"No, I mean all the way through. Every particle of it . . ."

Chris glanced at Katie, who shrugged. Arron continued to stare at the wood. "So," he said slowly. "It's just like everything else. I just need to . . ." He looked up at them, smiling broadly. "It's so simple. Why didn't I think of it before? It's just like everything else."

Chris turned to Katie again. "The genius at work." He indicated Arron with a dubious glance.

"Don't you see?" Arron said, very excited now. "It's just like making objects rise!"

"I'm sorry. I wasn't . . . eh, blessed . . . with your cunning little mind." Chris leaned forward on his knees. "So, stop thinking about what you figured out and do something with your newfound knowledge."

Arron nodded and began humming quietly to himself, then raised his hands over the wood. There was a moment where they all stared at the damp logs, waiting, then Chris started to laugh at the absolute absurdity of the scene, the three of them watching the wood with eager expressions, as if the logs were going to get up, reach for the matches, and light themselves. His laugh choked off, back in his throat, when the water on the logs began to spit and jump as if running from some evil in the wood. The logs grew red from the inside to the outside, spreading at a frightful rate. Suddenly they burst into flame, the wood snapping and crackling. Chris and Katie both pulled back.

"What's wrong?" The Roamer turned to them. "It's warm."

"It—it's not natural," Katie whispered.

Arron's face grew dark. "What do you mean? Do you mean it wouldn't happen on its own? Well, you're right and you're wrong. Not like this maybe, but it's the same kind of fire. It started the same way any other fire does except on a smaller scale. You just can't see the pure reaction. I can!"

Katie shook her head slowly. "You're playing with things you shouldn't. Men shouldn't do things like that."

"Even if it helps? We would die from cold without it. Don't think we wouldn't have."

"But how can you know the total consequences? Like with Chruston's finding out about his death. You say that's bad. How can you know that's bad and this is good? Both things are saving a life."

Arron sighed. "Because I can see it. It makes sense. It fits. I understand it. Can't you see—"

"No. I can't," Chris cut in. "But never mind, Roamer. Don't do it any more. I don't think you really know what you're doing. You're just trying to show off or scare us or something."

"I've been taught what's right and wrong," Arron started angrily. "I know this is all right!"

"Well, I've been taught right and wrong, too, and we have a few conflicts in those areas. So, don't do those things any more. That's what's destroying the world, these kinds of Roamer tricks!"

"What's upsetting the world is someone who doesn't know! Someone who didn't—"

"All right! All right!" Katie pushed her way between them. "It's too late for this now. We've got a fire. I suggest we stop questioning and just use it. We'll sort out later who's right and who's wrong. Until then, Arron, no more. Do you understand? We won't put up with any more of your magic. You are not to use it." She glanced at the fire. "Who knows? Every time you do something like that, you may be hurting the world somehow. You may just not know it. So, no more. Is that clear?"

Arron looked helplessly from one to the other, then sank down heavily on the far side of the fire. The flickering light flared uneasily in his dark eyes as he stared at it. He said nothing more.

Chris hesitated a moment, then sat down close to it, too, and Katie sat near him. It was very quiet for a while. Only the fire sparking and the sounds of the storm, muffled somehow from the inside of the cave, disturbed their verbal silence.

Katie cleared her throat once, then got up slowly. "I'm going to change into something dry," she announced quietly, took her pack, and went into the deeper recesses of the cave. Chris nodded to her briefly, but kept his gaze fixed on the fire.

"You think that I have no idea where we are, don't you?" he said, still eyeing the fire.

Arron looked up slowly. "What?"

"I know we're on the edge of Aetern Timber."

"So? Shall I applaud?"

"This is a rather long road to take to get to Sernet."

"It's the only road," Arron said dryly. He looked back at the fire between them.

"So, try and make me believe that Roamers only travel on the road. You must know a shortcut."

Arron leaned back and gazed at Chris a moment. "I'm going to change, too. I'm cold." He started to stand. Chris scrambled to his feet.

"No, you don't. You answer me! Why are you taking this route? You don't want us to get there."

Arron's eyebrows came down sharply, his eyes locked with Chris'. "There is a marsh in the middle of the loop of this road. I don't dare try to take you and Katie through it."

"Don't you think we can handle ourselves?"

"Frankly? No. But that's not it. You don't even trust me taking you down a damn road! How do you think I could lead you safely through a swamp?" He looked away.

"You're lying. There's no marsh. You have something else in mind."

"Like what?" Arron turned back to him.

"I don't know. And that worries me. But one thing I do know. You are lying. There is no way you could have gotten from Buernston to my house by this route and still have retained your so-called injuries. And I've seen you feign sickness. They never touched you up in Buernston. You've lied badly this time."

Arron caught him roughly by the arm. "I haven't lied! I came down through the marsh, I do know a way. It's faster, but not safe. Not at all safe for more than one person. You make too damn much noise! And I was on horseback. What did you think, that I carried my grandmother all the way from Buernston on my back?"

"And where would you get a horse?"

The Roamer's eyes slid away from his.

"You killed someone for a horse, didn't you?"

"Does it matter now?" he murmured. "I came down through the swamp on horseback. I didn't stop to rest, not once. I . . . I was sure I was going to die, but . . . I don't know . . . I was so sick, I didn't care, or even know. I just knew I had to bury my grandmother down here. That's all she ever asked for . . ." Arron stopped and stared at Chris.

"Why do you even bother to ask me questions?" Arron asked. "You never believe my answers. Why don't you just make up your own? That's what you end up doing anyway. Save me the trouble!"

Katie came back to the fire as Arron strode toward the back of the cave. She laid her clothes out to dry. Chris stared at her head now that her hat was off. She had cut her hair. It was cropped close like a little boy's. She returned his stare, but it wasn't Katie looking at him, it was some little boy. With the hat, he had seen in his mind that her hair was still there, she was still Katie. But now, it was gone.

"You . . . your hair," he managed.

"Do you think I'm so stupid as to risk my hat coming off at precisely the wrong time?" The little boy who had been Katie shook his head.

"I . . . I . . ."

"Chris, don't. Don't say anything. Just don't. I did what I felt I had to do. I don't think you can ever understand. And I'm not asking for that. Not for that." She sat down at the fire. "If I have to be a boy just to be me, I'll do it." She sat quietly a moment. "Sometimes I wonder why I can't be me and still be a girl; but they won't let me. They have to box everything. We always have to be one thing or another, never both." She looked back up at him as if demanding something of him. "And yet, we can be. And I am. Just don't say anything, please."

Chris got up abruptly and went to the back to change. Katie huddled miserably by the fire. She poked at it with a stick, making sparks fly up wildly. She watched as they winked out, then jabbed the fire again. She tossed the stick into the fire and sat back.

Hearing something, she glanced toward the opening of the cave. She stood and moved cautiously forward. Someone was out there, she was sure of it. Footsteps on gravel—the sound was unmistakable against the irregular sounds of the storm. It was more solid-sounding than the rain. She crept farther forward, straining her eyes to see into the gray-black backdrop.

Something moved so quickly out of the dark and grabbed her that she didn't have time to cry out. Hard arms pulled her tightly against a soaked body.

"Quiet, boy," came a hushed voice. "A few questions."

She didn't wait. Stamping down on his instep, elbows digging into his ribs, she leaned into him as he doubled in pain, raising his injured foot. He released her as they toppled, trying to break his fall. She rolled easily away and got up, her breath coming in gasps. Chris and Arron came running at the noise.

"What is it? Ka—" Chris started, but Arron nudged him sharply in the side, cutting him off.

An old man stood up shakily and eyed the three of them. He ran a bony hand over the leathery mask of his face. Dripping clothes hung on his spare frame. He stared wide-eyed and shivering.

"What do you want?" Arron demanded, stepping forward with his knife out. He glanced once at Katie to see if she was all right, then turned his full gaze on the man.

"Please . . ." The man began shivering all the more. He swallowed hard, blinking his eyes, and sniffled. "I just wanted to get out of the wet. That's all. Please?" He clasped his hands before him as if praying, then wrung them nervously. "You've got a fire. I'm so cold. It's bad out there."

"So, what did you grab him for?" Arron pointed to Katie.

"I . . . I thought you was thieves. I wanted to check you out, before I came in. I figured he wouldn't be too much trouble." He rubbed his ribs as he eyed Katie. "I wouldn't have hurt you, boy. I promise. Please don't hurt me, just tell me if you are. That's all I want."

"If we are what?" Chris came closer.

"Thieves."

"Do we look like Roamers?"

"That don't seem to matter much these days. If you be them, I ain't got but a cent. You can have it, though. It's yours. Anything you want." He nodded so quickly, it looked as if he might bob his head right off.

"I am not a thief," Arron said to the man. Chris got the idea he was speaking to him as well. "Now, I'm not so sure about you, though." He looked the man up and down. "I think you had better be off."

The man's mouth fell open, he looked wildly out at the storm, then back at Arron. "I'm freezing, boy!" He caught at the collar of his drenched coat and pulled it closer. "You don't know what it's like out there. It's so dark and . . . and cold. A man could . . . I'll die out there, boy!" He rubbed his hands over his face again. His fingers trembled as he looked outside once more and cringed. There came a flash of lightning and a crash of thunder. The cave was briefly illuminated, crazily tossing all their shadows against the walls. Arron took a step back and caught at his breath.

"Don't . . . Go on. You had better go."

"I'm soaked to the skin! Please, just a bit of fire. Just for a second, at least to warm my hands," he begged, wrapping his long arms about himself. "I'm no thief, I promise. I'm just a little desperate . . . It's so cold out there! I'm sure to die!" His voice pitched higher, seeing himself caught between the storm and Arron's knife. "Please? Please! I'm begging you."

Arron backed into Chris, who was behind him. His hand, holding the knife, trembled.

"Arron?" Katie started toward him.

The old man advanced on him, too, thinking he was about to give in. "Don't send me to my death, boy. You wouldn't . . ."

Arron dropped the knife, stumbling backward. Chris caught hold of him as he fell and lowered him to the ground.

"Arron? What is it?" The Roamer's breath came sharply, close to sobs. He was shaking all over.

The man was instantly at his side. "That boy is sick. He's very sick." He reached out to comfort him.

"No!" Arron tried to squirm away. "Don't touch me!" Chris pulled him close against him.

"He's been sick . . ." Chris said, looking blankly from the man to Arron.

Katie scooped up the knife and held it firmly in front of herself. "I think you had better leave," she said in her lowest voice.

The man turned and looked surprised.

"You're hurting him somehow," she said, looking at Arron who had covered his face with one shaking hand.

"But I'm doing nothing! He's sick. Don't send me back out there, boy. You'll kill me."

Arron moaned sharply. "Don't," he cried out.

"Tell them," the old man pleaded suddenly. "Tell them it's not my fault!"

"It's not," Arron gasped. "It's not." He grabbed at Chris' hand and squeezed it tightly. Chris stared at him, unsure what to do. "Get him away from me," Arron said through clenched teeth.

"You heard him. Get out," Katie ordered.

"No! Please!" The old man threw himself on Arron, grabbing his shirt and pulling him close. "Please, I'm begging you." The rain began to come down all the harder outside, the thunder so close it made the ground tremble. Arron groaned, trying to pull away from the man. Chris pushed at him, but he clung to Arron and would not be separated.

"There's a blanket," Arron finally gasped. "And the fire! Go over there and sit by it!"

"Oh, bless you! Bless you!" The man took Arron's hand. "You've saved my life, boy. You've saved me."

Arron yanked his hand away, trying to sit up and looking very pale. "No, I haven't," he said hoarsely.

"You have saved me and you'll not regret it, either. I'll not forget this." He tried to take Arron's hand again.

Arron pulled away and curled up, covering his face. "Take him away from me!"

Katie nudged the man. "Come on to the fire, before you catch your death." The man nodded eagerly, still looking at Arron. Chris had his hands gently on the Roamer's shoulders, trying to comfort him, to find what was wrong.

"I'll fix you a drink, boy, and you'll feel better. You'll see. I'll take care of you for taking care of me." He looked once more out at the rain and shivered, then looked at Katie. "Would you be good enough to get my pack for me? It's just outside. Please?" He stared fearfully out at the dark. Katie sighed, then went and got his pack for him. He took it, then said to Arron, "I'll fix you right up." Arron didn't look at him. He stayed curled up, shivering spasmodically.

"Come on, Arron. Come sit by the fire." Chris tried to help him up, but Arron shook his head.

"Not yet. Not yet. Let it pass," he muttered weakly.

Chris went and got a blanket, then wrapped it carefully

about the Roamer. "You'll be all right," Chris whispered to him.

Arron looked up at him hazily, his trembling stopping. He caught Chris' hand and squeezed it. "Thanks, Chris." Chris nodded and smiled, then felt Arron's forehead. It was burning.

"My God, you've caught pneumonia, I'm sure. You probably weren't completely healed from before." Arron just shook his head and let Chris help him up and to the fire. The old man beamed at him. Arron averted his eyes.

"You be sick for sure, boy. Here, you drink this, what I'm fixing for you, to thank you." He poured a reddish-brown, good-smelling liquid into a dented tin cup and offered it to Arron. Arron pushed it away with the back of his hand, shaking his head, and huddled down tighter in his blanket.

"Isn't poison, boy."

"I know." He had stopped shaking noticeably, but remained unusually pale. His dark eyes stood out all the more, but he kept them half-lidded as if the firelight bothered him. His hands trembled a bit. "I just want to sleep." Katie was at his side immediately.

"Come on. I'll fix you a warm place to sleep." She eased him up and stared intently into his face, trying to see how sick he really was. He looked away from her.

She had him lie down on her blanket and pushed some clothes underneath for a pillow, then carefully covered him with another blanket. "I'll bring a small fire over here to keep you warm," she said softly, then bent down close to him so the old man couldn't hear. "Should I get rid of him?"

Arron gave a small chuckle. "No, it's all right. This will pass, I promise you." Katie nodded and handed him his knife. Arron took it slowly. "You would have killed him, would you?"

"No!" Katie sat back on her heels. Arron nodded thoughtfully and closed his eyes. Katie stood and took up some wood lying near the fire to dry. She poked one stick into the fire until the end was well caught. She carried it torchlike to where Arron slept and set up a warming fire near him, then joined the other two by the main fire.

The old man was cackling gleefully at something Chris had said. Sobering, he looked at Katie and shook his head.

"Mmmmh." He continued to shake his head.

"What?" Katie sat nervously under his gaze.

"Can't get over you." He laughed slightly. "Thought you'd be the easy one. A regular fireball, ain't you?"

Katie raised her head. "I try."

That made him laugh harder. "So young, and already you're wanting to be a man." Katie glared at him and hunched closer to the fire.

"What's this little one doing out here with you? A might dangerous, I'd say."

Katie snapped her head up. "I took care of you, didn't I?"

"Ah?" The man's laughter subsided. "The cub's got pride, eh? Good, that's good." He rocked back and forth. He need only drool to complete the image of a madman. "You'll need it for life. But careful—it can take you, if you're not careful. It took me. So, you see me as I am today, without it." Katie sighed, not really up for a lecture. She poked at the fire.

"All right. I'll leave you be. I can see you're tired and I'll not push my welcome." He looked down a moment. Chris shifted positions and the man looked up. "Why, we ain't been properly introduced. I'm Durth, Tom Durth."

"Chris."

"I'm James."

Durth nodded to them each, then looked toward Arron. "Arron, I heard you say was his name." Chris nodded. "Is he going be all right?"

Katie shrugged. "He says he is."

Durth stared at Arron a moment more, then turned back to them. "So, what is it brought you so far from home?"

"Well, how do you know that we are?"

The old man laughed at him. "Your speech, Chris. Why, it screams southern. From under the shadow of the great mountain, no doubt. Yours and yours." He pointed at each of them. "Southerners you be. But his . . ." he trailed off looking at Arron. "Can't place it. Seems to me, I've heard it, but not for a while. He's traveled some."

"He's our guide. We're going north to find . . . relatives.

Our parents were killed, and we need family to live with,"
Chris said, swallowing nervously over the lie.

Durth nodded slowly, the loose skin on his neck swaying.
"Ah, the evilness in the land is striking at families now. Yes,
it's already struck mine. Yes . . ." He stared into the fire a
moment. "It's Roamer magic to be sure, lingering everywhere. They cast their horrible spells and destroy the land,
all for revenge."

"Why . . . why do their spells do that?" Katie asked.

"They're evil, boy! Contrary to nature. I seen them do
some strange things."

"Like what? Raise objects without touching them?"

"No, never seen them do that. But some can, you know.
Their most powerful could. Shakta. Have you heard of him?"
Chris nodded. "He could, but most can't. But they can mix
awful things in great kettles over their campfires. I seen them
bring a dead Roamer back to life with one of their concoc-
tions."

"Really?" Katie leaned closer.

"He was completely dead?" Chris asked.

"Not completely. But he would have been dead for sure
without their sorcery." Chris sat back slowly.

Durth's eyes sparkled in the firelight, pleased with his eager audience. "Some can even see a man's death, it's said.
The great Shakta could. He was their most evil, using his
devil power for the misery of the Homesteaders. It was his
magic what begun the decline, and other Roamers help to
keep it going."

Chris and Katie exchanged glances over the fire. The old
man leaned back, his mind wandering. "My grandfather told
me about the one time he actually saw the Roamer Shakta.
He told me these tales when I was a boy. He told me, it was a
time when Shakta was angry with my grandfather's neighbor. The one who had the best farm in the area, Shakta
hated."

"Why?"

"Why? Well, James, 'tis simple. Roamers, they have no
home, that's why they wander, forever searching for what
they want, but don't have. They don't care nought for each
other. And they hate that, that they don't care. And that's

why they hate Homesteaders. Nothing would make them happier than to see us care nothing for each other as well, to break up our families and cast us forever wandering in search of just that, our flesh and blood." Durth nodded to each of them slowly. They leaned closer as his voice grew hushed.

"Shakta, he hated this neighbor of my grandfather. Mr. Grell was his name. He had land. He supported a family. Shakta hated him. One day, he shows up there at the Grells' farm. Poof! Just appears out of nowhere!"

"Just appeared?" Chris raised his eyebrows.

Durth nodded. "Such was his power, boy. The simple, evil tricks of a Roamer were tenfold in this one. He and Grell had some big argument. My grandfather went over to see what it was all about. But Shakta was through talking by then. He spun about quite suddenly, an evil gleam in his dark eye. He turned to the great orchard and laid his evil eye upon it. Raising his arms quite slowly, he sang an evil Roamer tune." The old man paused, licking at his dry lips. "Then, he flashed his hands out over the orchard. First, there was nothing. Then a flock of birds scattered into the air in a panic, and the orchard burst apart. Every single tree splintered into shreds!" He nodded gravely at Chris and Katie. "Grell was ruined by the destruction of his orchard. The man was buried alone in a pauper's grave."

"I'll fix something to eat." Katie stood and went to her pack.

"Guess I scared him a little, huh?" Durth grinned and winked at Chris.

"Yeah." Chris glanced at Arron. Durth followed his gaze, then got up and shuffled over toward the Roamer.

"Where are you going?" Chris stood.

"To see how he is." He bent over Arron. "Ah, good. Sound asleep. Must have been near exhausted, what with the rain and being sick and all. Ah, and he's concerned about the two of you. Never seen a Homesteader so ready to protect. Thought he was going to kill me for what I done to James there. Not that I done anything. But still, wish I had such a friend." He bent to tuck the blankets more closely about the Roamer. Arron started awake, scrambling back from the man.

"Damn, boy! You scared me near to death," Durth exclaimed, jumping back. Arron blinked at him a few times, then shook his head, sucking in a deep breath. He began shivering again.

"Please . . ." he said weakly. "I need to sleep. Please, please, leave me alone."

"I'm making something to eat. Do you want some?" Katie asked, staring at him from where she stood by the fire. Arron watched her a moment without answering, then looked at Chris, and lastly at Durth. He lowered his eyes slowly, looking broken and old.

"Arron?" Katie said.

"No," he said at last. "My stomach isn't up to it."

The old man scrambled back toward Katie. "I'll have something if you've got it to spare. Then I'll need some sleep myself. Hope you're a good cook, boy."

"I'm fair."

Durth chuckled to himself. "Only good reason I could ever see for taking a woman along on the road. Eh?" He laughed nudging first her, then Chris. Katie laughed with him, then turned and added a handful of dirt to his stew and mixed it in. She gave it to him smiling, and Durth grinned back. She handed Chris some stew as well. He took it absent-mindedly, his eyes on Arron, watching as the Roamer covered himself with the blanket and closed his eyes. Chris rubbed his shoulder thoughtfully.

Katie blinked her eyes open and stretched slowly, her shoulders feeling stiff from the night on the ground. She sat up and stared at the bright sunshine streaming in the mouth of the cave. At some point in the night, the thunder had stopped, and the rain had ended. She could hear water dripping off the bare trees, and a strong wind rattled their branches. She got up and stoked up the fire. Durth opened his eyes at the noise.

"Why you little mite! If you ain't a bundle of energy, I don't know."

Katie smiled. "Breakfast?"

He thought about that for only a moment. "No, no, James,

I really couldn't take any more of your food." Katie shrugged.

Arron sat up stiffly, covering his eyes with one hand as if to protect them from the morning sunlight. "How are you, boy?" Arron just nodded.

"Is that breakfast I smell?" Chris' voice came muffled from under his blankets.

"No. That's the fire you smell. You're cooking." Chris sat up and stared at her. She stared right back. "Just because I'm the youngest doesn't mean I have to cook the whole time."

"That's telling him." Durth winked at her. Chris groaned and crawled out of his blankets.

They ate in silence. Durth changed his mind about eating as he watched Chris make breakfast. Arron ate very little; mostly, he sat against the far wall hugging his knees.

Durth stood at last, pushing his dirty plates inside his pack. He rubbed his back slowly. "Well, I'm off. Which way are you headed, boys?"

"North," Chris said.

"East," Arron corrected.

"Ah, staying with the road." Durth nodded. "Well, I'm going opposite, so I guess I'll take my leave now that the rain's come to an end."

"Well, it was nice to meet you, Durth," Chris stood and shook hands with him.

"Same to you," Durth said. He shook hands with Katie, then walked over to Arron and stuck his hand out. "Much thanks to you, boy. You really did save my life last night. I'm a trifle embarrassed about the way I acted and I hope you'll forgive a man for his fears. Not much on storms, you might say. So, this was much appreciated. Why, if I had something to give you with which to thank you, I'd gladly give it. I haven't, though." Arron turned away from him and began folding his blanket. Durth looked down at his still-extended hand, then rubbed it on his pants, shrugging.

"There's nothing to thank me for." Arron stopped folding the blanket and clutched it against him. His hands were shaking again. "If you're going, then go. Or else stay awhile and talk with us while we ready ourselves."

"No, I'll go now. Good-bye all, it was nice to meet you.

Wish I was traveling in a group so close. And I hope you're better soon," he added to Arron.

"I will be." Arron busied himself with packing, then turned suddenly to Durth. "Hey, be careful out there, Durth. The ground is slick . . . and . . . and . . . the soil's probably loose from all the water."

Durth stopped just outside the entrance. "How'd you know my name?"

"I heard you say it last night as I was falling asleep."

Durth nodded, smiling. "You've a strange accent, boy. Can't place it. Ah, well, it'll come to me. Take care and thanks for sharing your shelter with a lonely old man," he yelled back to them.

Chris and Katie waved to him as a rumbling sound began above them. They all looked up. Durth stepped back, his eyes wide, then he tried to run. Chris made a dash to try and save him, but Arron caught him roughly by the arm and held him back.

Durth screamed out in fear and pain as loose rocks and dirt from above came down upon him, tumbling him down the slope in front of the cave. Chris and Katie rushed out and down the hill and began trying to dig the man out.

"He's dead," Arron said, coming slowly down the hill after them. The wind ruffled his hair.

Chris stood up and stared at the Roamer. "You did this! You did this because you heard him last night."

"I didn't do this!"

"Then why didn't you let me try to save him?"

"You would be under there, too, if I had."

Katie stared numbly at the rocks. "We don't even know where he was headed, or who to contact—"

"He has no one." Arron stayed frozen where he was, standing not quite down the hill. "His farm failed long ago, too much of doing nothing. Most of his children are dead." Arron stared intently at the mound of rubble. "The rest ran off when his wife left him. He was alone." Arron pulled his gaze from the rocks. "Why anyone would want to hang on to that kind of life . . ." He stopped, ran a hand through his hair, and bit on his lip. Chris and Katie simply stared at him.

"This wasn't my fault!"

"You knew he was going to die, didn't you?" Chris said softly.

"It's not my fault."

"Didn't you?"

"I . . . Chris . . ."

"Didn't you!"

"Yes!" Arron turned away from them, burying his face in his hands. "Damn it, yes."

"Why didn't you tell him?" Katie asked, stepping back, away.

"I can't do that. Don't you see? I can't."

They shook their heads slowly.

"Well, I can't!" He hadn't looked at them. He stood still a moment, then, at last, he turned to them. "Let's go."

"We have to bury him," Katie said, starting to pull at the rocks.

"He's buried."

"No, but I mean properly."

"You don't want to see him." The Roamer started up the slope. "He's buried. Let's go." He turned back to them at the top of the hill, his black eyes fixing on them. Chris and Katie hesitated.

"I'm bringing you to your grandfather! That's what you want, isn't it? Well? Isn't it? Let's go!" He charged back into the cave.

"Is it?" Chris muttered, staring up at the cave. "Or is it what you want me to want, Roamer?"

XI

DAYS OF TRAVEL WENT BY, AND THE ROAMER SAID NOTH-ing. He simply stopped and set his pack down when he deemed it time to rest for the night. He ate little, then went to sleep. He woke them with the sound of his packing in the morning, then started off, silent still, when they were ready to go as well, leading them eastward without a sound.

Chris stared after him as they walked along, telling himself it was better this way, far better that the Roamer distance himself. He hadn't realized the danger he had been in.

Arron had seemed so vulnerable back in the cave, collapsing that way. Right then, all his doubts about the Roamer had fled, and he would have done anything to protect him.

Anything! Chris rubbed at his shoulder as it tingled. His father had accused him of being in league with the Roamer. That wasn't true. He wasn't working with the Roamers.

He just needed to go along with him for a bit. If he wanted to save his family, and he did, he had to get Arron to his grandfather. The Shaktas were his enemy. They had killed all of his family. Only he and his grandfather were left.

He couldn't side with Arron, no matter what, no matter how it seemed. The Roamer only wanted revenge. Durth had made that apparent to him. Even Arron had admitted he intended to kill Chruston. He'd made it clear that he was against all Chruston's family. How could Chris side with him? How could his father have accused him of that?

No. He would save his family and show them all. He had not betrayed anyone and never would betray them.

He concentrated on the angry silence Arron maintained. It was this which would allow him to remember that Arron was a Roamer. Vengeful. He could not get tangled in those other feelings. He rubbed at his shoulder as it tingled.

As days passed, he and Katie passed the time chatting, walking down a road that did not seem to end. To either side, a mottled forest grew fitfully. Arron strode on just a bit ahead, sometimes gazing quietly at the rotting trees, other times staring up the road. Chris and Katie watched his pack, bobbing directly in front of them, as they whispered stories and ideas to one another.

The Roamer's silence began, at last, to unnerve Chris. Katie, too, had grown quiet by this time, the oppressive atmosphere finally taking its toll on even her high spirits. Chris watched her for a while as she walked with her head down, then looked up at Arron still ahead of them. He caught up to the Roamer and caught hold of his arm in desperation.

"Come on, enough of the silent treatment."

Arron pulled his gaze from wherever it had lost itself and looked at Chris. "I thought you preferred me quiet."

"Yes . . . well, this whole place is so—so dead. It's getting on my nerves." Chris spread his arms as if to take in the barren trunks and empty branches that clawed at the dull sky. There wasn't even a breeze to knock and clack the branches against each other.

Arron smiled at him then. "Sorry, I guess I've been a little preoccupied."

"I'll say." Katie raised her eyes skyward. Arron stretched out his arms, laughing, his attention now with them, as if he were just coming awake. "What have you been thinking about?" Katie asked, smiling back.

"Nothing." His terseness made her smile fade. "Hey, look," he said, noticing her face. "Look, why don't I teach you some songs?" He grinned hopefully, thinking of the afternoon they had enjoyed on Mount Klineloch doing just that. Chris and Katie glanced at each other, remembering poor Durth's words about Roamer singing.

"No—" Chris started.

Arron turned away from him, pressing his lips together. He strode a few steps away, then stopped. "Can't we just be people for a moment! My hair is light like yours. For just this moment, can't you forget that I am a Roamer?"

"No." The word leaped from Chris' mouth. He could not forget. He must not forget.

Arron turned as if to snap at him, but only sighed. "Okay. Okay," he said gently. He thought a moment as they all eyed each other. "Say," he brightened. "Why don't you teach me your songs."

Chris hesitated, thinking that over. "Okay, that sounds safe." Arron winced. "Sorry." He shrugged.

"Do you have one, Katie?" Arron turned to her.

"Yeah, I know one my dad taught me. We used to . . . He used to sing it when he worked in the shop."

Arron nodded encouragingly. "Go ahead."

Katie smiled and cleared her throat. She began singing, softly, a song with an odd rhythm to it, erratic, as if in time to a mixture of sawing and hammering.

> Saw dust, splinters
> Payment for my labors
> Callused fingers
> Gifts from hard-spent hours
> Can't complain, cannot gripe
> Can't explain the feeling right
>
> The fine finish of the wood
> How it charms the eye
> Can't you see it, feel the shine
> Ample treasure for the pain
> Sawdust
> Splinters
> Callused fingers
> Payment for the surface glow

Katie grinned, finishing.

"That's an interesting one," Arron said, laughing. "Now, let me see if I've got it."

They continued to share songs for quite some time, even delving back to little twiddles they had learned as children. Arron picked up their tunes quite easily and even played some on his kithara. As the day wore on, and they all began to relax again with one another, they asked for songs from Arron. And he taught them, carefully picking light, funny tunes. By the time the sun was getting low, peeking through the branches of the trees, they were walking along, arms linked, laughing like children, heedless of what had passed and of what was to come.

Arron slowed down and released himself slowly from the other two. "I suppose we should camp, before it gets dark." Katie and Chris agreed somewhat reluctantly. They were not really ready to stop walking.

"It looks clearer to this side." Katie pointed to the left. It looked as if there might be a clearing just beyond the close line of trees edging the road. They pushed their way through. Arron set his pack down to one side.

"Looks good to me." He watched the two of them a minute, then started for the woods. "Get set up. I'll go and get some wood for the fire."

Chris set his pack down slowly and opened it, taking out his cooking gear. Katie set about clearing the area of loose brush.

"He wasn't so bad today, now, was he?" Katie said.

Chris looked up at her. "What?"

"I said, Arron's not so horrible as you keep thinking he is."

"I think? You feel the same way." Then Chris smiled down at the pan in his hand. "No, he's not so bad. I never said . . . It's not him. I like him . . . It's just, sometimes . . ." He paused, thinking a moment, then rubbed his shoulder. It had healed pretty well, but late today it had begun hurting him again. He stared off in the direction Arron had gone. "There's something inside of him, something bad. We can't trust him. We really can't," he added in a low voice. "I think he just wants to . . . We just can't trust him, that's all."

Katie looked at him quizzically, then shrugged.

They continued clearing the place for camp in silence. Arron was a long time in coming back. But when he returned he had a large sack, not firewood.

"What's that?" Katie asked.

"We were low on provisions, so I thought it was time to replenish our supply." He opened the bag to show them the food he had gotten.

Chris stared into the bag, then stepped back. "And just where did you get all that? This isn't something you conjured up out in the woods. We warned you—"

"No. I can't do that!" Arron raised his eyes skyward. "I ran back to that farm we passed."

"But how did you get this food? You have money?"

Arron lowered the bag, shaking his head. "No, but—"

"You stole that?"

Arron frowned and didn't say anything.

"You did steal it! I can't believe you." Chris threw his hands up and walked away.

"And just where did you think we were going to get food?" Arron snapped. "See much of it lying around these woods?"

Chris turned on him. "Is it so ingrained in you that you can't even think for a moment that there might be another way to get it? I have some money. Not very much, but we'll use it until it runs out, and then we'll work for the food. But we are not, I repeat, *not* going to steal it! Is that clear?"

Arron looked down.

"I have quite a bit of money," Katie added in a quiet voice. Both Chris and Arron looked at her in surprise. "I've been saving it," she said in answer to their blank looks. "For when I finally did something like this. I've always been intending to, you know."

Arron nodded as if he did know. Chris just stared at her blankly.

"You would have just left your family for no reason?"

Katie just sighed and looked down. "No, Chris, for many reasons." She turned away from them and went to her pack. She pulled out some money and handed it to Arron. "Now, go back and pay for the food. And when you come back, why don't you get the firewood you originally intended to get."

Arron turned without a word and went back into the woods.

Chris stared after him, frowning. "He didn't even ask if we had money. His first thought was just to steal it. I can't believe it."

Katie sighed and sat down against her pack, watching Chris begin to prepare dinner.

She got up abruptly as three men appeared from the woods. They were cloaked, their heads covered with hoods, faces hidden in shadow.

"What do you want?" Chris said, striding to Katie's side.

"Just relax, boys. We're not going to hurt you, so long as you stay calm," the center man said. He stood about a foot taller than the other two. "We're just asking for some food, and money, perhaps."

"We don't have anything you want. We haven't anything to spare," Katie snapped. Chris put a hand on her shoulder to quiet her.

The broad man on the left laughed at her and said something to the tall man. Chris and Katie couldn't understand what was being said.

"Well, we'll check to make sure," the big man said firmly. He looked about him. "Hey, wait one minute, there are three packs. Where's the third one of you?"

"Uh . . ." Chris hesitated. "He . . . uh . . ."

"Go find him. We don't want him surprising us now." The broad man nodded and crept off. "Now, search that pack," the speaker said to the remaining man. Katie moved as if to protect her pack, but Chris jerked her back.

The man by her pack pulled out his knife and waved it at them. "No games," he muttered.

"Got him," the broad man said, coming back from the woods. He pushed Arron in front of him, a knife pressed against his ribs. He shoved Arron over to Chris and Katie, then turned and grabbed at Arron's pack. Arron started forward, but the tall man forced him back at knife point.

"Let's not be stupid, now." Arron stared down at the knife and then helplessly at the man going through his pack. He was lifting the kithara out. He slid it from its cover. Chris took a tight hold on Arron's arm.

"Don't," he hissed at him.

The broad man stared at the instrument a moment, then called the other two over to him. "Look here!" The thieves bent over it curiously.

Arron shook off Chris' hand and took a step forward. "That's mine," he said sharply. All three men looked at him. The tall man advanced on him again, his hand clenching the knife handle so tightly that the bones stood out in his knuckles. He pressed the knife against the soft part of Arron's throat.

"How'd you get it, boy?" His voice came out as if he were choking. "Tell me, boy, and then I'm going to kill you. You deserve—" He stopped as if something else had caught his attention, then he took hold of Arron's hair at the base of his neck and forced his head back so the low sunlight caught his eyes. He released him almost immediately.

"Shakta!" He backed up slowly, lowering the knife. The other two looked at Arron, then they, too, backed up with their leader. The broad man carefully laid the kithara on the ground. Arron looked from one to another while Chris and Katie shifted from foot to foot behind him.

"Take down your hoods," Arron ordered. The three did so quite quickly, revealing dark hair and dark eyes.

"You thieves!" Chris started forward, fists clenched, but Arron stopped him with a hand out.

"I'm Jarra," the tall Roamer said, then pointed to the smallest of them, a scrawny man with a large gold ring in his ear and a tangled, dark beard. "This is Penclo, and this . . ." He indicated the broader Roamer on his left.

"Is Madran," Arron finished for him.

The three Roamers nodded to one another. "Indeed, it is Shakta," Jarra said quietly. "We thought you were dead." They all bowed to Arron. Chris and Katie looked first at Arron and then at each other.

"Are there others?" Arron asked eagerly, ignoring their apparent desire for formalities.

Penclo shook his head. "We've seen none but ourselves . . ." He paused. "We'd given up hope." He stared at Arron a moment as if unable to believe he was real. His eyes

fell at last on Chris and Katie behind him. He took in Chris'
pale blue eyes and Katie's hazel ones.

"They're Homesteaders."

"That's right."

Madran smiled suddenly, making his flat, broad face jump
and quiver. A quick look from Arron made the smile fade.

"They saved my life."

"Homesteaders?"

"Yes. Homesteaders. They're not like the others, and I
won't have you thinking that way. Understand?"

Madran and Penclo nodded, cowed. Jarra took a step
closer to Arron. He towered over him, but he had an odd
look, as if it were he who were looking up, rather than
Arron.

"Interesting method of disguise," Jarra said thoughtfully,
examining Arron's hair. "I never would have thought of it."

"And neither would I," Arron said, eyeing Jarra as the
man walked around him. "Chris did." He pointed to Chris.

"It won't last long, though," Jarra said, giving Chris only
a cursory glance. "It's growing dark already, close to your
scalp."

"It will last long enough. I'll wear a hat."

"Well, you've got us now. We'll protect you, Shakta," Jarra
said, backing up to the other two. They all tossed their knives
at Arron's feet. He made no move to pick them up, he just
shook his head.

"I'm much safer with these two, for a while."

"Homesteaders?"

"Yes."

The three Roamers eyed Chris and Katie again, then began to discuss something among themselves that Chris and
Katie could not understand.

"That's enough," Arron said sharply. "Now, you're welcome to spend the night with us. We need wood for a fire. I,
uh, meant to get some a moment ago . . ." He looked point-
edly at Madran.

"Forgive me," Madran said quickly. He took up one of the
daggers that still lay at Arron's feet, then went off into the
wood. Jarra and Penclo followed him, taking their knives.
Arron watched them leave, then shook his head, smiling.

Chris grabbed Arron by the arm and spun him around. "They're thieves! They would have killed us!"

"They're like any desperate men," Arron said protectively.

"You go with them. You belong with them," Chris said quite suddenly.

Arron remained silent a moment. "Gladly. More than you could ever know. But I've something to take care of first."

"You want to kill more of my family!"

Arron didn't answer him. He just turned, picked up his kithara, and put it back in his pack. Katie smiled hopefully at Chris, trying to get him to regain some of his earlier good spirits. He turned away from her.

The three Roamers came back a moment later with plenty of wood. Katie watched them start the fire, but they did it just as she would have. No magic there. They noticed her watching. Jarra smiled at her and stood up. Katie took a nervous step back, as the man seemed three times her size. Then she stood her ground.

"How do you fit in here, little man?" he asked in his deep, bass voice.

"I wanted to come."

"Aha? And what did your mother think of this? Eh?"

"She didn't know."

Jarra boomed out a laugh, then ruffled Katie's hair. "Shakta'll make a Roamer of you yet."

"No, he won't!" Chris stood up and pulled Katie away from them. "You just leave us be. If I had it my way, you'd be on your way right now."

Jarra cocked an eyebrow. "So, we see the Homesteader after all."

"Leave them alone," Arron said, coming over. Jarra raised his hands in submission.

"Shall we cook?" Penclo asked.

"I'll cook," Chris said firmly.

"Ha! He doesn't trust us," Madran laughed, his flat face winking at Penclo.

"Damn right I don't," Chris muttered under his breath as he squatted by the fire.

"What do you think, boy? We'll poison your food? Hmm?"

Penclo whispered close in Chris' ear, his beard tickling his neck. "Cast an evil spell on your dinner?"

"Now knock it off!" Arron pushed Penclo roughly away. "I won't have you doing this." He glared at the three Roamers. "You don't know what you're doing! I'm traveling with these two and I won't have you casting suspicions in their minds. They don't need any more than they already have. You don't know what you're doing!" The three Roamers looked nervously at him, then nodded slowly, mumbling apologies.

"Hey," Jarra said softly. "We'll stop. It's just, you know . . ." He shrugged. Arron nodded and looked at Chris. He was bent over the fire and refused to look up at him. Arron sighed and glared at the Roamers.

"Shakta . . ." Jarra started.

"Arron," Arron corrected him through clenched teeth.

"Arron, then. I must have a word with you." Arron nodded and stepped away from the fire.

Jarra leaned back against the trunk of a tree and stared at Arron, shaking his head.

"What?"

Jarra smiled and looked down. "I'm sorry, Shakta—I mean, Arron. I just can't get over the fact that you're standing here. You're not dead." He shook his head again and looked up at the now-black sky. "You don't know what it means to us to see you. We'd given up hope."

"I think I do know." Arron reached out and gripped his arm. "I was afraid I was the only one left. To see you three . . ."

"Really?" Jarra smiled and rested his hand on Arron's shoulder. "Well, you're not the only one." The big man gave a short laugh. "And I was ready to kill you when I thought . . . I can't believe I was so blind. You look like him, almost like a mirror into the past."

"What are you talking about?"

Jarra watched him a moment. "Yes, that's what I thought. You don't know. Well, I guess that brings me to what I wanted to tell you. It didn't occur to me until just when you said to us that we don't know . . . You see, there is something I don't think you are aware of. I knew your grandmother long ago, back when you weren't even thought of yet. Well, not true. Some of us knew you were to be—"

"The point."

"Ah, yes, forgive me. Well, your grandmother gave me something a long time ago. Now, I'm not sure if she foresaw this meeting of ours. She did have a bit of foresight, too, not quite your ability, but adequate. But, on the other hand, she may not have foreseen this, and then what I'm about to do is against her design. A bit of a dilemma. Hmmm." Jarra stopped.

"Tell me."

"Well, now I'm thinking that maybe I shouldn't have brought it up. But I'm also not sure that her designs were, well, as they should be . . ."

"I don't see the problem. Just get to the point."

"I'll tell you the problem. There is something that may cause some difficulties. By difficulties, I mean the creation of more of an imbalance than there already is in this world, if you can imagine that. It's not something you can—well, it's in you, Shakta. If she was thinking one way, the wrong way, then perhaps she never meant to tell you, and then I definitely should. But if she was thinking another way, perhaps I shouldn't. I can't foresee. I'm blinded in that respect. Do you see my problem?"

"No."

"She surely would have told me, if I was to tell you. Perhaps she was giving it to me to protect you . . . Hmm." Jarra began muttering to himself.

"Tell me!" Arron caught at his arm, then stopped, turning to look out at the road.

"Who's there?" a voice from the road called. "Who's in there?"

"Run," Arron whispered harshly to the three Roamers. They stared at him stupidly as two men pushed their way into the clearing. Their hats were pulled down tightly, and shotguns hung loosely at their sides.

"Roamers," the younger of the two gasped. The elder swung up his shotgun, as if on reflex, and fired. Penclo fell heavily. Katie dropped to the ground, pulling a wide-mouthed Chris down with her.

Jarra grabbed Arron's arm. "No time to tell you. But you must know that you may not do anything about what is to happen here. You must know that." He looked straight into Arron's eyes and saw the doubt. "Damn! She's told you nothing. She was thinking wrong! Be careful then, Shakta. There's something wrong in you. Think of this." He pressed something warm into Arron's hand. Warm? It burned! Arron tried to pull away.

"Leave that boy be!" The younger man raised his rifle and fired just as Madran leaped in front of Jarra, taking the shot, his eyes wide, taking death.

"Run, damn it!" Arron jerked his hand away from Jarra, closing his fist on the object.

"Think about it, and you'll know what it's for." Jarra turned and ran as the elder man fired after him. The bullet stopped mid-flight, as if hitting a wall, and fell. Chris stared at Arron. He had heard the snatch of the song, saw the quick movement of the Roamer's hand as he gently brushed the bullet from the air. The two men, not noticing, were after Jarra in a rush, crashing through the dry, leafless undergrowth.

Katie got up slowly and looked at the two unmoving Roamers. Madran stared back at her with frightfully wide eyes. She turned away with a gasp, her mouth falling open as the horror crept into her. They seemed to be her own eyes, when she was finally dead.

"Katie?" Arron touched her gently. She shivered. "Hey, it's all right. You're all right," he said with a funny sort of catch in his throat.

"His eyes . . ." Katie mumbled, carefully keeping her gaze averted from Madran's hard stare. Arron pulled away as if she had slapped him.

"Don't think about that, Katie," he warned, backing up still farther. Katie turned to him, bewildered that his concern for her could switch so suddenly to coldness. He continued to back away from her. She turned to Chris, who stood now between the two Roamers.

"Well, they're dead all right."

Arron strode away from him to the far side of the clearing. Chris and Katie looked after him, wondering what he would do. He was shaking his head slowly, unable to look at either of them. He raised his right hand, opened it hesitantly, and stared down at a glowing red gem.

"What's that?" Chris asked.

"Leave me alone, Chris," Arron warned, still not looking up.

"You're going to do something to those two men, aren't you?" Chris demanded.

A shot rang out, not far off. Arron stiffened up, clenching his hands. His right fist flashed red suddenly. He gasped, almost dropping the stone. He turned to glare at Chris. "No, I'm not!" He let out a sharp breath. "Damn you." He looked down again, wiping angrily at his eyes with his left hand.

"Arron . . ." Katie started over to him, but he held her off with his closed right hand, the red of the gem flaring again, glowing dangerously through his clenched fingers.

The two men came back a moment later, dragging Jarra behind them. They grinned at the three, waiting to be congratulated.

"No need to thank us," the older man said, beaming. "We've been tracking these three for quite a ways. Knew they was thieves, thought they was Roamers. And we was right, eh, Brent?" He turned to the younger man. Brent nodded.

"A fine week's work, I do say," the older man went on. He stuck his hand out to Arron, dropping Jarra's foot. It thudded against the ground. "I'm Carl."

Arron hesitated. The gem was still in his right hand. "I'd shake," he said, "but I think I've torn a muscle in my right arm, in the scuffle. Anyway, I'm Arron, and these two are Chris and James." The men shook with Chris and Katie, who were staring at Arron. He showed no trace of any emotion except gratitude toward the two men.

Brent turned back to Arron, a concerned look on his face. "Here, let me see to your arm," he said gently. Chris and Katie again looked nervously at Arron. What was he to do now? But he only nodded and carefully removed his shirt, dropping the gem in his pocket as he did so. His arm looked painfully swollen. They stared on, surprised.

"Mmmm, that looks real bad," Carl said, examining the

arm. "I hope you're not in too much pain." Arron shook his head.

"I'll fix it up good as new," Brent promised. "Don't worry. Just sit down and relax." He was extremely gentle as he tended it.

"There you go. You'll feel better in no time," Brent promised at last. He squeezed Arron's shoulder warmly. "We've all put up with a lot from the Roamers." He smiled then. "But this is a time to be celebrating! We've just rid the world of a few more. Hey, who knows, maybe they were the last!"

Arron grinned back at him. "You're right," he agreed heartily and pulled on his shirt.

"Let's have a toast, then." Carl pulled a bottle of whiskey from his pack. He winked at Brent. "Saved it for when we bagged them. Knew we would, you know. Come on, boys, get your mugs. It's a celebration for us all."

Chris quickly scooped up three mugs. He handed one to Katie, who took it very quietly. She didn't look him in the eye. He handed the other to Arron and was surprised by the lack of hesitation on his part. He seemed quite eager to drink to the death of the Roamers. Lying came so smoothly even at a moment like this. Or was it that he really felt nothing for the three? Which emotion was the act after all? Who was he acting for?

"To the good life!" Carl raised his cup high.

"To the good life!" They all raised their mugs and drank. It was strong homemade for sure and burned all the way down. Chris blinked back the tears that stung into his eyes.

"To the end of the Roamers!" Brent threw his mug up, some of the whiskey splashing out onto his brown hand.

"The end of the Roamers!" They all drank again. Carl began refilling their mugs, stepping carefully over the bodies.

Katie rolled over. Someone had just walked past her. Sitting up, she saw the form disappear into the woods. Chris still slept at her feet, and Carl and Brent, she could see, were on the far side of the fire embers. Their snores filled the empty night air. Arron's blanket lay in a heap.

She got up quickly and followed where he had gone, shivering as her bare feet tested the cold, damp ground for footing. She continued after him, a hand out to protect her face from unseen branches. She could hear him shuffling just ahead of her. Then the sound of his movement stopped, and a moment later she almost stumbled over him, sitting huddled by a fallen tree.

"Katie!" He looked up.

"Arron, what are you doing out here?"

"I'm sitting out here by myself, what does it look like?" he muttered.

She shrugged and slid down next to him. "I just wanted to see if you were all right." He felt her cold hand fumble against him, then clasp his, her comforting thoughts flowing into him. He stifled a sob.

"Oh, Arron," she whispered.

His free hand went up to his face. "Oh, God! I could have saved those three. I could've . . ." he mumbled to himself. "I could have just killed those two men." He clenched her hand so tightly it hurt. "Everything, everything within me said to kill those men! Kill them! It would've been so easy. So easy! And I could've saved those three."

"Why didn't you?" Katie managed, taken aback.

Arron shook his head. "It wasn't right. I wasn't to save them. I wasn't to do it. But I could have! The power was there. I could feel it pressing—no, demanding! I could have! I saw how. So easy! So easy . . ." He stopped, releasing the pressure on her hand slowly. "Sometimes . . . sometimes, I feel I can topple every tree in this pathetic forest. And . . . and I want to try . . . to see . . ." Katie felt her stomach muscles tighten. He began fumbling for something with his other hand. He held it out to her. The fine, smooth, red gem lay on his palm, glowing like a charcoal ember.

"What is it?"

"A carbuncle," Arron said softly. "Jarra pressed it into my hand before he ran. He knew I could have saved him. He also knew that I mustn't." He stared almost horrified at the gem. "That I wouldn't. That I would just let him die . . ." He closed his hand on it, his fist glowing red in the dark, and pressed his forehead against his drawn-up knees.

"I can't stay in that camp, not with . . . Oh, Katie! What

if they were the last ones? I may be . . ." He didn't finish. He began to weep. Katie pulled him close against her; his sobs wracked his entire frame. She tried to comfort him as best as she could.

XII

XII

As the sun began to lighten the sky, Katie gently shook Arron, asleep with his head in her lap. He woke, his eyes widening suddenly in surprise.

"Katie . . ." he began to apologize.

"Don't worry. It's all right."

He scrambled up and held out his hand to help her up. She took it hesitantly. He pressed the warm, round gem into her hand.

"For you," he whispered.

"No . . ."

"Yes," he said firmly.

"Arron . . ."

"I don't want it, Katie. It's a reminder, one I don't want." His black eyes seemed to grow darker still as she met his gaze. She pulled her hand quickly from his and stared at the gem in her palm. She backed slowly away from him, pressing a hand against her stomach. It was as if she could feel his hatred pouring into her through the gem.

"I had some thinking to do last night. It's done. I want no reminders. I've made my decisions. I'll do as I've always meant to do." He stared at her, his mouth a thin line. "There is nothing wrong with me."

She opened her mouth as if to reply, but instead held the carbuncle out to him.

He jerked back, his left hand coming up to the place on his arm that he had somehow injured yesterday.

"Did this do that?" Katie asked, staring first at his arm, then at the gem.

"I said there is nothing wrong with me. That means nothing! Keep it or throw it away. I don't care." He turned away from her, shooting angry glances about the area, but no longer able to meet her eyes.

"You can't hate everything," she whispered, then turned and ran back to the camp. Arron stared at the barren trees that framed her fleeing figure. He cursed under his breath, then began to walk angrily back to the camp. He could indeed hate everything.

They were all still asleep at the camp. Katie was kneeling by the fire and stoking it up for breakfast. She didn't look at him as he returned. He sat down quietly on his blanket and eyed the two men sleeping near him. His hand strayed to his boot. Chris stirred. He sat back again.

Chris finally woke up and saw Arron contemplating the men. "You hate them, don't you?" he said, pushing his blanket away stiffly.

"Why shouldn't I?" Arron turned to Chris now.

"Well, I should hate you."

"And don't you?" The Roamer raised his eyebrows.

Chris thought about it a moment. "No. I don't hate you." He watched Arron a moment longer. "I should, though. It doesn't seem to always work as it should, does it?"

Arron gave a slight laugh. "That sounds like something I should have said to you."

"Breakfast?" Katie pulled a pan out of her pack. Arron shook his head, glancing at Jarra, then shuddered. Chris nodded hungrily and went to the fire to help. Carl and Brent stirred at the lively sounds around them.

"Did someone say something about breakfast?" Carl said, sitting up slowly.

"Want some? I'm just starting it now." Carl nodded, smiling, and Brent sat up immediately, nodding as well.

"How's the arm?" Brent got up and sauntered over to Arron.

"Better, thanks."

"Anytime. Anytime at all. So, are you three fixing to join us? What a celebration there'll be when we bring these three back." He pushed at Jarra with his foot.

Chris turned to them. "They should be buried." Carl and Brent both stared at him. Arron stood slowly.

"What do you mean? They're Roamers," Carl said, spitting.

"And we're Homesteaders. Homesteaders don't do those kind of things."

"What do you mean, boy? I hang foxes I kill on my fence and watch the vultures pick them clean. That's all the treatment they deserve. Same with these three."

Katie glanced at Arron. He was riveted by his pack. She turned to Chris and saw an odd, obstinate look to his face. He wasn't going to give in on this.

"We bury them."

"They was going to kill you, boy, leave you to the dogs, maybe even cut you up into little bits."

"And that is exactly why we bury them. If we don't, then we're no better than they are. I refuse to be like them. I'm not. And I certainly hope you aren't, either."

Carl and Brent looked at one another, and then at the sky and ground. Arron remained very still.

"He's right. You know he's right," Brent said uneasily, looking at Carl for approval.

"Yeah," Carl said grudgingly.

"We'll bury them while James makes breakfast," Chris said quickly, not letting them change their minds. "The graves won't be marked anyway, so it's no honor." Carl and Brent nodded slowly.

They each took hold of a Roamer, Chris and Arron taking Jarra. As Chris bent to lift Jarra's feet, Arron caught him by the shoulder.

"Thanks."

Chris shrugged Arron's hand away. "I did it for me, not you."

Arron nodded. "Thanks anyway."

* * *

Carl and Brent had left them, promising them that they were going to miss the best celebration of the year if they didn't come along. They declined anyway. Carl and Brent waved then, turning south, while they kept going east.

Once the two Homesteaders had left, none of them spoke about the three dead Roamers. Katie didn't want to think about it much. Chris was afraid, strangely, of allowing Arron to think that he might be the last living Roamer. It bound them too closely—being alone. Chris would then remind himself that his grandfather might be alive. He, himself, might not be alone . . . And there still might be other Roamers.

The dead forest around them never seemed to end. Did it end? Chris wondered. Katie told him it did, to the north. But they didn't go north. East! The Roamer led them east, claiming a dangerous marsh lay in the loop of the road. Three weeks of moving east went by, the weather growing hotter with their tempers. Chris grew more certain that the Roamer had some evil planned.

"I never saw any marsh on the maps I looked at," Katie whispered to Chris, pushing back the short hair that clung damply to her face. He had told her about his suspicions as they walked along. Arron was far ahead, wandering by himself, leading them, but very separate. He had kept to himself since Carl and Brent had left them three weeks ago.

"My father's maps were marked all forest." She shrugged, then stared up at Arron who had stopped fifteen or so feet ahead of them, his hands clenched into fists. They walked slowly toward him.

"That map you hold in such high esteem was made before the decline in the land!" He spat on the dry dirt of the road. Chris and Katie stopped. He couldn't have heard them, so far away. Was he always listening to their talk? He waved his arms to encompass the dead trees. "Surely you can't consider this a forest!" He continued to glare at them. Chris took a deep breath and strode forward.

"Damn you! Mind your own business. Were we speaking to you? You've got no right!"

The Roamer opened his mouth for an angry retort, then

closed it. He wiped the sweat from his face and sighed. "I'm sorry. I forget. Your accusations come right into my head. What defense have I got?"

"Well, just think before you start yelling at us. If you know what we're thinking, fine. Keep it to yourself. It makes us uncomfortable."

Arron lowered his head. "And what are you willing to do for my comfort? I can't block your accusations from my mind. It does hurt, Chris. I have feelings, believe it or not. Can you think about that, maybe?"

Chris shrugged and turned silently to Katie.

"Maybe we should set up camp now. It's too hot to keep going, and it's late besides," Arron muttered, turning from the road.

Katie rested a hand on Chris' shoulder. "Everything will be fine," she whispered. Chris nodded, and the two of them followed Arron into the brush.

"Look what I found." Arron was standing next to a broad stream. The water was mucky, but it was moving.

"A stream! God, I haven't been in one of these since—oh, Chris, since ours dried up!" Katie pulled her shoes off and waded in. "It's not real cold, but after today's heat it feels great. And it is moving."

"Well, I'm for setting up camp right on the bank. I could do with a bath." Chris waded in after dropping his pack. "How did this survive? I thought there was only underground water left." He splashed the water up onto his face, sighing.

Arron sat down in the sand. "We're near a large body of water."

"A lake?" Katie turned to him, wide-eyed.

Arron shook his head, laughing shortly. "A swamp."

"That's enough, Arron," Chris warned, wading ashore.

The Roamer shrugged and got up to get wood for the fire.

"Do you remember, Chris?" Katie splashed water at him.

Chris laughed. "It seems so long ago. Thomas and I, every day we'd be down there. Until it was gone . . ."

Katie waded out and dropped to the sand at Chris' side. "I remember when that last little bit disappeared. I wanted to cry."

Chris sat forward. "This has got to change. This stream is disappearing, too. It used to be up to there." He pointed above them to where the line of erosion from the water ended. Arron came back, dumping the wood to one side.

"Do we really need the fire?" Chris asked, sticking his feet in the stream. "It's still hot." Arron ignored him, bending to start the fire. Once the wood caught, he sat back.

"You want a cold dinner?" the Roamer said finally.

"It's just so hot, that's all."

Arron nodded. "It'll cool down soon, and it's getting dark." He pulled his kithara from his pack and began fiddling with the strings.

"What are you doing?" Chris peered at him.

Arron glanced up. "I'm preparing to destroy this stream entirely."

"What!"

"Well, damn it, that's what you expected me to say, isn't it!" Arron hunched back over his instrument. "I'm doing nothing! I am occupying myself. I'm just keeping this in tune. All right?"

"I just don't . . ."

"Trust me. I know!" Arron stood. "Well, you're plotting more in your head than I've ever thought about plotting in mine. You're hiding something from me. Don't think I can't see that." He turned and strode away from them.

"Where are you going?"

"To play some music. I need—your accusations are stifling me!" He disappeared, running upstream.

"We're not being fair," Katie whispered after he was gone.

"Fair! And is what he's doing to the land fair?"

"Are you sure it's him?"

Chris rubbed at his shoulder. "Pretty sure. Oh. No, I'm not. I don't know."

"Let's go apologize." Katie stood and pulled Chris to his feet. She squinted at him, watching his face. "Why did you agree to come with him? What are you planning?"

"Nothing! Let's go apologize. Okay?"

"Okay." Katie followed him down the stream.

The bank was sandy, and the Roamer's footprints were

clear in the evening light. They plodded along in silence for a bit until faint hints of music came to their ears.

"Listen. Do you hear that?"

Chris nodded.

Katie stood still, listening. "That's really pretty. He's never played like that for us, just those funny, little tunes. Listen to that . . ."

"It's Roamer music. You probably shouldn't listen." Chris hesitated, stopping to listen himself.

"Chris, what if we're wrong? What he's playing . . ." She quieted, listening again. "It's really . . . How can that be evil? When the land was as beautiful as my mom says it was, was that evil, too? It was wonderful, just like this music. Listen."

Chris started walking again. "Beauty has nothing to do with it. That's not how you can tell. Some nice things really are nice, but some aren't. You can't lump them together because they all seem nice."

"Well, how are we supposed to tell, then?" Katie turned to look at the murky water. "How are we ever going to know?"

"Something will give it away. We'll know." He shrugged. "I hope. Come on. Let's go see if this music is actually as good as it sounds. Who knows what he's doing with it."

The Roamer stopped playing immediately upon catching sight of them. "What do you want?"

"To apologize, Arron," Katie whispered. She looked down, seeing the hard look in his eyes.

He laughed shortly. "Oh, Katie . . ." Then shook his head. "Never mind. There's no need." He stared out at the stream flowing slowly before him. The toes of his boots reached just to the edge of the water. "It's nice here, don't you think?"

"What were you playing?" Chris lowered himself to the sand.

"It was really pretty," Katie added.

"Nothing. It was nothing." He pointed over to a dense patch of bushes on the far side of the stream. The moon just broke the tops of the trees, its dim light playing across the mucky surface of the water. "Grandmother and I camped there once, in the winter, when it was cooler." He continued to gaze at it. "The stream was a bit swifter then. Cleaner, too."

Chris shrugged. "It's all right the way it is now. Looks just the way our stream looked."

Arron smiled briefly. "The Roamer children played in that stream, too."

"Really?" Katie looked over at him. "We never saw you."

"That I don't doubt; you always ran away." Arron plucked at a few of the strings. "The only Homesteader to ever stay was you, Chris."

"Only because I had to stop you from stealing our fish."

Arron nodded and began to play the tune he had been playing earlier. "I was impressed, at any rate. I had thought you all cowards. You always ran."

"What did you expect? We thought you were with the devil. You would torture and kill us. Who wouldn't run from that?" Katie laughed.

The Roamer stopped playing the tune. "Yes. I know that." He looked at Chris. "And you still stayed."

Chris looked away. "I only did it because my father would have expected it."

Arron turned the instrument in his lap and stared at its face. "It doesn't really matter why. Whatever the reason, it still took courage."

Chris peered at the Roamer. "To my father's thinking it was stupidity, not courage."

"Then you weren't really doing it for your father, were you? You stayed for yourself." Chris stared at the Roamer. Arron nodded, then smiled—not to mock him, Chris sensed, but more in approval. Chris looked down. When he finally looked up, it was over at the thick brush on the far side of the stream. It was only a looming mass of shadow now. The Roamer had once stayed in that darkness. Arron began to play his kithara again, one of the lighter tunes he'd played for them before.

Katie leaned forward and tossed a flat rock across the surface. It skipped three times, then plunked into the water. "My brother and I used to skip stones across our stream. He taught me how. I remember him showing me how to hold my hand just right." She tossed another rock. "That stream was

the only good thing that town had." She stood up and paced
some distance away.

"Katie . . ." Chris stared after her.

"Play what you were playing before, Arron," she whispered from where she had stopped.

"Maybe later." He set the instrument aside.

She didn't seem to hear him. "It was a nice stream, for
being so shallow and mucky. We had a lot of fun there." She
looked back at Chris. He smiled at her, not really sure if she
could see it in the dim light. She smiled back though. "Silly,
aren't I?"

Chris laughed then. "No. God, no. Thomas and I did everything down there. But when that was gone, our friendship
seemed to go with it." He pushed at the water's edge with his
toe. "We fought a lot, but just the same, we had so much fun.
All the things we discovered or built or destroyed together.
But no more . . ." He looked back over at the dark mass of
brush on the other side. Who had the Roamer played with in
this stream? His grandmother? That strange, old woman.
"Who was your best friend, Arron?"

Arron sat forward, clasping his arms about his knees.
"I . . . I didn't play with the other kids much. They didn't
. . . Well, we traveled a lot, and it was most often just me
and my grandmother. And my parents, for a while."

"Oh," Katie said softly. "What happened to your parents?
Chris said you just lived with your grandmother when he
met you."

The Roamer took a slow breath, as if debating. He looked
over at her. "My father was killed by three men on horseback. I was six. They had an argument about—about something. They killed him."

"I'm sorry," Katie whispered.

"It was a long time ago."

"What about your mother?"

Arron scooped up a rock, tossed it, and watched it skip
and splash across the water, shattering the smooth glow of
the moon on its surface.

"Arron?" Chris looked at him expectantly.

Arron turned to him. "Yes?"

"What . . . what happened to your mother?"

"I'll play that song for you, Katie." He pulled the kithara back into his lap.

"But . . ." The Roamer strummed softly on the instrument, and Katie let her protest die. It wasn't any of her business if he didn't want to tell. She sat down in the sand, listening to the gentle flow of notes as they splashed down from his fingers. It made her think of the clear streams her mother had told her about, the water singing as it flowed along, bubbling and clean. It was as if she could see this stream just that way. Little fairy lights played across the surface. The water danced, splashing up and back, rising and falling, the droplets frolicking in the moonlight.

"Shakta!" Chris had bolted to his feet.

Arron stopped playing. The stream stilled itself. Katie started then. It hadn't been in her mind. The Roamer had worked his magic on the water.

"What were you doing!" she gasped, staring in horror at the surface of water. She expected at any moment the stream would drain completely as their own stream had.

"I've done no harm."

"No harm! How do you know?" Chris caught hold of the instrument and ripped it from the Roamer's hands.

"Chris!" Arron leaped to his feet. "Give that back!"

"No." Chris backed to the water with it.

Arron advanced a step, then drew back. "Chris . . ." He raised his hands helplessly. "Please . . ."

"I won't have you destroying this stream."

"I wasn't!" The Roamer made a dash for him, then dropped back again when Chris retreated into the water. He stared at Chris, then dropped to his knees. "I thought I could help it. Katie had an image in her mind of what it should look like. I . . . I thought I could make it that way."

"We told you not to use any more magic, Shakta. You've used it several times since we told you not to. You complain we don't trust you. You've given us no cause to!"

The Roamer nodded. "You're right," he whispered. He stared down at the sand a moment, then looked up at the two of them. "I won't use it again. I won't do anything. No more. You have my word."

"The word of a Roamer? A Shakta?"

"You're killing me, Chris . . ." The Roamer lowered his head again. "Please . . . my kithara. Don't stand out there with it." Chris waded slowly ashore, still keeping a safe distance from the Roamer.

Arron looked up at him at last. "I could just take that from you if I wanted. But I'm not. It's the only thing I have left in this world, but I'm begging you, instead of forcing you . . ." He stood slowly. Chris took a step back. "You have my word. I won't use my magic. That's the best I can do. Have I asked as much from you?"

"Give it back to him, Chris," Katie said. "The stream looks all right. He's given his word."

Chris nodded and handed it to him. Arron took it and pulled it close. "You're going to kill me," the Roamer whispered. "It was as if I could taste it just then." He turned and walked back to camp.

Chris stared after him. "I'm not going to kill anybody!"

"Come on, Chris." Katie pulled at his sleeve and started back to camp, too. He followed, shoving his fists deeply into his pockets.

XIII

ARRON WOKE THEM BOTH VERY EARLY THE NEXT MORN-
ing. "Let's get an early start, it feels as if it's going to be even
hotter today. Come on, I've got breakfast ready."

Chris rubbed the sleep from his eyes and stared dismally at
the plate before him. It was hot already, and humid, and the
sun wasn't really up yet. He dreaded to think what it would
be like at midday. He groaned and stretched, feeling stiff.
"What I wouldn't give for a bed and a roof. Everything
hurts. I thought you got used to this."

Katie stretched. "Maybe not." She splashed water from
the stream on her face and the back of her neck, hoping it
would cool her a bit, and took up the plate Arron handed
her. She smiled at him and sat down next to him. "How do
you feel this morning?"

"Same as always. I'm used to living like this. It's all I've
ever known."

Katie shrugged. "Actually, I'm kind of liking it."

"You're a Homesteader, Katie." Chris lowered his plate.

"Yes, Chris. I know that."

"I'm sorry," he muttered. "I didn't . . ." He started eating again and stared out at the stream.

Arron pointed to a package over on the far side of the fire.

159

"I got more supplies this morning. After your breakfast, take whatever you can fit in your pack."

Chris eyed him. "And just where did you get those? We haven't passed a farm in a while."

Arron pointed up the stream. "It's common practice for Roamers to leave a cache of food when they leave a place. Grandmother and I hid this one up the river when we left there. Time was, when there were more of us, you couldn't go anywhere without coming across one. Everyone was free to use them, provided they replenished them before going on. Now, the only ones we'll find, I'm afraid, are the ones Grandmother and I left." Arron sat back, frowning.

"Well, it's a good thing there are a few left," Katie said gently. "We were running kind of low on food."

Chris eyed the package. "Are you sure the food's still good?"

"Yes." Arron got up. "What point would there be in leaving behind perishables?" He shook his head and bent to rinse his dish in the river.

"Hopefully this next bit of news will put you in a better mood." He turned back to Chris. "We start to go north today."

"After four weeks, I should hope so!"

"Chris!"

Chris waved his hand at Katie. "I'm just tired. Sleeping on the ground . . ."

Arron shrugged and began to pack up, kicking out the fire. "Maybe, after four weeks, I'm getting as used to your thoughts as you are to sleeping outside." He jerked his pack over his shoulders. "I'll wait out on the road. I wouldn't want to make your breakfast any more uncomfortable." He started for the road, then stopped, glancing back at Chris. "You were awfully quick to eat the food I prepared. Who knows what I put in it to coerce you." The Roamer flashed his quick grin and strode off.

Chris set his plate down and covered his face with his hands. "What am I doing?" He shook his head slowly, groaning. "I can't believe the things I hear myself saying!" He glanced up to see Katie staring at him.

"Chris, what's wrong?"

He threw his hands up, then stabbed a finger out in the direction of the road. "I don't trust that Roamer!" He lowered his hand. "But I—I think I'm really hurting his feelings. Roamers aren't supposed to feel. I didn't think . . ." Chris hunched forward. "But I've got to . . . Oh, I'm so confused, I don't know what I want!"

Katie knelt next to him and put her arms gently about his shoulders. "Don't worry. If he really does feel, I'm sure he understands."

"I don't want to hurt Arron. Damn! I don't trust that Roamer!" He stood up, pulling away from her. "Let's just go. Let's get away from here." He rinsed his dishes, shoved them into his pack, took up the remaining supplies, and started out to the road.

The heat was worse than it had ever been. The air was thick with it, making the road before them swim hazily in the distance. They plodded along, speaking little. The energy needed even for talking seemed too much. They breathed in gasps through their teeth, keeping out the tiny insects which buzzed ceaselessly about their heads, getting in their ears and eyes.

Katie sighed, wiping the sweat from her forehead. "Why's it so hot?" she groaned, as if the question might alleviate the heat. "I don't remember it ever being this hot."

Arron shrugged. "Rest?" He pulled to a halt and slid his pack off. He moved to sit in the shade, but the bugs were worse there. The three of them sat miserably in the center of the road.

Chris ran his arm across his forehead, the sweat dripping into his eyes. His face was smudged with dirt. "These bugs are driving me crazy!" He swatted at them a moment, then lowered his arm, sighing out his frustration.

Arron nodded. "It'll cool down a bit at nightfall."

"That's not for hours." Chris peered up at the sun, hazy in the humid air. "Can I have some water?"

Arron smiled and pulled the water bag from his pack.

"We can practically drink from the air," Katie muttered, rubbing at her chest. "I'm waterlogged."

Arron nodded. "I think that's why it's so hot; the humidity here traps the heat." He forced himself up again. "Come on, let's go. Which shall it be, shade and bugs, or heat and fewer bugs?"

"I'm for more bugs, less heat for a while." There was a thick, booming noise somewhere in the distance. Katie turned, looking. "What's that?"

Arron gazed in the direction of the sound, frowning. He shook his head. "I'm not so sure I want to find out. Let's go." He walked over to the shaded part of the road. "A lot more bugs," he muttered. Chris and Katie followed slowly.

The booming noises continued as they strode along, sometimes closer, sometimes farther away. Arron kept looking about. "Something's wrong," he muttered. "There's something . . ." He left off, shrugging. Suddenly, right in front of them, a tree shattered with that hollow, booming sound. Arron spun around, flinging his arms up to protect Chris and Katie from a barrage of bark and branches. They all stared at the scattered fragments.

"What the . . ." Chris walked cautiously forward.

Arron knelt by the remains of the tree. "It's too hot." He ran his hands along the trunk laying across the road, chunks of it blasted out. "I think the water inside the tree—" He spun about to look at Katie, who stood back from them.

"Katie!" He raised his hands and began to hum, then cut himself short, remembering his promise, and bolted from where he knelt, knocking Katie away as the tree next to her exploded.

Chris' arms came up to protect his eyes. When the littering of branches stopped, he peered cautiously about. The tree lay in ruin about the place, the huge trunk spanning the road. Arron and Katie lay fallen on the far side, the Roamer covering her with his body.

"Katie? Arron?" Chris leaped over the trunk.

"I'm okay. Get off of me, Arron." The Roamer started to get up, then, gasping, fell back. Katie crawled out from under him. "Arron?" His legs were trapped under the broad trunk. "Oh, God!"

"It's all right," Arron said, cradling his head in his arms. He took two deep breaths. "Just get it off. Nothing's broken. I'm just stuck, that's all."

"I could've been . . ." Katie started, staring at the scattered branches.

"Katie!" Arron cried out in alarm. "Go get something to lever this tree up. Don't think about that!"

She backed up. "I'm sorry—I . . ." She closed her mouth and turned to find something to help move the tree.

"Are you sure you're all right?" Chris bent to try and see Arron's face, but he kept it cradled in his arms.

"I'm all right, Chris. Go help Katie."

Chris stood, then hesitated. "You're not going to use your magic to move the tree are you? This damage could all be because of what you did last night."

"I told you I wouldn't use it!" The Roamer glared up at him. "I could've used it to help Katie, but I didn't!"

"Arron, I didn't mean—say, you are hurt." Arron's mouth was drawn tight in a grimace. Chris squatted back down. "Are you sure nothing's broken?"

"Yes!" The Roamer lowered his head again. "My foot's twisted and it hurts. It's not broken."

Chris nodded and squeezed Arron's shoulder. "We'll get it off. Don't worry." He hurried after Katie.

The two of them returned after a moment. Katie dragged a large branch that must have snapped off one of the trees. Chris pulled a thicker one after him. He shoved the branch farther down for better leverage. Katie lay the other underneath to act as fulcrum. They all started as another tree exploded into a thousand pieces.

"We'd better hurry," Katie whispered.

"Please do," Arron muttered into the ground.

"You pull him out when I pull down." Chris caught hold of the branch with both hands. Katie took hold of Arron. Chris gave a ready sign and hung down on the branch. Katie pulled, but Arron cried out. She stopped immediately.

"Arron, I'm sorry." The Roamer wouldn't look up at her.

Chris pushed the damp hair back from his face and swatted at the bugs buzzing around him. "This isn't going to work, damn it." A tree just across from them suddenly burst apart. Katie crouched protectively over Arron.

"I've got an idea," Arron whispered after the pieces from the tree had stopped falling.

"No magic," Chris warned.

"No magic!" Arron gasped and cringed against the ground. "God!" He took two quick breaths.

"Are you all right?"

"No! Now listen. Get something to dig with. If you can't lift the tree, lower the ground."

"I'll find something," Chris stood. "Get his pack off him and give him some water, Katie." He hurried away from them.

Katie bent and eased the pack first from one arm and then the other.

"Is . . . is my kithara all right?"

Katie opened his pack and pulled out the instrument. She slid it from its case. "It's fine," She held it out for him to see. He nodded and laid his forehead on his arms again. Katie put it back and pulled out the water bag. "Here, drink some." Arron shook his head. "Arron—"

"No, no water. Not yet. I don't want my foot to swell up any more than it's going to. Better that I'm dehydrated now."

Katie stared down at the bag in her lap. "I'm sorry, Arron. God, I'm sorry."

"What are you talking about? That tree wasn't your fault." Arron braced himself up on his elbows to peer at her. "It was my choice. You had no say in the matter."

"You could have used your magic."

"I gave my word, for all the good that is. Go help Chris find something to dig with." He lowered his head to his arms again. Katie put her hand gently on the back of his head, smoothing his hair, then went to find Chris.

They came back at last bearing two flat stones. Chris' face had a welt across it where he'd been hit by a branch when another tree exploded near him.

"You okay?" Chris asked, kneeling next to Arron.

"Yes. Please hurry. The trees are going crazy around here. I think it's getting hotter."

Chris nodded, jumping at another explosion. He and Katie bent to scrape away the dirt at either side of Arron's legs. They worked feverishly, the soil was dry and hard. The bugs gathered about them, as if more were released at each explosion.

"This is taking too long," Katie moaned, sitting back to wipe the sweat out of her eyes. She spat, tasting the bugs flying into her mouth.

"Just keep digging," Chris sputtered. He kept on, not stopping to pull the bugs from his eyes, or to wipe the dripping sweat from his face. "We'll get you out soon. Come on, Katie."

She bent, digging more furiously. Another tree went down just to the far side of them. Katie gasped, a branch knocking her across the back.

"All right?" Chris asked, not stopping.

"Fine." She scraped at the soil farther under the tree. They were making progress, but slowly.

"You'd better quit," Arron whispered.

"What?" Chris didn't stop.

"That tree there is going to go. I can hear it—feel it . . ." Arron stared up at it. "Go on. You'd better go."

"No!" Chris scraped more fiercely at the dirt.

"Chris—"

Chris threw the rock down. "Damn it! Shut up. Katie, take that arm."

"Chris, it's going to go soon!" Arron looked up at him, the streaks of dirt on his face making him look pale underneath.

"Shut up! This is going to hurt now. If nothing was broken before, it might be after this." He grabbed Arron's pack and tossed it to the far side of the trunk. "Pull hard, Katie. Really hard and don't stop till he's out, no matter what. When I say now." The tree next to them began groaning. They could all hear it. "Now!" The two of them strained back, clutching at Arron's arms. He cried out, then cut himself off, forcing his breath out in a hiss.

"Again." Chris yanked, and Arron slid out with a jerk, the tree releasing him. The three of them tumbled back a minute.

"That tree!" Arron gasped. They grabbed at him and, tumbling forward, hauled him over to the other side of the trunk that had trapped him. The tree groaned loudly once more, then exploded, littering them with branches and bark.

After a moment, Chris peered over. The broad trunk,

cracked and splintering, lay beside the one behind which they hid. He looked back at Arron, sitting with his head resting back against the tree. "Don't you ever just give up like that again. Don't you ever," Chris snarled at him.

The Roamer rolled his eyes to look at him. He nodded slowly. "I hear you."

Katie straightened, listening. "More trees are groaning. We've got to get out of here."

"It's hot," Arron muttered. "But not so hot the trees should be—that kind of heat would kill us, too."

"It's your damn magic."

"No."

"We'd better hurry." Katie stood up, then stared down at Arron. "Can you walk?"

"I don't suppose there's much choice."

"Come on, we'll help you." Chris helped him on with his pack. A tree across the road burst apart, raining branches on them. Then the one next to it went. Chris and Katie hoisted Arron to his feet. They started off, trying to run. The Roamer stumbled repeatedly, Chris and Katie keeping him up. They scrambled over logs and around trees, ducking the flying branches as more and more trees flew apart.

"What is this!" Chris gasped out.

"You've got to stop. I'm too heavy for Katie. It's too hot." Arron tripped again. They all went down, exhausted.

"Come on!" Chris pulled on him, blocking a branch with his right arm. He hauled the Roamer to his feet.

"Katie, you go on ahead, try and find some shelter, something. We can't go much farther. I'll bring Arron after." Katie nodded, darting off, dodging the pieces of the tree bursting up ahead.

Arron looked grimly at Chris. Chris glared back. "Don't you even think about that, Arron. Now, come on, help me. A Roamer might leave another behind, but a Homesteader wouldn't."

"A Roamer would never leave anyone behind!" Arron willed himself to move forward.

"Then just what was it that you and your grandmother did to all those Roamers in the camp before the Extermination? That wasn't leaving someone behind?"

Arron gasped, pulling to a halt. "You—"

"Never mind, come on. I don't really care." Chris shoved him forward.

They pushed on, scrambling over the large number of trees blocking the road. Arron's face was drawn tight as he forced himself to step down on his right foot.

"Lean on me." Chris pulled Arron's arm farther over his shoulder. "You can't do it yourself!"

Katie climbed back over the tree before them.

"There's a depression up ahead. A tree was uprooted and another's fallen across the hole. We'll be safe there." She caught Arron's other arm and helped Chris to get him there.

She pointed to the fallen tree she meant, then flung her arm up to defend herself against another bombardment of branches. Chris nodded, seeing the depression, and strove to push Arron faster. Reaching it at last, he shoved the Roamer down first, then sent Katie down, sliding in finally himself.

He shuddered, sitting back against the dirt, putting his hands over his ears to block the sounds of the shattering trees. "What's going on!"

Arron swatted at the bugs that had followed them into the hole. "Something . . . something . . . It's bad. But what, I can't see." The Roamer turned from his thinking to look at his right foot. Slowly, he reached for his boot and began tugging it off, clenching his teeth.

"Let me," Chris took hold of his boot and began to pull very carefully. He looked up at the Roamer's face as he tugged, easing his pulling when Arron stiffened up. "There. Oh, God, it's purple."

Arron stared down at his foot, then shook his head and leaned back sighing. "It'll be okay," he whispered.

"When? Tomorrow? Four more weeks? It's broken, I suppose."

"No! It's just bruised. Running on it didn't help much, either!" The Roamer stared up at the tree lying above where they crouched.

"Arron . . ." Chris shrugged, sighing. "It hurts, doesn't it."

"I'm okay."

"Thanks for taking care of Katie. I'm just scared, that's all. I just wish I knew what was going on here."

"We all do," Katie whispered. "Give me the water sack, I'll get some of the swelling down, if the water's cold."

"It's just that Durth told us a story about how Shakta once exploded all the trees in a man's orchard. That's why I thought maybe . . ." Chris cut himself off seeing an odd look cross the Roamer's face. Katie looked up, too, from wrapping Arron's foot.

"What?" she asked.

Arron didn't say anything for a moment. He watched Chris. "Shakta wouldn't ever do something like that. Durth didn't know what he was talking about. A Roamer wouldn't ever do that. He would know. Don't you see? I had nothing to do with this. There is nothing wrong with me. Do you understand? Nothing!" Arron dropped his gaze as Chris and Katie stared at him. "It's not something I've done. It can't be."

Chris shook his head. A tree above them broke apart, the trunk toppling onto their protector. They were showered with dirt and sticks, but their ceiling held.

Arron looked at them again. "Someone else, who doesn't know, might try this. The heat, it's from inside the trees." The Roamer's eyes held a dark look in the shadow of the trunk above them. They seemed to be the cause of the destruction.

"It's all the magic you've been playing with! It's having its effect. The whole damn world is finally falling apart. You—"

"I can stop it, Chris," Arron cut him off. "I know how to stop this." He leaned eagerly forward. "Let me try. Trust me for just one moment."

"No." Chris sat back against the dirt. Arron looked at Katie. She shook her head. Arron sighed, sitting back.

"I guess we'll just have to wait it out, then, and hope there's something left."

"You need to rest your foot anyway," Katie said.

"There's nothing wrong with me. I know what I'm doing. I do," he muttered more to himself than to them, shifting his sitting position, turning his back to them both as best he could in the cramped area.

They waited the day out, listening to the shattering noises of the forest going down around them. The insects swarmed around them, trapped as they were, wearing them out with their ceaseless buzzing and biting. As the day wore on, they abandoned almost all attempts to protect their skin. Exhaustion took its toll. They dozed on and off, waiting for the trees to quiet.

Arron woke them sometime past midnight. "It's stopped," he whispered. "Let's go."

"Can you walk?" Chris whispered back at him.

"I can walk."

"I'll help you."

"I can walk on my own." The Roamer pulled his pack up with him as he struggled out of the hole. Katie scrambled up after him, and then Chris. They all stared about them. The place looked razed, litter scattered everywhere. The moon cast a gray-white glow over all the fallen trees. Arron's shoulders sagged.

"Damn. Why did I listen to you. I could've . . ." He jerked his pack on, and struggled forward, limping over the shattered pieces of the forest. Katie came up to him, taking his arm to draw it over her shoulder.

"Let me help you."

"Leave me alone. I can walk. I'm a Roamer, remember. I don't feel a thing!" He pushed away from her.

Katie glared at him. "You sure are a Roamer! Down to the very bone. Help you? I wouldn't dream of it. You don't need anything. Why should anyone care for you? You trample on them!"

Arron stopped dead. "If you really wanted to help me, you'd help the way I need you to, not the way you want to." He pushed on then, grabbing up a stick to lean on as he staggered away from them.

When dawn finally came, they had passed out of the area of destruction. Whole trees once again lined the road, most of them barren and white, like grave markers. Arron shuffled along behind them, unable to keep up.

"Let's rest for the day," Chris suggested, looking back at the Roamer.

"No. I want to keep going."

"Arron—"

Arron tensed up. "You think I'm trying to delay this journey. You think I'm trying to take the slowest, most round-about route. Well, we'll keep going." He strode forward, forcing himself to walk more upright. "I'm trying to get you there by the fastest, safest way I know. We'll keep going until nightfall."

Chris stared at him in disbelief, then turned to Katie raising his hands. She looked exhausted, too. Chris turned back to the Roamer who had shuffled on some distance ahead.

"Arron, we're stopping. I'm exhausted, and so is Katie."

Arron stopped, his left hand clenching the stick he used for support until his knuckles grew white. "Okay. You want to stop? We'll stop."

"Yeah. I want to stop." Chris raised his eyes skyward and strode into the brush. Katie stumbled after him, then Arron followed. Chris kicked the brush out of a small, clear space to set up for bed. He turned to help Katie undo the ties on her pack and pulled her bedroll out for her, spreading it out.

"Do you want something to eat?" she asked, yawning.

Chris smiled and shook his head. "Lie down. You look like you're going to fall asleep standing up."

She smiled weakly at him, then sank gratefully down onto her blankets. Chris knelt and laid the blanket over her, smoothing it across her back. "Thanks," she murmured. He nodded, staying next to her as she drifted off. Only when her breathing had grown deep and steady did he move to go to his own pack.

He pulled his blanket out and noticed Arron was still standing at the edge of their campsite.

"Why don't you get some sleep?"

The Roamer nodded, but made no move. Chris frowned at him, then got up and went over. He took Arron by the arm, as if to move him into the campsite.

"Let me alone, Chris."

"No, I won't. You're dead on your feet. I can't for the life of me think what's keeping you up."

Arron looked away. "It's called hatred," he whispered.

Chris didn't release his hold on the Roamer, instead he

pulled the stick from his grasp, leaving him no alternative but to lean on him. He pulled him slowly into the clearing and forced him down. Arron glared, but didn't say a word. Chris pulled the Roamer's blanket from his pack and handed it to him. Arron took it and wrapped it about himself, hunching down.

"I can't sleep."

"Is your foot hurting you?"

Arron didn't answer.

Chris nodded and bent to pull Arron's boot off. Arron caught at his arm.

"Don't."

Chris ignored him, pulling it off quickly. Arron winced and looked away.

"Oh, Arron," Chris sighed, sitting back. "Why are you so . . ." He got up and gathered up a bunch of twigs, piling them into a tall stack. He put Arron's foot up onto it, elevating it.

"Lie down and get some sleep," he commanded.

"Sometimes," Arron whispered. "Sometimes, I just can't sleep, no matter how tired I am."

"We'll stay here a day or two, until you can walk properly."

"I can walk fine. You'll just think this is another scheme of mine to slow you up!" Arron struggled to get up. Chris held him down.

"Arron. You're hurt. You're really hurt. I'm not blaming you for anything right now."

"Except for the destruction of those trees." Arron pulled his arm from Chris' grasp.

"I don't think you did it knowingly. It's just that you're a Roamer. You can't help but—"

"Enough! Let's talk about something else, or just leave me alone."

Chris nodded. "I don't think it's going to be so hot today. It's almost chilly this morning."

"They're not trying to explode trees any more. They don't need the heat."

"They? You mean my grandfather, don't you? You think he's doing this."

Arron shrugged and looked away.

"Arron, it's more likely a side effect of your magic than the magic of a dead man." Seeing the Roamer turn to respond angrily, Chris added, "I'm not blaming you! I'm just saying, you can't know."

"He's not dead," Arron choked out.

"Well, even if he is alive, that still doesn't mean—"

"All right! So, you're sure it's me. Why don't you kill me?"

"Let's talk about something else."

Arron struggled to his feet. "No, damn it! We'll talk about this." He limped away. "They've taken everything else. Why can't they take my life and make an end of it!" He stopped, catching at the tree to support himself. "They take everything! Then—then they give me you in return. Oh, and it works so well! Giving me hope. You make me think you care! And then . . ." The Roamer pressed his forehead against the tree. "Get some sleep, Chris."

Chris moved to his side to lead him back to his bedroll. "Not until I see you're asleep."

"Ah," Arron laughed slightly, limping back toward his blanket. "The carrot. You care, huh?"

"You're not making any sense. Now, go to sleep. Put your foot up there." Chris held the blanket out to him. Arron took it, lying back.

"I almost believe you really do care," Arron muttered.

"Of course I care."

"But?" Arron said, sitting up again. "You were about to say it. But what, Chris?"

"Go to sleep, Roamer. We'll move on in two days, when you can make a more reasonable effort at walking."

XIV

THREE DAYS LATER, CHRIS FINALLY DEEMED ARRON FIT to travel. The Roamer mocked gratitude at Chris' decision. Chris frowned at that and gathered up his pack, starting for the road.

"He's just joking," Katie said to Chris.

"Is he?" Chris slapped at the dust clinging to his clothes. "You're so sure?"

"Yes. Aren't you, Arron?"

The Roamer grinned and wouldn't answer.

"Fine." Chris rolled his eyes. "Well, at least we're going north."

"Yes, we are doing that." Arron limped slightly as he walked along with them. He began whistling.

"Cut that out."

Arron shrugged. "You could join me. It's not quite so annoying then." He continued to whistle, picking up his pace slightly.

"Well, at least you're in better spirits," Chris muttered.

The Roamer nodded, then winked. "Or is it a lie?" He laughed at the look on Chris' face and began whistling again.

"I don't care one way or another," Katie laughed with him. Arron surprised her by linking arms with her.

"It's a whole new day, and I'm going to win your trust one way or another." Arron grinned at Chris. "Ask anything, and I'll do it."

"I'll ask you to leave Katie alone."

Arron unlinked arms with her. "Fine. Anything else?"

"Stop acting so giddy."

"Okay." Arron sobered a bit. "Anything further?"

Katie started laughing and linked arms with Arron again. "The two of you are ridiculous." She caught Chris' arm and made him match their pace. "Let's just enjoy the day. It's not so hot anymore. I don't think I can take this new form of bickering, no matter how good-natured you're trying to make it appear, Arron."

The Roamer shrugged and laughed for real. "Sorry, didn't know my guises were so easily seen through."

"They are this time." Katie slowed them up a bit. "Let's not ruin your foot the first day, okay."

"It feels all right, just a bit stiff."

"Well, no harm will be done if we slow down." Katie took a deep breath and let it out slowly. She stared off into the distance awhile, the dirt road they followed twisting out of sight up ahead. "I don't know how you Roamers did it," she sighed after a while of plodding on in silence.

"It's not so boring all the time," Arron murmured, knowing in his way that she was speaking of the length of their journey. Chris and Katie decided to let it go. "No more so than it is keeping a farm, I suppose, but then I don't really know."

"Yeah, that can be pretty boring, too. But, it's safe and . . . and comfortable." Chris said, kicking at a stone, pulling his arm from Katie's. He was remembering a time when their barn had burned down. His mother stood at the corner of the house wrapped in her robe, the fire showing the tears that streamed down her face. His father was on his knees before the blaze, that tiny, useless bucket he had used to try and douse the flames lay at his side, a trickle of water still dripping out of it. It was like the end had come. And it would have, too, but the neighbors suddenly came running from everywhere, with pails and blankets and water. They kept the fire from the house. And the next day, even after working all night, they were there, ready to rebuild. There were no questions. There were no words at all. Nothing needed to be said.

"You know where you are and what's expected. There's a kind of bond between people . . ." Chris added turning to the Roamer, expecting one of his taunts or derisive comments.

"That's important to you?"

"Yes!"

"Why so defensive? I only asked."

"Well, you always . . . Why would you understand? Is there anything that's important to you?"

Arron nodded. "Plenty."

"What could possibly be of importance to a Roamer—oh, aside from himself?" Chris muttered.

"Perhaps the very same things that you care about, comfort and safety."

"Oh? And so you wander about the country? How comfortable and safe is that? Lies!"

Katie stopped, pulling away from the two of them.

"Why do you do this?" Arron stared at him, shaking his head. "What have I done, today anyway, and even the last few days, to get this rise from you? Chris, just tell me what the problem is and get it over with."

"I don't even recognize you, Chris," Katie whispered, pleading. "From a Roamer—" She looked at Arron. "Well, I'd expect it, I suppose. But, Chris . . ."

Chris lowered his head, his left hand came up to rub at his shoulder, tingling suddenly. He looked up at last, jerking his hand down to his side. "I . . . I don't know," he muttered. "Maybe I'm tired. I really want to sleep in a bed again. Maybe I'm worried. I've got things to think about."

The Roamer nodded. "Things that worry me, too, Chris. I wish you'd tell me."

"No!" Chris took a step back. "You wouldn't understand. You just wouldn't."

Arron frowned, then turned and began limping forward again.

"He wouldn't." Chris said lamely to Katie, who was still staring at him.

"I would." She turned on her heel and ran to catch up to Arron.

When Chris finally caught up with the two of them, they were chattering about something and laughing. He smiled his apology at them, and they smiled back easily, no questions asked. He sighed, thanking them silently for accepting his moodiness. It was as confusing to him as to them. The Roamer's smile became gentler as, Chris realized, he heard the silent thanks. Arron's ability to see into his head irked him, but the apparent compassion with which he saw smoothed some of Chris' irritation.

"Tell us about your grandmother," Chris said suddenly.

Arron looked at him, surprised. "About my grand-mother?"

"Yes. If it's all right. You hold her in such high esteem. I'd like to know more about her."

Arron was quiet a minute, staring up at the grayish sky. "She was as much an enigma to me as to you." He looked at Chris. "You're asking yourself, why did that old woman give me that box? What did she have to do with my mother? Why did she send Arron back to Mount Klineloch in order to bury her? What did she expect of me?" The Roamer stopped to let the questions run through Chris' mind.

"You know, she never told me anything—not what she wanted, what I was to do, nothing. Little warnings. Cautions. She kept secrets bottled up inside of her. I'm afraid even ones that, perhaps, she should have told me." He walked silent awhile, thinking about something he apparently had no intention of sharing. He sighed after a bit. "I suppose it was good training for her end . . .

"No," the Roamer sighed. "She never explained a thing. But do you know what she did do?" He asked as if he were daring a response from them. "She protected me with her life. Everything she did seemed to be for my safety or comfort.

"I remember"—he laughed slightly, staring off up the road —"she always used to have a snack ready for me in the afternoon. I'd go off in the morning, collecting herbs for her, or some other chore. She'd pack my lunch. 'Be home before it gets dark, Arron, my boy,' she'd say. And I'd go off, come back late in the afternoon, and there she'd be sitting, a little snack for me on the table next to her. To tide me over until dinner, she said.

"It wasn't very much, really. But sometimes I could tell, especially when I got older, that some of those little snacks took quite some time to prepare. Little nothings that took an awful lot of work and got no appreciation until it was too late . . ."

He glanced at Chris. "I doubt that's what you wanted to hear. I can't answer your questions. Sorry. I've too many of my own. Far too many." He shook his head as if to clear away some thought. "What she did for me then was only the least of the things she did for me, suffered for me, because of me—because of Shakta."

Arron glanced up at the sky, squinting as a slight drizzle had begun. The weather had become freakishly unpredictable. He swung his pack from his back and pulled out his rain cape. Chris and Katie followed suit.

"Nice," Katie murmured, casting her eyes skyward.

Chris shrugged, accepting it. He turned to Arron again. "She never said anything about giving the box to me?"

"She never said. I knew, though. You told me. Your thoughts flashed out at me that day I walked you back to the river. I knew from you that she'd given you a small, gray box with something wonderful inside it. And frightening. It scared you.

"I think she gave it to you to keep it safe." Arron tried to answer the question that was in Chris' head. "She had foresight. I think she knew what might happen."

Chris nodded.

"Sounds like you were pretty close to her," Katie whispered when Arron grew moodily silent.

"She was my mother." Arron shrugged. "Or she may as well have been. She raised me. Mother *and* father, in a way. My dad was gone by the time I was six. My mom, when I was four or five." He stopped, peering up the road. The rain was coming down harder, graying out the trees around them. The Roamer stared through it, seemingly beyond the bend in the road.

"Someone's in trouble," he said quite suddenly.

"There's no one—" Katie started.

"Around the bend." Arron hurried forward.

There was an old woman trying to right her overturned cart. Her clothing clung damply to her with the rain and mud as she knelt in the road, trying to force the cart up. The horses stamped about, kicking up their heels, dragging the cart sideways through the muddy road. Bags and packages from the cart lay everywhere. The three of them instantly knelt at her side, adding their strength in raising the wagon.

"Oh, my, you dears. I would have never gotten this upright without your help," the woman exclaimed as the cart fell back on its wheels, splashing them all with brown water. Arron caught at the horses and calmed them, placing his hands gently on their noses, whispering to them. They stopped dancing and kicking, and stood with their heads low and still in the rain.

"What happened?" Katie asked.

The woman pushed back a gray-white strand of hair streaming water across her face. "Why, the horses spooked and darted off, and when I finally caught up, well, you see. My, I thought I'd never get home."

Chris lifted one of the grain bags into the wagon, then leaned against the side. "Well, I'm certainly glad you weren't in it."

"My, I didn't even think of that." She thought about it a second, looking a bit shaken. "Oh, thank the Lord it was me getting the groceries. I get out of the cart to walk that rough stretch back up the road; most of the others don't get out of the cart there, they just chance it. If it had been one of them . . . they would have been killed." She stared at the wagon, righted; it seemed to horrify her to think of what might have been.

Arron dropped the bag he was holding and stumbled over it. He struggled to get up quickly and get the bag into the wagon.

The old woman turned. "My dear boy, what's wrong? You haven't hurt yourself at my expense, have you?" She reached over to him. He pulled away. "Why look at you! You're shaking all over. Why you're burning up! You shouldn't be out in the rain with a fever."

"It's all right." Arron pulled back further, struggling to get the bag into his shaking arms. It slipped repeatedly, coated with mud and water.

Chris took the bag from him and set it into the wagon. He watched Arron closely. He didn't like these fits that the Roamer had—an illness that ate away at other people, it seemed. The horror he saw in Arron's eyes settled deep in his stomach.

"I want you all to stay at my place, until you are well, at least," she said, looking at Arron.

"No, that's not really necessary."

"Nonsense. In this weather! There's no other place to reach by nightfall. I offer much more comfort than the forest does."

"Thank you, you're very kind." Chris smiled at her, wiping water from his eyes.

"Good, then climb on in. I'm Anna." She got up into the wagon with a helping hand from Chris.

"I'm Chris." Chris climbed in after her.

"And I'm James." Anna pulled Katie up.

"You're awfully young to be going about with these older boys, aren't you?" Anna said softly.

"We take care of him," Chris said, pulling Katie next to him.

"Come on," Anna said sternly to Arron. "No more traveling about for you until you get dried out and get some rest. So tell me your name and climb in."

Arron stared up at them miserably, the rain streaming down his face, plastering his hair flat on his head; sighing, he climbed up. "I'm Arron," he said softly, avoiding the hand she held out for him.

They went only a short way up the road, the trees on one side suddenly giving way to a very large cottage. Castle-sized was more appropriate, but the build of it made it look small and homey. Even with the rain drizzling down, the glow from the windows promised warmth and happiness. People had begun to gather on the broad front porch, waving and smiling.

"We're a big family," Anna explained. "We take in all

sorts. Anyone who needs a reason just to carry on. Well, we can always come up with one." She smiled at the people and called out to them. "I've brought friends for dinner, so set some extra places. Three. And a big fire—we're drenched to the bone."

The group split apart, some going back in to prepare dinner, others splashing out to help unload the cart. A man took the horses and cart away, and Anna held the door as the unloaders filed in. Things were set in their places, and people began to crowd around the newcomers, eagerly greeting them and calling out their names. Chris felt Arron's hand tighten on his shoulder.

"Calm down, will you?"

Arron nodded, then started, hearing his name called.

"Arron? Did you say his name was Arron? Are you sure?" A woman came closer and held her hands out to him. He held back from her, interposing Chris between himself and her.

"Oh, my Lord! It is you! I can see your mother in you. In your face, your hands, the way you carry yourself. Your eyes." She pushed past Chris and came close to Arron. "Do you remember me?"

Arron stared, unsure. "I know your name is Bess. But I don't think—"

"Of course you don't, dear boy." She laughed, hugging him, ignoring the wet. "Oh, it's amazing, the resemblance—amazing. But you were only four when you met me. Your mother and I, well, we grew up together."

"But—but . . ." Arron stopped, at a loss.

"Yes, I know," she whispered. "Things were different in some places. And so were the circumstances. Your grandmother took me in as a child. Oh, it's like seeing family again!" She hugged him once more.

Anna pushed her way over to them. "Oh, Bess, you know Arron already, I see. That's wonderful. Now these two are Chris and James." They nodded to Bess, who had her arm firmly about Arron's waist.

"Why don't you take them off somewhere. Get them some towels to dry off. Show them their room so they can put on some dry clothes. I'll go and change and see about dinner."

Anna turned to go, then glanced back. "Oh, Bess, watch Arron a bit. He was burning with fever on the road. Seems a bit better now."

Bess looked at Arron, then back at Anna. "It's nothing to concern yourself about, Anna. The boy is like his mother. She used to burn a high fever for no reason, too." She looked back at Arron. "Inherited that, too, did you?" She leaned closer to him and indicated Chris and Katie. "Do those two know about you?" Arron nodded.

Bess showed them their beds, piled high with thick, soft-woven blankets, and the marble wash basin and anything else they might want or need. She handed them towels, rubbing Arron dry herself until he pulled away, taking the towel from her. She gave them a chance to change, then sat on the bed, pulling Arron to sit next to her. She shook her head staring at him.

"I just can't get over the resemblance." Chris and Katie sat gingerly on the other bed.

Arron stared at her, trying to place her face in his memory.

Bess smiled. "Yes, things are rough sometimes, I know. But your mother was so sweet and caring. My, never was there anyone so much in love as she was with your father. And so much love she had for her little boy." Bess sighed. "And now, to see you all grown up, I could cry. And you, so much like her. Except the hair," she added wryly.

Chris stared, amazed. Was that really how the Roamers were? Bess painted such a different picture. Or had she been deceived? She said she'd been raised by Arron's grand-mother, hadn't she? Who knew what that had done to her perceptions of what Roamers were really like.

She put her hand to Arron's forehead. "Still a touch of fever. You see someone's death, no doubt." Arron tried to pull away from her, but she caught him by his upper arm.

"I remember being with your mother when she had such a fever . . . when she foresaw your father's death."

Arron's eyes opened wide, her face suddenly coming into focus in his memory. He jerked away from her. "That's enough."

"Your mother foresaw your father's death?" Chris asked in a horrified amazement.

Bess took hold of Arron's hand. "I'm sorry, dear, I didn't mean to upset you. We old people sometimes like to reminisce the tragedies. Sometimes, it seems, that's all there are."

"She didn't tell him?" Katie stood up. "If she loved him as much as Bess says, she still didn't tell him?"

Arron looked down, running his fingers through his hair.

"I'm sorry, Arron." Bess pulled him closer to her again. "It's just the memories. You and your mother stayed with me that night. She cried and cried. I couldn't get her to stop. Do you remember?"

"No!"

"You do, then. I'm sorry." She pulled him closer still. "But you do see someone's death. I recognize the fever. Who is it? Anna?" Then she looked at Chris and Katie. "Or maybe . . ."

Arron pulled back, his hands rising, a soft humming passing his lips. Chris cringed, but the Roamer bit down on his lips, and clutched his hands in his lap, surprise coloring his face at what he had been about to do.

"We're not going to talk about this. Do you understand? I'll not talk about this. I'm not like my mother," he said in a very low voice.

"Ah, but you are," she cried, looking him over again with pitying eyes. Then she shook her head. "Not a trace of your father in you. Everything is her."

"Stop it!"

She smiled gently, the lines by her mouth deepening, then she turned to Chris and Katie. "Well, now. I've been prying for a time. Why don't I tell you a bit about us? There are about fifty of us making do here. We gain some more people now and then—and lose some." She took a quick look at Arron. His eyes opened wide, and then his eyebrows came down sharply. She turned back to Chris and Katie. "But it really is wonderful here. Anna, well, I don't know what we would do without her. She has a hand in just about everything. Why, the woman never rests! No, we couldn't get along without her."

Arron got up abruptly and strode over to the window. He

stood staring out at the barren landscape, at the pitiful vege-
table garden growing below, struggling to get some nourish-
ment from the wretched soil. Some of the people who lived
here were busy chasing away the crows that haunted the
patch even in the rain, food was so scarce.

Bess sighed and smiled weakly at Chris and Katie. "Well,
are you brothers?"

"Yes."

"No."

"Same father," Katie added quickly, then turned on Chris.
"You're always like that! It's not my fault Father remarried. I
wasn't even born then!" She turned back to Bess. "He's such
a jerk sometimes! He blames me that Father married my
mother when his died."

"You wouldn't understand," Chris mumbled.

"Now, now," Bess said quietly. "It's a blessing your father
remarried. I'm sure you and your younger brother have had
some good times. Haven't you?"

Chris nodded. "Some."

"It hurts sometimes, but things are all for the best. Think
of the fun you would never have had if your father hadn't
remarried."

"Yeah, yeah." Chris turned to Katie. "Sorry." She beamed
up at him, like an adoring younger brother.

"That's it." Bess stood up. "Why don't we see about
dinner."

"Good idea," Arron said, turning away from the window,
a determined cheerfulness on his face.

XV

DINNER WAS SERVED IN A LARGE ROOM WITH MANY TA-
bles. The three newcomers sat at a long table with Anna and
Bess.

"I'm sure Bess told you all sorts of lies about me." Anna
leaned over to them, passing the meat. "I don't suppose she
said anything about herself? She started this home, you
know. Took me in after my husband died. Oh, I was a wreck.
But Bess, she can show you the right things to look for, the
way to go on being happy. She seems to be able to point out
the way to life." Bess laughed at what Anna was saying and
shook her head. Anna just waved her hand at her. "It's true.
She's given every one of us here a reason to hang on."

"Anna, you can't say I've done this all myself. You've had
the largest hand in this for quite a while. Oh, you could run it
yourself."

"Oh, no!" She paled slightly. "No, not alone. We've done
too much together."

Bess laughed again. "Oh, look at the way two old people
do go on." She shook her head again, then caught Arron's
eye. He started to look away. "Arron," she said quickly. "I
want to introduce you to Ian." She indicated a man two
chairs down. "Ian, this is Arron. He plays, you know." She

looked back at Arron. "As I recall, you were already quite accomplished at four."

"Really?" Ian leaned toward Arron. Arron turned to look at the man. Ian's chin stuck out from his face like a hook and forced his mouth into a permanent smile. Arron found himself staring uncomfortably at that.

"Yes, he was," Bess added quickly. "His mother taught him as soon as he could hold the instrument."

"Really?" Ian said excitedly, his chin bobbing. Arron pulled his eyes from it and looked into Ian's. They sparkled from a mixture of enthusiasm and extra moisture from age. Arron nodded numbly.

"You and I, then, we will do a duet after dinner?"

"Oh, yes!" Anna caught hold of Arron's hand and squeezed it. "Please, we'd love to hear it. Ian has many lutes. He's been waiting for someone else who can play." She pulled Arron closer to her. "Please. He needs you to do it," she whispered.

"I'd love to," Arron said, turning back to Ian.

"Good, good. Perhaps I may teach a bit, and we will play very well."

Arron grinned. "Very likely."

Anna clapped her hands together. "Oh, Bess! You always know what to do. To think after all these years you would remember. Ian will be so thrilled." She stood up. "Listen, everyone. Ian's finally gotten someone to play along with him tonight. That may be a relief to those of you who he's been trying to coax into learning." Some laughed, while others groaned at the memory. "So, after dinner we'll all meet in the living area and, hopefully, be entertained by Ian and Arron."

Katie nudged Arron. "Can you play a lute?"

Arron nodded slowly. "My mother taught me a lot of instruments. They're all the same in principle, mostly."

When dinner was over, Chris picked up his plates to help clear the table, but Anna snatched them away. "I'll not hear of it!"

"But you've been so kind. It's no trouble."

"Nonsense. Bess, take them into the living area. We'll all be in shortly. Now, James, put that plate down." And she turned and went into the kitchen.

"You'd do well to listen to her." Bess laughed. "Come along. If I know Ian, and I do, he'll already be scrambling about his room, gathering up his instruments and what-not."

The living room was spacious, with large, cushiony furniture. Katie sank down into one and cried out in pleasure. "Ah, this is a great way to soothe travel-worn muscles. Let's stay here forever."

"Then you wouldn't have any travel-worn muscles to soothe, you lunk." Chris flopped down next to her. "Hey! This is great. I agree, let's stay here forever."

Ian came scuttling down the stairs the next moment, hugging two instruments to his chest and a whole bunch of sheet music. Some of it got loose and floated down about his feet. He stood staring miserably at it, clinging tighter to what was in his arms, causing more to fall. Arron knelt down and quickly scooped up the sheets, then gingerly took the rest from the man's hands.

"I've got them."

Ian nodded and followed Arron to the two chairs set out in front. He put an instrument on each chair, then rifled through the sheet music. "We will try something simple, and I will see what I may teach. Then, when the kitchen cleaning is done, we will be ready to play."

"Okay." Arron looked over the music Ian had selected.

"This is for you to play." Ian handed him the lighter-colored instrument. "I played it at your age." Arron took it slowly. Then the two of them sat down.

"On the four, then," Ian said, sitting spritelike on the edge of his seat. "One, two, a one, two, three, four . . ."

Katie smiled at the melody they played. It was charming in a way. The two instruments seemed to chase each other's melodies as if in and out among the trees. She thought about the picnic they'd all had, running about the mountain until— she glanced at Chris. He was rubbing his shoulder thoughtfully. The melody stopped, and she and Bess and Chris clapped. Ian bowed, beaming, then turned to Arron.

"You play better than at first I thought."

"I told you, Ian, he was very good at four," Bess said.

Ian nodded gravely. "Perhaps you will teach me."

Arron laughed at that. "I don't think so. I believe you are in fact my master. The music you've written is beautiful."

"But this is nothing!" Ian pushed the sheet away.

"Play some more, please," Katie said, sitting up somewhat. "Arron can do it, Ian. And I want to hear more."

"We will play this." Ian slid some new music before Arron, who quickly looked it over and nodded. "One, two, a one, two, three, four . . ."

The music flew along happily, a couple dancing in front of a fire, the flames warm, happy, the house clean, safe, the music dancing with the pair, joy in everything. Chris nodded and smiled at Katie. She smiled shyly back.

The tune smoothed into a wonderful contentment as the two melodies bound together and joined into one. Quite suddenly, one instrument slowed and all but stopped, becoming a background melody of sadness, and Arron's went on in anguish, so suddenly alone.

Arron stopped and turned away. Ian struck an off chord and looked up in surprise. "Too difficult?"

"No, no. I'm sorry, Mousikos."

Ian stared a moment. "But—but why do you call me that? My wife called me that . . ." Arron cringed against the instrument, shaking his head.

"It was beautiful," Katie whispered.

"Sad." Chris nodded.

Bess sat nearer to them. "He wrote it after his wife died. A duet. But no one could play but him . . ."

"You do not like it?" Ian asked a bit timidly, staring at Arron, who crouched over his instrument.

"No, it's beautiful."

"We will play something else."

"No!" Arron turned to him. "No, no, we'll finish this. I'm sorry; we'll finish. I'm a little tired, that's all. Let's start again." He nodded to Ian, who nodded back. They raised their instruments together.

This time the listeners could make out an undertone of longing in the happy part that they had missed the first time, not knowing what was to come. The tune was a memory after all. Ian's cheeks were wet with tears as they made their way to the end, but his mouth, as always, smiled. Arron kept his head down.

The music faded off slowly, Arron's anguished melody fading, at last, into Ian's, and they both ended. The applause startled them. Chris and Katie turned to see that the others had joined them.

"Oh, Ian, that was beautiful!" Anna wiped her eyes and clapped again.

Ian nodded and squeezed Arron's shoulder. "We will play something lighter for our audience, eh, Arron, my boy?" He changed the music before them when Arron nodded, still not looking up.

"Ready? Okay. One, two, a one, two, three, four . . ." And off they went, all trace of sadness gone. Katie thought that the tune must have been one Ian had written while his wife was still alive. She tried to imagine him young, dancing to this before the fire. But she only saw her own self, old and unwell, alone. She looked over at Chris.

"Dance?" he whispered.

"With your brother?" she whispered back, very slowly.

Chris made a face, then stood and turned to Anna, bowing. She laughed at him, then the two of them danced out onto the floor. Other couples joined them quickly. Bess walked over to Katie, who was watching the people dancing and laughing.

"Come on, James, don't be shy."

Katie shrugged and stood, then imitated Chris' bow, and she and Bess joined the other dancers on the floor.

The dancing went on late into the night until, exhausted, they all flopped down on the couches, too tired to crawl upstairs.

"It has been long since I have played such music." Ian laughed, his hand lovingly stroking the lute in his lap.

"It's been long for me, too." Arron smiled over at the old man. "Your music, it's so full of life—"

Ian held up his hand, wrinkled, but strong from playing. "You made it such. I only wish you wouldn't leave. To play like this every night, it would be like before."

"Perhaps I'll come back, sometime."

"And perhaps I will not be here when you do."

"I wish you wouldn't—"

Ian put a hand gently on his arm. "It is only because you are so young. There are things much more frightening to those of us who are old. Do not think of it as bad."

Arron sighed and nodded slowly, then looked about the room at the quiet clusters lying about. "I think they've had enough of our music."

"And I've had enough playing. I must go to bed. Good night, Arron. Sleep well." He carefully gathered up his things and made his way upstairs. Arron watched him a moment, then stood up and stretched. Bess got up quickly and came over to him. Seeing her approach, Arron turned to go, but she touched him lightly on his arm to stop him.

"Thank you. You made him very happy."

"His music is beautiful. I wish I could write music like that."

"Your mother did. She wrote a lovely song about your father. Do you remember?"

"Yes." Arron answered slowly, as Chris got up and wandered over to them.

"I wish she'd saved that music for you. She ripped it up that night."

Arron stared at Bess, horror slowly changing his expression.

"I tried my best to help her. She was so upset. She loved your father so much. It hurt me to see her like that. Her pain was killing her."

"You told her to tell my father." Arron's eyes were opening wider.

Bess looked down. "You inherited that, too, then."

"How could you? Do you know what that might have— You had to know she might have been weak." Arron watched her. "You knew she *was* weak."

"Now, Arron, what's so wrong with telling? She loved him so much. She would have died without him."

"And now! Now you're trying to play on me, to find my weakness!" He leaned toward her violently, as if he were going to strike her. Chris reached forward to stop him, but the Roamer drew back from her on his own. "I'm not like my mother," he whispered. "Do you know what could have happened if she'd told? Do you?" He clutched his hands firmly in front of himself. "But I think you do know what happened because she was going to tell. Because of you! You do know what happened, don't you? Well, don't you?" He turned and dashed up the stairs.

Bess looked down at her hands, then took a deep breath and looked at Chris. "Well," she said softly. "I'm afraid James has fallen asleep." She pointed to Katie.

Chris nodded. "Yeah. I'll carry him upstairs. He's not one for endurance, I guess. Good night, Bess, and thanks."

"Good night, Chris, and . . . please, have a word with Arron. I didn't mean to upset him so. It's time he got some things out of his system." She paused. "I wanted him, you know, to bring him up, that is. When his mother . . . died, I offered to take him. I pleaded with his father. That old woman . . . I was afraid she would bind him the way she bound her daughter, his mother. So many mistakes. It's wrong. Wrong and they can't see it. Oh, and especially wrong what that old woman did to that poor boy. So gifted, and she's twisted him so. Teach him, Chris. She taught him too much about death. Show him life." She turned away from him and walked over to Anna. Chris rubbed at his shoulder, then went to Katie, knelt down next to her, and lifted her up. She opened her eyes in surprise.

"Awake?"

"Mm-hmm, barely," she murmured as Chris started up the stairs. "I can walk, please."

Chris shrugged and lowered her to the steps. "They all think you're a little boy," he whispered.

"Well, there's not much to indicate otherwise." She gave a sharp laugh that made Chris look at her, sensing her bitterness. "There never really was."

He stared at her as they climbed the stairs. She was small, all around, and strong, amazingly so for her small size, like a little boy would be, one trying to be a man. "Well, I know you're a girl."

She just nodded.

"Just because you're not—well, you know—that doesn't mean anything. You're just as much a girl as, say, Sarah Anne. Just because you don't always act it—"

"Chris, please."

Chris shrugged. "Sorry, I was just—"

"I know!" She walked into their room without looking at him.

Arron was already there, sitting over in the corner, his kithara cradled in his lap. He was playing, softly, one of the songs he and Ian had played earlier.

"Drowning your sorrows?" Chris said, standing in the doorway. Katie's sharpness still stung him.

Arron looked up at him and stopped playing. "I guess I am." He shrugged, then slid the kithara into its case.

"Bess wanted me to—" Arron cut him off. "I'm going to bed." Arron cut him off. "I'm tired."

"She says you're wrong, Arron. Your grandmother lied to you. It's not—"

"What does she know?" Arron turned on him.

"Arron—" Katie stepped toward him.

"And you leave my grandmother alone," Arron snapped, ignoring Katie.

Chris walked slowly into the room, watching the Roamer. How anyone could think Arron was a Homesteader was beyond him. His dark eyes glared so from his impassive face. The hair, now, seemed to do nothing for a disguise. "Is Bess right, then? Do you see someone's death?"

"I am not going to talk about this. Good night!" He sat down heavily on his bed.

"How can you be like that? Someone is going to die, and you can stop it! How can you be so inhuman?"

"I'm a Roamer, remember!" Arron snapped his head up, then something gave way in his face, and he turned away, burying his head in his hands.

"Hey . . ." Katie reached out to him, but he shrugged her hand off his shoulder.

"I don't believe your mother wouldn't tell your father." Chris walked around the bed to face Arron. "I just don't believe that."

"Chris . . ." Katie looked at him pleadingly.

Arron pressed his hands to his ears. "I don't want to hear it."

"I can't understand how you can just let them die. You

saw how much everyone loves Anna. She'll do more good if she's alive. They need her." Chris knelt down in front of Arron. "Listen, I'm not trying to bully you. I understand that this is what your grandmother taught you. Okay? I'm just trying to get things clear between us." Arron looked at him now, nodding. "Now, look. If what you say about my grandfather is true, well, that wouldn't happen with Anna. You know it won't. She's so good. Maybe Chruston wasn't so good, but Anna wouldn't be like that—"

"I'm not like my mother. I'm not like Shakta. I'm not like them," Arron whispered softly.

"Chris, let him be." Katie tried to pull him away from Arron.

"Why? He should tell her. I think he should tell her. Who does he think he is? His mother was going to tell. Bess said she was. Why didn't she?"

Arron closed his eyes tightly, to block them out. But the darkness only pulled him away from himself. And he couldn't remember where he was, the voices buzzing around him and in his head. Then the wagon was very dark. But, no, there was a light, at the table. Grandmother and Mother were there, eating. He had sat on the tall stool and watched Grandmother make the food, adding powder from a bottle he had firmly been instructed never to touch. Grandmother wasn't eating, she was talking, quickly. And her thoughts were nowhere, he couldn't find them. Mother was eating.

She stood up, grabbing at her throat, her stomach. Her eyes stared at Grandmother. "I wouldn't have told," she gasped.

"I see Shakta in you," the old woman said.

"I tell you, I wouldn't have—oh!" She was clawing at her stomach now, her knees buckling. Grandmother looked away, but he could only stare.

"Please . . ." his mother begged, falling on her side, shivering. Wide eyes caught at his, and she reached for him, pulling him tight against her twitching body. Her arms tightened once, convulsively, trying to take him with her, then they relaxed, loose, limp, like thick ropes.

He felt his grandmother's arms encircle him, pulling him from his mother. She was crying, and inside she was cursing the world for what it had made her do. Hating. Hating. "Don't be weak, like them. If you must have the gift, pray the weakness did not come with it."

"Arron?" Arron opened his eyes. She had her arms about his shoulders. He stared at her, blinking.

"Grandmother?"

"Arron?" Katie shook him slightly.

"Ka—" He sat a moment trying to place himself again, then pulled away. "Good night."

"Just like that?" Chris stared, incredulous.

"Just like that." Arron rolled over. "I'm not going to breakfast tomorrow."

Chris strode over to him, but Katie caught at his arm. "Leave him be."

"But—"

"Let him alone, Chris. We don't understand, so we can't judge."

"I think I understand quite well. Someone's going to die, and he doesn't give a damn. Just like for poor old Durth, remember?"

"Does he really look like he doesn't care?"

Chris turned away. "Then how can he let them die?"

"Everyone has to die sometime."

"Why?" He turned to Arron when she didn't answer. "How can you not tell them if you really, truly care? Didn't Bess convince your mother to tell your father because of her love for him? Isn't that what Bess said?"

"Yes."

"And didn't your mother tell him?"

"No."

"Well, why not?" Chris demanded.

"Chris, please," Katie begged him. Arron only pulled the blankets tighter about himself.

"I'm asking you a question." Chris leaned over him.

"One that isn't any of your damn business!"

Chris grabbed Arron and forced him up. "You had better tell us, Roamer. You wouldn't be so closed about it if it weren't some horrible Roamer deed, something you know would turn us against you."

"Chris, leave him alone!"

Chris leaned closer to Arron. "But you'd probably lie to us anyway, wouldn't you?" Arron's mouth fell open a moment, then he snapped it shut, anger and hatred growing in his face.

"I haven't lied to you. Not once!" He pulled out of Chris' grasp.

"Then tell us, damn you, why didn't your mother tell?"

Arron bolted upright. "Because my grandmother killed her before she could do it! There! Is that what you wanted to hear? How barbaric the Roamers are? It is and you know it. But maybe, through all your horror and disgust, you can see how important it was for my mother not to tell. Her own mother killed her!" He sobbed, finishing, then cut it off, turning over. "Goddamned Shakta curse!" He pushed his face deeply into the pillow.

"Oh, Arron." Katie went over to him.

"Leave me alone," he screamed from the depths of the pillow. "You've done enough. Just leave me alone!"

"How can you be sure that—" Chris started.

"Chris," Katie said sternly. "I'd like you to fix up some sort of separation here. I'd like a little privacy." Chris looked at her and then at Arron. "Please."

He rubbed his shoulder, then nodded and went to get a rope from his pack and a blanket from the bed.

Katie opened her eyes and stared at the blanket that hung between the beds. She traced the pattern on it with her eyes for a bit, then got up and got dressed. She could hear the faint sounds below of people working in the kitchen, the banging and clattering of pots and pans at odd intervals, and the steady breathing on the other side of the blanket. She drew it back and saw Chris sleeping soundly, one foot sticking out of the blankets. Arron's bed was empty.

"Chris! Chris!" Katie caught hold of his shoulders and shook him.

"What! What?"

"Arron's gone."

"What!" He leaped out of bed and began digging through his pack. "Damn! Why'd we trust him? Why? I should've turned him in when I had the chance. Now he's taken it and run off."

Katie sat down on his bed, her reason returning as her surprise wore off. "His pack is still here. He wouldn't leave that. And his kithara."

"Well, he's taken my box! I don't trust him. He lies. He's a Roamer."

"Chris, it's in the bottom pouch. You moved it last night after Arron fell asleep."

Chris pulled it out meekly. "Oh, yeah."

"Chris, why won't you tell me what's wrong? You've been acting so strangely, downright nasty sometimes. The way you were driving into Arron last night . . . You could see he was upset. I don't blame him for running off this morning."

"Katie, that could all be an act. Likely he's playing at being something he isn't just to deceive us."

"I think he was upset for real last night."

"But you're not sure, are you?"

"No, of course not. How could I be?" She shook her head. "But . . . I don't know. Chris, what if it is true? You're too hard on him. You were never like that before. You always seemed to want to care." She turned to undo the rope, then she folded the blanket and threw it onto Chris' bed. "It seems now you want to do just the opposite. You seem to see only the things that make you distrust him and you drive into him so that all he can do is be nasty back. I think it just takes some time to understand."

"Do you know how my father died?" Chris asked.

"My father said he was hunting, and his gun backfired."

"Hunting what?"

Katie turned to him, coiling up the rope, unsure where he was trying to lead the conversation.

"He was trying to kill Arron," Chris said, seeing her loss. "And Arron foresaw the gun backfiring. But did he utter a word? No! Nothing. He just let him shoot . . ." He turned to stare out the window. "My father, Katie. He just let my father die. How could he do that? And right before that, my father had said that Arron and I were . . ." Chris bowed his head, pressing the palms of his hands against the glass.

"Well . . ." Katie started and stopped.

Chris turned back to her. "What would you do if he foresaw my death? What if it was really horrible? Worse than getting your head blown off, like my father, or worse than dying like he says his grandmother did. What would you do if he wasn't going to tell me?" He leaned toward her. "Hmmm?"

"Chris, please. I don't know. Right now I'd be logical, but that's emotional—so just stop it."

Chris stared at her, puzzled. "What are you so afraid of?"

A light tapping came on the door and Bess peeked in. "Morning. How did you all sleep?"

Katie turned to her. "Great. Billions of times better than sleeping on the ground."

"Where's Arron? He's not still upset with me from last night, is he?"

"He . . . uh . . ." Chris started.

"He hardly ever eats breakfast. I guess he went for a walk." Katie shrugged.

"Ah, I see. Oh well, he'll miss one terrific meal. Come on down whenever you're ready." She smiled and closed the door.

"Well, get dressed, and I'll see you down there." Katie quickly went out the door, closing it softly behind her.

"Okay," Chris said to the closed door.

It was in his mind that he saw Anna as she stumbled up the stairs and pushed her way into her room. He watched her now in the dark; she didn't bother with the lamp and left the drapes closed. An odd wailing from below followed her into the room. She pressed the door closed and wove her way to the desk. She struggled with the top drawer, pulling on it, tugging it. Oh, it was stuck! Jerk it open! She was groping inside; he could feel her trembling hands grasping the smooth handle of the knife, one she had put in the back long ago. She pulled it out and held it up, staring at it. He saw in her mind, her husband had made it. He had carved the handle, made it silky smooth. He had said he didn't want anything to ever hurt her. No blisters for his wife, no pain, not ever—not so long as he was around to keep her safe, he had promised her. But he'd died. Oh, he'd died!

She was turning the blade slowly in her hands. A thin stream of light coming in through the crack in the curtains glinted off the shiny metal and illuminated the face that was watching her from across the room.

"Oh!" She dropped it. The knife thunked hollowly against the papers stacked in an even pile in front of her. She glared at Arron, sitting curled up in a chair across from her. "You . . . you weren't at breakfast," she accused.

"I know what happened."

She nodded, accepting this, then quickly put her hands over the blade, as if to lean on the desk. "I'd rather be alone right now."

"Why don't you cry?"

"I said, I'd like to be alone!"

Arron jumped up and caught her small, wrinkled hands between his. She tried to pull away. "I'm not going to let you do it, Anna. There are other people besides yourself."

"Damn you! I need to be left alone!"

"That's just it. You don't want to be alone. I'm not going to let you. I'm going to stay here until you know you're not."

"I said! I–I said . . ." She sat down slowly in her chair. Arron leaned over the desk with her, still holding her hands as she began to cry.

"Oh, she left me. She left me!" Anna shook her head back and forth, back and forth. "I can't do it by myself. I can't! She was always there when I needed her. Always with a good word, a good thought, a direction. Now I'm alone. Oh, God!"

"It's all right. You're not alone, not really. You'll get along."

"No! No! I don't want to! Don't you see! Can't you see? She was the one who mattered, not me! When I met you on the road, I was thinking, Thank God it was me who went for the groceries and not her. She might have been killed in that cart. I was thinking . . . She would've left–left me alone!"

"Anna, I know. I know." He let go of her hands and straightened up. "But there are some people downstairs who are as confused and frightened as you are. But you're the only one with the authority to pull them together. Bess expected that from you, she was counting on you."

"No! I can't! Why don't you see that? They'll all go. One by one, as I get close to them. One by one they'll leave me!"

Arron slammed his hands down on the desk. "No, they won't! Not all of them. Some will, sure. But, Anna, they need you. They need you right now, and you're failing them, and you're failing Bess."

"I don't care. I don't care. I don't want to be alone. Old and alone."

She leaned back in her chair and stared at the ceiling. "When I was young—and I was once, you know—my grandmother, she used to just stare out the window and mutter names. I used to dream that it was me, muttering names in the dark, all alone. I prayed to God I would die when I was thirty. Why couldn't I have? Well, I want to die now."

"You don't want to be alone!" Arron swung the door open again so she could hear the people crying below. "They all depended on Bess, like you. They all did. Now they're waiting for you. You won't be alone down there." He pressed the door closed so that it grew dark again. Only the thin slit of light from the curtains vaguely illuminated his face. She was shaking her head.

"Anna . . ."

"Let me alone!" She grabbed up the knife suddenly.

He jumped forward, catching at her hands. He jerked her toward him, yanking her halfway over the desk. "If you die up here, damn you, you'll be alone *forever!* I promise you. I'll make sure of it!"

Anna's eyes opened wide as she stared at the sudden demon before her, gripping her wrists tightly, till her fingers grew numb. His eyes were so dark as they glared at her, blacker than the ravens that croaked out on the fence. He stood over her, sucking in the darkness of the room, standing out blacker than it all, vengeful and evil. "Wh–what are you?" she whispered faintly. The knife clattered to the floor, her fingers losing all feeling.

He released her immediately, backing up. "What do you mean?" His left hand clenched his right, trying to stop the flow of blood from where he had cut himself when he had grabbed for her. He became once again the young boy she had met on the road, in pain and needing help, looking more frightened than she had imagined him frightening. She reached vaguely for him. He pulled farther away.

"Anna, don't you see? You're just like your grandmother when you sit up here, muttering empty names. Come downstairs," he pleaded. "They need you so much. And you have to find someone, like Bess found you, someone to take your place when you go. And you will. Everyone . . ." he paused. "Everyone does."

She hesitated, listening to the confusion below. She nodded and stood up, reaching for his hand. "Let me help you first."

He pulled back and shook his head. "It's okay. I'm all right."

Anna frowned. "You're like Bess. Helping, but unwilling to ask for any yourself. Unwilling to take it if it's offered. Did she ever feel alone? I wonder. She never told me." She wiped a tear away. "Help me down the stairs, will you?" Arron took her arm very slowly. His right hand dripped blood onto the carpet.

"You're very strange," she said softly as he led her down the steps. "I can't place why, but part of me thinks you're not seeing things where I see them. In some ways, that's good—but there is the other side. You may not see the obvious." She stopped at the bottom of the stairs and took his face in her hands. "I'm afraid of you," she said frankly. "I came down here because you frighten me." She paused. "And in this case, you are also right." She looked about at the clusters of people, all sobbing and looking bewildered. "They do need me. And I really need them."

Chris and Katie had started over toward them. Anna saw them and took Arron's hand. Before he could protest she bound her handkerchief around it. "You're afraid, too. I can feel it," she said, then kissed him gently on the cheek. "You are like Bess, giving me a direction." She turned away from him and went to the closest group and put her arms about them.

Chris and Katie reached the stairs. Chris grabbed Arron by his upper arm and began pushing him up the steps.

"Hey, cut it out, that hurts," Arron said, trying to resist.

"Good!" Chris shoved him into their room. Katie followed. She couldn't look Arron in the eye so, instead, chose to stare out the window. Chris forced Arron down onto the bed.

"Well, you got your petty revenge, didn't you?"

"What are you talking about?"

"Oh, yes, you did save yourself from the show, didn't you. While all those other people had to watch her choke to death at breakfast! How could you? I could kill you!"

"I had nothing to do with—"

"You knew, didn't you?"

Arron kept quiet.

"Didn't you?"

"Yes."

"Then you could have saved her!"

"No! No, I couldn't! It's wrong. It's wrong!"

"No, Arron!" Katie spun around. "You're wrong! What you're doing just can't be right. If I saw a man about to be bitten by a snake, and I had a gun . . . shouldn't I kill that snake? Shouldn't I?"

"Oh, no, Katie, this is different," Chris said, mocking bitterly. "Oh, so different!" He spun on Arron. "This was for you! You wanted her dead because you blame her for your mother's death, don't you? Blame her, instead of the person who really killed her."

"I don't have to take this." Arron stood up, but Chris shoved him back down.

"Yes, you know it's true. Now, if it had been someone else, someone who meant something to you—if anyone does— well, then, the story would have been different, wouldn't it? Wouldn't it!"

"No, it wouldn't! You don't know what you're talking about."

"And all those people had to sit there and watch her die! That's why you didn't go to breakfast, so you wouldn't have to see it and suffer like the rest of us. We're all going to keep on seeing her—seeing her die—like that. But not you, oh no, you saved yourself from that!"

"You think I didn't see it? I saw the whole thing in more detail than you ever will! I have a memory of more deaths than you can even imagine. And a memory of their pain and fear, and the pain and fear of all the people who loved them! Don't tell me about your painful memories!"

"Stop it! Both of you!" Katie pushed Chris off Arron.

"This can't be right, Arron. It was so . . . horrible. It just can't be," she pleaded with him.

"I only know what I've been taught!" He folded his arms firmly across his chest.

"And I know what I've been taught!" Chris pushed Katie out of the way. "All life is precious."

"And so is the ability to die!"

"Well, I'm not so sure that ability is lost by being saved from a horrible death. Old age will take over where accident hasn't."

Arron threw his hands up into the air. "So? What are you going to do? I won't tell. Ever! No matter whose death it is." He looked at Katie, and she looked away. "So? What are you going to do?"

Chris rubbed his shoulder, frustrated. "What if there is no Chruston?"

"There is."

"Well, what if there isn't? That means this is all untrue. Then will you tell?"

"Yes."

"Okay, then we'll find who's leading this Dempter guy, and if it's not Chruston, then—then will you tell?"

"Yes."

Chris nodded. "Okay, then we'll find him. And then you'll see what's right."

XVI

"ARE YOU SURE YOU KNOW THE WAY?" CHRIS ASKED, poking at the fire. It had been two weeks since they'd left Anna's. They'd stayed for the funeral, and Anna was so nice to Arron, it rankled Chris. But then she didn't know the whole story about Arron anyway.

"Yes, I know the way."

"It all looks alike." Katie said, gazing around, her eyes briefly falling on the trail they had been following. It was merely a faint etching in the brambles they had been pushing through.

"Well, it doesn't if you've traveled a lot, like I have. Roamers move around a bit, you know."

"You couldn't get a wagon through here," Chris muttered.

"We don't always take our wagons."

"Why do Roamers move around so much?" Katie asked, tilting Arron's head with her left hand as she trimmed his hair. He would have to wear a hat after this.

Arron shrugged. "Oh, I don't know. We learn too much about the people around us, I suppose. Get bored with them."

"Learn when they're going to die and don't want to face the fact that you don't want to tell them," Chris murmured.

"Look!" Arron started forward.

Katie held the scissors up, almost cutting him when he moved so suddenly. "Shhhh!" She snipped the scissors closed with a snap. "Listen . . ." Chris and Arron fell silent, trying to hear what Katie heard. Chris peered through the thick undergrowth, trying to see into the gray, tangled mass of thorns.

"I don't hear anything," he whispered.

Arron listened a moment longer. "Nor do I."

Katie shrugged. "I heard voices. Maybe you two are making me go crazy!" She snipped quickly at Arron's hair. Arron sat nervously still until she calmed down, then he smiled sheepishly at Chris.

"Hey, I'm sorry."

Chris nodded. "Me, too. Sorry."

"You're done," Katie said, stepping back.

Chris groaned. "Oh, God, you look like a Roamer again."

"This will help." Katie pulled a hat down over his head, covering the dark top.

"A little," Chris murmured.

Arron took the scissors. "Thanks. Shall I do yours?"

Katie thought about it a moment and ran a hand through her hair. It was still short enough to pass for a little while. "No," she said softly.

"It's not really safe out here—"

"What do you want her to cut it for?" Chris snapped. "Just because you don't want to be the only one living a lie?"

Arron pointed to his hair. "This was your idea, not mine."

"I did it for your safety."

"And I'm doing it for hers."

"It's short enough," Katie cut in. "No one is going to think I'm a girl, so stop arguing about it!" She turned and walked back into the brambles.

"Katie . . ." Chris scrambled to his feet.

"Let her alone for a while."

"But—"

"She can take care of herself."

Chris stared at where she had gone, then sighed and sat back down and began poking at the fire again. Arron pulled the hat off his head and lay back on his blanket.

"You sure you know where we're going?" Chris asked after a moment.

"Yes."

Chris stirred the fire a moment more. "Well, why'd we leave the road? It was going north, wasn't it?"

Arron sat up slowly. "But we want to go northwest. We went east for a while, remember?"

"Yes, I remember! But this all seems so roundabout!"

"You didn't want to be on the road when we were! And now, when we're off it, what are you complaining about? No road! Damn! I can't do anything right, can I?" Arron got up and strode back and forth in front of the fire a moment, then he dropped to his knees beside Chris. "Tell me," he pleaded. "I'll do it. What do you want from me?"

Chris got up. "I'm going to find Katie."

"Don't you leave here without answering me! You answer! I'm asking you," Arron shouted from where he was kneeling. Chris hesitated at the edge of the firelight.

"There's nothing you can do." He turned to follow where Katie had gone.

"Someday," Arron warned, "someday, and I hope to God it's soon, you're going to feel this. You're going to feel what it's like not to know where to step, not to know what to say, to be unsure. You'll be all alone. Ask me for help then!"

"Is that a threat or a prophecy?"

Arron stared at him a moment and then looked away. "That is a prayer," he whispered.

"Katie? Katie!" Chris called out to her, trying to pick his way through the thorns.

"Shhh!" Katie came up against him suddenly.

"What?"

"Shhhh!" She put her hand up sharply, then indicated for him to follow. Chris crept behind her and peered through the brush to where she pointed.

There was a large group of men camping out in what had to be a graveyard. The earth came up in mounds with small doors in the sides as if for the dead to walk out.

"Who are they?" Chris whispered. Katie shrugged. Some of the men were arguing amongst themselves, others were cooking over one of the many campfires scattered among the graves. Some of the men were even sleeping, apparently unconcerned about the proximity of the dead.

"There's a lot of them."

Katie nodded, then her mouth fell open. Chris followed her stare to one of the clusters of men. A man staggered away from them, a knife sticking from his chest, and collapsed, blood spurting everywhere. Chris went to cover Katie's eyes. She pushed his hands away impatiently. One of the men pulled the knife from the man, pushed him out of the circle of their firelight, and bent to scoop up the dead man's belongings.

"Let's get out of here," Katie whispered. "They're just a band of thieves. I don't think it would be a good idea to get involved with that." She turned and crept away. Chris followed.

They burst back into the camp. Arron looked up from the fire. "Let's get out of here," Katie said quickly. "There's a band of thieves or something over to our left."

Arron stood up. "At the barrows?"

"Yes," Chris said guardedly. "How did you know about that?"

"Because I've been there before." He paused a moment, thinking. "Yeah, it probably is thieves. They use the barrows as a campsite because it's safer for them. No one would bother them there—"

"Well, let's get out of here." Chris started kicking out the fire.

"Don't! Don't." Arron pulled him away.

"Why not? Do you want them to know we're here?"

"They already do. Do you think they didn't see it already? If you kick it out, they'll know we're leaving. Just clear away the brush and let's go."

They quickly gathered up their packs, and Arron led them away from the fire. They picked their way along the path that only the Roamer seemed to see. Then Arron stopped so abruptly that Chris and Katie, tight on his heels, banged into him. They peered fearfully around him and made out a large group of men in front of him.

"Is there something I can do for you?" Arron asked in a steady voice.

"Yeah." The man in front grinned. Two teeth were missing, as if they had been knocked out in a fight. He was heavy and dirty. "We'd like to have a look through your packs."

"No!" Katie stepped forward angrily.

The men all laughed. "Pretty spunky, boy. Maybe we'll let you join us, instead of—but we always need a few good laughs." Chris pulled her back against him.

"We don't have anything you'd want except maybe food and water. You're welcome to that," Chris said.

The front man smiled again. "I think we'll decide what we want and what we're welcome to." He looked from Chris to Katie to Arron. "So, let's have it." Arron watched them all a moment, then unslung his pack and set it on the ground.

"What are you doing?" Katie snapped.

"He's being smart." The front man laughed at her and bent eagerly to the pack. Arron grabbed him and pulled him against himself, his knife to the man's throat.

"Now we'll talk."

"Wait—wait now, boy," the man stammered.

The other men stepped forward.

"Get back or I'll kill him! I've done it before, so don't think that I won't.

The men looked at each other. Arron froze in surprise. They didn't care. It hadn't occurred to him that they wouldn't have any concern for the man's life. At the moment, the only ones who cared if the man lived, Arron realized, were the man—and Chris. Arron glanced at Chris, who stared back with cold eyes. Arron looked quickly back to the other men, daring them forward. He saw they held back only out of surprise. No Homesteader would do what he was doing.

"Listen—listen to me, boy. What's your name now? Maybe we can work something out," the man in his arms was saying.

Arron pushed the man away from him. "Go on, I'm not going to kill you." He looked back at Chris again, then pulled his pack closer. "But don't touch my pack." The men laughed again, and one of them swung his rifle up.

"No!" Chris jumped forward to block Arron.

The front man knocked the gun away. "Cut it out."

"We're going to do it anyway, Brades," the man sneered, picking up his gun.

"Brades?" Arron looked more closely at the man.

"Yes, that's my name."

"You . . . you knew my father then."

"Oh, yeah?" Brades eyed him unconvinced.

"Deruth. Do you remember him?"

"Yeah." Brades nodded, still eyeing Arron. "But . . ." He caught Arron roughly under the chin and forced his head up to see his eyes in the moonlight. "You were the little three-year-old boy?"

"Six years old." Arron pulled back from him, watching the other men who were shuffling about behind him. They were curious about this. It might mean more for them—or more fun.

"In your mother's arms."

"I think I was clinging to my grandmother's skirt."

Brades nodded. "Yeah, you're him all right. Yeah, I knew your father, but I was paying off a debt when I hid you all. I don't owe you a thing now."

"I could've killed you a minute ago."

Brades stood a moment, watching Arron, and something, a memory perhaps, came dimly to the man's eyes. He smiled suddenly and slapped Arron heartily on the back. "Okay, you're safe then."

A large, red-bearded man pushed past Brades and took Arron by the arm as if to welcome him. "I think we ought to have your friends stay with us for the evening. They might need some protection from thieves." More laughter, and the other men agreed.

"No, we really have to go." Arron tried to pull his arm from the man's grip.

"Oh, no, no. We insist you stay with us. It's late." The man's eyes locked with his. Arron shivered, seeing something in them that the others couldn't see—all the people the man had killed; the ways he had killed them.

Arron turned to Chris and Katie, raising his hand slightly in question. Should he do something? Chris scowled and shook his head fiercely. He wouldn't have any more of the Roamer's magic. The Roamer had promised. Katie made no response at all.

"We insist." The man touched the knife at his belt lightly.

"All right, then," Arron agreed.

Brades pushed the man away. "As my guests." He led the three of them back toward the barrows, keeping his body between them and the other men, as if he were protecting a treasure. He pushed them toward one of the fires at the center of the yard and sat them at the doorway to one of the graves. Katie hunched down, her back to the door. It looked as if it had been recently opened. Chris sat quite close to her, and Arron on the other side. The other men stood about, watching them.

"Excuse me, sir?" Chris said slowly. "But . . . what are you going to do with us?" He pulled Katie closer to him.

"Just stick with me, boys, and you'll be all right."

"What do you mean?" Katie asked.

"I mean stick close to me."

Katie looked around at all the men scrambling about trying to find a place within the firelight. Their shadows flew up over the graves as if they were ghosts, arising at the intrusion. Brades grabbed her roughly by the shoulder and pivoted her to look at him. "Keep your eyes here, boy!"

"But—"

"But nothing. Take my advice and don't notice nothing. Just keep your concentration right in our own little circle here." He stabbed a stubby finger into the ground in front of him. "They'll take notice of you watching 'em. Trust me, you don't want 'em to notice you. That's the last thing you want. I seen 'em do some things that I can't speak of to one so young. Give you nightmares for the rest of your life. And they'd just love any excuse to do them things to you, being so little and all."

Katie nodded, looking down.

Arron leaned closer to Brades. "You have no authority over them."

"We have no leader. Just mutual respect."

"They were going to let me kill you. You call that respect?"

"Don't make me angry, boy!"

"I'm just trying to make our situation clear—to both of us." Arron pulled his pack closer. "As soon as they get their courage up, they'll kill us all."

"Really?" Katie sat up.

"Really."

"But . . . but he knew your father." Chris pointed at Brades.

"He has no pull with these men."

"Well, what do they think we've got?" Katie asked. "We don't have anything!"

"They think we do, because Brades got so protective. You see, they know he would never do that unless we had something he wanted." Arron eyed Brades a moment, then rubbed his eyes with his fingertips, sighing.

"Well, why'd you ask him for help, if he can't help us?" Chris said sharply.

"I thought he was their leader. I made a mistake."

"What happened to your farsightedness?" Chris turned on him angrily.

"I told you that it doesn't work that way, so just shut up."

Katie stared at Brades a moment. "Why are you helping us? You said you paid your debt."

"It's the least I could do," Brades said softly. "I remember his family pretty well. They were a good group."

Arron narrowed his eyes. "That's very kind of you." He tapped his boot. "And you can be sure I'll reward you for any further kindnesses."

"You're just as bad as anyone here," Chris said, watching Arron's hand as it tapped against the boot.

"Perhaps you should have let them shoot me?"

"Next time I'll remember!"

"Cut it out!" Katie snapped. "All you ever do is fight. I don't know what's wrong with you!"

"Shhh," Brades said nervously. The three of them looked up at a small gathering of men.

"Once they get a group large enough for their own safety, they'll go for us," Arron whispered.

Chris closed his eyes, resting his hand on the pouch with his box.

"There's only three of us," Katie said confused. "Why don't they go for us now?"

"They're not afraid of us," Arron whispered. "They're afraid of each other. You see, they all want whatever it is Brades wants from us, but they need a group large enough to protect them from the rest of the thieves once they get whatever it is."

"I just wish they were afraid of us," Chris said miserably. "Then I doubt they could get enough men together who would trust each other."

"Afraid of you." Brades looked at Chris, then at Arron, and back to Chris. "Hey, I think you just said the key words here, boy."

Brades stood and glared at the tightly clustered group of men. "We know what you're fixing to do, Ganche," he said to the tall man who had insisted they stay.

"Don't!" Arron scrambled to his feet.

Brades caught his arm and pulled him forward. "This is what I'm talking about, right here. I know because I knew his father. With the hat you can't tell." Brades pulled it off. "This here's a Roamer."

The men grew silent and formed a ring about them, staring blankly at Arron. "Don't you know what that means?" Brades said to them.

"Yeah, there's a reward out for them. You wanted to keep it for yourself, eh, Brades? But now that boy's going to make us all rich. Dead or alive." Ganche grinned. His teeth looked incredibly white through his beard.

"No, that's not what I mean. I mean, well, didn't I ever tell you what his father done for me?"

"No."

"Well, I was in a fix, I'll tell you. Cornered by about ten men I'd done no real harm to, but that's beside the point. His father took them all on and killed them. All of them."

Ganche spat on the door of the nearest tomb. "So, he was a big man. This kid ain't nothing."

"No, his father wasn't no bigger. He done it with magic." Brades whispered the last word. "Magic killed them."

"Brades," Arron grated, trying to pull away.

Ganche looked down at Arron, laughing. "Yeah? Well, let's see him take me on. Not ten, just one."

"Go ahead, boy." Brades shoved him forward. Arron stumbled and fell. The men started laughing, crowding in closer and closer.

"Oooh, look at the scary Roamer! Oooh, eeek. Help me, Brades! Call him off," a thin man with loose, hanging skin shrieked nearby. The laughter grew. Chris and Katie scrambled to their feet. Arron got up slowly, eyeing the crowd. He stared widely at them, hemmed in by the doors to the graves and by the bodies of the thieves, crowding closer still.

Ganche slashed at him with his knife. Arron leaped back. Ganche croaked out a deep-throated laugh. "Come on, boy. Scared? Let's see your magic. Come on. I'm going to kill you, but you know that." He lunged at him again. Arron backed into Brades, who pushed him back out at Ganche.

"What's the problem, Roamer?" Ganche laughed and slashed at him again, just barely missing. "Come on, it'll hurt, but that's the way it goes, now, isn't it?"

Arron grabbed his knife from his boot and made a feint for the thief's weapon hand, then switched direction as Ganche dodged, and sliced through the man's shirt, cutting across his stomach. Ganche leaped back, howling his surprise. The other thieves yelled theirs, pulling back, then the crowd pushed in as Ganche charged again.

"It'll be worse for you now, Roamer boy. You'll wish you'd just stood still to begin with. Is this your magic? This won't be good enough." He ducked Arron's next attack, but again Arron seemed to foresee the man's defensive move, and cut across his shoulder. Ganche pulled back, the men had quieted down.

Arron stood still, holding his knife before him. "Let's leave it at this, Ganche."

The thief stared at him; the men whispered to each other, then began to egg Ganche on again.

"Two times his size, and Ganche can't pull it off. No magic, either." They laughed. Ganche turned on the man, hurling his knife; it caught the speaker in the throat and he crumpled. Ganche turned back on Arron.

"I'm not through yet, Roamer. Not until you're dead, boy." He pulled a knife from the belt of the man nearest him and dove for Arron, aiming for the right shoulder. Arron brought his knife up to block, but Ganche's left hand also came up, catching Arron's knife hand. He jerked Arron around, knocking his hand again and again against a grave door until he dropped the knife. He pulled the Roamer about again and pressed his blade against Arron's throat.

"Don't, Ganche," Chris cried out. Brades held him back.

"It's a good trick, don't you think?" Ganche whispered close to Arron. Arron tried to turn his head away, choking. "But then, it only works on lefties, they never think us right-handed people can use our left. But, me, I can use both." He smiled at Arron and shoved him back. Arron crashed against, then through, the rotted doors of a tomb. Ganche caught at his leg and yanked him back out.

"Amazing magic this Roamer has, eh boys?" The men all laughed in agreement. "Let's make this entertaining, then."

"Please . . ." Katie begged. "Please don't."

Ganche looked at her. "Don't make it entertaining? You just want him killed, then." Ganche frowned and leaned over Arron. "Well, it's my choice. You're mine, Roamer." He gripped the front of Arron's shirt and hoisted him up. "I think it should be fun—for us anyway." He shoved him back against the side of the mound.

Arron turned desperately to Chris and Katie, the question in his eyes. Chris stared back in surprise, then shrugged. Katie nodded a firm yes.

Arron immediately slashed his hand up, humming. Ganche's hand, as he went to cut across Arron's chest, seemed to smash against an invisible wall. He drew back in pain and surprise, releasing the Roamer. The others, who had crowded closer, pulled back with him.

Ganche hesitated only a second, seeing triumph in the Roamer's eyes. Growling, he raised his knife again. Arron flashed his hand up, then brought it down in a slicing motion, slapping it against his thigh, his humming pitch rising. With the movement of Arron's hand, Ganche flew into the air and crashed down in the midst of the men surrounding them.

Five men rushed forward to try and make a grab for Arron, but he toppled them easily with a gentle swing of his arm.

The wind began to pick up and gust about them. The Roamer slowly raised both hands, his face growing dark, eyebrows drawn down, his mouth in a tight line, his humming pitched higher still. The doors to all the tombs suddenly exploded outward, the rotted stench from inside flooding out in a rush.

"Arron!" Chris broke away from a dumbfounded Brades and grabbed the Roamer by the shoulder to stop him. He jerked his hand back as if he had touched a hot oven. The Roamer sparked at his touch.

"Arron, stop it! Stop it! Stop," Katie screamed at him. The thieves were running, trampling one another to get away. She grabbed him, ignoring the sparks, trying to pull his arms down. "Stop it!" He turned to look at her. She pulled away at seeing such darkness, such horror, in his eyes. She backed into Chris, catching at his arm as a creaking, groaning sound began deep within the earth, from inside the tombs.

Arron dropped his arms abruptly and took a slow, deep breath, sagging to one knee. "No, I won't," he whispered. Everything grew immediately silent. "There's nothing wrong with me. There isn't. There isn't!" Chris and Katie and Brades stood there staring at him. Arron looked up at them. "It's all right." He stood stiffly.

Chris shook his head, wordless. Arron ignored him. He pulled on the hat Brades had dropped and bent to pick up his pack, then scooped up his knife and shoved it back in his boot. "We'd better go."

Chris and Katie hesitantly got their packs. Brades quickly began to gather his things as well.

"What are you doing?" Arron asked.

"I'm going with you." Arron started shaking his head. Brades caught hold of his arm. "I can't stay here. They won't let me stay with them anymore."

"You are not going with us."

"You can't leave him. They'll kill him." Chris stepped toward them. "You couldn't let them do that." He paused, staring at Arron. "I can't let them do that."

"All right. All right! Let's just go, then," Arron snapped.

He turned away and strode into the bushes. The rest of them followed hurriedly. Some remaining thieves stood watching, too afraid to stop them, but too greedy to let them go without second thoughts.

XVII

THEY WALKED ALONG IN SILENCE FOR A WHILE, FOLLOW-
ing Arron's back as he moved dimly ahead of them, finding
their trail. Brades caught up to him and picked his way beside him.

"Boy, I just want to say—well, wow! I didn't realize
Roamers could—I mean—well, your father, he never did
that much."

"He never did anything at all," Arron snapped. "My father couldn't do that."

"So, I exaggerated. But I saw your grandma light a fire
with no matches. And there are stories and all. So I knew
you Roamers were magic. Your dad didn't use his when he
helped me, but I knew he could've."

Arron stopped. "No. He couldn't. Only some Roamers
can."

"I was only trying to help, boy."

"You paid your debt, as you said. Don't help." Arron
pushed on again.

"What exactly did you do for them?" Chris asked, stepping around some briars that were barely etched in the darkness.

"Well, as I told you, his father did save my life. Not quite

as I said." Brades nodded to Arron. "But, he did help me in a
bind, and I do return favors like that. I do have some principles." Arron snorted in contempt. Chris glared at him,
knowing the Roamer could probably hear his thoughts, even
if he couldn't see his face.

"Anyway, I came across him a short time later. He looked
real worn, and desperate. And the sight of him, all afraid like
that, made me think of that desperate night of my own when
he'd saved me. So, I approached him like a friend, smiled and
all, asking his trouble. He needed a place to hide, him and his
son and the grandmother. Begged me to help them. I was
willing though, so he needn't have begged. But he was desperate and all." Brades nodded to each of them.

"So, I hid them," he went on. "Hid them in a little place I
knew of; stood guard. I'll never forget. No wonder he was
scared. A lot of men came through, searching and asking
questions, threatening me. And the whole time, you know, I
felt little prickles at my neck, like there was something else
searching, something else trying to catch them. Something so
horrible clamped in my mind, so horrible . . ." He stopped.

"But, I won out, you know," he added after a moment. "I
made it through that night. Felt like I'd done battle. Strange,
huh? But you know how it goes when you're doing something dangerous, risking your life for people you hardly
know. But, as I said, I got my principles."

"Do you remember, Arron? What those men wanted?"
Katie tried to see his face in the faint light. Scraggly bramble
shadows from the moonlight lined his face and made him
look old. She shivered slightly.

"A little," Arron said softly. "Very little. My grandmother
was holding me . . . and I could hear whispers in the
air . . ." He closed his eyes, letting his feet find the path as
they had so many times. Walking it with his grandmother,
with his father. Running. And his father was frightened, unsure where to go. The need—he could feel his father's need to
move to safety. To save what?

Grandmother held him close, and it was dark in the cave.
His father was pacing. Grandmother pulled him closer at a
noise outside. He listened, reaching out of the cave to find a
stranger's mind. The mind of the man with whom his father

had spoken. It was a frightened mind, it saw itself dying, and yet death wasn't upon it.

But the mind bargained, bargained away the thoughts of death. The cold fright of the man crept into him, but Grandmother held him tighter still, crushing the thoughts from him, calling him back to her.

"Not yet," she whispered. "He'll not have you. You'll win out. You'll beat them all." His father took him from her, his fear taking the place of that of the man outside the cave. But this was different, tinged with a warmth, fearing a loss of something other than self.

Someone came into the cave then, a shadow . . . so large! It reached for him. But they ran deeper into the cave and hid in the darkness where, without light, there could be no shadows. Here they waited for a time when it would be safe. He slept in that darkness for a long time.

There came a shadow looming before his closed eyes. Arron opened them and made out the dim form of a man standing in front of him.

"I think we ought to stop here for the rest of the night. You need to sleep sometime. The way you're walking, boy, I don't think you could go much farther. I doubt they followed."

Arron shook his head, focusing on Brades. "I suppose you're right."

"Are you okay? Ganche didn't hurt you any, did he?"

Arron flexed the fingers on his left hand. "I'm bruised, but nothing more."

"Let me take a look," Katie said hesitantly.

"I'm fine." He swung his pack gently from his shoulders and leaned it against a tree. It was dead. Its branches rattled hollowly in the slight wind. He squatted down next to it.

Katie and Chris slid their packs off and sank down. "Damn brambles!" Chris leaped up again. "They're everywhere!" He kicked at the ground, then sat down carefully while Katie laughed at him. The sound of her laughter was quickly lost in the empty night air.

"Just in case they did follow," Brades said, leaning against a tree, "I'll keep watch."

"No, I will." Arron stood again.

"No, boy, don't worry, I've done it before. Remember?"

Arron watched him a moment, feeling the fright of the strange man seeping into him. He was getting pulled back again and lost. Where was he?

"Oh, Arron, come on! Just go to sleep," Chris groaned. "You can take second watch. Good night." He slid down and pulled the blanket he had taken from his pack over himself.

"All right, Arron?" Katie sat looking at him.

"Oh, all right." He took his blanket out, wrapped it about himself, and lay down.

Arron rolled over nervously. He couldn't quite remember what he'd been dreaming. He felt sick now. He was hot and winded, as if he'd been running. Someone had been trying to cut out his brain or something, he was remembering. He sat up, shivering, wondering what time it was. It was still so dark.

"What?" He started. Something was standing over him. "Brades?"

"Yes."

"What? What do you want?" Arron struggled to get his hands free of the blanket that had twisted itself about him.

"It's your turn for watch."

"Oh." Arron pushed at the blanket, and it came uncoiled. "I . . . I was dreaming. Did I make any noise?"

"Quite a bit. I was worried."

Arron looked up at the man standing over him. A cold wave of fear washed over him as parts of the man's thoughts trickled in with his own. He reached for his knife, but Brades jumped on him, pinning his hands to his side before he could reach it.

Chris sat up at the noise. "What's going on? Arron?" He stood. Katie sat up.

"Arron?" she said, standing as well. "Arron, are you all right?"

"Yes."

Katie glanced at Chris, shaking her head. She moved to go closer, then backed up abruptly. "Chris!" she called as she caught sight of the glint from a knife in the darkness.

"Okay. Stay right where you are. I want someone to light a

fire, so I can see you more clearly," Brades said slowly. "Do it, Chris!"

"It . . . it may take a moment."

"No, no it won't. The wood here is very dry. Use some brambles as kindling."

"Use your magic, Arron. Why don't you use your magic?" Chris urged. Was he dead?

Brades started laughing then. "Just light the fire, boy."

"No. Arron must be dead."

"Oh, he's not dead." Brades laughed harder. "No, not dead. But Roamer magic is useless without their hands. Come on now, Arron, my boy, tell them you're alive."

"Chris. Listen carefully." The Roamer's voice came smoothly across the darkness. "I want both of you to take the packs—mine, too. Do you understand, my pack, too—and then go. Just run, please."

They hesitated, then Chris bent and began to scoop up brambles for a fire. Katie got out her matches and pulled some wood over. She lit the brambles, blowing gently as they caught. The wood began to crackle, and the area glowed brighter. Brades took his knife from Arron's throat.

"That's better. I can see you. Now, get over there." He pointed to the other side of the fire, away from their packs.

"But . . . but you . . ." Chris stared openly at Brades, then looked hopefully at Arron, but his hands were tied behind his back, his face drawn tight in anger as he watched Brades.

"I what?" Brades asked.

"I thought, I mean, you said you had principles and all. You knew his father, helped them." Chris looked about helplessly.

"Well, yes. But there are other debts to be paid." Brades looked at Arron.

The Roamer closed his eyes. "Why didn't I see?"

Brades slapped the flat of his knife against his thigh. "Perhaps you should have, but it's too late. Now, you two get over there!" Brades pointed the knife over to the side again. Chris and Katie backed up. "And stay there. I wouldn't want to have to kill anyone."

"You . . . you're not going to kill Arron, are you?" Katie asked in a choked voice, her throat constricting.

"Nope, that's not part of the bargain." He reached for Arron's pack. "But, for my own safety, there's a few items I have to take care of," he said, opening the pack slowly.

"Bargain? What are you talking about? With whom?" Chris glanced at the pocket in his own pack holding the box. It cried out for protection. His heart began pounding the way it had when his mother's bony hand reached for him that last time.

"You bargained the night you helped us, didn't you?" Arron spat out. "I heard you. It was you, then, wasn't it? You came into the cave."

"To take a child, yes. But now the child has gotten a little too dangerous for me. So, I'm to take the toys first." Brades lifted the kithara from the pack and gently slid it from its case. He looked at it carefully, turning it. The firelight glinted off the gilded neck.

Arron sat forward as if a rope about his neck had jerked him. His face drained of its color. "What . . . what are you doing?" he asked hoarsely.

Brades smiled. "This is a toy, is it not? And I am going to smash it." He swung it up over his head violently.

"No!" Arron struggled to get up. Brades swung it down fiercely. "Brades!" The man pulled up at the last second and stood laughing at Arron, who was close to tears.

"You've lost your cool composure, Roamer boy."

"Brades," Arron gasped. "Please. Please!" Katie covered her mouth and pulled back against Chris, hating the panic in Arron's voice.

"Whatever he gave you, I'll give you more. Please! Please, Brades," Arron begged desperately. Katie felt tears of shame stinging into her eyes. She wiped them away angrily, hating that Arron was begging, hating Brades for causing it.

"You'll give me more? You?"

"Yes, please!" Arron tore his eyes from the kithara to look at Brades. "Please," he whispered.

Brades' smile broadened. "Just like your father, begging me to help him. So. This is as important to you as you were

to him. You need your voice so badly, then? It's like he said."
Brades swung the instrument over the fire.

"Brades!" Arron cringed, closing his eyes.

"What'll you give me, Roamer boy? What'll it be, huh?
What he gave me?"

"Anything! Yes. What did he give you?" Arron looked up
at him, hope lighting his face. He didn't dare look at the
kithara still suspended above the fire. "Yes, I'll give you
whatever he gave you."

Brades swelled his chest triumphantly and pulled the kithara from the fire, laughing. "He gave me my life, Roamer.
My life."

Arron stared at him in disbelief.

"He was going to kill me and didn't. Can you give me my
life, Roamer?" His voice was low in anticipation.

Arron licked his lips, looked at the kithara, then at Brades.
Katie moved closer, slowly, watching Brades. Chris stared at
Arron with narrowed eyes. Arron lowered his head, moaning
softly.

"No."

Brades looked disappointed a moment, then started laughing again. "I would have had to smash it in any case. He told
me it aids your magic. You're dangerous enough without it."
He raised the kithara over his head to smash it.

"Don't!" Arron cried out in agony.

Katie leaped forward, her fist closed and swinging, smash-
ing Brades full in the face. Brades recoiled, surprised, dropping both the knife and the kithara, his face dripping with
blood. Katie fell back, crying out in pain, clutching her hand,
blood oozing from the joints.

"I'll kill you for that, you little—" Brades tried to spy the
knife, but the blood on his face, in his eyes, blinded him. He
scrambled after her anyway, to throttle the life from her.

Chris grabbed his arm to stop him. Brades punched him in
the stomach with his free arm and kicked him violently
away, then went after Katie again. Chris coughed out blood,
choked on it, then spat it out. He struggled to get up and
spied the knife, its blade catching at the firelight, shining at
him.

Katie screamed, striking at Brades with her good hand.

Arron was yelling at them, unable to stop it. Chris grabbed the knife and ran after them. He jumped on Brades' back, reaching around to slice through his throat. The body crumpled beneath him.

Katie pulled herself from underneath, choking and gasping for air. Chris lay on top of Brades.

"Chris? Chris!" Katie grabbed hold of him and turned him over. He stared at her blankly, blood all over him. "Chris?" She struggled to find a pulse.

"I killed him," Chris mumbled softly. He looked at the bloody knife in his hand and flung it down with all the force he could muster. "Oh, Mother, what have I done?" he moaned.

"You saved us." She gently wiped the blood from his face.

Chris scrambled up, jerking away from her. "I killed him!" He turned and ran out of the circle of firelight.

"Chris!" Katie stood up. "Chris?" She turned to Arron, bewildered.

"He'll be back. He left the box. He . . . he's just upset."

Katie looked slowly about for the knife he had thrown. "But he had to. He saved us."

"He'll realize that in time." Arron put his head back against the tree. "It's my fault. Why am I so blind sometimes? Everything is always shadows and whispers," he mumbled miserably.

Katie spotted the knife and lifted it with her good hand. She went to Arron, kneeling to cut the ropes. It was sharp and cut them easily, even with the awkwardness of her left hand.

Pushing the ropes away, Arron took her right hand gently. She sucked in her breath. "Hurts, huh?"

She smiled faintly and nodded.

"I think . . . I'm afraid it's broken, Katie."

"Yeah." She laughed slightly. "I guess I did it wrong."

"It was quite a punch. I think you broke his nose." He straightened her fingers carefully. She stared up at the tree branches, her mouth set in a firm line. "I want to thank you. You risked your life, you know," Arron went on, looking at her, then back at her hand.

"I do dumb things sometimes." She watched as he carefully bound her hand with some cloth from his pack. "I really didn't think about it. I shouldn't have . . ." She paused, thinking.

Arron looked up from her hand again. "Why would you compare yourself to Sarah Anne? She . . ."

Katie drew back from him in surprise; she hadn't spoken aloud. Then remembering what he was, she waved him off. "I would like to think that it's better to compare oneself to someone who is alive. And Sarah Anne is a lot like Julie was . . ."

"Your sister?"

Katie nodded, then laughed bitterly. "I know it's silly, but I sometimes wonder what I would have been like if James and Julie hadn't . . ."

"I should hope you would be exactly the same."

"But I wouldn't have been." She looked as if she might cry. "Things might have been better somehow."

"How?" Feeling her torn-up feelings creeping inside of him, Arron went to put an arm about her, but she stood and walked over to the fire. Arron got up and followed closely.

"Oh, I don't know. I'm just crazy sometimes." She shrugged helplessly. "But, you know, maybe I would have been more like Sarah Anne."

"She doesn't care as much as you do," Arron said, coming up close beside her. He touched her cheek gently, but she flinched away as if he had burned her.

He turned sharply to stare into the brambles. "Damn your prejudices."

"I can't undo everything I was taught."

"No, I suppose not." He left her there and scooped up his kithara. He ran his fingers over it, then plucked one of its strings and listened to it a moment. Katie watched, curious.

"That's pretty important to you. I mean, I thought you were going to tell him how he was going to die."

Arron looked down, embarrassed. "I thought I might, too."

"What's so important about it?"

Arron stared at it a moment, then shrugged.

"I see," Katie said slowly.

"I don't weave spells with it!"

"Did I say—" Katie stopped and raised her eyes skyward. "I'm going to find Chris," she said finally.

"Katie, you . . . you don't understand. There's so much I can't explain. Not because I don't want to—it . . . it's because it's not all quite clear to me yet. Really. I'm just reacting to what I've been taught." He paused, holding the instrument close.

"This is all I have left. My kithara. Why, it's almost like a person, now. More, it's my history, my family. This . . . this is what Shakta bargained for when he . . . he told Chruston his death. He held out from breaking long enough to be sure this kithara was given to my grandmother. Somehow, it meant something, something that's just on the edge of my consciousness. I can't let it go. Don't you see how alone I'd be?"

"I'm trying to see." Katie whispered, then watched him a bit longer. "I'm going to find Chris." She looked at the knife still in her hands. "Is this yours?"

Arron shook his head.

Katie nodded and thrust it into her belt. It wasn't quite comfortable, but she felt much safer. She turned to go after Chris. The firelight behind her flickered oddly through the tall patches of brambles, making monster shadows grow steadily about her and then dissolve into nothing as she moved on.

Chris hadn't chosen the best path, and Katie was soon cut and bleeding from the sharp thorns, but it was easy to follow his trail with the bushes crushed and broken from his passing. Then she saw him crouched in the brambles before her.

"Chris? Are you all right?"

He moaned softly, turning away from her. "Please, go away."

"Chris." She knelt next to him. "I was worried. There might still be some of those thieves around."

"I'm fine."

"You had to do it. I don't understand what's wrong."

"I don't want to talk about it."

"You sound just like Arron now."

"Well, I'm not like him!" He grabbed her arm and shook her. "Do you understand? I'm not!"

Katie pulled back, rubbing her arm. "Okay, I'm sorry. I didn't mean it like that."

Chris stared at his hands. "I didn't mean to get so angry." His eyes fell on her hand. "You're hurt?"

"When I punched Brades. Remember? I broke it, I guess."

He took her hand gently. "Arron took care of it?" Katie nodded. "It'll be all right then. He knows what he's doing. Does it hurt?"

Katie gave a short laugh and didn't answer.

"You shouldn't have punched him," Chris said.

"You didn't warn me ahead of time."

"That's not funny, Katie. He could have killed you. He would have, too, if . . ."

"Someone had to do something."

"Over an instrument? You would have died for that?"

"Arron seemed like he would."

"And you want to be just like him."

Katie looked away. "That's not it, Chris. Arron was so upset . . . and there was nothing he could do. You were just going to let Brades smash it."

"Enter James to save the day."

"That's not fair, Chris!" She pulled away from him.

"You're right. I'm sorry. I didn't really mean it." He sighed, nodding, then caught sight of the knife in her belt. He gestured loosely toward it. "You weren't man enough with just your fists?"

Katie stared dumbly at him for a minute. Then she stood slowly and walked back to camp without a word. Chris lowered his head down on his knees. "Oh, damn!"

"Katie?" Arron stood, setting aside his kithara, as she came back into the firelight. She shook her head at him and squatted down next to the fire. Arron hesitated, then stepped closer to her. "He didn't mean what he said. He just wanted to hurt someone the way he's hurting. He doesn't really think those things are true."

Katie started, surprised again by his insight, then narrowed her eyes. "Well, they are true. And what does it matter? There's nothing wrong with me. Ha! It's just the rest of the world."

"That's right."

Katie's left hand clutched at the knife handle. "Don't you patronize me. I don't need you to tell me what's right or wrong. I know perfectly well."

"Katie, why are you trying to cover up your feelings with more anger? I know he hurt you."

Katie got up abruptly and strode a little away from him. "Roamer, Roamer, what may my fortune be. Tell me, thou, what my heart doth truly hold . . . Isn't that the way that old poem goes?"

"I'm speaking to you as a friend."

Katie turned on him. "A friend is told when the other person is upset. A friend doesn't pry into the other person's thoughts!"

"I'm sorry, I guess we have different definitions. I thought a friend was someone who cared." He took a step toward her, stabbing a finger into the air to enunciate his words. "But there are two requirements, now, aren't there? I must care, and I must be a Homesteader!"

She turned away from him, embarrassed. "I . . . I'm just not used to people being able to see inside my head. Before, I just had to watch what I said, to be sure it came out the way I meant it. Now, I have to watch what I think as well. I'm not so sure I can handle that."

"I don't see the problem. What are you so worried about?"

Katie stared up at the dark sky for a long while. "Me," she said at last.

"Katie . . ."

She pulled farther away from him. "Go get Chris," she said, staring at the spot where Brades had been lying. "Good, you moved him. I don't think it would've helped much for Chris to see him again."

Arron turned to see where she was looking. "But, I didn't . . ." He moved to the spot then stared at Katie. "Chris did kill—I mean, he was dead, wasn't he?"

"Yes, he was dead. Chris slit his throat. I saw the blood. There was no way he could've . . ." She looked at the spot again. The ground was dark with the blood. "You must have moved him."

Arron shook his head, shivering. He peered nervously out

into the brambles. "Keep the fire up high. I'm going to get Chris. Check for the box, will you?"

"All right. Chris is just over—"

"I know where he is," Arron said quickly, moving into the brambles. He stopped and looked at Katie. "I don't do it on purpose, you know. It's not really something I have any control over." He stood as if waiting for something.

"Just go get Chris."

Arron nodded and disappeared into the briars. He made his way hurriedly to Chris and stood silently by him.

"What?"

"Chris, come on back. There's no sense in you sitting out here. It isn't doing anything."

Chris didn't say anything a moment. "What do you know? You kill for the fun of it, at a whim."

"I've never—"

"You would've killed every one of those thieves if we hadn't stopped you, even if it meant raising the dead to do it. I know it, and you know it." Chris picked up a twig and bent it between his fingers.

"No, I . . . I . . ." Arron looked down, then turned away, looking into the briars for an answer.

"And you want to kill my grandfather. You want me to. You want Katie to. You want us all to be part of your big revenge. I'm not going to do it, Arron. I'm not going to." He ran his fingers along dirt. "You can't deny that you want to kill my grandfather. You can't."

Arron took a slow breath and turned back to him. "Chris. You didn't kill Brades. He's still alive."

"Yeah, right. Go on and change the subject, Roamer. Why don't you lie about my grandfather, instead of lying about Brades? Why don't you say 'Oh, no, Chris, I'd never do a thing like that! Not little innocent me'?"

Arron grabbed him roughly by the collar and pulled him up, standing. "I'm not lying! Brades is gone! Do dead men walk away? And I won't lie about Chruston, either. Yes, damn it, I'll kill him if I can. But that's not now. Now is Brades! He's gone, and I'm worried about you being out here alone."

Chris laughed slightly. "Why? Am I going to die or something?"

"Stop it!" Arron released him immediately and backed away, covering his eyes. "I don't want to know! Don't do that to me!"

"Arron?" Chris went toward him. The Roamer was shaking so hard, he could barely stand. Chris reached out to steady him. "What is it?"

"Don't!" Arron pulled away.

"Arron . . ."

"What are you thinking about?"

"You, for the moment. What is it?"

Arron tilted his head back, breathing out. "Come back to the fire, will you?"

Chris hesitated, then nodded slowly. "All right. I will. Are you all right now?"

"Yeah, now I am."

"Did you see my—"

"Chris! Don't! Please, just think about something else. Please." Arron pulled away again.

"You did."

"I didn't! But stop, or I will. Please."

Chris took his arm gently. "Okay. Come on. Let's go back to camp."

Katie was staring intently into the fire when they returned. "The box is still there. Brades didn't take that."

"Good." Arron sat down, pulling his kithara into his lap, turning it carefully, then tuning it. Chris continued over to Katie.

"Katie, I . . . I didn't mean what I was saying. I was upset. I wouldn't ever . . . I mean . . ." He stopped and stared at her miserably.

Katie stirred the fire. "I really don't think there's anything to apologize for. I believe we both know what you meant and why you said it."

"Then you do understand."

Katie turned to him without smiling. "Perfectly."

"Oh, God, what did I say to you?" Chris groaned.

"Nothing but the truth."

"Katie, don't pull away like that! You can't—"

"Chris. I don't want to talk about it."

"Nobody wants to talk about anything here! I can't talk to anyone!" He glared at her. "And I can't think anything!" He turned on Arron, then pulled back gasping. "Arron!" He pointed at the dark figure behind him. It was blending in with the brambles one minute and then reaching out, a tree come to life, the next, its scraggly, dark limbs snaking out to enclose Arron.

XVIII

Arron turned, too late, as the form grabbed hold of him roughly. The fire, lighting them, showed the tree to be Brades, back from wherever he had gone, the ugly gash across his throat glinting with blood in the firelight. Nothing could live like that.

Katie stifled a terrified scream and rushed forward, pulling the knife from her belt.

"The box," Arron yelled, struggling against the dead man.

Chris stood, mesmerized by the horror, watching Katie plunge her knife into the man again and again with no response from Brades, as if he didn't feel the holes created in his flesh.

"Chris! Please!" Arron pushed against Brades' chin, and the gash in his throat opened, allowing the head to slip sideways out of Arron's grasp. They rolled over onto the ground, Katie with them, dropping the knife and trying to pull the thing off Arron.

Chris ran to his pack and tore the box from its pouch.

"What do I do with it?" He held it uncertainly.

Arron cried out in pain, twisting, shouting to Chris. "Open it! Just open it!"

Chris fingered the catch, his shaking hands fumbling with

it, but it snapped open. The firelight caught at it, and it began
to hum.

"Nothing's happening!"

Katie pulled on Brades, pounding him. Arron struggled to
get his left hand free, flinging it out, groping for his kithara.
Between gasps, he was humming the note the box sang. He
finally grabbed the handle and twisted the kithara around,
plucking two of the strings. It wasn't as rich-sounding, but it
was distinctly the same note. It echoed into the sphere, making it ring louder and louder, shaking, vibrating Chris' hands.

The firelight suddenly gathered into the sphere, knocking
Chris back. The light swung together in one beam and bore
itself into Brades until he glowed, then stiffened like any
corpse, and lay perfectly still. The sphere grew dark, and the
clearing completely silent except for Arron's quiet sobs. Katie pushed Brades away and pulled Arron close against her.

"Are you all right?"

He caught at his breath and held it, nodding fiercely.
"Sorry," he gasped.

Chris closed the box carefully and knelt down next to him.
"You're cut." He touched Arron's forearm.

Arron tried to sit up, but Katie held him down. "No, no.
We're going to patch that first. That's not a cut. That's a
gash."

"He—he bit me, I think."

"He bit you?" Chris raised his eyebrows and stifled a
laugh, then stood up and got the bandages. Arron stopped
him when he bent to wrap it.

"I feel funny." He stared at them, his face quite pale.

"Funny, how?" Katie bent closer and peered at him.

Arron looked vacantly at the fire a moment. "He was
dead," he whispered. "Dead. How could he be alive?" He
shivered spasmodically and looked up at Katie. "He was
dead. You stabbed him, but couldn't hurt him. He was
dead—" His breath became more shallow. Katie turned to
Chris with wide eyes.

"Arron . . ." Chris shook him slightly.

"How? It doesn't make sense. I can't see . . . can't . . ."
He stared off again. "Dead . . . like the people of the barrows. I was going to . . ." Then he started to laugh, a harsh

laugh, strange and hard. He shook his head and stopped, staring up at them, very frightened.

"Arron?" Katie felt the blood draining from her limbs at the terror in his face.

Arron licked at his dry lips. "Something . . . something's wrong with me." His voice cracked slightly.

"No, no there isn't. You're just under some stress or something," Chris said quickly. He pushed the box inside his shirt.

Arron began laughing again, then shivered and took a shaky breath. "I think I'm poisoned." He nodded. "I think I am." He started to laugh again, but gritted his teeth and struggled to get up.

"No, no. Lie still." Katie caught at his shoulders with trembling hands.

"No," he said sharply. "I have to get something to tend the . . . the poison. I have to . . . to . . ." He stumbled over to his pack.

"We'll do it," Chris said, steadying him.

"No . . . you don't know . . ." He paused, staring at the kithara lying on the ground. He grabbed it, swinging it up as if to smash it.

"Arron!" Chris caught hold of his arms while Katie took the kithara from him.

He stared at them, the whites of his eyes standing out against the dark irises. He ran a hand through his hair. "I've got to hurry. Oh, my God." He pulled things quickly from his pack and laid them out before him. His eyes wandered from the jars to his boot, the fingers on his left hand slowly flexing.

"Take my knife!" He clutched his left hand tightly in his right. "Take it!" Chris reached for it, grabbed it, and stepped back.

Arron took three jars, quickly now. "My bowl, get it. Please hurry."

Katie pushed it in front of him. He poured some of the contents from the jars into it, spilling much of it over the sides. "Water . . . where's some water?" Chris pulled the water bag over. "Just a little." Arron turned and wandered toward Brades.

"Arron!" Chris caught him by the shoulder and pulled him back. Arron looked at him blankly. "The poison." Chris pointed at the gash in his arm. Arron stared at it impassively, as if it were on someone else's arm. Then his eyes focused on Chris again.

"Stir in some water. Heat it. It turns—turns dark. Smear it on . . ." Chris nodded and hurried to do as he said.

Arron wandered about listlessly as it cooked. It turned as black as Arron's hair. Chris looked from it to Arron. "Is this right? Is this how it should be?"

Arron stared down at it and started laughing again. Katie turned to Chris looking as if she might cry. "What do we do?"

Chris took the bowl to Arron. "No! No!" Arron pushed him away.

"It's got to be right. He's crazy. Hold him. I'll put it on."

Katie nodded, grabbing hold of him.

"Hold his arms down, he could use his magic," Chris said, hesitating as he looked at the black stuff. It smelled foul, and Chris was unsure what it might do to him. Who knew with this Roamer stuff?

Katie had her arms all the way across Arron's chest, but he lifted her from the ground. Chris set the bowl down and helped Katie force him to the ground.

"I'll kill you," Arron shrieked. "Kill you!"

"Sit on him," Chris ordered, grabbing up the bowl. "Hold that arm, while I get this one." He knelt on Arron's arm above the elbow, pinning one side to the ground. Katie lay on top of him, using her whole weight to hold him down.

"Kill you! I'll kill you!"

Chris thrust his hand into the stuff and scooped out a big handful, then all but dropped the whole thing at the almost painful tingling sensation that shot up his arm through his neck into his head. He smeared the stuff onto Arron's arm, trying to wipe as much off as possible.

They struggled with Arron a moment more, then he stiffened up, just as Brades had, the tendons in his neck and wrists distending. They pulled back in alarm. Chris dropped the bowl and grabbed him by the shoulders.

"Arron?" The Roamer shook at his touch, his face turning from white to an asphyxiated blue.

"Oh, my God! Do something!" Katie caught at Chris' arm.

Arron's eyes rolled slowly back into his head. He shuddered, tensed up once more. His breath seemed to stop a moment, and Katie and Chris caught at theirs as well. Then he gasped, sucking in a breath, and began screaming a piercing, high-pitched wail that rang through the dead forest around them, black smoke pouring from his mouth with the sound. Katie covered her ears, screaming herself. Chris shook Arron, yelling at him, trying to snap him out of it.

Arron's head flopped back, the blue color leaving his face, his whole body falling limp. Chris sat numbly silent, holding the limp body in his arms.

Katie had her hands over her mouth, stifling her own screaming. She stared wide-eyed at Chris, pulling her hands slowly from her face. "Is he . . . Oh, God, is he dead?"

Chris fumbled to find a pulse in the Roamer's neck, placed a hand on his chest. "No," he said after a moment. "He's breathing . . . and he's got a pulse." He swallowed, then bent over the Roamer and wept. Katie moved closer to him and stroked his hair.

"It's all right."

They sat there for a moment, then Katie stood, taking a deep breath. "I'll get him a blanket."

Chris nodded and watched her as she moved to her pack and took the blanket next to it. She stared to the east a moment where the sun was coming up. She turned back to them and laid the blanket over Arron.

Chris held Arron's head in his lap. He stared down at the Roamer and smoothed his hair. "Funny how you forget your anger when you're terrified."

Katie smiled and nodded. "All of it."

Chris held out his hand. She took it and knelt next to him. "The other one, too," he said softly. She held out her bandaged one. "You didn't hurt it more, did you?"

"I guess pain is forgotten, too. No, I didn't. It's really well wrapped."

"You did pretty well with your left, trying to kill Brades . . ."

Katie looked down, pulling her hands from Chris', but he held onto her left one tighter. "I'd want you next to me over Sarah Anne any time."

"Chris—"

"I mean it, Katie. And I don't just mean in battle."

She looked up at him questioningly.

He tugged gently on her hair. "Your hair has gotten longer. You won't be able to fool people much anymore. You should cut it, I suppose."

Katie looked down, shaking her head. "No, I think it'll be all right. I don't need to cut it." She looked at Arron's hair. "His will be all grown out, too. A hat may not do any good."

Chris pushed Arron's hair away from his face, nodding.

"Why do you do it, Chris? You seem to hate him so much, sometimes. Do you hate him? Or don't you?"

Chris shrugged. "Nothing makes sense."

"What doesn't?"

Chris watched Arron, whose face was calm, his breathing quiet and steady. "He's a Roamer . . . I—I hate him for that. I have to . . . what they've done to my family . . ."

"Why? Why were we taught to hate them?"

"It was Shakta," Chris said softly. "It wasn't so bad until Shakta. He ruined everything. He destroyed my family. My mother was sick and died because of him. So did her father. Anyone of Chruston's blood does. I will." He stared up at the slowly lightening sky. "It was Shakta's fault."

"How?"

"From the trouble between Chruston and Shakta. Shakta cursed Chruston's family. All those born of him, we languish and die, waste away, the same way the land does. Some— someday, that's what is going to happen to me."

"How do you know?"

"Chruston wrote about his life, about what happened to him and to our family. It tells all about how Chruston and Shakta were friends, how Shakta betrayed Chruston, about the curse . . . and the cure."

"Cure? Then you don't have to worry. What is it?"

Chris put his hand against Arron's forehead. "A Shakta must go to a Chruston."

"What . . . what does that mean?" Katie looked at him worriedly.

"A Chruston must kill a Shakta, just as Shakta has killed so many of Chruston's kin."

"And Arron is a Shakta."

Chris nodded.

"But Chris, you're not a Chruston."

"No, not in name. I have the blood, so I will die. But I am not a Chruston. But if my grandfather is alive . . ." Chris bent his head. "How can I turn over someone I care about?" He looked up. "But how can I betray my family and allow these deaths to continue? My father said that I—"

"What did your mother have to say about all this?"

Chris stared down at Arron. "All life is precious." He covered his face suddenly with his hands and began to sob. "Oh, God, what have I done? I killed a man."

Katie stared in surprise. "Chris, you had to."

"Had to? Then I should have killed Arron. He killed my father, my mother. He's a Roamer, a Shakta—"

"He didn't kill them, not really. He didn't kill them, Chris."

"My mother made me promise . . . when she was so sick . . . she whispered so Father wouldn't hear. 'If you love me,' she said to me. 'Do as I would wish. Show me you do understand what I have taught you. Do not kill. No matter what you may think of the being, no matter how horrible . . . Its life is as precious as mine is to you. Promise me.' And I did. I wanted to love her." Chris paused, his eyes still on the Roamer. "But my father . . . I owe him, too. He wanted revenge for my mother's death. Would want revenge for his own. I get so confused." He stared off at the red sun sending its pink rays through the brambles. "And now, worse, my own feelings complicate it all. I feel for this Roamer. Not as my mother would like. Certainly not as my father would like. But my own feelings . . . I don't know. I wanted—I did love them. I do. I owe them, owe them both . . ." He let his words die off. Katie squeezed his hand.

"You don't, Chris. You only owe yourself. You'll do what's right. It'll all sort itself out."

Chris nodded and remained silent.

Arron moved slowly, stiffly. They both leaned eagerly over him. He rolled his head slightly and moved a hand carefully to his face, then opened his eyes. He stared blankly up at them, then looked slowly about the camp. He opened his mouth to speak, then caught at his throat with his hand.

My throat.

"Yeah, it'll be sore for a while," Chris said gently.

No. I can't talk.

"What do you mean you can't . . ." Chris stopped, staring. "What did you just say? No, wait, you didn't say it. Your mouth didn't—"

"Chris? Who? What are you talking about?" Katie looked from him to Arron and back.

"Talk to me like that again," Chris demanded.

Like this?

"Oh, my God."

You can hear me?

Chris nodded slowly.

How come?

Chris stared about him at a loss. "I can hear what he's thinking, Katie. I can hear him! It's so strange, almost as if he were talking aloud."

That's right. Almost. Arron sat up slowly. *How come? What happened to me? My throat . . . My voice . . .* His thoughts trailed off, the words themselves consumed in worry and fear. Chris caught hold of Arron's shoulders, the feelings of the Roamer so intensely expressed.

"You were poisoned by that cut on your arm—"

Yes, I remember, Arron's thoughts interrupted.

"I put some of your poison cure on it."

You did? Did . . . did it feel strange?

"Yes, yes it did. It did this? Did it?"

Arron was staring off. *But my voice?*

Chris tightened his grip on Arron's shoulders. The terror and pain in his words—it was so strange. "You screamed, Arron," he whispered. "It was loud, really loud. Blackness poured from your mouth. I think you just strained your voice box a little."

Or snapped my vocal chords! Arron's eyes fell on his kithara, lying on the ground where Katie had placed it.

Chris slowly released his hold on the Roamer. "Arron . . ." There didn't seem to be anything he could say to rid Arron of the hollowness he could feel in him. Arron turned to look at him. Chris felt the Roamer's sudden awareness of what he could hear. A wave of realization washed over him, then bitter, bitter anger. A firm black wall rose up in Chris' mind, blocking Arron's thoughts from him.

"Hey!" Chris pulled back, the hatred startling him. Arron only turned away from him.

"What is going on?" Katie pulled at Chris.

"I could hear him, Katie. It . . . it's so strange." He watched the Roamer. "Make some of that stuff so Katie can hear, too."

Arron shook his head.

"Why not?"

Arron shook his head again.

"Talk to me." Chris caught at his arm. Arron shrugged him off and got up, moving to the far side of the fire. He stood staring at his kithara.

"Now you know what it feels like to have people listening to your thoughts. Don't like it very much, do you?" Chris snapped, clenching his fists.

And now you can see that you cannot read my mind! I must send to you. Arron's reply shot back, seeming to burn white in Chris' mind, a naked stream of anger rather than words. The mental wall sprang up between them again.

"No, Chris. I don't want to hear Arron's thoughts," Katie whispered, turning to Arron. "Really I don't." She walked slowly around the fire, picked up his kithara, and held it out to him. "You'll get your voice back." She paused, still holding the instrument out to him. He didn't move to take it. "And you'll be able to sing again, just as well as before." Arron stared down at the kithara. He turned away, his fingers flexing just slightly.

"Arron. Don't torture yourself. Take it. You'll get your voice back." She reached for his shoulder. "Really."

He hesitated, then grabbed the instrument from her and carried it carefully to his pack. He stood holding it against his chest a moment, then laid it gently in the top of his pack.

"I don't need to read his thoughts to know what's going through his mind, Chris. Don't worry about it."

Chris shrugged and nodded. "I didn't want you to be left out."

"I know. But, I'm not."

Let's move to another spot, Arron's voice crept softly back into Chris' mind, the dark wall melting away. *Then you can get some sleep, how does that sound?* The anger was all gone, and only that odd emptiness was left to his words.

Chris turned to Katie. "We're going on just a bit farther, away from here. And then, could you do with a bit of sleep?"

"Could I! I don't even think the light will bother me." She looked wearily about at the gray briars surrounding them, then squinted up at the sun. "I like it better here with light."

Katie sat up stiffly. The sun had gone down. She stretched, listening to soft strains of music. "That's pretty." She turned to Arron. He was sitting on the far side of the fire he had built while they went to sleep. The light played on his face and gleamed off the neck of the kithara. He nodded slowly to her, smiling in a vague, dreamy sort of way, and continued playing. Katie sat content a moment, her arms clasped about her knees. She watched Chris, who was sleeping soundly with his back to them.

"It sounds sort of like Ian's music, you know. The one he wrote for his wife." She looked back at Arron. He nodded again. "Is it about someone?" Another nod.

"Who wrote it?"

Arron stopped playing and frowned. He studied her over the fire a minute, then shrugged and continued playing, his head down, in shadow.

"Sorry," Katie whispered. "I wasn't thinking. It isn't one Ian wrote, is it?"

Arron shook his head.

Chris rolled over, groaning. "It's a song his mother wrote about his father." Arron started, then nodded. "You woke me." Chris sat up. "Trying to send . . . to her . . . it seemed."

Arron shrugged.

"You're too moody." Chris pushed away his blanket and

rolled it up. He put it in his pack, then slid the box from his shirt and tucked it in, as well. He glanced over his shoulder to see if the Roamer was watching. He was. Chris pulled the strings on his pack firmly and turned to face Arron.

"How much farther?"

A week. No more.

"A week! Katie, we're close. Arron says only a week more." He turned on Arron. "Then we'll see. We'll see who's right."

Arron nodded wearily. He stood and placed his kithara in its case, then in his pack. *I will be right.* His voice rang with a sharp edge into Chris' head. *I will.*

"You? Oh, no," Chris said, standing. "You can't be right."

I will be right! He pulled the strings on his pack closed with a hard tug.

Katie stared at them. She hugged her legs more tightly against her chest, watching them glare at each other. Why? Why? She put her forehead against her knees, then let out a startled cry as she was grabbed roughly from behind. Chris and Arron turned about and peered past the fire.

"Katie!" Chris stepped forward, then pulled back. "Ganche!" He grabbed Arron's arm. "It's Ganche. It's those thieves!"

Arron nodded slowly.

"Do something," Chris hissed at him.

"Yes, do something, Roamer." Ganche laughed at him, then looked at Katie. "This one will get whatever you throw at us. So, don't try it." A thickset man next to him held Katie tightly about the waist, up off the ground, her hands pinned to her sides. Ganche glanced at her. "Katie is an odd name, boy. Or is it the boy that's odd?"

Idiot! Arron shot at Chris.

"Do something," Chris pleaded, ignoring the last. "You can do something without hurting Katie, can't you?"

Arron ran a shaking hand over his face. *My throat. My voice. I can't. I can't!*

Chris stared at him in horror. "What do you mean, you can't!"

Ganche grinned broadly and strode forward. "Go ahead, boys, search their packs. They won't hurt you, not unless they want to lose this one." Katie struggled to get her arms free. She had one hand on her knife—if she could just get it loose!

Ganche took another step toward Arron. "Got something for you, Roamer." He swung his fist at Arron quite suddenly, catching him hard in the jaw and sending him sprawling. Arron lay there dazed, blinking, his hands catching at the dirt as if to steady the world.

"Do something, Chris!" Katie kicked at the man holding her.

Chris ran to stand in front of Arron, blocking him from Ganche. "Leave him alone," he said in a low voice.

Ganche just smiled patiently. "Wait your turn, boy. I'll take care of you next. Now, move aside." He went to push him out of the way, but Chris ducked, butting his shoulder full into Ganche's stomach. The big man doubled over with a soft sound and the two of them toppled. The others had turned to watch, laughing and rooting Ganche on.

Ganche kicked Chris away. "I said I'd get you later!" Arron struggled to his knees, one hand on his chin, an ugly, purple welt growing under it.

"First you." Ganche grabbed him by the collar and hauled him up, leveling another swing at him. Arron twisted, ducking the punch. He snapped his own fist into Ganche's throat. The man staggered back without releasing his hold on Arron's shirt; he dragged Arron with him. Catching at his breath, he swung Arron about by his shirt and sent him flying into the brambles. The other men opened a path as he hurtled toward them.

"Do something, Arron," Katie screamed at him. "Never mind hurting me. Do something!"

Chris charged Ganche again as he continued after Arron. Ganche saw him coming and caught him easily. He swung him up off the ground and into some of the men. They caught at him and held him back as he tried to go after Ganche again.

Ganche pulled his knife from his belt and advanced on Arron, who was struggling to get out of the briars, painful gasps coming from his mouth as he breathed.

"And now, Roamer, you die." Ganche smiled. "But don't

worry. I'll send you a friend to keep you company." He
glanced at Chris. "But not all of your party need go." His
eyes slid to Katie, then he looked at Arron again and pulled
him roughly from the bush. "But you, Roamer, you get the
privilege of dying by my hand—by my methods." He
slammed him up against an old tree. Arron struggled to keep
from blacking out as his head knocked against the hard, dry
bark.

"Don't, Ganche! Don't," Chris cried out, pulling against
the men.

"Oh, you'll enjoy it, Homesteader. I'll make it quite entertaining. He's a worthless Roamer, after all."

Katie worked her arm free as her captor's attention left
her, to follow Ganche's activities. He really couldn't expect
any trouble from her, after all. She pulled her knife up as she
slid her arm out, slicing into his arm. He dropped her with a
howl. She rushed at Ganche as soon as she touched ground,
stabbing him deep in the forearm as he tried to fend her off
and still keep his grip on Arron.

Arron yanked himself free as Katie attacked again.
Ganche turned full on Katie. "If that's the way you want it!"
He knocked her to the ground and raised his knife, aiming
for her chest. Chris tried to jerk free.

"Katie!"

Arron let out a weak, keening sound which grew rapidly
louder. Everyone immediately clapped their hands to their
ears. Ganche reared up from Katie with a cry. She scrambled
to her feet, hands protecting her ears. Chris broke loose from
his captors as they, too, clapped their hands to their ears.
Arron grabbed him and pulled Katie close, too, the whine
dying off. The thieves turned on them, their eyes wild with
pain and hatred.

"Do something!" Katie pulled on Arron's arm. He looked
at her frantically, his eyes begging her not to ask. He gritted
his teeth and looked away, taking a deep breath, then began a
low-pitched, rough-sounding note. He raised his hands
slowly.

Chris clenched his hands to his head. Pain! Pain! His fingers caught at his hair. The Roamer's mind was open to him!
The pain! Arron's thoughts filled his mind.

Katie stared at Arron as he raised his hands. The air seemed to thicken about the three of them. Arron's face grew pale, the hue of dead-man's white. Tiny beads of sweat stood out, glowing in the firelight. The air grew thicker.

The thieves began gasping and clutching at their throats. Katie watched, horrified, as they fell to their knees all around them, an invisible demon striking them down.

Their mouths gaped as they thrashed, sucking at the air like fish drying in the sun. They clawed at the ground—for air! It all seemed to gather about the three of them, leaving the others in a vacuum. Chris was on his knees with the thieves, cringing, trying to block the Roamer's thoughts of pain.

They all fell still at last. Arron's note broke off with a cry. He collapsed, sobbing soundlessly, clutching at his throat as if for air himself.

Chris clutched at his own throat, screaming out the Roamer's pain. Arron saw him, as if through a haze. He reached vaguely for him, then, realizing what it was, blocked his thoughts.

Chris let out a sigh of relief as the dark wall rose, cutting him off from the agony of the other's mind.

"Arron . . ." He took hold of him.

"I . . . I want to get out of here," Katie whispered harshly, staring at all the wide-eyed, distorted figures about them. "I have to get out of here."

Arron nodded, shivering. He tried to stand, but his knees buckled under him.

"No," Chris said suddenly. He steadied Arron. "No, Katie. He's hurt himself, badly. We have to wait."

Katie looked around her, then closed her eyes. "Okay," she managed.

"Rest, Arron. Take a moment."

Arron shook his head, then lowered it to the earth. He pressed his forehead against the ground, breathing unsteadily, pounding one fist in the dirt.

"What's wrong?" Katie looked to Chris for an answer.

He shrugged slightly. "He—his throat. I . . . I think he's really hurt it. I mean really."

"What choice did you have?" Katie knelt next to Arron

and put an arm about him. He shoved her away, knocking her down. Chris bent to catch her, then gently helped her up, his eyes catching hers.

Let's go! Arron's voice snapped into Chris' head.

"What—"

Let's go, the voice insisted again. Hatred.

Chris stared at him. "He wants to leave now," he mumbled to Katie. "It's not my fault." He turned on Arron. "Don't you blame me!"

Damn you, there's nothing wrong with me! There can't be.

"Did I say . . ."

Arron turned away from him and spun on Katie, glaring at her. She pulled back from him, moved behind Chris. *Damn you both!* He turned away from them. Stepping over the bodies, he grabbed up his pack and walked away. Chris watched him disappear into the brush. Katie caught at his arm.

"What is it?"

"I . . . I don't know. Something. Oh, Katie, I think we've been led on and lied to the whole way. He's a Roamer. He's so thoroughly a Roamer. I thought that . . ." He shook his head, kicking out the fire. "And we have no choice now but to follow." He shrugged. Katie lifted her pack, glancing briefly at the stiffening forms lying about, their eyes vacant. She turned and ran after Chris, remembering how Brades had come back to life.

XIX

"A WEEK! A WEEK YOU SAID! WHAT HAPPENED? IT'S BEEN over a week." Chris shoved his breakfast plates back into his pack.

Arron looked up from the fire. *I took a detour.*

"What? Why?" Chris turned to Katie. "He took a detour!" *We are near Buernston as well as near Sernet.*

"So?"

Arron looked down, the wall up again, then down in a flash of rage. *They know me there!*

"We're near Buernston, he says. If that means anything to you." Chris shrugged at Katie.

"That's the town where Craftan was from," Katie said suddenly. "They would know Arron there. That's where he . . . his grandmother . . . It was probably for the best that we detoured," Katie said finally. Arron stared at her with cold, black eyes, then turned to Chris.

Sernet is just over the next hill. Less than a half a day's walk.

"Really?" Chris sat forward. "A few hours, Katie, and we'll be at Dempter's."

Arron shook his head, smiling at Chris' excitement. He

245

pulled the hat firmly down over his head. *Not much help, is it?*

Chris laughed at the wistful way the question came across. "We'll see." He rocked back, eyeing the Roamer. "Okay. So, what do we do when we get to Sernet?"

You go to Dempter and tell him who you are, that you're related to Chruston. Tell him about the disease and that you must see Chruston to talk about the cure.

"The cure? You . . . you know about the cure?"

Yes. Of course.

"What . . . what is it?"

Chruston must die. Arron's voice rang hollowly in Chris' head.

"I see," Chris whispered, rubbing the scar on his shoulder. It had begun to tingle again. "I tell Dempter who I am, and he'll send me to Chruston."

We hope.

Chris nodded and turned to tell Katie what Arron had said. She stared at him openly, waiting for his thoughts on the subject. But he only stood and reached for his pack.

"Let's go, then."

Chris sighed, staring about him. The land had gotten marginally better since they had left the briars. The ground sloped gently upward with only a few gravelly places where they could lose their footing. He stopped when he reached the top and looked at the village that lay below.

"Sernet?"

Arron nodded.

Chris gazed down on it a moment more. It seemed no different from his own town—a little bigger, perhaps, less rural. But like his town. They probably had the same bad times and good ones. He remembered picnicking on Mount Klineloch with his parents. The food had seemed to taste so good. His father tossed him up onto his shoulders, and they chased his mother, laughing, all about the meadow. Hadn't he loved them then? Yes, he had. Hadn't he?

"Well, what are we waiting for?" Katie asked and started down the hill. Chris and Arron followed closely. Arron pulled his hat down tighter. Chris noticed he looked pale and wouldn't catch his eye.

The town was dusty. The windows were all coated in a thin film of dirt. The dust seemed to settle on them as well, heavily.

"Excuse me," Chris called out to a man crossing near them. "Sir? Can you tell me where Dempter's house is?"

The man pointed down the main street. "On the right. No way to miss it." He took a second look at them and went on his way.

Chris nodded his thanks and started down the road. Arron caught at his arm. *Give Katie your pack. We'll wait for you at the stable over there.*

Chris hesitated. "You . . . you're not coming?"

Arron watched him a moment with the strange look in his eyes Chris had not seen since that morning the Roamer had first awakened in his house. Arron looked away and shook his head.

"Why not?"

I think you'll get better results if you go alone.

Chris still hesitated.

You won't be inhibited by my presence.

Chris stepped back. The hatred had surfaced again, as if the Roamer blamed him for something. Anger and . . . and disappointment . . . disillusionment, like his father's. But anger . . . Chris slid his pack off and handed it to Katie.

"Arron wants you to wait with him. I'll be back shortly." He turned and went the way the man had pointed, glancing back once to be sure it was Katie's pack he saw Arron taking from her, and not his.

Dempter's house was not what he had expected. The man said he couldn't miss it, and he was right. Chris stood still a moment.

The gate said *Dempter* on it, so it was definitely the house. The front yard was amazingly well kept; the whole house was. In this dusty town, not unlike his own, he was surprised to see neatly painted shutters, a yard so spotlessly kept. It seemed the dust from the streets was not permitted past the gate. There was something oddly comforting in the tidiness, the order a relief from the disrepair all around it. He realized he would like this man.

Quickly he brushed the road dust from himself, before touching the gate. The metal gate was cold and swung on its hinge without squeaking. Chris' eyes traced the lines of the trim brick walkway, following them in a sweep up to the steps of the porch, which looked wide and airy, as if it would be cool in the hottest of summers.

"Yes?" came a sharp voice from the porch.

Chris straightened abruptly.

"What is it, boy?" A taut-faced, gray-haired woman stood impatiently. Her hair was drawn back tightly, as if pulling her face and her whole body up.

"I came to see Dempter. Is he in?"

"What about?"

"It's personal."

"Personal, is it? So personal you can't even tell Dempter?"

Chris blinked and looked at her, confused. "No, no, of course not."

"Well. I'm Dempter."

"You? Oh . . . I . . . sort of . . . expected a man."

"Well, you expected wrong. Now, what is it? I certainly don't have all day to stand about with you."

"Couldn't we go inside?"

"Not unless you're the grocery boy, come to put my groceries in the cellar." Chris shook his head. "Well, then, out with it, boy."

"I . . . I have the Chruston family disease. I have to discuss the cure with my grandfather. I was told you could help me find him," Chris blurted out, afraid she would leave him. But she sat down slowly on the porch chair, her face softening suddenly, her young, blue eyes filling with tears. She put a shaking hand to her mouth.

"I think we best go inside," she said at last.

Chris nodded and started up the steps. She held the door for him, and he went inside.

She indicated a comfortable armchair. He sat slowly, staring, amazed at the richness of the room. It was well decorated with expensive-looking furniture, evenly coordinated in different shades of cool blue. He never imagined houses could really be like this. He turned back to Dempter. She sat opposite him, her eyes trained on his face as if unable to believe he were really, truly there.

"You are a Chruston, then?" she said when he didn't speak.

"No, my mother was. She was Sheila Chruston."

"Then you must be Chris."

He nodded slowly.

"Well, then, Chris, what is it you want?"

"I . . . well, this is probably going to sound silly, but I was told my great-great-grandfather was still alive." He watched her a moment.

"Who told you this?"

"Well . . . I sort of . . . you see, the cure says a Shakta must go to a Chruston . . . so there must be a Chruston living . . . in order to be cured. So . . . so I asked around and was told he was still living . . . you see." Chris stopped and looked at her nervously.

"What do you want of him?" She sat back, her arms rising slightly as if to protect someone behind her, to protect with her life. "Who told you this?"

"My father."

"You're lying."

"All right. A Roamer, then!"

"You've been led here by a Roamer?"

"Is my grandfather alive?"

"Was it a . . . a Shakta?" She stood. "Is there to be more deceit? And from his own grandson!"

Chris checked himself at that and swallowed, staring up at her, pleading with her. "My grandfather? Is he alive?"

"Why do you want to know? What do you think it means, that a Shakta must go to a Chruston?"

"My father said it meant a Chruston must kill a Shakta since so many of Chruston's blood have been killed by Shakta."

She sat forward, searching his face. "What do you think?"

"I don't know! That's why I must talk to my grandfather. Is he alive?" Chris stood up.

"Bring the Roamer to me; only then will I take you to your grandfather."

He was alive! Chris' heart thudded woodenly in his chest, then faster. He was alive! He stared at Dempter. But she bargained for Arron. "I . . . I don't have a Roamer."

"But you have been dealing with one."

"No." Chris stepped back from her. She was watching him so closely. "Why? Why is it so important?"

Dempter stood, too. "I don't trust your intentions. You would guide a Roamer, free, to your own grandfather? Don't you know what the Roamer intends?"

Chris shook his head, blocking all of Arron's past words from his mind. Arron wouldn't . . . he wouldn't really . . . Chris struggled with that thought. "I don't think you can be of any help to me. Thank you for your time." He started for the door. She caught at him with both hands.

"If you walk out now, you'll waste away like all the rest. I can help you. Don't you want to live? Your grandfather, you don't know the torture he feels at these deaths. Don't do this to him. Don't," she begged him. The desperation in her voice frightened him, but not so much as his own desperation. Was he really doomed to waste away as his mother had? Arron would know. Arron could tell him.

"Do you want to die just when your life has begun? Why —how could you protect a Shakta? They have taken more than enough of Chruston's blood. It must end." She squeezed his shoulders, her eyes wide, taking him in. "It must."

"Is it true? Is it true my grandfather tortured Shakta until he told him his death? Did he do that just to find out his death?"

"Is that what the Roamer told you?"

Chris nodded.

"And you believed? A Roamer?"

Chris shrugged. "But if my grandfather is still alive . . ."

She laughed slightly and lifted her head as if to talk to the air. "Oh, Chruston, wouldn't you just die if you heard this? Your own grandson."

"Is it true?"

She took his hands gently. "No, it's not true. And I think I'll leave it to your grandfather to explain. It is involved. But do trust me on this. The Roamer lied to you. Your grandfather is not evil. He is so completely honorable . . . You should be very proud to be related to such a man." She squeezed his hands. "What I am saying is true. You must believe me. But you'll see as much when you meet him yourself. There is no one better than Oliver Chruston. Really, Chris."

"Really?"

She nodded. "Now, have you been dealing with a Shakta?"

"Yes."

"Will you bring him to me?"

Chris looked down at his hands still clasped in hers. "Yes."

She pulled him closer in joy. "Thank you! You don't know what this means to him, your grandfather. You're going to save him." Then she paused, watching him. "You wouldn't happen to know if this Roamer had anything of note about him. Something small? A box, a gray box."

Chris pulled his hands away and backed toward the door. "I . . . I have to make sure I can still get this Roamer. My . . . my cousin would know. I'll get back to you." He ran out the door before she could stop him and raced down the street to the stables. Dempter watched him from the porch, concern lining her face. She shook her head and went slowly back inside.

"Chris! What happened?" Katie stood up as he rushed into the stables.

He ignored her, looking around. "Where . . . where's Arron?"

"He went out for some water. We're out. He was thirsty, I guess. He should be back soon, because he's been gone a really long time. But anyway, tell me, what did he say?"

"Dempter is a woman. And she didn't say much. My grandfather is alive, but she didn't say where. She—" Chris broke off when Arron stepped back into the stables.

"Why didn't she tell you where?" Katie asked.

Chris shrugged, walking slowly toward Arron. The Roamer stopped by a post, grabbing it. "Am I going to waste away like all the rest of them?" Chris asked. "Is that my fate?"

Arron backed up.

"Chris? What are you doing? What did she say to you? What's wrong?" Katie reached for him.

"I have to know, Katie. I don't know what to do, so I . . . I have to know." He turned on Arron. "You have to tell me."

Arron shook his head fiercely, grabbed his pack, and ran from the stables.

"Chris! What are you doing?" Katie yelled at him.

"I have to know, Katie."

"No, you don't, Chris! You just want to know!" She glared at him a moment, then chased after Arron.

"Arron," Katie called out again. She felt herself beginning to go hoarse. She had been looking for him for hours; he seemed to have just vanished. She couldn't find him anywhere in town, and now she was searching along the outskirts. "Arron! Where are you?"

It was already beginning to grow dark, and she had started to worry long ago. Damn Chris! Why did he have to start this up now? They were so close to the end. The least he could have done was come out here and help her find Arron.

She bent down to look at the dirt; there were marks as if someone had run by. Oh, but it could have been anything! She followed anyway. Chris probably would only have made matters worse if he had come. The way the two of them went back and forth with their endless bickering . . . She studied the dirt again, running her fingers through the dry topsoil as if it might give her the answers.

At times the two of them seemed oddly close. But then, just as she was sure they would finally come to an understanding with each other, one or the other would suddenly pull away. She shook her head, standing up.

She could understand Chris a bit more than Arron. He, even more than most of the Homesteaders, had a reason for hating the Roamers. The whole town had seen the way the Roamers had destroyed his family—if it really had been the Roamers who destroyed his family. She turned to climb to higher ground for a better view.

He kept so many things bottled up, and just when she was sure he was about to give in to his feelings, something deeper inside seemed to reach up and grab him and pull him away.

Was it guilt? Or maybe he had just never learned how to reach out. She frowned.

And the Roamer, he was harder for her to understand. He did have feelings, she felt certain, though she had been taught that Roamers didn't have any emotions. He seemed to be striving much the same way Chris was striving. But something troubled him, too. She wondered if the same self-doubt that she felt was consuming Chris could be stopping the Roamer from reaching out, as well.

But there was something in him, something she felt the Roamer himself recognized as not being right. Was that what ate at him, kept him apart from them? And whatever it was that was in him . . . could any of them really trust him? Could even she ever trust him?

She shook her head, hoping that when she found him, if she ever did, and she got him together with Chris, this could all be sorted out, once and for all. All the misunderstanding and distrust—was there really a reason for it all? Or were they all just incapable of showing themselves for what they really were?

She sighed out her frustration, trudging forward. She stopped suddenly, coming to the top of the slope.

"Arron?" She saw him crouched by a stone that seemed to jut from the ground like a grave marker. "Arron, what are you doing?" He didn't look up at her. "You can't just run away like this. Not now. Not when we're so close." She bent down to squat next to him. "Are you all right?"

He nodded.

"He's just confused, you know. He doesn't mean what he says. You told me that yourself, remember?"

He nodded again.

"So, why don't we go on back. He's had plenty of time to cool down. I'm sure he'll be much calmer."

Arron shook his head violently.

Katie pulled gently on his shoulder to turn him toward her, but he resisted. "You didn't see his death, did you?"

Arron got up abruptly and walked a little distance away. "Did you?"

He looked her in the eyes now and shook his head. Katie stood and walked over to him.

"Let's go back, then."

His eyes slid away from hers, he shrugged, shook his head, then covered his face with his hands.

"Arron . . ." Katie put her arms about him. "Arron, he won't ask again. I won't let him. I'll tell him not to. He'll listen." She stroked his hair gently.

He pulled away after a moment, his mouth open as if to speak, then he snapped it closed and stared off at the graying hillside.

"Now you're the one who pulls away," she whispered.

He nodded slightly.

"Come on." She took his hand.

He hesitated, looking back toward the town.

"We have to go back. We have to finish this." She watched him, his eyes growing wider, then he closed them, tightly, shaking his head. "What are you so frightened of?"

He turned to her and took a deep breath. He squeezed her hand tightly, raising it between them. He held her hand there a second, up, and stared at it. Then he looked at her, begging her, begging her—but he couldn't tell her for what. He lowered her hand slowly then and dropped his eyes, shaking his head, looking beaten.

"Can we go back?" He shrugged. Katie slid her hand from his. He stared at the space between them and held back. She took his arm then and led him back to the stables.

"Well? Where is he?" Katie looked around the stables. "Chris? Are you in here?"

Arron walked slowly about the area.

"You don't think he ran off? Do you think he went back to Dempter?"

Arron didn't move, didn't attempt to answer.

"Look!" Katie pointed to the floor over by one of the stalls. The hay that covered the floor had been kicked up. "There's been a scuffle of some sort here." She looked about a moment more and then in horror at Arron. "You don't think . . . Chris? Chris!" She spun about. Arron grabbed her roughly before she could run off. He held out a steady hand, telling her to be calm. He tapped his own pack and pointed about the stables, then began looking in all the corners.

"You . . . you're looking for Chris' pack."

Arron nodded.

"For the . . . that box?"

He nodded again.

"Is that all you care about? That damn box!"

He looked up.

"That's all the two of you seem to care about. That's what all this distrust is about. Who cares! Who needs it! I just want to find Chris!"

Arron walked over to her and took her arm. He mouthed the word *please*. Katie stood there shaking her head. But he was looking past her. He walked quickly to the stall behind her and lifted Chris' pack up onto the rail. He fumbled with the pocket, then pulled the box out, raising it triumphantly.

Katie snatched it from his hand. "Chris didn't want you to have this!"

He stared at her.

"Don't you look at me like that! I'm not sure that you'll look for Chris if you have this. You . . . you might just leave. And we've got to find Chris, we've just got to. Arron?"

He just kept looking at her.

Tears stung into her eyes in shame. "I . . . I'm sorry. I just . . . I don't trust you. I want to . . ."

Arron ripped the hat angrily from his head and clutched a handful of his dark hair.

Katie looked down, wiping at her eyes with the back of her hand. "Yes. It's because you're a Roamer." Arron strode away from her, throwing the hat at her in his rage. She jumped back, startled. "And because of the way you act."

Arron looked at her from a distance.

"You . . . you act so violent sometimes. It scares me."

He stabbed a finger toward the knife in her belt. She looked down at it.

"But . . . but I'm a . . ." She stopped, looking up at him. His face grew flat, eyes remote. He nodded slowly, his chin raised slightly.

XX

UNCONSCIOUSNESS LEFT CHRIS SLOWLY. IT WAS DIFFI-
cult for him to determine when it did, exactly. The blackness
didn't go away at all. He spent some minutes floating in his
thoughts, unclear, drifting in nowhere. Then it struck him
that he was blinded. His other senses seemed clear. But as his
rationality began to return, he realized he was blindfolded.
His hands, he became aware, were bound firmly behind his
back, and he was gagged. Lying on his side . . . somewhere . . .

What had happened? He had been in the stables, wondering what to do about Arron. He . . . he had . . . he didn't
remember!

And now—now where was he?

What was that? He strained his ears, making out what he
thought might be footsteps. He listened harder, but there was
nothing more. Was he in a room? How big? Where in the
room was he? Near the wall? Out in the center? An incredible sense of vertigo enveloped him, as if someone had spun
him around and around and around . . . He lay there
shivering, unable to think what he should do, what he could
do.

He forced his mind calm again—calm—and took a deep

breath through his nose. The air was cold, damp, and it smelled musty. The floor beneath him was cool as well. Smooth stone or tile, not wood, nor dirt. The air felt still on his face, no warmth of sunlight. He must be inside, he decided. Underground? In a cave? Oh, God, what was happening? Where was he? Who did this?

He stopped thinking and strained to hear again. It was the footsteps . . . Someone was there, not far off, but not in the same room—if he was in a room! The steps sounded echolike, as if in a long corridor . . . Where was he?

Maybe he could attract their attention? Did he want to attract their attention? And how? He kicked his legs back and forth in hopes of knocking something over. The way was clear, nothing was there. But the scraping of his boots seemed very loud. He waited. Loud to him perhaps, but not to whoever was nearby. No one came.

Whoever had taken him, did they have his box? He felt the panic beginning to rise in him again. Then a sudden thought struck him. Who wanted that box but Arron!

Arron, his mind cried out angrily.

Chris? came the immediate response, as if he were waiting and nearby.

Why have you done this to me?

Where are you? Are you all right? Chris? The voice was smooth, devoid of any feeling.

What do you mean, where am I? The realization of what had happened to him suddenly hit him. He didn't really know who had taken him or why. He had no way to find out. He was completely and totally helpless—he couldn't even describe his surroundings to Arron.

Arron! He panicked. He desperately wanted to hear the Roamer's familiar voice.

I hear you, Chris. It's all right. We'll find you, now don't worry. The calm in Arron's voice flowed smoothly into Chris' mind. *Now, tell me what you can about where you are.*

But further anxieties had crept into Chris' mind, ones that the Roamer could never calm. *The box? Do you have it?*

Katie does.

Katie does? Are you sure it's Katie? And not . . .

It's Katie! Anger and frustration. *Now, tell me about where you are,* he added a bit more calmly.

I . . . I'm inside. It's cool and the ground is smooth and damp. It's underground, I think. Arron?

Yes?

You'll never find me, will you? There's no way . . . where would you begin?

We'll find you, Chris. We won't stop looking until we do.

Arron . . .

Yes?

I think I ought to tell you. I . . . He could feel his own fear and embarrassment seeping out with his thoughts.

What?

I told Dempter about you. I said I would bring you to her. She . . . she knows you're a Shakta.

Nothing.

Arron! Arron, I left giving her the impression that I wasn't going to bring you. She asked about the box . . . Arron? Arron, are you there?

Yeah. Yeah, I'm here, Chris.

Arron knelt down in the dirt and wrote carefully with his forefinger. Katie bent beside him and read.

" 'We're going to see Dempter. Chris told her about me. I think she may know where he is.' " Katie stared at him as he stood up, smearing the writing with his foot.

"You're going to give yourself up?"

He shook his head and scooped up the hat he had thrown down. Slapping the dust from it, he pulled it over his dark hair and started from the stables. Katie shoved the box deeply into her pocket and followed him out into the dimly lit street. They walked quickly down to Dempter's.

Arron didn't pause at the gate. He pushed it open and left Katie staring at the yard as he went up onto the porch.

"Arron? Don't you see? Look at this yard." She stared at the yard and back out at the dusty street. She smiled up at Arron. "Can you imagine the time it must take to keep it clean like this? This is like something my mother would have done, sweeping and sweeping until there was no sign of dust."

Arron stared at her a moment, questioning. Then he shook his head slowly and held a hand out to her. Katie smiled again and took it, coming up onto the porch. "If she had seen this yard, she would have been so envious. The hours she spent . . . I'll never forget . . ."

He shrugged and knocked on the door. Katie watched him, pulling her hand from his.

"Yes?" The gray-haired woman answered the door.

Katie turned to Arron, expecting him to speak for some strange reason. Then remembering, she turned with a start back to the woman. "Oh! Are you Dempter?"

"That's what it says on the gate. Right?"

"Yes. Yes, it does. Look, we're trying to find a guy named Chris. He came to see you this morning."

Dempter looked more closely at Katie. "Who are you? His cousin, perhaps?"

"No. This is his cousin." Katie pointed to Arron.

"And you are?"

"I'm Katie."

Dempter looked her over slowly, noting her male attire, the ragged cut of her hair.

"Traveling is rough for a girl." Katie looked down.

The old woman nodded, smiling gently. "I know." She watched Katie a moment, then looked at Arron. "Well, cousin, do you have a name?"

"It's James," Katie answered. She realized Dempter might know a Roamer name.

"What's wrong, James? Afraid to speak for yourself?" Dempter asked Arron. He kept his eyes carefully averted.

"He's mute."

Dempter left off with him at that and considered Katie again. "You said you're looking for someone, then."

"Yes. Chris. He's disappeared. Last we saw, he was going to talk to you about . . . uh . . ." Katie stopped, unsure if it was wise to let Dempter know she knew the reason for the visit.

"About his grandfather?"

"Yes."

"Is he a blood relative of Chruston as well?" Dempter indicated Arron.

"No. No, he's from Chris' father's side."

"I see. Well, come on in. There's no sense in us standing out here in the dark." She held the door open for them. Katie hesitated, then walked in with Arron close behind her. Dempter let the door slam shut.

"Have a seat." She pointed to the chairs, and they sat down.

"So," Dempter said, turning around. "You're looking for the young man who came to see me. Well, I'll tell you, he promised to bring me a Roamer. Oh, don't look so surprised. Yes, there are still some living."

"I . . . I just don't understand why he would promise a thing like that."

"Because, my dear, he wants to live." Dempter leaned close to her and put a hand lightly on her shoulder. "Survival. It's simple."

"But I don't see how getting a Roamer—"

"Do you know the story about Chruston and Shakta?"

"Some."

Dempter nodded and wandered a moment by the bookshelf, running one finger across the backs of the books lined up on the shelves in perfect rows. She stopped and flicked out a well-worn, brown-covered book. The pages crackled as she opened it. She held the book out to Katie and pointed out a passage. Arron leaned over in sudden interest.

" 'His mind completely gone by this time, Shakta laughed maniacally, then grew silent and would stare blankly. Blank, yes, as he had but one thought left in his mind,' " Katie read slowly. " 'All else had been told or was lost. But he held to the last on that one thought. His treasured jewel. The cure to all his curses. What is it? Tell us. We demand to know! Chruston will not live by this curse. "Aha," screamed Shakta. "Live you must, it seems. But I'll tell you." His voice dropped to a tremulous whisper. "Yes, I'll tell. A Shakta must go to a Chruston." He jumped up at that. "But I'm done. It'll not be me!" He ran to the open door in the tower and flung himself from the height—' "

Dempter snatched the book from her hands. Katie and Arron looked up with a start. Arron looked down again quickly. Dempter was looking at him.

"I don't understand," Katie said.

"It means Chris must bring a Roamer, a Shakta, to his grandfather for justice. That is the only way he can save himself, the only way to stop the Chruston family deaths, to stop the failing in the lands."

"Oh."

"And he was going to get him . . . except he said he had to speak with his cousin first, to see if he could still get the Roamer." Dempter turned to Arron. He lowered his head. She had enough experience, she would know from his eyes.

"Well? Did he come talk to you?"

Arron shook his head. She caught him under the chin and forced his head up. "Afraid of an old woman, James?" Their eyes met briefly, then Arron looked away, jerking his head from her hand.

"No, he didn't come talk to us. I was with James. Chris never came back from seeing you." Katie stood up.

"Maybe he went to get the Roamer, then, and something happened," Dempter said slowly, watching Arron. "Eh, James? Is that it?"

Chris stiffened up hearing the approach of someone . . . something. "You awake then? Eh?" A man's voice, rough from too much drink, perhaps. Like his father's, Chris thought. Chris hesitated, wondering if he should feign sleep. He nodded, quickly then. Maybe the man would remove the blindfold . . . he was feeling so sick, dizzy. And his head was hurting him.

"Hmph, thought so. Hungry then, eh?" Chris felt the man lift his shoulders, gently, carefully moving him into sitting position. His head began spinning from the disorientation and pain. The back of his head and neck were so stiff. The pain pressed dully forward against his eyes and the blindfold.

The man's arms felt thick around his shoulders. Then he was leaning close against the man's chest. Stomach? It felt soft and large, but rose and fell with the man's breathing. He smelled strongly of flour and grease.

A hand reached clumsily behind Chris' head. Hope for removal of the blindfold died when only the gag was yanked down. Chris gulped the cool air into his mouth, licked his dry lips.

"Who . . ." Chris started, but a spoon was pushed into his mouth. He choked on the food, tried to spit it back out, then swallowed. It was dry and tasteless.

"Mouth is for eating." And with that the spoon was pushed back into his mouth.

"Please! Please," Chris sputtered.

The man shook him. "No talking! Say more, and no more food for you. Ever." Chris opened his mouth to protest, then snapped it tightly shut.

"Good." The man pushed the spoon back into his mouth. "It's good for you. Medicine for your poor head. Good for you."

Chris ate in silence for a while, feeling like an infant with its mother, enormous in comparison, unfathomable to the blank mind of the child, feeding him dutifully. But he didn't have a blank mind, not anymore. He would be dead now if they didn't need him alive. They wouldn't starve him to death, he thought. Whoever they were . . .

"Just tell me where I am in this room. I . . . I feel so sick. I'm all disoriented," Chris managed between mouthfuls. He heard the spoon clatter into the dish with a frighteningly permanent ring. The man tugged the gag upward.

"I'm begging you! Please! Plea—" The man forced the cloth between his teeth and lowered him back to the ground. Chris could feel his entire body trembling, every muscle wanting to grab the man and make him listen. But he couldn't. He could do nothing to force him, to tell him, to beg him. The man couldn't even see his frustrated tears absorbed unnoticed by the blindfold.

"Well, our cousin here doesn't seem to know anything about a Roamer." Dempter turned to Katie. "Do you?" Katie shook her head.

"No, huh?" Dempter thumbed through the book in her lap. "Roamers fool you, you know. Shakta fooled a lot of people, every way possible. He tangled everyone in his lies, all those who loved him." She looked away. "Especially Oliver Chruston. Oh, God, they were so close—like brothers!"

She stopped and turned to Katie. Katie stared back, recognizing the pain in Dempter's eyes, so like her mother's, longing, wishing things were different.

"Then Shakta turned on him. He always had to be on top." She flipped more pages, her fingertips flicking at the worn corners. "Roamers are like that, you know. Such a warm, loving side, at times sad and pitiful. Your heart just opens up and pulls them in. That's what any Homesteader would do." She leaned close to Katie. "But their hearts, my dear, are Roamer. They don't pity. They do not love. They mimic for power. You'll see their violence now and again, the hard interior breaking through the cracks in their shell, the pride in their skills that leads them to power."

"Pride in their skills?" Katie thought back to Arron's boast of toppling every tree in the forest, the chilling look on his face when he killed all the thieves.

"Oh, yes, their marvelous skills. Shakta, oh, he had conceit all right, but he masked it and still wormed his way into Chruston's heart. Homesteaders, they blind themselves when they don't want to see. That was Chruston's downfall. Here's a sketch of the two of them together. Complete trust. You would never think Shakta was scheming even here. He was." She held the book out to Katie.

Arron hesitated. He knew he should run away now. Now! It was going wrong. It was all going so wrong! He leaned over to look at the book anyway. His throat constricted as he looked at Shakta. It was as if someone had drawn a picture of himself. Like a mirror into the past, Jarra had said, and now he understood. He glanced up. Katie and Dempter were both looking at him.

"I suggest you tell us where Chris is," Dempter said slowly. Arron stood abruptly, making an attempt for the door. Dempter caught his arm and swung him back into his chair. He sat there staring and shaking his head.

"I know you've done something with him. Where is he?" she demanded.

Arron turned frantically to Katie. She was up and pulling back behind her chair. She was thinking of the box—that he wanted it, that it had a lot of power. She had seen what it had done to Brades. Was it true, what Dempter said? No, it couldn't be. The Roamer mouthed her name pleadingly.

"Ah, that's the way it is," Dempter said. She took Katie gently by the shoulders. "Oh, Katie, don't. You'll be hurt too much. Let me show you the scars." She held Katie's eyes a moment, and Katie saw something there, something else she recognized. The woman pulled down her collar, revealing a long, pulled scar along her throat. "Chruston saved my life. I was young then, like you. I trusted a Roamer, pitied him, cared for him. I thought he cared for me. You see, I was special. He told me secrets, his feelings, his needs. He needed me. Oh, and I needed him! He gave me such wonderful things. And I was the only Homesteader he cared for. I should have questioned that. I was the only one because he wanted something. You see, I knew where Chruston was. Well, this is what I have to show for his love!" She touched the scar. "Are you and Chris the only ones? What do you have that this Roamer wants? Does he just want to use you to get at Chruston?"

Katie put her hand in her pocket. Her fingers brushed the box. That's what Arron had looked for when Chris had disappeared. Her fingertips grew warm as they touched another object, round. Dempter's eyes fell on the pocket. Katie pulled the object out, held it up, then dropped it into the palm of her bandaged hand. It sat nicely in the slight depression of her palm, glowing red against the white bandages—the carbuncle Arron had given her. A bribe.

"What's that?" Dempter's eyes opened widely. "Why, a carbuncle! Chruston spoke vaguely about this . . ."

Katie stared at it in horror. It was burning through her hand, the fire flaring into her fingers through the bandages. "My hand!" She dropped the stone, crying out in fright and then in wonder. "My hand?" She flexed her fingers against the stiff bandages. "But—but they were broken." She started to undo the wrappings to look at her fingers.

Arron leaped upon the stone, clutching it, and held it against his throat.

"No!" Dempter grabbed him, shoving him backward. The stone flew from his hands as he lost his balance. He struggled up, pushing Dempter as she reached for the stone. He jerked her about by the arm, catching at her throat, his eyes flashing.

Katie caught his arm. "Arron?" She wanted him to say it wasn't true. But with him standing over Dempter, ready to kill her, she knew it had to be.

He stared at her. What could he say to her? He pulled away, roughly, and glared at her.

Dempter scooped up the carbuncle. She turned to Katie, taking her arm gently. "The pain does pass, my dear. It really does. And something better fills it, I promise you." Katie nodded, keeping her eyes on Dempter's face. She would cry if she were to look at Arron now.

Dempter turned to consider him. "Maybe he had to get rid of Chris to get his hands on this." She held up the gem. "Could this be what he wanted?"

Katie shrugged, then shook her head. "I think—"

Arron turned on Dempter suddenly, a low hum from his throat. The stone had healed him, too, somewhat. He slashed his hand upward, and Dempter flew back, crashing over a chair.

"Arron!" Katie backed against the door.

Dempter shrieked as she stood up. "I've dealt with your type before and learned a bit myself. You've misjudged here!" She flashed her hand out.

Arron let out a cry, clapping his hands to either side of his head. He fell to his knees, cringing, stifling his cry to protect his still-weakened throat. Dempter lowered her hand. Arron snapped his head up, shaking it.

"You," he whispered, choking on the pain in his throat. "You were in my grandmother's mind. It was you. You tore her mind apart! You killed her!" He struggled forward, but Dempter held her hand up again. He collapsed in pain.

"Arron!" Katie ran over to him. "Stop it. Stop it!" Dempter dropped her hand. Arron stayed down, shivering.

"How . . . how did you do that?" Katie asked, looking at Dempter. "You're not a—"

Dempter was staring at Arron in wonder. "No, I'm not a Roamer," she said, distracted. "But their tricks can be learned. It was one of the things Shakta told Chruston."

Arron pushed himself up on his hands and knees. "It's

wrong," he whispered. "You shouldn't have ever used it. You . . ."

Dempter watched him a moment and then moved closer. "So, you were one of the Roamers they had at Buernston."

Arron nodded slowly, his hands clenching into fists.

Dempter shook her head as if unable to believe it. "A Shakta. No, two! There were two of you, and I didn't know! I had only thought you might have information. It never occurred to me that you might be—but, of course! That's why the old woman closed you out. I would have known when I touched your mind." She shook her head again. "Chruston looking all over for you, and I had you, but didn't know it. It never even occurred to me. But I do have you now, and all this can be settled."

"I'll kill you. I'll kill you for what you did to her," Arron said in a quiet voice.

"Oh, no. For now, Roamer, you are going to tell us where Chris is."

"I am going to kill you." Arron started to hum softly, but Dempter raised her hand immediately. The tune broke off with an agonized cry. Arron doubled over.

"Not so long as your voice is weak. And you'll lose it again, if you're not careful. Now tell us where Chris is." She lowered her hand at last. Arron sucked in a sharp breath at the release, then shook his head, trying to clear the ringing. Katie watched the two of them in horror.

"I–I don't—" Arron stuttered.

"You had better tell us, Roamer. I have no room for principles when a young man's life is at stake, especially Oliver's grandson. If you've hurt him, if you've done anything . . ." Katie could see it in her face. Dempter was in love with Chruston. "Chruston taught me a lot," Dempter said slowly. "A lot on how to make Roamers tell the truth."

Arron pushed himself slowly against the wall. He shook his head and pressed himself closer against it.

"No!" Katie stepped in front of Arron. "No, don't. I couldn't bear it. He'll tell me. He will." She turned to him quickly now. "Tell me, Arron. Enough lies. You don't want her to have to hurt you. Tell me, and I won't let her."

Arron narrowed his eyes and pushed himself upright. He

stood slowly. "You think I would hurt Chris." A hand went to his throat.

Katie looked from him to Dempter. "He couldn't have done it," she said at last.

"No? You mean he has never done anything violent, never done anything for his own power, his own feelings. Never?"

"But . . ." Katie turned back to Arron. His back was pressed flat against the wall. He watched her now with wide eyes. "Oh, Arron. Did you? When you left me in the stables, was it to get water? Really? Or—or did you speak to someone? Did you? Did you do something with Chris?"

His mouth tightened into a thin line. He glared at her with the horrible eyes that had looked on the thieves. "Torture me and find out! Then you tell me who's violent! Tell me—" He stopped, gagging on the pain in his throat.

"Arron, you know I wouldn't . . ." She reached for his hand. "You know that."

He took a sharp breath, jerking away from her. "Do I?" He buried his face in his hands, shaking his head. "Why did I ever think I could trust a Homesteader?" He looked back up at her, tears of anger glittering in his eyes. "Go ahead! Go—" He tried to clear his throat, but no sound came out. He simply glared.

Katie turned away from him, back to Dempter. "No. You'll not touch him. He didn't do this. We'll find another way."

"Well? Eat now? Not talk, eh?" Chris stiffened up, hearing the man speak. "Good food. It's good. Medicine for your poor head. Good, eh? You eat now?"

Chris shook his head. He would talk as soon as he could.

"Then you get no food," the man said, the voice coming from directly over him. Chris swung his legs in the direction he thought the man to be. The man grunted in pain or surprise as he struck him.

He leaped upon Chris. Thick, angry fingers tightened about Chris' throat. Chris' hands were crushed against the floor. He kicked his legs up wildly. He would be dead in the next second. But the man only shook him.

"Don't try that! Don't do that!" He knocked Chris' head

against the floor. Chris' mind swam hazily with the pain. Then the man stopped and sat breathing heavily over him. Chris lay still a moment only, then kicked at the man again.

"Hey!" The man grabbed his ankles as Chris raised his legs to kick him again. "You don't give up, do you?" Chris shook his head.

"Okay. Okay, tough, talk then." He yanked the gag down.

Chris gasped, then cleared his throat. "Who are you?" he asked at last. The man said nothing. "I said, who are you?" Still no answer. "Why don't you answer me?"

"Talk, I said. Go ahead."

"You answer me! Answer me," Chris shrieked, kicking his legs from the man's grasp, knocking him with his knees. "You answer me! Answer me!" He kicked angrily for a few moments, then let his legs flop back to the ground with a sob.

He felt the man's arms move gently about his shoulders. One thick hand stroked at his hair. "So, this is the other side, eh, tough?"

"Wh–what's going on?" Chris sputtered, trying to shrug away from the man. "Who are you?"

"Pehter, tough. My name is Pehter."

Chris lay confused, with Pehter comforting him. "Why are you answering me?"

"You asked, tough."

"Why did you do this to me? What do you want?"

"I? I am doing nothing but orders. I do not do this to you."

"Well, who? Why?"

"I was told only that they want you to suffer as they have. To feel the pain. To understand."

"Can you take off the blindfold?"

"No."

"Why not!!"

The man yanked the gag up over Chris' mouth. "You shout now. I said talk, eh. No more talk!"

Chris kicked at him again, but Pehter had moved out of reach and apparently out of the area. Chris stopped kicking and lay there frustrated. Who would want him to suffer as they had? Who had suffered? Arron. Chris closed his mind tightly, knowing the Roamer could hear at a distance.

* * *

"All right, Katie, what do you suggest be done to find Chris? He could be hurt, or even dying. Who knows what this Roamer could have done." Dempter looked at her openly. Katie glanced over her shoulder at Arron. He stood with one hand rubbing his throat. She turned back to Dempter, feeling sick all over. What if he had hurt Chris? She didn't know what to do. It was all so mixed up!

"Well," she forced herself to speak slowly, calmly. "I think I would like to look around the stables a bit more. Perhaps I can find something there."

"But that Roamer knows where he is! How much time do you think we've got?"

"I don't know! I just know that I can't be a part of what you're suggesting. If he isn't willing to tell me freely, then my only alternative is to try another method—another nonforceful method. Do you understand that?"

Dempter nodded. "All right. Go ahead, then."

Katie hesitated. "What about Arron?"

"He's a Roamer, Katie. He can't go about freely, especially not now. He will stay here."

"You won't hurt him will you?"

"No."

"Promise?"

"What games are these? If I were going to hurt him, promising or not won't stop me."

"But you really won't?"

"No, I won't."

Katie eyed her a moment, trying to decide if she could trust her. She realized that she had to. She had to go and try to find Chris. Dempter certainly wasn't going to let her take Arron with her. Nor was she any too certain she actually wanted the Roamer along.

"Okay," she sighed. "Then I'm off. But I'll be right back."

Arron caught at her arm and looked at her pleadingly. The anger was gone now, only fear remained. Fear. She felt like crying. She had seen him fake his emotions to others. Had he done it with her? Was he doing it now? She wanted to be sure —and she couldn't be.

"Come on now, Arron. She promised. Now, let go." Katie

disentangled her arm from his and walked to the door. Arron stared pleadingly after her, until the door swung shut. He sucked in a short breath and clenched his hands into tight fists.

Dempter peered out the window, then locked the door and slid the key into her pocket.

"Now then," she said, turning back to Arron.

His eyes grew wide, seeing her thoughts. Arron stood still a moment, then shook his head firmly.

"Oh, yes," Dempter whispered. "You'll tell me. I'm not about to let that damn curse turn Chruston into a shell. He deserves better than that. I'm not about to let him live tortured and alone because of you damn Shaktas."

Arron straightened, smiling grimly. He shook his head again. No.

XXI

KATIE WANDERED ABOUT THE STABLES TRYING TO FIND something, anything, that would lead her to Chris. But her mind kept wandering back to Arron, alone with Dempter. She wouldn't do anything to him, would she? By leaving them, Katie felt she had in some way given Dempter permission to go ahead. The thought kept eating at her that, by turning her back, she was saying it was okay. And what was worse, she wasn't entirely sure she had not meant it that way. If he had done something with Chris, they had to find out what, and by the quickest way. That would certainly be quicker than this.

But had Arron really done something with Chris? He wouldn't have, he couldn't—and yet, he was a Roamer. How could the entire Homesteader population be wrong about the Roamers? Maybe Dempter was right. Maybe they all were. Maybe it was all an act, so Arron could get the box. Chris was very careful about letting Arron near it. Maybe Chris knew Arron only wanted it, and Chris was just pretending to like Arron so he could get him to his grandfather to cure the curse. But wouldn't Chris have told her? He would have, unless he was afraid Arron would read their minds. Maybe Arron *had* read Chris'.

She wandered back to stare at the scuffled marks in the dirt and tried tracking them again. But again they led back deeper into the stables. They didn't go out . . .

She had a sudden thought. Maybe that's where Arron had somehow arranged to have Chris taken. He had insisted they leave the stables rather quickly. She hurried into the even darker interior of the stable and set the lamp she had lit on one of the bales of hay. She moved slowly along the back wall, testing each panel.

Chris heard Pehter's slow footsteps starting toward him again. Would the man let him talk again? He hoped it wouldn't be another fight. His back and especially his hands were sore. Maybe this time he could get him to remove the blindfold.

"You eat something now, eh?"

Chris shook his head.

"You want to talk then, eh?"

Chris nodded.

"Why? I told you all I know. Talk isn't going to keep you alive. Food is. Your poor head needs medicine. It will be better to eat. Eat first, then talk, eh?"

Chris debated. He was hungry. He really had no idea how long he'd been there. His head had been throbbing since he'd come to. He nodded.

"Good." Chris sensed that Pehter was kneeling down next to him, from the way the man's breathing grew louder and unsteady. The gag was pulled away. Pehter raised him gently, easing him into a sitting position.

"Can't you please just tell me who told you to do this to me?" Chris begged. Arron had done this. He wanted him to feel helpless. Had he done something to Katie, too? Did he have the box?

"Eat first, eh?"

Chris bit down hard on the spoon Pehter pushed into his mouth. His frustration was beginning to consume him now. *Arron!*

Chris? There was worry in the Roamer's voice. Worry, as if he knew Chris understood what he had done. *Chris, are . . . are you all right?*

Who has the box? Who?

Katie does. I swear, Katie does.

I don't believe you. You did this to me! You can't fool me, Roamer.

I did . . . The Roamer's voice disappeared quite suddenly.

Blocking your thoughts, huh? Trying to block the truth?

Chris, I promise. The words came back quite weakly, as if he had been struck in the mouth and was mumbling, but the feeling behind them, his hatred, nothing could block that. *You know I would—* The block came up again, but loosely. The Roamer shot something at him through the gaps he'd left in the block. Chris' mind went numb with pain.

Roamer! What are you trying to do to me?

You . . . can't you understand? Arron's voice was faint and far away. But it brought with it a stab of pain, lighter than what he'd shot at him through the block. A stabbing probe of the Roamer's anger and hatred, aimed right at Chris.

Let me alone, Roamer! You've done enough!

Damn you and Katie both! The block went up again and did not come back down.

But Chris didn't care. He didn't want to talk to Arron anymore. He wanted to kill him.

Damn that Roamer, how could he have done this to them! It had all been a lie. The Roamer wanted only to kill his grandfather, wanted to trick them into helping to kill his grandfather. Chris' throat ached. He tried to squelch the horrible emptiness that was once again rising in his chest.

Chris thought about the knife he had in his boot, Arron's knife. He had taken it, back when the Roamer was sick from that thief Brades. Now he carried it like a Roamer would, and he would use it on a Roamer. His father had been right, not his mother. He'd avenge her, too. He had disobeyed her once because of Arron, when he had killed Brades. Now he would make it right by avenging them all—and himself. And if Katie wasn't still all right . . .

"I'm not hungry anymore, Pehter." Chris felt his shoulder beginning to tingle in the spot where he had been bitten. That Roamer had put something in it. He would get him for that, too. Now he just wanted to rub his shoulder and make the sensation go away. But it wouldn't stop.

Katie stood there, staring up at the bare walls at the back of the stable. The scuff marks ended here. She stood there cursing the Roamer. It was a trick, a trick to hold her off and keep them from questioning him. She had been gone so long now—it had to be way past midnight. Maybe Dempter had already questioned him. Maybe the answers were already available. But wouldn't Dempter come and get her?

She pushed against the wall again, then knocked, and pushed again. She stared dejected for a while. Now what? Her eyes wandered up and down the wall. She got the lantern and held it up a bit. Funny. She noticed a slight mismatch in the grain of the wood up near the top. Her father had taught her to watch for such imperfections in the make of wood-craft. But now that imperfection meant something else to her. She turned about to find something to climb with. She could stack the hay bales.

She set the lamp down again and began to drag a bale over. It wasn't so much that it was too heavy, as that it was so awkward. She was so small, it was hard for her to get her arms about it. The second one was harder still. And she was trying to hurry!

"No, Pehter, wait," Chris said, as the man began to pull at the gag. "I'm a Homesteader, like you—right?" Chris suddenly had second thoughts. Maybe Pehter was a Roamer, too. "Are you?"

"Am Homesteader."

"Well, then you should be on my side and let me loose. Why are you working for a Roamer?"

"Pehter no tell you who he work for."

"Why not?"

"Shame me."

"Then it is a Roamer?"

"Pehter not tell."

"Tell me! I have a right to know!" It was Arron, he was sure of it now. "It's a Roamer boy, isn't it? You've been with him, I know."

Pehter said nothing now, apparently consumed with his thought of betraying another Homesteader.

"Pehter, let me loose and—and you'll be forgiven for your shame. Pehter?"

"No! You tempt me, but danger . . . Magic danger. I am afraid."

"Pehter! Pehter, I'll . . . I'll protect you."

"You have magic, too?"

"N–no, only Roamers have magic."

Silence.

"Pehter, did you—you didn't do anything with a girl? Did you? She's very small, dressed like a boy. Really tough. Did you do any—"

"A girl?" Chris heard the man spit. "No," he said gruffly. There was no mistaking his distaste for women. Chris was thankful that he had not taken Katie as well. Who knew what he would have done.

"Pehter, let me go."

"No."

"Pehter—"

"No! Afraid. Bad magic. No. Do not tempt me!"

"Listen, I have better than magic. Listen to me. If you just bind their hands, they can't make magic. Then you'll be safe."

"No!" He yanked the gag up. "No more talk! You get Pehter into trouble!"

Katie leaned against the bottom of the stack of hay. She had hay splinters stuck in her hands and tangled in her clothes and hair. It didn't feel steady as she leaned against it. She didn't have time to make it steady. She forced herself away from her resting post and caught hold of another bale, carted it over, then slowly pushed it up her stairway of bales. This was it. Or rather, this had to be it, this had to reach; she couldn't drag another up. And that wood-grain difference had better be a door and not a craftsman's mistake.

She pushed the last bale into place and clambered up on top of it. She hesitated before standing to reach for the spot, a queasiness settling in her stomach as the bales shifted slightly below her, and the ground . . . so far away.

Chris. She set her mind on Chris. Pressing her hands against the wall, she straightened her body, bit by bit, pressing it, too, against the wall. She reached slowly for the place, her cheek flat against the panels. She went up on tiptoe, pushing the wall with her hand. It moved in! She gave a cry of relief, then another of fear as the whole stack under her shuddered. The bale she was on started sliding, tipping under her lopsided weight.

Her fingers clawed at the edge of the now-open doorway. She caught at its lip and pulled herself painfully upward as the top bale slid off and the stack swayed back and forth. Her face came up into the square hole, her chin over her fingers. She pushed with her feet against the wall to find a grip; they slid against the wood of the wall. The slight friction, though, gave her enough force to pull herself up, one arm inside. She pushed down on the floor inside the hole, heaving herself up and getting the other arm in. One final effort, then she lay gasping on the small platform of the opening.

She sat up and looked into the darkness. The light from the lamp below provided her a shadowy view of the area. There were the tips of a ladder on the other end of the platform. She crawled slowly over to it and climbed down.

It was totally dark below, and damp. The floor sloped downward. She could hear rats scuttling back and forth, squeaking their wretched stories to one another. One scrambled over her feet. She pulled back, drawing her knife.

She began to walk cautiously down, her knife gripped close, her other hand out in front. It took only a short while for her sense of direction to go, especially when the slope leveled out. She couldn't even judge how far she had walked. Then she thought of the box in her pocket, thought of the glow it had given when Chris opened it. She wondered. Carefully she slid it from her pocket. It glowed eerily and cast her shadow oddly upon the dripping walls. She moved along more quickly then, able to see.

She slowed up again when the hall widened into a circular room. A form lay in the center, not moving. She stepped closer, slowly.

"Chris," she gasped, rushing fully into the room and over to him. "Oh, Chris!"

The form stiffened up and raised its head slightly. Katie went to kneel down next to him, but was struck violently sideways. The box flew from her hand as she spun against the wall. Almost instinctively, she gripped the knife tighter.

It was only a moment before she was on her feet again, facing a huge man who was laughing as he looked at her. She felt her slight size here against this man as she had never felt it before. She swung the knife in front of herself.

"He's my friend. Stay away or I'll kill you," she warned.

Chris kicked his legs, trying to stop this. He knew Pehter's strength. And he knew Pehter would kill Katie with the pent-up fury he had felt in the man's hands. He knew Pehter hated her as violently as he now hated the Roamers.

"Puny, you would hurt me, eh?" Pehter stepped closer to her. He reached out angrily for the knife. Katie slashed quickly; the knife was sharp and went deeply through his fingers. He howled and fell back, clutching at his hand, sizing her up once more.

"Who told you to take him?" Katie asked quickly. She had to know. "A Roamer?"

Pehter held his hand tightly, trying to stop the flow of blood. He was trying to wrap it with a filthy rag from the floor.

Katie still hesitated. She knew this was the moment to get him, but she had to know. "Tell me, or I'll cut them all the way off," she demanded. "Was it a Roamer?"

"Evil magic, magic made me. Kill you because of it," Pehter spat out. He ran his small eyes over her, then charged.

Katie ducked under his flailing arms and slashed at his side. She realized by the way he put his arms out to grab her that he would crush her if he caught her. Her arms would be much too short to reach around his back to his kidneys, if he caught her like that. He was enormous. She was unsure if her knife could even reach through his flesh to his heart. His throat was her only choice—but to reach that he either had to fall or . . . or lift her up.

He was charging at her again. This time she let him grab her, holding her arms up carefully, to keep them from being trapped in his.

"Pulp! Puny pulp," he laughed, squeezing her convulsively. She gasped in painful surprise, then stabbed her knife into his throat and face, whatever she could reach. The flesh was too thick. She felt her breath going from her, her ribs pressed back against his arms, a weak effort, cracking. She slashed him across the bridge of his nose. He shrieked, dropping her and stumbled away. She fell where he dropped her and lay sucking air into her pain-filled chest. She forced herself up again and went after him. He stumbled about, blinded by the blood in his eyes. She jumped up on his back, he spun around, throwing her off, then stumbled over her and fell. She leaped on top of him. His arms immediately closed about her, crushing her against him. But her knife was already at his throat, digging its way to his jugular, to his windpipe, anything! There was a sudden rush of blood spurting all over him and her, and his arms flexed spasmodically.

"Shame," gurgled the last of his breath.

She rolled off him and lay a moment, trying to breathe without pain. Then she struggled up again, remembering Chris.

Her hands tore at the gag, pulling it away. She yanked the blindfold off and hugged him against her.

"Oh, Chris! Oh, my God, you're all right," she sobbed, hugging him again. She bent and cut the ropes at his hands and feet. His arms circled suddenly about her, and he pulled her into his lap.

"Katie, Katie—I thought you were dead. I heard him, he was crushing you. Katie . . ." He hugged her tightly and kissed her, then hugged her again. She cried out in pain at his tight hold.

"He did hurt you! Did he break your ribs?"

"Just bruised," she laughed. "I'm only bruised."

He hugged her at that and then apologized, thinking he had hurt her again. Then he held her back and looked at her thoughtfully. He stared for a long moment, and she looked away uncomfortably.

"How long?" he asked. "How long have I been here—wherever we are?"

"A day and a night . . . forever. God, I was scared. Chris, did . . . did you know Arron was only after the box?

Or were you as taken in as I was?" She blinked back the tears that started anew in her eyes.

"I was taken in. I . . . I still can't believe it." Then he looked at her more sharply. "The box? Do you have it?"

"Oh!" Katie pulled herself from his arms, looking around. The sphere lay in the corner, glowing, the box at its side. She picked up the box and rolled the sphere carefully back inside. She shivered, touching it, feeling Pehter's death grip about her body again, then it soothed her sore ribs. She set the box in Chris' waiting hand. He took hold of her hand with the box.

"Lead me out of here," he said, smiling and standing up. He tottered unsteadily, his head spinning, then he pulled her closer to steady himself. "How'd you get in here?"

"This way." She led him back up the dark passageway.

"Arron is with Dempter?" Chris asked as they neared the front gate.

Katie nodded. "I was afraid to leave him—"

"You don't think he'd hurt her, do you?"

"Oh! No. She wanted him to tell us where you were. She was going to—"

Chris knocked on the door. No one came. He knocked louder, then banged and tried the door. It was locked. He looked nervously at Katie. "She was going to what? You sure he wouldn't hurt her?"

Katie tried to peer in at the window. "She was going to make him tell where you were. But Chris, he's gotten his voice back. That stone—oh! It's too complicated. But he has his voice back! You don't think . . ." She caught at Chris' arm, thinking of the horror in the Roamer's eyes.

"Stand back." Chris moved her out of the way, took a running start, and crashed shoulder-first into the door. He bounced back, sprawling on the porch.

"Chris!"

"I'm all right—all right." He got up and stared at the door. "We've got to get in! We've got to. He'll kill her. I'll never find my grandfather!"

"The window! Come on!" Katie caught hold of the chair and smashed it through the window, her arms coming up to protect her face. Chris kicked away the extra glass. He climbed in and pulled Katie in after him.

The living room was a mess, the chairs toppled, books pulled from the shelf. They stared, shocked, then Katie turned and ran down the back hallway.

"This way," she called to Chris.

She skidded to a halt as Dempter came hurrying toward her. "Katie? Is that you? The Roamer knows where Chris is! But I can't get him to tell. We'll have to—" She stopped, seeing Chris come up behind Katie. A hand went to her chest with a surprised intake of air. "Oh! You've found him." A smile quickly covered the shocked look on her face, and she reached out to take hold of Chris. "Oh, thank God you're all right!" She squeezed his shoulders gently.

"We—we thought Arron had done something to you when you didn't answer," Katie said. "We broke your window. Sorry."

"Oh, my, that's quite all right. Just to see you safe. But look at you, you're both covered with blood! What happened? You weren't hurt were you?"

Katie shook her head. "We—I had to dispose of a guard. But, where is Arron?"

"Back here." Dempter led them into a room. Arron was sitting in the corner, his hands shackled in front of him, head bent down against the wall. He looked up at them slowly.

"I . . . I asked you not to hurt him," Katie whispered.

"I know, dear. And I wouldn't have. But I was frightened, and you were gone so long. Fear makes you do odd things. I'm sorry."

"No. No, it's all right. We were all rather frightened."

"And now," Chris said softly. "You have your Roamer. Take us to my grandfather."

"Damn you!" Arron forced himself more upright.

"Me? You're the one who's damned!" Chris turned on him. "How could you! How could you do that to me? To Katie? All those lies! All those tricks! Go ahead and deny it. Go ahead! I dare you."

Arron shook his head and looked away, leaning back against the wall.

"All right, one of you go on to the stables and tell the

stable master to prepare my wagon. I'll go and get some food ready. It's about a two-week ride to the west."

Chris nodded and turned to leave. Dempter looked back at the Roamer huddled in the corner. He was watching her closely, his eyes so very dark. She felt a tiny knot of terror coil about her stomach. As if he knew what she felt, he smiled, ever so slightly. She raised her hand to strike him. Chris caught at her wrist.

"I think you've done enough to him. That's something a Roamer would do, not a Homesteader."

"Oh, no, not a Homesteader," Arron said in a low voice. "Never a Homesteader. What do you think she is? Look what she's done. You've seen what other Homesteaders have done to me! Show me what the Roamers have done! Show me!"

"Shut up!" Chris walked to him and stood over him. "You killed a whole group of men just a week or two ago, Roamer!"

"Thieves! They would have killed us."

"And you would do anything to save our lives. Even raise the dead?"

Arron stared at him, then looked down. "I—" He stopped and covered his face with his hands.

Chris turned away from him when the Roamer had no answer. "Get him ready to go. Keep his hands cuffed. I don't want any of his magic."

XXII

THE WAGON RATTLED ALONG WITH CHRIS AND KATIE sitting up in the front with Dempter. Arron sat far in the back, very quiet. Katie glanced back once. He was trying to reach his kithara, where it lay on top of the pile of baggage. She thought about going back and moving it from his reach —hadn't Brades said it made him more dangerous? But Arron's eyes caught hers and stared at her so accusingly, she turned away. Chris glanced at her and took her hand. What is it? he seemed to be asking. She shook her head.

"How much farther?" Chris asked Dempter.

"Very near."

"How long?"

"An hour or two."

"Really?" Chris turned to Katie, squeezing her hand. "We're close, Katie. We're really close. And then everything is going to work out right." He looked about at the barren landscape. "All the confusion we've felt will be cleared up."

He twisted about, suddenly, hearing the soft, plucking sound of an instrument. Arron had reached his kithara and had it in his lap. He held it awkwardly; it was difficult for him to spread his hands. But he had gotten it right finally, or as best as he could.

Chris hesitated, deciding whether or not to go back and take it from him. The Roamer began singing softly. His voice, still scarred from the poison, didn't sound as glorious as it once had. It sent chills to Chris' spine as it mimicked the bleak landscape around them. The notes didn't flow well, with his hands bound, but their meaning was clear as Arron began the old lullaby.

> It comes to you desired, tired or not
> Sleep, my boy, 'tis a blessed thing
> Trouble will go, light will follow . . .

Chris got up, his boot stamping hard on the seat as he climbed over, crawling through the baggage to get at the kithara.

The Roamer quickly changed what he was playing. The notes became smoother as he grew accustomed to his disadvantage, his voice, with use, becoming stronger and full.

"Trouble will come. Ancient desired relieving his mind. Trust in him!" Arron spoke the last of it as Chris yanked the kithara from him.

"Trust who!" Chris tossed the kithara to the front of the wagon, watching the Roamer flinch as it landed with a thud. "Trust who? Who, you? After your lies? After all you've done!"

"Chris, I didn't." The voice was thin, barely audible. The wagon went over a bump, knocking Chris flat on his back. He got up slowly and made his way back to the front. He didn't look back at the Roamer. He hunched down next to Katie.

"Do you know what that song means?" she whispered to him.

He shook his head.

"Trust your grandfather," Dempter said softly. "He is undoubtedly the ancient referred to in the song. Trust the ancient." She stared far ahead, her blue eyes seeing something else beside the black, dry land. "I'd trust that man with my life."

Chris watched her. "He really is a good man?"

"The best," she said very firmly, then frowned. She was

silent for only a moment, thinking. Then she said, "Oh, Chris, he's the very best there is. You must believe me." Seeing him nod, she turned forward again, repeating to herself. "The best."

The horses continued to trot on. They hadn't even the slightest interest in the fields beside them. There was nothing for them here, no vegetation to catch their thoughts. The gray land spread out all around them and seemed to fade off into the sky, with no distinct boundary for any of them to say where the land ended and the sky began.

Katie turned about, trying to find something that stood out in the landscape. "What's that?" She pointed to a dark patch on the horizon to the south. There a line of haze rose darker above the land.

"That's the Derthlan Slough," Dempter said, nodding toward it.

"A . . . a swamp?" Katie asked, forcing herself not to look back at the Roamer.

"Yes."

"Is . . . is it possible to cross it?"

"Oh, my, yes. It's large, but very shallow. After all, it's very recently formed. It's the quickest way between the north and south towns. People go back and forth over it all the time."

"That's a lie."

Dempter looked back at the Roamer in surprise. "Why do you say that? You know as well as I do that it's easily traversed. That's where the men from Buernston found you. Now, if it were dangerous, how could you have been living in there, and how could those men have gone in there to find you?"

"Three of those men died in quicksand. And we were near the edges at the time!"

"There is quicksand, yes. But those men knew where. And apparently so did you. Those men died because of you. You pushed them, isn't that right, Roamer?"

Arron's mouth fell open. "But . . . but what they were going to do to my grandmother . . ." He lowered his head, then jerked it up again. "That swamp is not safe to cross, and you know it! Don't twist my words with my past deeds."

Dempter watched him openly, then, shaking her head, looked at Chris and Katie.

"He lied to us earlier about the swamp," Chris answered her unasked question. Dempter nodded, understanding suddenly. Arron grew quiet again.

"My grandfather really lives out here?" Chris stared sadly about.

"Yes, really. I know what you're thinking. He hates it, too. There. You can just make it out up ahead." She pointed. Chris looked up and saw, very far in the distance, a small, squat building. As they approached, it rose slowly, becoming a turret for a massive stone building, as dead-looking as the land around it, bone white.

"That's it?" Katie said doubtfully.

"That's it," Arron answered from the back of the wagon. They all turned to look at him.

"How do you know?" Chris asked. The Roamer shrugged and looked away.

"I . . . I've seen it somewhere," he said vaguely.

Dempter pulled the wagon to a halt in front of the tall double doors, and she, Chris, and Katie climbed out. She rapped firmly on the door, the knocker booming both into the castle and into the air.

Chris and Katie stared about them, taking in the massive stonework. Traces of long-dead ivy still clung limply to the cold granite walls. The windows, made of intricately cut glass, were covered by thick layers of dust and grime, marring their beauty. It seemed sure that no one could live here.

But the door began to open, and an old man stood before them, blinking in the light. Chris recognized something in the man's eyes, faint reminders of his mother through all the wrinkles.

"Ulna, my dear, how kind of you to visit." He took her hand gently and turned to look at Chris and then at Katie. He looked back at Chris. "You! You are a . . . a grandchild of mine, perhaps?" He reached out and touched him.

"Yes, yes I am, if you are Chruston. I'm Chris."

"And I am your great-great-grandfather Chruston. Yes." The old man continued to gaze at him. "Ah, I've waited so

long," he whispered, then a troubled look passed his face.
"But . . . but not to lose you," he murmured. "No, please,
not to lose you. I couldn't bear it."

"Grandfather?"

The old man looked up and smiled. "It's nothing, nothing,
Christopher. I'm afraid I have a great deal of fear for things,
things I wish were otherwise. It will pass, this fear, God
willing." He turned to Katie then.

Chris took her hand and pulled her forward. "This is Katie. Katie Topkins." He placed her hand in his grandfather's.

"A pleasure, my dear. Indeed a great pleasure." His eyes
wandered away from her face and out to the wagon. He
gasped. "Shakta? Oh, my friend!" He stumbled to the wagon
and took Arron's face lovingly in his hands. "Oh, my friend,
I forgive you. You didn't know, you didn't see. Oh, I forgive
you."

"No, no. Grandfather, it's not . . ." But Chruston spun
to face them.

"Why is he shackled? And who has abused my dear friend
so? He is full of pain, and his face—who has beaten him?"

"It's not Shakta, Oliver," Dempter said. "It's his grandson, Arron Shakta. He is cuffed because he means to kill you,
to kill us all."

"Is this true? You would betray my friendship with your
great-great-grandfather?"

"It's already been betrayed." Arron strained forward. "By
you! And I would kill you if I could."

Chruston stepped back from the Roamer, his mouth falling open. "He is confused. Someone has mistaught him."

"That old woman who kept him close at her side. Away
from you, so she could fill him with her poison. It's a crime
what she did to a child. She should have been put to death
for that." Dempter went to Chruston's side.

"Well, you took care of that!" Arron spat at her.

"And is this why you brought him? To teach him my kind-
ness?"

"No, Grandfather. For the cure to the curse, the curse for
which you just forgave him. The cure that says a Shakta
must go to a Chruston. He is here. Do whatever you have

to." Chris paused. "I . . . I don't want to waste away like the others have."

Chruston turned to him suddenly and caught his arm, pulling him close. "No. Never. I'm not going to lose you now that I have you with me. I won't let that curse keep taking from me! My family will live." Chruston looked thoughtfully at Arron. "And a Shakta has indeed come."

Dempter smiled and took the old man's arm. "They brought you a gift." She nodded to Katie, who brought him the kithara. "It belonged to Shakta."

Chruston took it from Katie. "Oh, yes. He played it often and gave me much pleasure. He had a beautiful voice and such skill—"

"It's mine!"

Chruston turned back to Arron. "Is it? Can you play?"

Arron looked at it and then at Chruston, a funny look in his eye. "Yes!" He reached for it, but Dempter intercepted him.

"I would take care before letting him near this instrument," she cautioned. "For your safety, Oliver. You must remember, he does not understand that there was once a closeness between you and Shakta. There is such hate in him! I think it best we go in. We've traveled a long way, and it is late."

"Oh, yes, my dear, yes, we shall." Chruston looked at Arron again. "The curse, yes. We must do something about that, too, mustn't we?" He looked at Chris.

Chris nodded. "I don't want my children or theirs to have to live under what I've lived under."

"No," Chruston whispered as if in pain. "They mustn't. Gaeth! Gaeth," he called into the house. A moment later a tall, gaunt man stepped from the doorway. He was pale, barely there, it seemed. His hair was bleached white and his eyes. It was as if someone had taken an eraser and wiped all trace of color from the man.

"Sir?"

"See to the Roamer, then to the bags."

Gaeth nodded and walked silently to the wagon. Arron stiffened up, staring at the man.

Gaeth leaned against the wagon, stretching a hand out to Arron. Arron pulled back, seeing the man smile.

"No," he whispered. "I–I'm not—you stay away." He scrambled back over the bags. Arron turned his eyes wildly on Chruston. "I'll go where you tell me. Just . . ." He looked back at the pale man, climbing toward him over the baggage.

Chruston watched them, confused. Arron jumped suddenly from the wagon, when Gaeth reached for him, and began running across the dark field. Gaeth leaped after him.

"Whatever is the matter?" Chruston turned to Chris, who shrugged.

Dempter raised her hand quickly, and the Roamer collapsed in pain. Gaeth caught hold of him and lifted him up.

"Ulna! Don't do that! Don't do that to him." Chruston shook her.

"He was running. I wanted to stop him."

"Where could he go?" Chruston said softly. "You needn't have done that."

"He's gotten away before." She turned to the door. Chruston shook his head slowly and led Chris and Katie inside.

"Something to eat, perhaps? You're probably hungry." Chruston led them through a great hallway and into a grand living room. The furniture was rich looking, but worn with age. The windows were shuttered closed. Chris wondered how it might look cleaned up, warmer, with more people— how it might look in happier times.

Gaeth entered the room from a back doorway. Chruston signaled him to get some refreshments for his guests. The man nodded once and left.

"You're here alone except for him?" Chris asked.

Chruston nodded sadly. "I wish it weren't so. But any relationships I would care to make . . . Well, nothing lasts forever except—me." Dempter reached for his arm, her eyes not leaving his face.

"The cure? It will allow you to die?" Katie asked.

"No," Chruston said softly. "That is now permanent."

"I . . . I want to help you." Chris put his hand on his

grandfather's arm. The man looked so thin and frail, as if he needed Chris' protection.

Chruston patted his hand. "Perhaps you can, my boy. But we'll leave that talk for later."

Dempter sipped the wine Gaeth had brought and eyed Chruston and Chris. She stepped carefully between them. "I think we ought to sit down." She took Chruston's hand and set him in a thick armchair, then took the one next to it.

"No offense, my dear, but allow my grandson to take your chair. I would like to speak with him further." Dempter opened her mouth, then closed it, nodding. She got up, indicating the chair for Chris, and joined Katie over on the couch.

Chris sat down slowly, and Chruston put his hand gently over Chris'. "It does me good to see you. It's been so long . . ." He stared off a moment, then focused back on Chris. "You remind me of myself, Christopher, as much as that Roamer reminds me of Shakta." He leaned back slowly in his chair and sighed. "Oh, to be with family." He squeezed Chris' hand. "And I'm not going to lose you. I won't give you up. I've lost all the others, helpless. My sons, my daughters, your beautiful mother—but not you." He looked Chris over. "We have a Shakta—a true Shakta, mind you. There is a difference." Chruston's mind wandered away from them again.

"What difference?" Katie asked.

Chruston looked at Katie. "He is as my friend Shakta was with all the powers Shakta had—more, in fact. This one is extremely powerful. But I don't think he knows, yet, not his full potential. He's too young. Shakta was much older. And I realized almost too late. Almost. This time, however, I know, and the Roamer does not."

"So, not all Roamers can—" Chris started.

His grandfather shook his head. "Not all. Oh, they have some magic. But it runs extremely powerful in the Shakta family, and amazingly strong in certain individuals. So very strong . . ." He watched Chris closely.

"But that Roamer you brought has an ability Shakta did not have. He can undo what Shakta has done. He can right the land."

"The Dark Prince," Katie whispered.

Chruston glanced at her. "The Dark Prince is death, my dear. The Roamer, I am sorry to say, will not, cannot, live through the undoing. He may not be aware of it yet, but somewhere within his mind is the secret to the cure for the lands."

Katie nodded slowly. "I think he might know. He talked a couple of times about understanding how to fix things."

"And the curing of the lands will cure me, too?" Chris asked eagerly.

Chruston grew silent a moment. "Chris, we have to get the Roamer to tell your death. Only then will you live. And if you live, the curse on our family will be broken, destroyed."

"What?" Katie stood up. "But—but Arron said that your living forever is what is causing the destruction in the land. Surely Chris living forever, too, would only . . ." She stopped and looked at Chris and Chruston. "Wouldn't it?"

Chruston shook his head. "My life is just another part of the curse, not the cause. And a single living Roamer has the magic to perpetuate the curse. Especially if that Roamer is a Shakta—and the most powerful I've ever seen, at that."

Katie nodded and sat down. "I just can't believe Arron lied to us all this time."

"Only the deceitful suspect deceit, my dear," Chruston said gently. "It is no fault."

"There are so many conflicting stories." Chris leaned back, rubbing his eyes. "I just don't know what to do."

Chruston nodded. "I may be able to help you find the truth. There are ways to know what it is. But, will you agree to the cure, my boy? It is truly the only way."

"Can I think about this?"

"Of course! Take all the time you want, and more. Whatever you need. I know what kind of problems these decisions cause, believe me. But you're tired. It's time we turned in." He rang a little silver bell at his side, yawning. "Gaeth, please take my guests to their rooms for the night."

Gaeth nodded and led them up the long main stair.

Chris flopped down gratefully on the big bed. It had been so long since he had last been comfortable. He stared up at the ceiling for a while. It felt strange, too, to be alone. Yes, it had been long since he had slept alone. He'd gotten rather used to having Katie and Arron nearby, to hearing their quiet breathing at night, or maybe their idle chatter as he was drifting off.

He rolled his head about on the pillow. He couldn't believe he had fallen for that Roamer's act. And now, it just ached inside.

One of the funny songs Arron had taught them came to his mind, one about a man dancing with his sheep, or something. It seemed so long ago now. They had all laughed together. Arron had seemed oddly grateful for their laughter and had quickly played another. Chris rubbed his forehead with his fingers, trying to press the memory from his mind. God, he really had cared for him. Damn.

He shifted positions. It seemed terribly quiet. This house carried its own loneliness. And his grandfather had lived here so long, alone.

Chris? The Roamer's voice came as a whisper in his ear, strained with fatigue. *Chris?*

Go away.

Chris, what did he tell you to do to me? You're blocking something. I can feel it.

I'm not the first one to block something.

Chris—

Shut up! I won't have you confusing me! I can't let you confuse me anymore, filling me up with your lies! Shut up! If I can block my thoughts to you, I can surely block you from me. I won't hear any more of your lies. You've caused me enough grief. My grandfather says he can make you tell the truth, and then I'll know.

What? the Roamer's voice snapped back. *What can he do? What? Chris—*

Frightened? Well, I am going to learn some things, then. I believe my grandfather. And I'll do what he says. He knows what's best for a Homesteader—not some damn Roamer! I'll do what he says, even if it means killing you. And I won't hear another thing from you!

There was a long, quiet pause, then Arron's voice rang so sharply into his head, it was painful. Hatred and anger shot through, overriding the bitter hurt. *No, don't worry, my good friend! You won't hear another thing from me!* Chris suddenly felt a strange sensation pressing into his head. As if . . . as if it were expanding, folding out upon itself, as if each little thought added itself to the others, making a new kind of sense, meaning something more than they had when they sat side by side. An added factor seemed to have pressed them together, but instead of becoming more condensed, they grew and grew, meaning more, saying more.

In that moment, he saw in detail the way his and Arron's minds were connected, how it worked, why it worked—and everything that could alter and change the pattern. Everything. But each part was qualified, as if it had a bit extra that said what the consequences would be if the pattern were altered . . . the consequences to—

Arron blocked the vision suddenly, and Chris realized then that it had all been in the Roamer's mind, not in his own. He tried to remember what exactly he had seen, but it had disappeared like vapor. Chris started to wonder about it, but the Roamer's voice shot back into his mind, white-hot, burning any of his own thoughts with its hatred.

No, you won't hear another thing from me! It's my power that allows this connection, and mine that will put a stop to it. I was going to search that whole town for you when you were missing. I risked my damned life by going to Dempter's! Why would I do that if I knew where you were? Well, no more, damn you! You can go ahead and kill me, if that's what your grandfather asks. But, mind you, that's all you'll get from me. My life—not yours! Damn you!

Shut up! Shut up! Chris yelled back at him. But it felt strange now, like before. *Arron?* The strange, tingling extension was gone. The Roamer had stolen it back.

Chris rolled over, slapping his hand against the pillow. He got up and paced a bit. Finally he opened his door and peered down the hallway. It was empty, like his room, like the whole house, and the land around it.

He stepped out into the hallway and carefully shut his door. He tiptoed a few doors down and knocked softly, waited a moment, then knocked again. He turned and started back to his room, stopping a few feet down when he heard a door click open.

"I thought I heard something," Katie whispered. "But if you meant to knock on my door, I was the next one down." She paused. "Did you?"

"Uh . . . yes." Chris stared down at the design in the rug.

"Well?"

"Well . . . my room seemed . . ."

"Lonely?"

"Yes."

"Come in, then. So's mine." She held the door open wider, and Chris stepped in sheepishly.

"Don't be embarrassed, silly. I was about to go down to yours. It's been a while since we've any of us slept alone. And this house seems so . . ."

"Very empty."

"Yes. Come on. Sit down." She tapped the bed next to her and sat hugging her knees. "I suppose Arron's somewhere alone, too."

"I suppose."

"I feel guilty."

"He's done wrong by us. We've got nothing to feel guilty for."

"But we do—or I do."

"We do." Chris stared about the room. "But, Katie, when I was kidnapped, I was so scared and . . . and frustrated. To think how he had . . . Katie, I don't see how even a Roamer could lie like that! Damn him, why couldn't he have just used his magic on us? Why'd he have to . . ." He ran a hand quickly through his hair, then flopped back onto the bed, his breath hissing through his teeth. "I told myself I'd kill him, when I was trapped there. Against what my mother taught me. I think that's what I'm feeling guilty about. I feel, oh, God, like I'm betraying her the way that Roamer betrayed us."

"No, Chris, you're not."

"And my grandfather, living in this lonely, empty house. I can't let him. I owe him—"

"Chris—"

"I think my mother would be happy if I did something about that. And I'd be stopping the curse. Think of that, Katie! She said all life was precious. Think of the lives I'd save. I'd be helping Grandfather and stopping the curse. Right? And like you said when I killed Brades, I had to, or he'd have killed us. Right?"

"Yeah, I did."

"This is the same. It seems to be one life for many. Does that seem right? And my grandfather, he's so kind. Not anything like I'd expected from Arron's picture of him. What did you think?"

Katie lay back next to him. "I like him. I really do, Chris. I don't think he should have to live like this, any more than you do. Don't worry, you'll do what's right. I trust you."

Chris turned his head and smiled at her. "Thanks."

"Now, I think we should get some sleep."

Chris nodded, getting up.

"You . . . you can stay here, if you want to," Katie whispered.

"There's only one bed."

Katie shrugged. "It seems like this house needs something —something like people being together, instead of alone."

Chris sat back down. "Yeah?"

She nodded and smiled, sliding across the bed to make room for him to lie down. He smiled back and lay down next to her.

"Thanks," he said, making himself comfortable. Then he lay back and closed his eyes.

Katie propped herself up on one arm, watching him a moment.

"It's a little cold in here, don't you think," she said in a very quiet voice.

He looked at her, then sat up. He reached down for the blanket at the foot of the bed, pulled it up, and reached to wrap it about her as she sat up with him. She leaned closer as his arms went about her shoulders. He looked down at her, almost surprised to find her face so close to his.

Suddenly he tightened his arms about her, pulling her close against him. Her arms came up, curling behind his neck. And for the first time, as he felt her pressing against him, he felt safe, less cut off, a feeling that he wasn't alone any longer. He bent his head to kiss her gently, then more urgently as she pressed him closer. He laid her back onto the bed, letting the blanket he had wrapped about her fall away from her shoulders. He stared down at her a moment as if finally recognizing something he had known all along.

"Katie . . ." he breathed.

"Shhh," she whispered back, smiling up at him. And he could see in her eyes that she understood, as she had always understood him. She pulled him down to her, and he realized he would never be alone again.

XXIII

"MORNING, GRANDFATHER," CHRIS SAID, JUMPING DOWN the last few steps.

"Ah, good morning, Christopher. You're mighty cheerful this morning. Where's your, ah, your companion?"

"Katie?"

"Yes."

"She's not down here? Hmmm. I thought she'd come down."

"Not that I've seen. But, not to worry, my boy, she could've gotten up before me."

"Yeah." Chris sat down across from the old man.

"Have you thought about what we discussed last night? Not to rush you; if you need more time, by all means—"

"No, no, I have thought about it. Katie and I discussed it last night."

"Katie and you?"

"Yes. This house is so lonely. Yes, I'll do it, Grandfather. I don't want you to be alone anymore."

"Well," the old man sighed, leaned back in his chair, and smiled at Chris. "I can't be too cursed." He shook his head, his eyes still on his grandson. "No. And it's a hard thing I ask you to do. You're very giving. I'm proud, proud of the way your parents raised you, proud of the way you've turned out."

"Thank you," Chris said, feeling his face redden a bit. "But you did say you could get the truth from Arron. I have to know the truth first. Can you understand?"

Chruston nodded. "Of course, my boy. I, too, once felt as you do about a Roamer—confused. It is the truth that helped me decide what I had to do. So it shall be with you."

Just then, the big front door boomed shut. A moment later, Katie strode into the room, her face flushed from the cold morning air.

"Ah, here's your companion now."

"Morning." She perched herself on the arm of Chris' chair. He reached up and took her hand, relieved. "Were you worried?"

Chris laughed and indicated the knife at her belt. "No." Then he looked at her. "Not at all, except that no one knew where you were." He frowned at that.

"Well, I told Gaeth where I was going. No one else was up, so I just went. I needed to take a walk." She leaned back against the chair. "This area is so barren, it's eerie." She glanced at Chruston to see if she had offended him, but he wasn't looking at her. He was checking his watch.

"Come. Let's go have some breakfast. Ulna has been in the kitchen this morning. She's in a good mood, too, and she just up and decided that was how she wanted to start the day. So we shan't disappoint her now by being late.

"Then, of course, we have a Roamer to consult, but I fear that won't be until late. So many things to prepare. Well, come along." He took Chris' arm and led the way to the dining room with Katie trailing along.

Chruston pushed his breakfast dish away and turned to Chris. "Now, let's go over your journey here, to try and sort out what it is you are confused about." Dempter cleared his dish away, casting odd glances from Chris to Chruston and back. Katie sat quietly in her seat, listening to the old man talk to Chris.

Chris nodded. "It's just that there are so many times he acted . . . well, like he cared about what happened to Katie

or me." He looked down at his empty plate. "He acted in
ways that for various reasons he shouldn't have."

"You can't be sure of all the reasons for the way a Roamer
acts. Their plotting goes deeper than you might ever suspect."

"Yes, I know. But he risked his life so many times for us.
Why? Why would he do that? Sometimes it seemed to me it
might have been more to his benefit if we were dead."

"That is why you need the truth from him," his grandfather said. "That will show you plots and schemes you
couldn't imagine. We will get the truth from him, and you
will know what to do." He got up and gathered some papers
he had left on the counter. He came back and sat close at
Chris' side.

"Now then, I want you to tell me all about your trip. I'll
jot down the questions that come up, and we'll put them to
the Roamer."

"But he won't—"

"He will give you the truth, I promise, Christopher." The
old man lifted his pen to show he was ready for Chris to
begin. So Chris began outlining the weeks that had passed
since he found the Roamer at the riverbed.

His grandfather interrupted him as he told him about the
bear attack on Mount Klineloch, how Arron had saved him,
and how he had put a strange paste in his wound to take out
some poison he claimed was in it. "Poison?" The old man
looked confused, then stood up and looked closely at Chris'
shoulder. It tingled when the man touched it. He sat back
down, shrugging.

"Strange this bear should bite you and then run off. But
poison . . ." He glanced over at Dempter. The woman's
face was as blank as his, indicating she had no explanation
for the strange behavior, either. He indicated to Chris to
continue with his story.

Chris went on, with Chruston watching him closely and
scratching down questions Chris asked about oddities in the
Roamer's behavior. He stopped him only a few times, once to
have him give more detail on the exploding trees, and again
when he told him about Brades.

"You say he came back to life?" Chruston said, an amazed look on his face.

Here Katie interrupted. "It wasn't really that he was alive," she said. "He was still dead. I mean, he couldn't feel anything. He was just—animated. His body was still being used, but the man inside was gone." She got up from her chair, thinking about it. "That's what it was—he still had something to do, and that was to kill Arron." She shivered. Chris got up and went to her side.

Chruston shook his head in disbelief. "Who would have thought?" he muttered. "That much power in a spell." He turned to Dempter then. "Get the girl something to drink, she seems badly shaken."

Katie turned around at that. "No, no, I'm all right. I'd just forgotten the strangeness."

"Come and sit down." Chris led her back to her seat, made sure she was comfortable, then sat down himself.

Chruston waited until they were settled, then picked up his pen again. "Let's finish up here. We still have to deal with the Roamer yet."

Chris agreed, took Katie's hand, and went on to finish his story.

It wasn't until late that afternoon that Chruston led them up the long, winding staircase in the turret they had seen coming up the road.

"I've chosen the room carefully. It is the same room in which Shakta cast the curse. I thought it fitting."

Chris nodded.

They rested three times before at last reaching the top. Chris tried to imagine how someone could build something so tall, and with each additional step, he began to wonder why anyone would want to. Finally they stood before a tiny metal door perched, it seemed, on the last step. Chruston was fumbling with a number of keys. He stabbed one into the lock and turned it until it clicked. He fiddled again, found another key, and turned it in the lock with a click. Katie gave Chris a bland look after the third key. Chruston swung the door open and stepped back to allow Chris to enter first.

The air was musty and hung about him; the room was

dark until Katie entered with the lamp. It cast its light fitfully about the place, revealing a vast emptiness attempting
to be filled with one small table covered with books and papers, a pitcher and mug. The kithara leaned against the leg,
looking oddly out of place. The floor and walls were stained
dark, making the room look even larger. An especially dark
track of stain led, as if someone had paced over and over,
from the table to the very center of the room, where a tiny
metal chair was bolted to the floor.

The Roamer sat stiffly in it, sideways, one arm hooked
through the back of the chair, his hands shackled in front of
him. He sat at attention when they entered, but his face was
lined with fatigue. Dark lines seemed worn under his eyes
and at the corners of his mouth. Katie stared at him in pity.

"Did . . . Where did he spend the night?" Katie turned
to Chruston, who took the lamp from her hand and set it on
the table.

"Why, right here, my dear."

"Here? But that's inhuman! We were all exhausted. How
could he sleep here?"

"Well." Chruston stared thoughtfully at the Roamer. "It
really doesn't look much like he did."

"Oh, Arron," Katie whispered.

"Leave me alone!" He forced his head up a bit higher.
"I'm not asking anything from you!" His chin dropped
lower, as if he had spent all his energy. "You've never given
me what I wanted in the past. I'm not expecting you'll start
now. Just leave me."

"Come now." Chruston gently pulled Katie back from
him. "Let's get on with this."

"Grandfather, I have to know the truth first." Chris
looked from Chruston to Arron. "I have to."

"Yes, yes, you must. Knowing that makes it easy to determine the direction one must go."

"Only if you know the whole truth," Arron cut in. "Bits
and pieces in the wrong places lead you—"

"I said quiet." Chruston turned on Arron. "He shall have
the whole truth. You are going to give it to him."

"I've told him the truth."

"Have you now? Never a lie? Never?" Chruston waited

expectantly. Arron stared at the floor a moment, then looked up slowly.

"And have they never lied to me?"

"No!" Chris practically jumped forward. "Never! I never lied to you!"

"To yourself, then!"

"Homesteaders don't lie! Not for evil selfish reasons, anyway!"

"Chris." His grandfather pulled him back. "Enough. No shouting is necessary. I have a way to get the truth, something Shakta told me about so very long ago." He turned to Dempter. "Ulna, if you would, please." She nodded and took up the cup from the table. She looked into it and rattled the contents around a bit, then poured water from the pitcher. A reddish fire seemed to lick up from inside the cup, flickered about the mouth, then died down. Dempter swirled the contents and handed it to Chruston. He looked at it and nodded.

Dempter turned to Arron; he eyed her nervously, trying to shrink into the chair. She shook her head, smiling slightly, and reached for him, taking hold of his chin and the hair at the base of his neck.

"What—what are you doing?" Arron tried to pull away.

Chruston went closer, holding the cup carefully. He put a hand on the Roamer's shoulder. Arron shrugged it off. "Don't worry, Arron. It's quite painless, so long as you tell the truth. The effects don't last long, either. The dose I'm giving you will last merely thirty minutes, no more. I'm very careful with this because more might kill you."

"And it's painless!"

Chruston bent closer. "I wouldn't hurt anyone unless I had to and I think you are aware of that. It could kill you only because you will fight it. Now, if you told the truth straight out—why, it would be as nothing." He straightened up. "But you will fight it, no doubt."

"How does it work?" Katie asked, looking nervously at Arron.

"Well . . ." Chruston thought a moment. "It works somehow in the mind, making the truthful paths the only way to answer without pain. Shakta explained it to me once. It is complex. Too complex, I'm afraid, for any of us to really understand. I am aware of its dangers, though."

"Are you?" Arron spat at him. "Are you really?" He took a few short breaths. "Chris, please. I've told you the truth. Just trust me. Please? Katie?"

"If you've told the truth, you don't have anything to worry about. But, Arron, I have to be sure. I have to know that you've told me the truth." Chris stared at Arron, biting on his lower lip. His grandfather said it wouldn't hurt him. He had to know which way to go . . .

Dempter pulled Arron's head back, opening his mouth. Chruston bent and poured the contents of the cup into his throat, the reddish liquid spilling as Arron tried to spit it back out. Dempter released him when they got it into him. Arron leaned over the chair, his breath hissing through his teeth.

"It doesn't taste so bad, now does it?" Chruston tried to lighten the atmosphere.

"It tastes awful!" Arron spat out, then straightened up. He stared at the old man, black eyes holding the man's light ones. The Roamer's hands strained against the cuffs, as if he wanted to curl them about Chruston's throat. The old man turned away.

"Now then, we'll give it a minute." Chruston fumbled in his pockets and pulled out a sheet of paper. "I'll try and make some sense out of these notes I took downstairs. Life is confusing, isn't it. Ah, think how simple it would be if people were born with this drug already in their blood." He shook his head and watched Arron a moment. "Feel anything, Roamer?"

Arron thought about it. "No." He appeared a bit relieved.

Chruston turned to Chris and Katie. "I told you, nothing to worry about. I won't hurt him. He'll be the one to hurt himself. Sadly, that seems the way it always is."

He turned and paced closer to the Roamer. "Well, let's start simply. Arron, do you want to kill me?"

"I never lied about—" Arron stopped, gasping. He clutched at the rungs of the chair, crying out. Chris started forward, his hands out as if to catch him.

"Oh, I forgot," Chruston said quickly. "Answer only what

I ask you. Then there will be no problem, no pain. A straight yes or no will do in this case. Do you want to kill me?"

"Yes," Arron hissed at him.

"And her?" He pointed to Dempter.

"Yes!"

"And then, Chris and Katie. Tell me. You would never kill them? Not under any circumstances?"

"No! Nev—" Arron cringed against the back of the chair, his words dying.

"Arron!" Katie pulled back against Chris.

"Then there could come a time when you would kill them?" Chruston walked around the chair. Arron followed him with his eyes, his mouth clamped shut.

"You must answer me."

Arron shook his head fiercely.

"You must."

The Roamer clenched his teeth together, lowering his forehead stiffly to the back of the chair. His knuckles showed white as he clenched his fists.

Chruston knelt beside him. "Don't do this. All we ask is the truth. Could there come a time when you would kill them?"

"Yes! Damn it!" Arron reared his head up.

"I knew it," Chris whispered.

"Parts," Arron spat out. He shuddered violently.

"Please, Arron, don't speak except to answer." Chruston bent over him worriedly.

"Under what condition would you kill us, Arron?" Katie asked.

"Quiet." Chruston turned sharply.

"He's right. You're just asking for parts of the truth."

Chruston shook his head. "No, Katie. Don't worry. I will ask your question, and any other you come up with. But it must be asked through me. It is the way this drug works. I'm not sure why. But it would cause him pain to answer to you."

"Oh?"

Chruston nodded and looked toward Arron. "I really don't want to hurt him—he's so much like Shakta was when he was young, when I loved him . . . But that has nothing to do with now, and I'll ask him your question. Yes, you're a

bit too logical-minded just to take my word. You're a bit
heartless to an old man, I must say," he joked.

Katie started, then looked down.

"Katie?" Chruston was at her side immediately. "I've
struck a soft spot—I'm sorry, I wasn't aware." He paused,
watching her as she shrugged. "You shouldn't feel that it's
bad. No, it's good, your logic. It's probably what saved you.
It helped you to distance yourself from this Roamer. I'll explain more later. I'll ask your question now, and any others
you come up with."

"All right, then."

Arron sat up nervously as Chruston approached him
again. "Any pain right now, Arron?"

"No."

"Good. Let's try and keep it that way. I'll make this question easy on you. I ask that you give one condition under
which you would kill Chris and Katie. What would be just
one circumstance where you would kill them? Give us the
most dire case, if you wish."

Arron tried to turn away.

"You had better answer. Don't do this to yourself. I'm
only asking for one reason. I could've dragged this out, asked
for more. Please, what is the answer?"

"If . . . if they . . . tried to stop me from . . . from
. . . killing you." Arron turned to Chris, his eyes begging
him.

"You would expect me to just allow you to kill my grandfather? You planned this whole thing! You wanted me to lead
you here so you could—damn it, you really did just want to
use me, so you could kill my grandfather. And Katie and me,
too, if we got in the way."

Arron stared up at him, then lowered his head. Chruston
took Chris by the arm and pulled him away from the
Roamer.

"It is only as we expected, Christopher. He will allow
nothing to stand in the way of his revenge."

"He said that killing you was the only way to right
things," Katie whispered.

"Yes, that's what he said." Chris had his eyes on the black
wall.

"Is that what you told them?" Chruston turned to Arron. "Yes."

Chruston nodded. "And Chris was telling me earlier that you said that it was only through my death that he would be able to live. This is what you have been telling them, is it not?"

"Yes," Arron said with only slight hesitation.

Chruston shook his head slowly. "Then here is yet another place where you have lied to them." Arron tried to shake his head, but his neck muscles were stiff.

"Yes, it's true, you lied." Chruston looked away and ran a hand over his face.

"Grandfather?"

"It's nothing, Christopher. It—oh, damn! It's just the memories, Shakta and me . . . God, he hurt me, with all his lies. Now it's just hurting all over again." The old man took a deep breath and turned on Arron.

"Roamer, you know and I know that the actual way to stop that part of the curse is for Chris to find out his death." Arron stiffened up. "You know as well as I do that is the only way to save him. You can't deny it. He will not die then, correct?"

Arron tried to pull away. "Yes," he gasped out. "That's true." He turned quickly to look at Katie. Her mouth was open. She turned away, covering her face.

Chris walked to the wall and stood facing it. He finally looked back at Arron. "I trusted you," he whispered.

The Roamer's eyes opened wide. "You nev—" The words choked themselves off.

Chris nodded. "You didn't ever care what happened to any of us. I thought sometimes that maybe you did. But you didn't! So now you'll just have to forgive me if I don't care what happens to you."

The Roamer stared hatefully at him a moment, then looked down, making no attempt to speak again.

"No, Christopher, I'm sorry. I found this out as you are now. I know that doesn't take away any of the pain. But, no, he never did feel anything for you. He used you and your trust to get to me, all for his revenge."

"No!" Arron started up then fell back against the chair, crying out in pain.

"Oh, so you are trying to salvage some of your lies, Roamer? Tell me this. Tell me, you never had one thought of revenge? Tell me that, Roamer."

"I—I—" He seemed to be trying to press himself close against the chair.

"Can you truthfully tell me that you never thought that killing me would be your revenge for what you thought was an injustice against Shakta? Revenge for the entire population of Roamers, for your parents, your grandmother? Can you say that, in truth, Arron?"

"Chris!" Arron turned to him.

"Can you say it?" Chris whispered.

Arron shivered and tried to say he could. "No. I . . . I couldn't."

"I thought not," Chruston said. He stared down at Arron, who sat weakly pulling against the cuffs about his wrists. The old man put his hand gently on Arron's shoulder. The Roamer jerked away immediately and stared with hatred at the man. Chruston looked oddly hurt a moment, then nodded sadly.

"It could have been so different, so much more gentle, if only that old woman had allowed it. But she would not let anything stand in the way of her revenge. Nothing, not even the thought of ruining a child's mind and destroying his emotions, twisting them sour. She had a cold heart, that one."

Arron opened his mouth to retort; but, remembering the pain, he snapped his mouth shut. Chruston smiled down at him. "Good. I don't want you to hurt yourself."

"Grandfather, the time . . . Ask him about his spells," Chris urged.

"Ah, yes." The old man nodded to Chris and turned back to the Roamer. "Your singing. I understand you are quite good. Shakta was, too. But he turned that gift to evil purposes. And I fear you have already begun on that path, from what these two tell me."

Arron stared at Chris and Katie. Still he kept silent.

"Yes, Chris told me of many episodes of your making magic with your tunes. Most interesting was that of your working on people's minds with your music. In particular, he told me of a night when you played an old lullaby his mother once sang to him."

The Roamer's eyes narrowed as Chruston moved to stand in front of him. "Chris tells me he felt as if he were in a trance at first, lulled in some sort of way. Drawn, you might say, to you."

"No . . ." Arron started, then cut off as the fire of the drug burned through him again, and once again at even the thought of speaking out.

Chruston caught him by the shoulders. "Arron, don't speak. Please, don't." The Roamer looked down as Chruston continued, the old man's hands still steadying him. "He says that he barely broke out of that trance, and then only at the shock of seeing you and not his mother. You were trying, it seems, to confer his love for his mother to yourself."

Arron raised his head, looking sick.

"Don't try to deny it, now. You used your singing to lead these two to your side. All their feelings for you were because of the magic you worked on them. You can cast spells on people, can't you?" Chruston asked at last.

The Roamer's eyes opened wide at some horror only he seemed able to see. He choked back the truth, snapping his teeth together.

"Arron." Chruston bent down until his face was even with the Roamer's. "Can't you?"

"Yes!" The answer forced its way out.

"Then you did sway these two with your spells." Chruston shook his head. "With your singing, you cast spells, don't you?"

"I—I—" The answer screamed in his head. His mind was on fire! He was trying to shake his head, but nothing seemed connected, rigid with pain, fluid with the fire. "But, I didn't—"

"Answer, Arron. Don't do this to yourself."

"Yes! Yes," he cried out, collapsing over the back of the chair. Chruston poured a cup of water from the pitcher.

"So you see," he said to Chris and Katie, "much of what you feel for this Roamer is due to his spells." He held the cup to the Roamer's lips. Arron drank some of it, then spat it back at him. Chruston started back. Chris leaped at the Roamer.

"No! No, it's just water, my boy." He pulled Chris away, brushing at his coat to dry it. "No harm."

"You're only making it worse," Chris snapped at Arron over Chruston's protective arm. "I had my suspicions back when you played that lullaby, but now I know."

Arron shook his head stiffly. "He asks . . ." He stopped, doubling over again.

"Please stop," Chruston begged. "I don't want you—"

"You stop! You . . ." Arron stopped, groaning.

Chruston looked away, frowning and shaking his head. "I was afraid he would be like this. Damn! I shouldn't have used this drug. Why! Why did I use this on him? It's too much. It's too painful. How could I expect him to give the truth freely after the way that old woman raised him?"

"It's all right, Grandfather." Chris caught his arm. "You had to. You really did. I had to know."

Chruston nodded grimly. "I suppose I did. But, still . . . I wish I didn't have to. Well, on with it, then. Time is running short." He glanced again at the paper he had put on the desk.

"Oh, yes, about what you did to Chris in Sernet." He turned to Arron again. "Yes, there is a bit of confusion about what you did there. It's not why you had him taken, though. On that he's quite clear. It seems you had threatened him earlier, told him you wanted him to feel the way you felt. So, that part is clear."

"No—"

Chruston sighed as the Roamer doubled over. Chris put a comforting hand on the old man's arm. Chruston smiled weakly at him and waited for the Roamer to recover.

"No, it's not why you kidnapped him. It's why you went to Dempter. Yes, why . . ." Chruston thought about that a moment, then looked at Katie. "And this, my dear, is why you should be highly praised for your logical thoughts. You see, as you may no doubt understand by now, this Roamer needed your blind trust to get to me and wreak his revenge. But you didn't fall into that trap.

"And I suspect that this is exactly why this Roamer went to Dempter after he had Chris taken."

Arron stared up at the man, his mouth falling open.

"Yes, Roamer. You did it as a last attempt to get their total trust. You didn't count on this young woman being able to see through you. You didn't count on Dempter's extreme concern for my grandson's welfare. Yes, to gain their trust—that was the reason for your taking them through that whole circuitous route to get here: for a little more time to trick them into trusting you."

Arron let out his breath slowly and pulled back from them all.

"You can't say it isn't so, Roamer. You felt that by going to Dempter's, by risking your life, you would prove to Chris and Katie that you were trustworthy, that you would do anything to help them. It's true. Weren't you thinking, as you made your way to Dempter's to turn yourself in, weren't you thinking that this, if anything, would get them to trust you? Weren't you?"

Arron stared at him, horrified. He bit his lips together and tried to shake his head.

"Isn't that what you were thinking?"

"Katie," Arron cried out, pleading.

"Is it true?" She only stared back at him.

He turned to Chris then, but the coldness Chris was feeling didn't need to be spoken.

"Answer, Roamer."

"You—you ask—" Arron stuttered, his eyes filling with tears. "That's not—"

"You'd best answer, Arron," Chruston said. "We're almost done. Is that what you were thinking?"

"Yes! Yes, I was. I was thinking that." Arron cried out at last. He looked from Chris to Katie, then pressed his forehead to the back of the chair, wiping his eyes against his shoulder. "It's true," he sobbed, looking down.

They all grew quiet a moment. Chruston shuffled his notes about. Dempter and Katie watched Arron as he wept silently, huddling close to the back of the chair. Chris watched his grandfather.

"That clears things up," Chris said. "It all makes more

---

sense now. He wanted to kill you, and he needed our help, our trust."

Chruston nodded sadly, then glanced at his watch. "Just a little bit of time left. Any last questions?"

"Well, why don't we ask about my death now? He'll have to tell."

Arron straightened instantly.

"No!" Chruston pulled Chris back from the Roamer. "No, Chris, you'll kill him. Careful. Be careful."

"I . . . I don't understand."

"It's simple," Dempter said from where she had been sitting the whole time, on the corner of the table. "He has in his head the knowledge of your death, and what he sees in his mind is a true vision. But if he speaks of it, then you can get out of it, and it is no longer your true death, so he would be lying."

"Yes," Chruston added. "He must speak, because the drug tells him he must, but on speaking, that truth becomes a lie, so he cannot speak it. It would rip his mind apart."

"Oh, I see. I'm sorry."

Chruston nodded. "So am I. I wish it were so easy. Well, is there anything else?"

"Yes," Katie said suddenly. "Yes. Ask him why his kithara is so important, why he's so protective of it—the real reason."

Arron shook his head slightly at her, mouthing her name, begging that there be no more. She met his gaze easily. He had deceived them all with his words. She wanted to know everything now.

"Yes. That's a very good idea. It became very important to Shakta, too, at the end. He would never tell me why, though. He bargained that it be given to his granddaughter. I couldn't say no; he had once been such a good friend . . ."

"All right, Arron, only one more question. Tell us the reason why you protect that kithara? Give us the most important reason. Why is it so important that nothing happen to it?"

The Roamer hooked his trembling fingers about the rungs in the back of the chair and shook his head firmly.

"You must answer, Roamer."

Arron set his teeth together and gripped tighter at the rungs. His neck was too stiff to allow him to shake his head again. He held on. His eyes burned with the pain behind them.

"Arron, don't. Don't do this . . ." Chruston pleaded suddenly.

"Only . . . a . . . minute—" Arron gasped out. He pressed his forehead against the back of the chair and locked his feet about the legs. He bit down on his lips, forcing the reply back into his throat.

"But—a minute! You could die in a minute!"

"Good—" Arron choked out through clenched teeth.

Chruston was down on the floor next to him. He caught wildly at his arm. "Tell us. You must! Don't—don't do this."

"Take back the question," Katie cried out.

Chruston looked up at her. "I can't. He must answer. I can't take it back! Arron! Please!"

But the Roamer was gone from them. The blood pounded so hard through his ears, Chruston's words came in a blur. The chair seemed to reel and tilt. The answer couldn't come now if he had wanted it to. And now, he wanted it to, wanted to scream it out, just to be free from the pain—the pain.

The rest of them all stood pleading with him, horrified, watching the Roamer, each counting off the seconds in their head.

"Arron, please—oh, please," Katie begged once more. She caught at Chris' arm, but he didn't seem to notice, staring at the Roamer, watching him shudder, clinging to the back of the chair.

"Arron!" Chris called out to him.

The Roamer relaxed suddenly, falling limply against the chair. Then slowly, so slowly, he raised his head to glare at them. His hair clung damply to the sides of his face.

"It's done," he murmured. A trace of a smile touched his lips.

"You were lucky," Chruston said, climbing to his feet. "I've seen that amount of time kill stronger."

"I'm stronger," Arron gasped, lowering his head to the back of the chair again. "And now, Chris, you do not know the whole truth."

"I know enough to know what to do." Chris turned to Chruston.

"All you have to do, Christopher, is ask him about your death. It'll take a moment, but the more you think of it, the sooner he'll see it. Now is the time to do it, since he's so weak."

"Is that why you always got so angry when I talked about death?" Chris asked Arron.

The color was just beginning to return to the Roamer's face. "Yes."

"Angry, no," Chruston whispered. "Frightened is more the word. You know, Shakta was a brave man—one of the many things I admired in him. But, when asked about death . . . well, I'll never forget the times I saw him with a vision of death in his mind. Oh, he would pale and quake. When I saw him see mine, that was truly frightening . . ."

"Did you want him to see your death?" Katie watched him.

Chruston nodded. "Yes."

"But . . ." Chris pulled away from him. Arron smiled at him as if to say, I told you.

"Yes, Chris, I know what you are thinking." Chruston reached out to him. "But it is not as it would seem."

"It never is," Arron said softly. Chruston turned on him.

"You, Roamer, do not know it all, either." Chruston went on explaining to Chris. "As I told you before, Shakta had amazing powers, the strongest I had ever seen, until—well, never mind," he said, glancing at Arron. "Shakta also had a weakness, one that no other Roamer seemed to have. He could feel his strength. He knew what he could do with it, the good . . . and the bad. And something gnawed at him to try it, to use all his powers, to try anything—to see, he said, to know." Katie stared at Arron, remembering their talk in the woods.

"We were close then," Chruston went on. "And he told me about these feelings. But I knew, of course, he would never use his powers for evil. He would always stay to the good. He was good." Chruston walked around Chris.

"Then all that began to change. Slowly, so slowly I didn't notice at first. Then it became very noticeable—destroying people's crops, massive fires, altering the weather, and even people's minds! I became very cautious. I had, at all costs, to remain his friend until I could find a weakness . . ." Chruston sighed and turned back to Chris.

"It was this fear of the visions of death that gave me hope. It was this, I began to realize, that would destroy him. You see, he did anything. He would use his power any way, try all forms of it, except that. Never would he speak of the death he saw. It frightened him. Why? I began to realize it was because he knew it would destroy him. By telling, he would bring about his own ruin. I had to . . . had to destroy him before he destroyed everything! Chris? Can you see? This was the only way I could do it."

The old man turned away and shuffled to the wall. "And it did destroy him. But it didn't stop what he had started. His curse lives on, in the land, in my family, and in his family." He turned to Arron, who was staring open-mouthed at him. "This Roamer here, this Shakta, will undoubtedly follow the same path. Oh, not through his own conscious thoughts. It is the power. It engulfs them. It becomes so that they can see only the power. Shakta, my God! He was my closest friend. To have that happen—damn! I never wanted to believe it. But his power, it took him."

"That's not true! That's not true!" Arron tried to stand up. "You're lying to them. Don't believe him!"

"It is true!"

"Then I would have heard something about it! I would have heard! My—my grandmother, my mother, my father, they would—"

"They all carefully prepared you to carry on in Shakta's steps. They lied to you!"

Arron shook his head madly. "No. No Roamer would do what you say Shakta did. We know. We see. We see things on the whole scale, a clear picture. We have the total logic that the Homesteaders lack. Shakta couldn't have—"

"Shakta was my brother! He was my father's son, my half brother. Half Homesteader! He could not see as you claim the Roamers can. That bit of Homesteader blood—"

Arron sat back, away from him. "No . . ."

"You know it's true, Roamer. And you, like Shakta, cannot see entirely. You have that blood. You will follow him. Undoubtedly. And you know that as well."

Arron's face had grown gray-white. His dark eyes opened their widest, seeing nothing.

"Your great-great-grandfather would have tried to destroy the world simply on a whim, to see if he could do it. A mad fancy! And you know that's true."

Arron shook his head, pressing himself down as if he were trying to disappear.

"Look at me!" Chruston bent close to him. "You know it's true, don't you?"

Arron stared up at the man who was fiercely daring him to deny it. Chris, Katie, and Dempter were standing close now. He was suffocating! He lowered his head to the back of the chair. "It can't . . . can't be . . . And, yet—it is," he moaned. "It's true. God, they lied to me!" He sat quite still, madly thinking, then looked up at them all. "But I won't be like him, I tell you . . ."

"Arron . . ." Katie walked away from him. "Yes, you will. You will. Oh, can you blame us for thinking that, after the things you've done? What you did to Chris? I know you will become like Shakta. You've said things like that. Can you blame us for what we must do?"

He didn't answer her, only stared in horror at his own hands, shaking his head ever so slightly, not wanting to believe it was true.

Chruston nodded to Chris to go ahead.

"But how will I know if he really sees it? He could fake it."

Chruston shook his head. "No, Chris, there is no faking it here. Ulna, would you please."

She nodded, opening a book on the desk.

"I was careful to record everything that happened when I dealt with Shakta. Maybe even then I realized it might not be the end." He nodded to Dempter.

She began reading in a lilting voice. " 'And I asked him again to tell me my death. He said he could not, he did not know. And then his mouth fell open, wide like his eyes. He stared, like death itself, unseeing, yet seeing all. His face, pale, bloodless, dead. His breath became shallow, and he looked at me in fright, shaking to rattle the very bones of the reaper . . .' "

Chruston nodded. "You will know when the Roamer sees it. Now, ask him."

Chris turned to Arron. "Are you going to tell me? My death, I mean. You saw my father's; can you see mine?"

Arron sat a moment, trying to regain some of his past calm, "No," he whispered. "I can't." He turned his head weakly, to stare at Dempter. For all his fear and pain, he had not lost the horrible dark look in his eyes. They had only grown darker still. She pulled back, a hand against the wall.

"Go on, son." The old man put a soft hand on Chris' shoulder. "Go ahead."

Chris turned back to Arron. "Look, you're going to have to tell me. I'm sorry. But some things are too important. Sometimes one person really doesn't matter. You have to tell me."

"Whether I matter or not makes no difference now. I can't see your death. I won't be able to. I can only see one death at a time."

Chruston moved Chris away from the Roamer. "What do you mean? You see someone else's death?"

Arron smiled grimly at him, the hatred he felt for the old man, for what he had done to him, plain on the Roamer's face. It seemed to strike out at the air between them, striving to reach the man. "Not quite what you expected, is it?"

Chruston grabbed him by the arm and yanked him up until the cuffs strained against the chair. "What do you mean?"

"I mean, I see another person's death, and another vision cannot replace it. Not until I tell, or it is fulfilled."

Chruston slammed him back down in his seat. "Whose death do you see? Hers?" He jabbed an accusing finger at Katie. Arron only smiled. "Whose?" Chruston raised his hand as if to hit him.

"Then you'll treat me as you treated my grandfather? Your dear friend."

Chruston stormed away from him and stood staring at Katie. "Did you speak of your death to him, girl?"

"Why, no," Katie stammered.

Arron laughed at them. "Why do you think I came to you so battered? Someone has already attempted your methods of finding their death. You know the method. A mix of physical pain and bribery. Using something—someone—that I care for to get me to tell." The Roamer looked piercingly at Chris, then turned slowly to Dempter. "Didn't you?"

XXIV

"ULNA, DID YOU?" CHRUSTON SPUN ABOUT TO FACE HER.

"Dear, yes. Yes, I did. I did it for you, so we could be together forever. I didn't want you to be alone."

"But you—you didn't consult me on this."

"No, I meant it for a surprise." She smiled hopefully.

"But you knew my plans. You understood this was the only way to save my family, to save the world."

"I love you—I . . . And you won't be alone. You'll still be able to save the world . . . Oliver?"

He walked over to one of the doors on the far side of the room, unlocked it, and swung it open. Cold, crisp air flowed in. It had already grown dark outside. "I think we need some air." He stared quietly out onto the balcony.

"I . . . you see—"

"You've doomed my family, Ulna. You've doomed my grandson."

"Couldn't we get the Roamer to tell my death . . . and . . . and then his?"

"He'll barely survive the first telling. He won't be able to do two."

Dempter looked at Arron who nodded and grinned. She

jumped toward him, grabbing him about the throat. "You tell me! You tell me!"

Arron pulled back, her nail marks standing out red on his skin. He shook his head. "Oh no . . . oh no. This is one death I want to see. You took everything! Everything I worked for. You destroyed it all, everything that I loved! My father! My grandmother . . . and—" He broke off, turning to look at Chris and Katie, who stood by the side, not moving. He snapped his head back to glare at Dempter. "The only thing I want now is to watch you die the death I've seen for you, the death you made me see for you!

"You see," he said, quite calmly now, quite distantly staring off, "you've left nothing for bribery. And the pain?" He gave a short laugh. "I feel nothing. What could you expect? After all you've done, after everything done to my people? Well, now I'm what a Roamer is supposed to be! All I want now is to see you die, and Chruston suffer." She slapped him.

Chris caught at her arm and spun her about to face him. "Why would you do that to me? Why did you . . ."

"Why?" She opened her eyes until they looked perfectly round. "Why? Do you know how I've worked? Slaved for this man for years. Years! I've done everything he asked. Killed. Hunted. Searched through mountains and pits!"

"For what?"

"Him!" She jabbed her finger at Arron. "To cure the damn curse! To save you!" She strode to the wall, then swung back to glare at him. "But what about me? What about it?" She waited. Chris glanced at Katie, who only stared back.

"Yes! That's right. Nothing! Well, years, I've given. My love! I've given. For what? To hear him speak of you! Only of you, never of me. Never!" She took a slow, deep breath, clenching her fists in front of her stomach.

"I kept thinking he would say something about . . . loving me. Maybe?" She glanced at Chruston. The old man was staring blankly at his hands.

She turned back on Chris. "Well. I was helpless! Nothing! Nothing I could do would make him feel what I felt. You did nothing for him, and he gave you his love. I did everything! And what did I get? So I wanted you to feel that cut off, that alone, that kind of fear, that pain! That's why I made Pehter put you away. I wanted you to suffer as I did!"

"You used my grandson!" Chruston looked up at last.

She stared at him, shaking her head slightly. "I loved you. You . . . you never . . ."

Chruston walked over then and took her arm gently, lovingly. "All right. Enough. We're all just a little surprised. Plans have to be changed. Let's discuss this where we can clear our heads." He led her toward the open door. "We're getting a bit crazy. Perhaps we can get the Roamer to speak of both. He is younger than Shakta, and much, much stronger. Really, what is our alternative?"

Dempter nodded quickly and gave Arron a triumphant look. The Roamer stared back oddly, knowingly. She could hear his handcuffs rattling strangely. His hands—they were trembling.

She stopped, staring at the balcony. She took a step back. "I . . . I did it for you, Oliver."

Now Chruston turned to look at Arron. "Damn you! You couldn't make this easy, could you?"

"It's never been easy on me, has it?"

"Shut up."

"Oliver, please, listen." Dempter put her hand on the man's shoulder.

"You, shut up and get out there!" He pushed her toward the balcony.

Katie caught at Chris' shoulder. He pulled her close against him.

"No!" Dempter backed up. "You're not going to kill me, because I know."

Chruston shook his head. "Everyone knows right before they die. You have to know farther ahead, way ahead, to make plans."

"Please! I only did it because I—I love you. Why would you want him?" She stabbed her finger toward Chris. "Listen. You could use him as a bribe, as I did. I'm sure the Roamer still cares for him. He must! If you use him, the Roamer will tell you everything, all his power tricks. All of them! And then, then we can be together, forever," she whispered.

"Use my grandson? Use my grandson!" Chruston thundered. "Get out there! Get out there now!"

"No!"

The old man's eyebrows fell together. "No? No!" The room seemed to grow darker as his voice rose. A wind picked up from nowhere, pouring from inside the room out through the balcony door. Chris let go of Katie, rubbing at his shoulder. The coldness in the wind seemed to come from there.

"You don't love me!" Chruston pushed Dempter toward the door. "It's only power that you love! You would understand why I do what I must, if you loved me. You never loved me. Never!"

"Don't! Please," Dempter screeched as the wind kicked up about her, knocking her toward the open door. She caught at the frame. "I did! I did love you! But you—you never—" She screamed, losing her hold. Her wail filled the room, then stopped, quite abruptly. The room became silent. Silent.

Chruston leaned against the door and shut it, tightly. He blinked back the tears that had come to his eyes. "Ah, Ulna. Why did you make me do that? Why?"

"That wind—it just sucked her out. It didn't touch us. How?" Katie looked at Chruston, then at Arron. "Oh, Arron. She did—you didn't . . ." She moved close to him and knelt down. "I'm sorry. We're sorry. You didn't." She took his hands gently and sat there staring at the ground.

Chris hadn't moved. He watched first them, then his grandfather. His grandfather—family. He was family. Chris felt for him, living in this lonely house—felt something close to love. He turned back to Arron and Katie. The Roamer had his head down against hers. "Don't worry," he was whispering.

"Now then, Christopher." Chruston touched his shoulder gently. Chris started at the tingling sensation. "Christopher, we must get back to where we were. Nothing has changed. That Roamer will become so powerful that if we don't do something now, it may be too late. His mind is clear. Go on, son." He turned him toward Arron, then noticed Katie leaning, as if for protection, against the Roamer's leg.

"Hey, girl! Get away from him. I said, get away!" Chruston grabbed her arm and jerked her back.

"Grandfather!" Chris caught at his shoulder.

"She was falling under his spell. I know only because I, too, fell under the spell of a Shakta—but not for long."

Chris stared at Arron.

"Go on, son. Ask him if he has the power to do that."

Chris hesitated, then took a step toward the Roamer. "Can you—could you cast such a spell?"

There was hatred in the Roamer's eyes. "Yes, I could."

"You—can you—could you become as powerful as Shakta? Do the things he did?"

Arron didn't say anything. He stared at his own hands, biting at his lower lip, then, as if deciding something, he looked up at Chris. "It seems I can do more."

Chruston moved to Chris' side. "Hurry, Christopher. You must get him to see your death—quickly, before he sees someone else's." He looked at Katie.

"Mine? But—" She shrank back against the wall.

"Don't, Katie! Don't think about it," Arron cried out.

"Quickly, Christopher! Turn his mind before he sees hers. He'll have to tell her then, or—"

"Arron, my death! What is it?" Chris said immediately.

"Please. You don't have to—you mustn't!"

"Will it be painful, like my father's? Or—or horrible, like my mother's? Arron, just tell me."

"Chris!" The Roamer started up. "Chris, don't!"

"Chris!" Katie reached for him, but Chruston pushed him forward, out of her reach, toward Arron.

"I can feel it's going to be horrible, isn't it, Arron?"

"Don't do this to me! Don't . . ." His voice fell off, his eyes misting strangely. He clutched at the chair a moment, then bolted up with a cry. "No! No," he screamed, straining to stand, but the chair was bolted to the floor. He dropped back down, shivering, sobbing.

"Ah, he sees it now," Chruston said softly.

"He does?" Chris stared at the Roamer, a knot of terror coiling tightly in his stomach.

"Yes. Now, to persuade him. It won't be easy, but easier since he's a Shakta, with that bit of Homesteader blood gnawing at him, making him wonder what could be the harm in telling. If he cares for you, all the better."

"I won't tell!" The Roamer's voice came raggedly with his breath. He stayed crouched over the back of the chair, looking sick. But every moment the defiance in his face grew. "This is what they trained me for. They taught me as a Roamer. My grandmother was very careful to teach me. She gave her life to protect me. Me! And now, I'll give my life to protect her ideals. She taught me with care, kept me safe. Always, she protected . . . and my father, too. They all—"

"For their destructive purposes! They wanted you—"

"They loved me! Can you say that? In your empty house? Can you? I won't betray what they wanted from me!"

"Then you'll damn the world! I won't let you. I won't!"

"No, not at first," Arron said calmly. "First I'll save it from you."

"And then what'll you do, Roamer? Destroy it yourself?"

"No," Arron said in a whisper. "Chris and Katie will contend with me. But you are the first menace. I'll kill you and then . . . then they must kill me."

"So you would convince them now. But when the time came, your quick tongue would find a way. As it is, the only way to save the world is to destroy you directly. Destroy you by finding the cure. And you will tell. Now ask him, Chris." Chruston took him by the shoulder. Chris stiffened up at his touch.

"What did you see, Arron? My death—is it horrible?"

"Chris." Katie was at his side now. "If you learn your death, you'll live forever . . . with him. I'll be left behind."

Chris turned from her to look at his grandfather, then he turned to Arron. "Can't you see her death, too?"

"Damn you."

Katie pulled on Chris, trying to move him away from Chruston. "Chris, this isn't right. Do you really want to be with him forever?"

Chris stared at her. "But, Katie, you don't understand. He —he's all I have left. I have to. I—he's my family, the only family I have left."

"After last night, I'm your family!"

"But the curse—"

"Damn the curse!" She strode over to Arron and put her hands firmly on his shoulders. "I trust him."

Arron started, his eyes meeting hers doubtfully, but she nodded firmly. He turned back to face Chris and Chruston, his head raised higher than his fatigue had previously allowed.

"Enough, enough," Chruston interrupted. He took Katie's arm and pulled her away. "I can't have you distracting these two." He pulled her over to the door next to the balcony.

Katie pulled back. "Stop it! Chris?"

"Grandfather, please—"

"Chris, this is too important." He opened the door to a closet.

"I am not going in there!" Katie pulled out of his grasp, but he caught her about the waist and lifted her easily off the ground.

"Yes, you are. You don't understand what you're doing."

She ripped the knife from her belt.

"Katie! No!" Chris ran over to stop her. But she plunged it wildly into Chruston's upper arm, a crazed look on her face. Had she gone mad? Chruston gave no notice. He shoved her into the closet, slammed the door, and locked it.

"Grandfather, your arm!"

Chruston put his hand over it. "It's all right, Christopher. She didn't mean to. It's quite all right. And she'll be fine in a little while, as soon as that Roamer leaves her alone."

"Arron! Did you make her do that? You made her do that, damn you! How could you?"

"What would you have me say, Chris?" The Roamer shrugged and looked away.

Chris turned helplessly back to his grandfather. The old man had taken his hand away from the wound—and it was gone! Healed!

"But—but how?" Chris couldn't take his eyes from his grandfather's arm.

Chruston glanced at where Chris stared. "This is one of the things I learned from Shakta. It will be the same with this one, no doubt. You see, once we get him to tell your death, he will be so distracted, it will be a simple matter to relieve his mind of the rest. We will learn so much! Oh, Christopher, you can't imagine! Most importantly, of course, we will learn how to heal the world, just as I have done with my arm. But, still, much much more—"

"Ancient desired relieving his mind," Arron sang softly.

Chruston spun about. "I'll have no singing here! You've wrapped your spell about that girl, but we're stronger. We know your tricks. No singing." He turned back to Chris. "Now, let me straighten my papers so we can get everything written down. Always keep a record, I say. You see, there will be many things that this Roamer will tell us that won't make any sense without studying. Amazing, truly amazing things." Chruston shuffled over to the desk and bent over the books and papers.

"Chris," Arron whispered. "The box, the sphere . . . It's his death. Quickly, it's your only chance. Katie's, too. He'll kill her, Chris, like he did Dempter. Undo my hands and give me my kithara. I'll take care of it, if you'll just take out the sphere. Chris! You want to take it out."

Chris pulled back from him. The box . . . it made sense now. They made him desire it. They made him secretive about it. If he had just spoken up earlier, then he would have gotten to his grandfather's sooner, maybe even when his mother was still alive. But they had tricked him! They made him think he must keep it all to himself, keep it away from his grandfather.

"Grandfather!" Chris straightened up. Arron's face grew pale, and he shook his head ever so slightly.

"Chris—" His name barely passed over the Roamer's lips.

"Grandfather, I have something for you." He held out the box.

Chruston's eyes opened widely. "But, where did you get this, Christopher?"

"From Arron's grandmother. She gave it to me."

"She trusted you!" Arron kicked at him. "I trusted you! And your mother—"

"You killed her!" Chris swung toward Arron, clutching the box close against himself, tight against his stomach as Chruston reached for it. "She wanted me to save my grandfather!"

"I didn't kill her! He did."

"No. You Shaktas did with your curses."

"He did! He is the curse. His being alive drains the land of life; more closely, he takes the lives of those that have sprung from him. You can't grow old because he needs back that bit of life he gave you. He takes it to keep going. Why do you think it's so barren here? Why do you think this house is so cold and—and dead! He's sucked all the life from it!"

"Shut up! Shut up!"

"And Gaeth, the only living thing we see—he's dead!" The Roamer shuddered. "Dead, Chris, like Brades was when he attacked me with the poison to make me weak, so Chruston could more easily take from me—"

"Chris!" His grandfather caught at his shoulder. "Chris, it's true. What he's saying—it's true."

"What?"

"Christopher, I'll not lie to you. I'm never, ever going to lie to you. So I tell you what he says is true. That's why you must get him to tell your death. You will live then! I won't be able to suck you in, like some horrible monster, the monster Shakta made me into. You'll live! That curse will be broken."

The old man stared up at the ceiling, and the lamplight showed the hope in his pale eyes. He caught at Chris and pulled him close, looking down into his face. "Ever since Shakta first cursed me in this way, I have waited, planned, for a way to save my family and the world. And then, when this one was born, I sensed him—so like Shakta. I could feel him as I could feel Shakta, we were so close. And I knew that at last there was a way to save my family—to save you, Christopher.

"But the old woman had plans of her own. Shakta's grand-daughter, Arron's grandmother. She strove to hide this one from me, because she knew he could heal the lands. She thought to use him instead for her own revenge, to continue Shakta's destruction."

"She never—" Arron started up.

"Quiet!" Chruston turned on the Roamer. "Yes, she hid you from me. And for years I could only find traces of your existence. I sent out hundreds of spies to find you. Nothing was too much to do when the fate of the world was at stake. I wouldn't let her win, let her destroy my family."

He turned back to Chris. "My spies carried a drug with

them, one Shakta had shown me long ago. If the Roamer had taken it, he would have turned against the lies his grandmother had told him and seen the true path. He would have come to me and shown me how to heal the lands freely, instead of forcing me to take this awful path, hurting him, forcing him to show me."

Arron straightened. "Poison—that poison in Brades. That almost killed me. Then you would have been shown nothing! You don't know what—"

"I do know what I'm doing, Roamer. It was that strong a dose because I had confirmation that you had been attacked by one of my spies and the poison had no effect."

Arron stared at him, then turned to look at Chris. "That bear . . ." He shook his head at the realization and swung back toward Chruston. "You don't know what you're doing. Can't you see that you have no control over . . ."

Chruston had pushed Chris back, away from the Roamer, and began speaking to him in a hushed voice. "When the old woman died at last, I could sense him again, but not like I could when he was a boy. No, now he had control of his powers and he could shield himself. Sometimes I would get a glimmer of where he was. And my only thought was to get him to me, to save you. When I sensed him, I would direct some of my spies in his direction. But then he would always disappear from my mind again. I couldn't hold him to one place and I couldn't see where he was going. It seemed I wouldn't be able to catch him.

"I tried to trap him on the road once; I got a distinct picture of a river. There aren't many left. So, I had the trees there fall to trap him, like a giant cage. Then I knew I would be able to get someone to him. But somehow I lost sight of him again! And strangely I lost my spies there, too."

"You didn't make the trees fall. You blew them up!" Arron yelled at him, hearing even though the man whispered. "Why can't you see? You don't know how—"

Chruston turned on the Roamer. "I do know! I know that you can show me the way to save my family, to save my grandson. I have done all this to save him. We will get you to tell his death and then . . ." He turned to Chris, pulling him close again. "And then, Christopher, you and I, we will search his mind for a way to heal the lands."

"For power! He doesn't want to heal anything! He wants power, that's all. Power. And someone—something—besides a dead man to share it with!" Arron turned his eyes on Chris. "He doesn't love you. He can't possibly. Why should—"

Chris leaped upon the Roamer, clapping his hand hard over his mouth. Dropping the box, he drew the Roamer's knife from his boot and shoved it up against Arron's throat. "Shut up. I said, shut up!"

Chruston dropped to the ground and scooped up the box. Arron remained still until Chris removed his hand. "He took the box, Chris."

Chris turned. "Grandfather?"

"We must be very careful with this, Christopher. We can't trust something that old witch gave you. This box contains the very essence of the curse. It is the source of their power. Perhaps it even holds the secret of the way to right the land! The Roamer will tell us the truth about it. He will have to, once he has broken. He will be unable to keep anything back. Get him to tell your death, and the secret will be ours."

"Arron?" Chris looked down at him, the knife still to his throat. He pressed it closer. "Tell me."

"Just kill me. I am not going to tell you." The dark eyes seemed to be reaching for him. "Kill me, like your mother asked you not to. I'm never going to tell you. Never. You can at least trust me in that. I am not going to tell you." He lowered his eyes. Nothing else moved. "Isn't my life also important?"

"But so is my grandfather's."

The eyes were back up in a flash. "His life is over! Long ago. Now he's living everyone else's! Look at the land."

"The only way to save the land is to get the secret from him, the secret implanted in his mind, so like Shakta's. Find out your death," his grandfather pressed.

"If you find out your death, you'll never get that box back. It won't ever be a comfort to you again," Arron whispered. "Forever out of reach . . ."

Chris pulled the knife away and stood staring at him. Was

the box truly a comfort, or had they tricked him. Tricked him.

"Give me my kithara," Arron said quickly.

"I should just kill you!" He raised the knife to plunge it into him as wildly as Katie had to Chruston.

"No! No!" Chruston grabbed at his arm. "Not yet. No, his mind. He . . . he can cure everything. You don't know, Chris. You don't realize the incredible—"

"Amount of power—that you want! Chris, please, listen to me," Arron begged. "Now, listen. I have this . . . this power now. But when you are done with me, when you're done—he will have that power." The Roamer stopped.

"So? That's much better. He cares. He feels!"

Arron lowered his head and began speaking in a hushed voice. "Well, why don't you try feeling for a minute. Why don't you think about the things we've gone through. The things we've been through. Together." He raised his head to stare at Chris. "I know what you've been taught. I know the way things look. But, damn you, don't you feel anything? Trust me. I see now what I have the potential to become. The bad, yes—and the good. Think of that, too."

"My grandfather can—"

"No, he can't! He has no control. None! He doesn't understand at all. He only sees it one way! Chris, he cannot see any difference between the good and the bad. They are the same to him. The same!"

"Chris, don't talk to him. We must get on with this."

"Right now, I'm the only one who can see any difference! Kill me, then, if you're afraid of what I'll become. Kill me! I'll welcome it. But we have got to kill him first!"

Chris pulled away, the knife hanging from his fingertips. He pressed close against his grandfather. The old man steadied him with strong hands about his shoulders. Steadied him as his father should have done so many times. Should have! "Yes, I understand, Christopher," he whispered in his ear. "He was a friend, in a way. I know. But the world, our family . . ." Chris let the knife clatter to the floor.

"How many single lives are there that must be given up for the good of the whole of which he speaks? How many? Dempter's, my grandmother's, the entire Roamer population, mine—those single lives add up. It's rapidly becoming many lives for one!"

Chris took a slow step toward Arron. His grandfather caught desperately at his shoulder. "Look, he cares for that girl. We could use her, then he'll tell."

"No!"

"She's not important to you, Christopher. Don't you care for me?"

"Of course! You—you're my grandfather, my only family left."

"Family . . ." The old man said faintly, a delighted smile crossed his lips. He pulled Chris close.

"Katie and I are your family, Chris," Arron snapped out. "Think of what we've been through! You've cared for us, loved us, haven't you? Can you really love him? Do you love him, or do you owe him?"

Chris opened his mouth to reply, but nothing came from it.

"You think he loves you? Why should he? He only feels he owes you. For what he's done to you. You saved my life, Chris, any number of times. And I've saved yours. We didn't owe each other anything—so why did we do it, Chris?"

"Shut up!" Chruston stepped forward, a protective arm coming up in front of Chris. "What would a Roamer know of love? Shakta knew nothing of it."

Arron watched him. "More than you do, I think. He loved your father—and you didn't, did you?" The Roamer smiled faintly. "And I? What do I know? Well, my grandmother . . . But no, I'll never tell you what you want to know." He looked past Chruston. "Chris, think. No, don't think—feel. Don't think about the circumstances, feel what we've felt."

"No more from you! I knocked your voice from you once before. I'll do it again if you're not careful," Chruston threatened.

"I don't think so," the Roamer whispered.

Chris backed up, watching the two of them, thinking of the light touch his grandfather had on his arm, so like his mother's.

Chruston clapped his hands together, and the air stirred up and began to blow about the room. Chruston yelled above the whirling. "You're not going to take my grandson from me, Roamer. I'll kill that girl in there if you won't tell."

"No!" Chris grabbed at Chruston's arm. "No! He'll tell me. Don't hurt her." He turned to Arron, the wind stealing the words from his mouth. "Arron, tell me! Don't . . . don't hurt Katie."

Arron raised his hands slightly, the cuffs catching on the chair. He looked up helplessly. *What have I done to you that was so terrible?*

Chris' mouth fell open, and he drew back from the Roamer. Chruston had turned to the closet door. The latch clicked, sounding oddly loud in the storm. The door slammed open. Katie stood still in surprise.

"My kithara," Arron shouted.

She ran immediately to where it was leaning, but the wind caught at her, grabbed her, and pulled her toward the door slowly opening to the balcony.

"No!" Chris ran to her and caught frantically at her hands, trying to pull her back. "Arron," he screamed at last. "Help her!"

Arron stared down at his hands, caught helplessly through the back of the chair. "Chris . . . you bind my hands. I—I can't."

"Stop it! Stop it!" Chris turned to his grandfather, shocked by the look of anticipation he saw on the old man's face. "Stop it!" he shouted again. "I'll make him tell. I'll make him tell you everything! But not unless you stop!"

Reluctantly, it seemed, the wind died down.

Chris breathed a sigh of relief, glancing at Katie to be sure she was all right. Then he turned to face his grandfather. He watched him a moment, then took a deep breath. "I think I know a way to make him tell. It's that box. That box will force him to tell." Chruston hesitated. "It will make him tell. You haven't seen its power. I have. He'll have to tell!"

Chruston drew it out slowly and handed it to him. His eyes narrowed when Chris gave it to Katie. "What are you doing?"

"I know what I'm doing! Just open it when I tell you." Chris walked over to the kithara and scooped it up. "Now, I have to smash this."

"Chris!" Arron struggled against the cuffs.

"Chris . . ." Katie said nervously.

"Shut up! I'm saving your life."

"I don't want it like this. This is wrong. Wrong! This house, that man! I stabbed him. It . . . it was like he was dead, or I was stabbing someone else."

Chris stood in front of Arron, the kithara slightly raised. "You'll show him everything. Do you understand?"

"Don't do it, Arron! Don't do it!"

"Everything!" He shoved the kithara into Arron's hands. "Play, damn you!"

Arron struggled to hold it, to reach the strings. He—he couldn't!

"What! What are you doing!" Chruston swung Chris about to face him. "Don't you understand? I wanted you to share eternity with me. I chose you! You, so much like me—always feeling alone, unloved. I chose you!" He shoved him out of the way trying to get at Arron.

Chris grabbed him, pulling him back from the Roamer.

"Play it, Arron! Play!"

"I can't get at it!"

"It's yours," Katie cried out to him. "You acted as if it were a part of you if anyone were to hurt it. There must be something more in your mind, there must be something . . ."

Arron snapped his head up, staring at her. "Yes," he whispered. "Yes . . ."

Chruston pulled Chris around, jerked him about to stand in front of him. Chris stared up into the old man's face, at the hatred there. Not like the Roamer's—no, this hatred was for him, completely and specifically for him. It flared out at him and sent him crashing into the far wall. Chruston turned quickly from him and knocked the kithara from Arron's struggling hands.

"No!" The Roamer tried to grab it, but was blocked by the chair.

Chruston caught at the Roamer's shirt and pulled him up to face him. "It's to kill me, isn't it?" Chruston whispered. "That's why you would not speak before!" Chruston released him, raising a foot to crush the instrument.

"Don't!" Arron strained to reach him.

Katie jumped on him, toppling him before he could touch the instrument. The box spun from her hands as they fell.

Chris pushed himself up, his hands pressing against the cold wall. "You lied to me," he shouted at Chruston. "Oh, you gave me truths, all right, the ones you wanted me to hear. But without the rest, they're no better than lies!

"You wanted to save the world from Shakta, yes. But you wanted it all for yourself. You may have rationalized it was for the world, but you wanted it for yourself! You wanted to be him. You could've just stabbed him, you could've—you lied to me. You never cared for me!"

"I did!"

"No! You didn't. You don't! You couldn't. I've given you nothing! And I can't love you. You've given . . . given nothing!"

Chruston shoved Katie away. "I wanted to love you. I did."

"That's not enough!"

Chruston struggled to stand up. "Then you shall die, too. And I will have it all." He bent for the box. Chris dove for it. Katie forced herself between Chruston and the box. She screamed at Arron.

"Arron! Play it!"

He looked up at the three of them, each trying to grab the box. The kithara lay just to his right, far out of reach. How . . .

There was a way, he realized suddenly, even with his hands bound. Brades had spoken about it . . . Something about—he concentrated on the instrument. It was his. It belonged to him. He had always had it with him. It was his, another part of him. The Roamer's face grew pale and damp.

Chruston held the box aloft, crying out in triumph. Katie struck his arm. He turned on her, eyes flashing. She crashed against the wall, knocked almost senseless. Chris caught hold of the box and backed quickly from Chruston.

The kithara gave a sudden ping. Chruston raised his arms, and the sound of thunder boiled through the room, echoing, drowning the simple pings of the instrument. But the music grew louder, richer.

Arron sat erect, engrossed in the instrument. One could almost see a thin line connecting them, a line of magic itself. The storm grew louder and with it came the music, swelling, engulfing them all.

Chruston tried to leap upon the instrument, to destroy it. But he was struck back by some invisible web of protection the Roamer had somehow set about it. He grabbed Arron then, struck him. The music faltered, then swelled again.

"Open the box," Arron cried out, his eyes never leaving his kithara.

"No!" Chruston grabbed the knife that lay on the floor where Chris had dropped it.

"Don't! Don't," Chris called out, seeing the man raise the knife over the Roamer. Katie was faster, leaping on him. The blow fell just wide of the chest, burying itself in Arron's shoulder. Chruston pulled it out, raising it to stab deeper. Katie pulled on his arms, forcing him back. He shoved her away.

"Grandfather! It's over!" Chris held the box aloft, his trembling fingers pulling at the catch. The old man flashed out his hand, sending a lightning thrust at him. The box popped open, and the sphere absorbed the blow Chruston sent, then sent it flying back at him. The man stumbled backward, falling over the Roamer.

Arron was crouched against the back of the chair, blood running down his arm. The only thing holding him upright was his chin resting on the back of the chair. His eyes seemed the only part of him alive, intent on the instrument.

The tune was familiar. The Roamer, though, was too far gone to sing the words, his mind one with the strings of the kithara. So it was Chris who began to sing, recognizing the tune.

> It comes, tired or not
> Sleep is a blessed thing
> Go, light will follow
> Sleep is starlight lit

Katie joined in, their two voices coming above the crashing of the wind and thunder, blending with the music.

Orb encircles sleep
Promise given you, by me, by him

All must sleep
All that was saved by lack of sleep
Must be returned to sleep
It is a blessed thing

"No!" Chruston pulled himself up. He had lost track of the knife and instead caught Arron about the throat. The orb flashed golden, blinding them all, deafening them with the thundering boom of the last note. Then the light went completely.

XXV

IT WAS DARK. CHRIS SAT UP SLOWLY, RUBBING HIS HEAD. He listened and heard only quiet breathing.

"Katie?"

"I'm here, Chris." He felt her touch him and he took her hand quickly, pulling her close.

"Arron? Arron?" There was no response. "We need some light." He felt Katie pull away and heard her stumbling about.

"The lamp's broken." She struck a match.

Arron was bent over in his chair, his shirt damp with blood. The only sign of Chruston was his dark robe, which lay in a heap where they had last seen him, by the chair.

Chris hurried to Arron, put a hand to his chest. "He's alive. Come on, help me."

The match burned Katie's finger and went out. She made her way over, her hands feeling in the robe for the keys. They undid Arron's hands and carefully laid him on the floor.

"Arron? Come on, please?" Chris bent over him, trying to see him in the dark. "Arron?" He shook him gently, then sat back, sighing. "What was wrong with me?"

"Chris?" Katie straightened up.

"I was just thinking," Chris murmured, "thinking about

how I could always see the hatred in him, could always feel it. I thought it was for me. With all the other things he had to hate, I just assumed it was for me."

"Yeah, me, too," Katie whispered. Arron gave a low moan.

"Arron?"

"Mmm?"

"Are you all right?"

There was a pause. "Chris?" came his voice. "Chruston? Is he . . ."

"He's gone."

"He's dead, then," Arron sighed, then added. "I . . . I'm sorry . . . Chris?"

Chris took his hand and squeezed it. "Don't say it. It doesn't matter. Now, can you walk? It's too dark up here. We've got to take care of your shoulder. It's bad. I think we ought to get out of here."

Arron was silent a moment. "You should have killed me."

"Arron!" Katie leaned over him.

"I mean it. Just leave me up here now. Go on down. Lock the door behind you."

"Cut it out," Chris said. "Now, come on. We'll help you downstairs." He and Katie pulled Arron carefully to his feet, one on either side of him. They found their way to the stairs. The air that came rushing in as they opened the door was cool and fresh.

"The box is gone, too," Chris said, feeling for the first step.

"Yes," Arron affirmed. "Sort of . . ."

Chris thought about that. "Arron," he said after a moment. "Am . . . am I going to waste away?" The Roamer shrank from him. "You don't have to—"

"That image has faded," the Roamer said hoarsely. "Please, don't replace it with another. Please?"

"No . . . no, I won't. I'm not like my grand—like Chruston."

"You are most certainly not," Katie said with strong assurance. They continued their slow descent. Chris smiled, feeling Arron lean more weight on him.

"What about Gaeth? How will we explain?" Katie asked as they reached the bottom steps. "We'll probably have to do

something with him, too. I don't think we'll be up to it."
Arron shuddered. "Arron?"

"Gaeth is gone, too."

"What's wrong?"

The Roamer didn't answer.

"Is it because he was dead? Like Brades?" Chris asked.

"The name Gaeth, it means nothing to you?" Arron's
voice whispered at them in the dark. Chris and Katie both
said no. "Gaeth," Arron paused. "Gaeth Shakta."

"What? But he was so pale. His hair, his eyes—"

"He wasn't a Roamer anymore. He was . . . nothing."
Arron stopped.

Katie drew her arm more firmly about his waist. "Arron, I
know what I said before. But you are not going to turn out
like that. You may feel some things the way he did, but you
understand more. Arron?"

"Yes, I suppose," he sighed, then tensed up a bit. "You
should have killed me!"

"Now stop that!" Chris shook him slightly. "Look, remember when you took away our mental link? Well, right
before, I saw what you saw. You didn't block it soon enough.
But, Arron, I remember, it was more than just how, it was
why. Isn't that right?"

"I don't know. I don't know!" Arron slumped back toward
the steps, but Chris and Katie held him up.

"Come on. We'll get you downstairs. We've got to take
care of your shoulder," Chris said softly, then remembered
how Chruston had healed his own arm. "Or can you do it?"

"You do it."

They went the rest of the way down without speaking.
They steered Arron into the living room, feeling their way,
and laid him gently on the couch. Chris left them to go find a
light and bandages. Katie knelt quietly next to Arron.

"You okay?"

"Yeah."

"Say, remember when those three Roamers were killed,"
Katie whispered to him.

"Katie—"

"I remember something you said to me, something I didn't
think of when I said you would turn out like Shakta, some-

thing I *did* think of when I said I trusted you." She smoothed his hair. "Do you remember what that was?"

"No."

"Well, I'll remind you. You said you wanted to kill them—"

"That I could see how to do it! That I could've! I could have! And I might have—" he sobbed.

"No, not that part. Don't you remember? I asked you why you didn't. And you said that you mustn't, that it was wrong. There had to be a reason why you said that, Arron. There had to be something else you saw when you saw how you might kill them. Isn't that right? When you see how to do these things, you see more than what we would see, or more than what Chruston saw when he got the knowledge from Shakta. And even more than Shakta himself. Isn't that right?"

Arron didn't answer.

"Arron, we were wrong when we said your powers were evil. They were in Shakta. They were in Chruston. But you *do* know. Arron?"

He said nothing.

Chris came back into the room. Arron didn't look up at him. Chris set the lamp on the table. The Roamer looked as if he were trying to sink into the couch. The fingers on his good arm fidgeted nervously with the edge of the cushion.

"Hey, we'll get you all cleaned up and then we'll see how you feel," Chris said gently. He didn't need the mind link now to feel the utter despair hanging about the Roamer. He set to work with Katie, dressing Arron's arm.

"There. How's that? Feeling better?" Chris said cheerfully. Arron nodded stiffly. Chris glanced at Katie. She shrugged.

"Do you mind staying here tonight?" Chris asked Arron. "I don't think you should be traveling anywhere."

"It's fine. We can stay."

"Good. We'll take you upstairs and put you to bed. I think we could all do with a bit of sleep." He stood and stretched, staring about the room. "But you know, it doesn't seem quite so cold and empty here." He walked over to the window and rubbed his sleeve over the glass. "Hey, I even think I can see some stars out there."

Katie helped Arron sit up as Chris came back to the couch. "Come on," she whispered. "We'll get you to bed."

They led him to Chris' room of the night before and put him into the bed. Chris stopped at the doorway as he and Katie went to leave.

"Look, Arron, I don't really know what you're thinking, but I think I can guess. And it's just stupid. Look, if you're going to become like him—well, what about it? We're not going to kill you. You're not going to kill yourself, are you? No. And if you aren't going to be like him, then you're wasting your time worrying, right?"

"Maybe . . . maybe—"

"Maybe what? There's nothing."

"Why didn't my grandmother tell me! Why didn't any of them tell me! If I had the potential . . . to become like him, why didn't they—I don't know. Kill me? Do you . . . do you think they wanted me to become like him? Why else would they—"

"Maybe because you were the only one to undo what he had done. You were to be the Dark Prince. That's why they kept you safe."

"Why didn't they tell me?"

"Why, Arron? It would have made you unsure. All your life you would have been unsure. You wouldn't have had the strength you needed to face Chruston. You would have been doubtful, like you are now. Right? You're wondering at each step whether to use your power, aren't you?" Chris set the lamp down firmly on the table.

"Yes."

"Well, what if you'd thought that all your life? You wouldn't have ever been able to destroy Chruston. You would have been too weak. It was awfully close as it was without you thinking there was anything wrong with you using your magic. And, Arron, your grandmother taught you to be careful of it. Why else was she so short with you on your mind reading?"

"Yes . . ."

"And finally, it doesn't really matter what they had planned. You've done what's right by you. Right?"

Arron looked past Chris out the dark window. "But—"

"Look. The short and long of it is that if Katie and I are willing to chance it, then you shouldn't be so concerned. We weren't easily won over, now were we? I'm sure you'll prove us right. I am not the least concerned."

Arron looked up at him quizzically. "You trust a Roamer?"

Chris laughed slightly and joked. "You have Homesteader blood in you, you know."

Arron looked down. "Yes, I know."

"Hey." Chris walked over to the bed. "But I'm betting on that Roamer logic." Katie agreed from the doorway.

"Do you think you can get some sleep now?" she asked.

Arron looked at them both for a moment and tried to smile. He looked down again, the fingers on his right hand catching hold of the blanket. "Don't . . . don't . . ."

"Don't what?"

"Please don't leave me in here alone . . . Please—" He cut himself off.

"Close your eyes. We'll stay." Chris said gently.

"Just until I'm asleep. That's all."

Chris walked leisurely down the wide main staircase. He'd had a good sleep, better than any he could remember. He took a deep breath and let it out slowly. The morning light filtered hazily through the dusty windows. It might have been beautiful here once, he was thinking to himself.

He stopped short when he got to the living room. It was bright, very bright. The windows had been polished until they sparkled, and the tables were dusted. The other furniture shone as well, and the floor was swept clean. Katie was sitting in a thick armchair before a crackling fire.

"Who did this?"

"Who do you think?" She shook her head, laughing.

"You?"

"Oh, and I really like the shock in your voice." She sat back smugly. "I was curious to see what it looked like . . . before. Look here, I found a picture of this place. It's beautiful." She held a small, gold-framed painting up for him to see. He stared at it for a while, the huge gardens, the neatly trimmed ivy . . . It was difficult to believe.

"Who would have thought?"

"I think we could make it like that again."

Chris looked up from the picture. "What? You mean stay here?"

"Well, it is yours now. Your grandfather is dead."

"Yes . . . yes, I suppose . . ."

"Look at this room. Now imagine the whole house like this? Let's stay."

"Stay? Here?"

"Do you really think you can go back? Live there, after all we've seen and done." She sat forward. "Chris, I can't go back to living like that. I won't."

Chris smiled and sat on the arm of the chair. "Okay, let's stay." He leaned back against the chair and ran his fingers through her hair. "How about breakfast?"

"How about you make it?"

"Yeah?"

Katie nodded.

Chris laughed suddenly. "Yeah, okay. I will." He stood up. "Should I make some for Arron, or wait until he's up?"

"Oh, he's up. I checked on him this morning. He was already gone. You suppose he's all right?"

"Of course. His stuff is here, isn't it?" Katie nodded. "Well, then, nothing to worry about."

"I just wish you hadn't . . . well, said that about him killing himself last night. No sense putting odd thoughts like that in his head."

"Oh, come on—" Chris stopped, hearing the front door boom shut. "See, there he is now."

Arron strode into the living room a moment later. He was dressed once again as a Roamer. He nodded good morning to each of them.

"What's this?" Chris indicated his attire.

Arron looked down at himself. "The charade is over. And it's time for me to be off."

"What?"

"I've got to go. Hey, two nights in one place, that's almost a record."

"You stayed longer than that at my house."

"That's true." He grinned suddenly. "Well, looks like I'm back to my old ways now."

"Where were you this morning?" Katie asked, sitting forward.

"I . . . I buried Dempter."

Chris looked at the Roamer's arm, hanging from the sling they'd fixed for him. Arron saw where he was looking.

"Yes, well, I don't need both my arms. One works just as well." He waved it in the air as if to cast a spell, then brought it down slowly and shrugged. "I had to . . . well, she needed to be buried." He stopped, staring at the fire, chewing on his lower lip.

"Arron—"

"Look. I felt—what I said to her before she—oh, damn. Well, I guess I meant it, but—"

"Listen." Chris caught him by the shoulder. "I don't blame you in the least. Who cares what you said or meant. That's all over. Are you going to have breakfast with us?"

Arron nodded, then grew serious again. He pulled something from his pocket. "There's something else," he whispered. The red gem sat in his palm. "I went to get this from Dempter. I want you to take it. It . . . it does more than heal. You see, it can kill."

"Kill? What does that have to do with anything?" Chris asked as Arron pushed the stone into his hand.

"The stone can act, well, to get rid of harmful things. That includes healing broken bones or working to eliminate whatever is harmful. You see—"

"And?" Katie stared at him.

"And . . . if I should . . . well, if I began to be like Shakta, you could use it against—what are you doing?" Arron gasped as Chris tossed the stone into the fire. It glared brighter, like one of the embers, then grew dark again, like any burned-out ash.

"What did you do that for!"

"Arron, I want you to stop this. No stone is going to keep you from becoming like Shakta. If you became like that, you would just kill me before I could do anything about it. I'm going to trust you, and I'm betting that you're not going to betray me. Just like you didn't betray your grandmother."

"But—"

"But nothing. Now, what do you have to say?"

Arron looked down at his feet for a moment. "Nothing," he said hoarsely. He looked up at them, then impulsively embraced Chris. "Not one thing."

Chris laughed and clapped him on the back. "Good. I don't want to hear it. I'm cooking, are you eating?"

Arron nodded, laughing. "If someone can feed me. I'm afraid I'll be rather clumsy with my right hand."

"We won't laugh." Katie slid her arm about Arron's waist and starting walking to the door.

"Not too much," Chris added, backing into the kitchen.

"So, this is it," Chris said, as he and Katie followed Arron to the front door. Arron nodded, sliding his pack over one shoulder.

"Isn't that going to be a little awkward?" Katie asked. "Stay."

Arron shook his head, frowning. "I've had it worse." He rested one hand on the door knob.

"You really don't have to rush off, you know."

"Chris . . . I have to see if there are other Roamers. Can you understand?"

Chris nodded. "Yeah, yeah, I can. And there are. Don't worry. They'll start to show up. Look, when you find them, send them here. They'll be welcome. Besides, this place needs all the help it can get."

"Are we going to see you again?" Katie asked, hesitating. She took Arron's hand.

He squeezed it and nodded. "Just try and keep me away. This is my home, too, you know—as much of a one as any Roamer could have. A relative of mine once lived here, eh, cousin?"

Chris laughed and shook his head. "Seems kind of funny how that worked out." He stared at the door a moment. "Hurry back, Arron."

Arron swung the door open. "Three months, and I'll be begging on your doorstep." He watched them both a moment. "It's going to be different traveling on my own, now."

He reached out and squeezed Katie's hand tightly. "Three months, no more."

"Don't be any longer," Katie whispered. She released his hand slowly.

He grinned and tossed his head back. "I promise. Now, come on, come walk with me a bit. Some wonderful things must be happening out here for the air to smell so clean."

Chris stepped out onto the porch, his eyes reflecting the blue of the sky. He caught Katie's hand and pulled her close. "Let's go look for tadpoles."

She laughed and linked arms with Arron. The three of them walked slowly down the front way. At the end of the main drive, Chris and Katie hugged Arron good-bye. They stood watching, arms about each other, until the Roamer disappeared.

ABOUT THE AUTHOR

LAURIE GOODMAN was born in Los Angeles in 1962, the second of six children. She grew up in the East in a variety of locations and remembers her childhood as a mixture of building forts in the living room and taking (one too many) trips cross-country in a station wagon crammed with eight hyperactive people.

She has always had a terrible habit of daydreaming when she should be paying attention, but finally found a use for this in high school when she began writing her ideas down in order to entertain her youngest sister. By college, the writing had become a necessary part of her life.

Her interests vary from theater to ancient Egyptian history, depending on where she is in the library. For now, she is trying to concentrate on educating herself in the sciences. She graduated in 1986 from Stanford University with a B.S. and an M.S. in biology and is currently pursuing her Ph.D. in biochemistry at the University of Chicago.